Don't Touch My
Petunia

Also by Tara Sheets

Don't Call Me Cupcake

Published by Kensington Publishing Corporation

Don't Touch My
Petunia

TARA SHEETS

ZEBRA BOOKS
KENSINGTON PUBLISHING CORP.
http://www.kensingtonbooks.com

ZEBRA BOOKS are published by

Kensington Publishing Corp.
119 West 40th Street
New York, NY 10018

All Kensington titles, imprints, and distributed lines are available at special quantity discounts for bulk purchases for sales promotion, premiums, fund-raising, educational, or institutional use.

Special book excerpts or customized printings can also be created to fit specific needs. For details, write or phone the office of the Kensington Sales Manager: Attn.: Sales Department. Kensington Publishing Corp., 119 West 40th Street, New York, NY 10018. Phone: 1-800-221-2647.

Zebra and the Z logo Reg. U.S. Pat. & TM Off.

First Printing: October 2018
ISBN-13: 978-1-4201-4628-8
ISBN-10: 1-4201-4628-9

eISBN-13: 978-1-4201-4629-5
eISBN-10: 1-4201-4629-7

10 9 8 7 6 5 4 3 2 1

Printed in the United States of America

To my daughter Maia,
for the magic and the laughter and the joy.
You light up our lives.

Chapter One

If a guy was going to fondle her petunias, the least he could do was act like he cared. Pawing at them with a big meaty ham fist while he stared absently out of her shop window was not cool.

Juliette Holloway frowned, swiping a lock of dark hair behind her ear. It was going to be a long day at Romeo's Florist Shop, and she still had two more flower arrangements to put together before the morning rush.

She leaned over the counter and called across the room. "Excuse me."

The guy messing with her petunia plant didn't move or turn around. He had broad shoulders, and his head almost reached the top of the door frame. In jeans, a gray T-shirt, and a baseball cap, he looked like one of those NFL athletes—completely out of place surrounded by the delicate summer blooms and hanging fuchsia baskets.

She called again, louder. "Hello?"

Nothing. He just kept running a giant hand over the fragile purple flowers.

Juliette bristled. The plant was her newest project. Normally, she could make anything grow and thrive. Like all Holloway women before her, she was born with a special gift. Hers was garden magic. A customer had given her the potted petunia after rescuing it from an office cubicle. The poor thing had been halfway to the grave, but she'd nurtured it back to life. And now some linebacker was mauling it.

She marched across the room and tapped the man firmly on his back. It was a rock-hard, muscular back. He was probably one of those gym guys who spent all day pumping iron. "Can you please not touch that?"

He swung around and pulled an earbud out of his ear. Loud, thumping music spewed from his headset. Even with a baseball cap and mirrored sunglasses, he looked vaguely familiar. Strong jaw with a light stubble, high cheekbones, full lips. A tiny prickle of recognition tiptoed down her spine.

She gestured to the pot of flowers. "Please don't touch my plant."

He frowned and pulled the other earbud out. "What's that?"

Juliette sighed. Gym rats. Brains in their biceps. She enunciated each word carefully. "Don't. Touch. My. petunia."

His lips twitched. "I . . ."

She closed her eyes, ignoring the flush of embarrassment creeping up her cheeks. *Way to set yourself up, genius.* Maybe he didn't notice.

"I'm not usually so forward." His deep voice hovered on the edge of laughter.

Okay, so he noticed. Big whoop. Whoever he was, he was immature, and she didn't have time for this. She grabbed the plant and turned away. The hem of her flowy skirt caught on the edge of a low shelf, and she yanked it free before escaping to the back counter.

"Have we met before?" he called.

She threw him a glance.

He gave her a slow smile that sent a jolt of physical awareness from the top of her head to the tips of her blue painted toenails. "I feel like I know you."

For a pickup line, it was pretty bad. But he had a million-dollar smile and knew how to use it. The face. The superhero physique. All he needed was a cape or a giant hammer, or something. He probably didn't have much practice with pickup lines because he didn't need any.

He sauntered toward her.

There was something familiar about the way he walked—like he owned the world—but she couldn't place him. When he reached the counter, she was glad to be on the other side. It wasn't that she felt threatened. At five feet nine inches, she was comfortable with tall people. But this guy towered over her, and when he looked at her like that, it was . . . unsettling.

He took off the baseball cap and mussed his tawny hair.

Juliette sucked in a breath.

Then he removed the sunglasses and fixed her with a gaze as deep and dark as the earth after a rainstorm.

Something inside her cracked open, and a trickle of long-forgotten feelings threatened to bubble to the surface.

Logan.

She took an involuntary step back, trying to hide her surprise by leaning casually against the wall. Supercool. She was an *iceberg* of cool. Except she misjudged the distance to the wall and stumbled.

"That bad, huh?" His mouth kicked up at one corner. It was the same cocky grin that had once made her naive teenage heart yearn for things that were impossible. Logan was four years older. He'd been far too busy with the cool kids to notice her. And when he finally did that night at his senior graduation party, it was only to judge her and find her lacking.

Stay icy. She gave a half shrug. "It's been a while."

"Over thirteen years."

She studied him from beneath her lashes. His face was deeply tanned, his features sharper and more defined. He had faint lines near the edges of his eyes, and there was a weariness in them she hadn't seen before. He'd grown up.

"Aren't you in the army, or something?" she asked. Three tours in Afghanistan, last she heard. But that was old gossip from years ago.

"I was." He shifted his gaze to the window. "But I'm done with that now."

She still couldn't believe he was standing there like some ghost from a past life. Pine Cove Island was about as small as any Pacific Northwest island town could get. The Logan she remembered had been a powerhouse of restless energy. He couldn't wait to leave. Nothing was going to stop him from getting out to see the world. Certainly not a fourteen-year-old nobody with stars in her eyes.

"What are you doing here?" she asked.

He shrugged. "I've come home. Going to fix up my grandfather's old house near the woods. It's on the other side of yours, I think."

She nodded vaguely, even though her heart thumped in her chest. When she was little, she used to wander those woods, spying on him and his grandfather through the trees. Logan always seemed larger than life. A great mystery she wanted to solve. What must it have been like to have a family like his? To have people involved in your life who loved you and stuck around?

"So." He stepped away from the counter, glancing around the shop. "You work here."

"Yes." A twinge of pride settled over her. Her floral arrangements were the best on the island, and her creative designs won first place every spring at the Flower Bud Festival. Everyone knew the plants from Romeo's Florist Shop bloomed well past their season. Her magic growth potions kept them healthy and vibrant. All a person had to do was look at them to know they were special.

But Logan wasn't looking at the plants. He was peering over her shoulder, frowning at the back room.

Juliette cringed. She knew exactly what he saw. Floral wire and paper scattered across the cutting table. Wilted flowers and greenery all over the floor. Stacks of packing crates blocking the closet with the broken door, and random baskets overflowing with gardening tools and cleaning supplies.

She shifted uncomfortably. "It's a work in progress back there."

His calculating gaze took in the cluttered cash register area, her coffee cup sitting on a stack of inventory papers, and the pile of broken plastic pots in the corner of the room.

Juliette resisted the urge to throw a tarp over them. Why hadn't she taken them out to the recycle bin yet?

He slowly made his way around the shop, stopping to check out the cracked tile on the floor near the door. She'd been meaning to find a doormat big enough to hide it.

When he jiggled a wooden shelf to test it for sturdiness, irritation spiked. She bit the inside of her cheek and grabbed her coffee cup. Why was he ignoring her gorgeous plants and only focusing on the shop's flaws? *Because he's still judging you. It's what he does.*

Juliette smoothed her thrift store tank top and sipped her coffee, glaring at him over the rim of the cup. The hazelnut chocolatey goodness was almost enough to quell the wave of annoyance building inside her.

The moment he ran his finger along the chipped paint above the door frame, Juliette decided she'd had enough. Maybe the place was a little shabby around the edges, but she loved it like it was her own. And if everything went according to plan, someday soon it would *be* her own. The last thing she needed was some drill sergeant strolling around, assessing its faults. She half expected him to break out a white glove and check for dust.

"Is there something I can help you find?" she asked. The exit door, for example.

He didn't answer. When he came to the recycled wooden bookshelf filled with her handmade bath products, he poked at the basket of soap, frowning.

Juliette felt as if he were poking at her. She didn't have to take this. The sooner he left, the sooner she could quit this messed-up stroll down memory lane and get back to work.

"Any particular plant you need?" she prodded.

He flicked a glance at the ivy spilling over the top shelf. "I'm not really into plants."

"Not surprised."

He turned to look at her. "Why's that?"

"I'm not sure you could handle them." The Logan she remembered could never sit still. He was always flying from one activity to another like a cyclone, leaving everyone in the dust if they couldn't keep up. "It takes effort and patience to keep them green."

"I have a plant," he said. "It's green."

Juliette gave him a dubious look. "Cactus?" Those things could survive almost anything. Even cyclones.

"Plastic." He looked almost smug. "The best kind, if you ask me."

Oh, the end. Juliette gritted her teeth. She set her cup down, sloshing her mocha on the counter. "If you're not here for plants, what do you want?"

He gestured to the black truck parked on the street. "Lumber delivery. I need to know where to make the drop this evening."

Everything suddenly clicked into place. Her boss had mentioned a supply delivery for the new deck and greenhouse they were building for the remodel. It suited Logan to work at the lumberyard. It would give him a chance to put those stupid GI Joe muscles to good use.

Juliette pointed to the fence near the front walkway. "You can just leave it out there."

"I think it's better if I take it around to the back."

She pointed to the fence again. "Right there is fine."

Logan frowned. "Are you the only one here? I should talk to—"

"—I'm the manager," she said testily. "I'm in charge of this place."

He cocked an eyebrow.

"Yup." She threw her arms wide. "Just little old me. The manager. And I'm telling you to leave it out front near the fence."

Logan seemed about to say something, then decided against it.

She crossed her arms and stared into his dark eyes.

Neither of them spoke for several long moments.

Neither of them blinked.

It was a silent battle of wills. She wasn't going to look away, either. She could stand there all day, if she had to. Even though her delicious hazelnut mocha was sitting right in front of her, growing cold. Even though the extra vanilla whipped cream was probably already melted by now.

She licked her lips.

He blinked. His gaze flicked to her mouth.

Score.

When he turned to leave, she felt a surge of triumph. She was in charge. She was The Decider. So what if he crushed her silly hopes when she was young and vulnerable? He probably didn't even remember. And none of that mattered now. She was twenty-seven. All grown up, and nothing he said or did could get under her skin.

At the door, he paused and glanced back. "There is one plant I can handle just fine." A spark of mischief lit his eyes, but his expression was all politeness.

Juliette didn't trust it. "What would that be?"

"Petunias." He shot her a crocodile grin. "I'm really good at handling petunias."

Chapter Two

After Logan left, Juliette threw herself into creating floral arrangements and helping customers. By noon, she'd already forgotten his visit. At least five or six times. Yup, everything had slipped back into business as usual. In fact, on a scale of one to ten, she'd give the day a solid seven. If it weren't for accidentally running a drug cartel, it might have even been an eight.

She peered through the ferns lining the florist shop window and lifted a small marijuana plant from its hiding place. It was gorgeous and healthy, of course. Why wouldn't it be? She'd unknowingly been watering it with her magic growth potion for the past week.

"You're not supposed to be here," she whispered.

The seedling didn't explain itself, but it didn't have to. Her new employee did.

Juliette marched to the back room, hating this part of her job. All her life, she just wanted to be around plants, and aside from her cottage by the woods, Romeo's Florist Shop was her favorite place on earth. Plants were her "family." She loved them and cared for them, and they grew roots and stuck around. People, on the other hand, weren't as dependable.

"Kevin," Juliette said. "We need to talk."

A lanky teenage boy with swoopy hair leaned against the back door, tapping on his cell phone. In rumpled pants and the same AC/DC shirt he'd worn three days in a row, he looked like he just rolled out of a mosh pit. "What's up, boss?"

"You don't have to call me boss. I told you, Juliette's fine."

He didn't glance up from his phone. "My mom said I have to be respectful or you'll cast a spell on me."

Juliette rolled her eyes. "I don't cast spells on people." Why did she bother? People would believe what they wanted. Holloway magic was subtle, and only used to help others. It didn't even work directly on herself. Most of the locals laughed it off as silly superstition, but some— like Kevin's mom, apparently—didn't want to take any chances.

"What about those potions?" he asked, still tapping away. Screenagers. Never let it be said they lacked focus.

"Those are essential oil blends," Juliette said in exasperation. "Made from things in my garden. To help people. I don't make anything dangerous."

"You make bath grenades," he said through a yawn.

"Bombs, Kevin," she sighed. "Bath bombs. For relaxation."

"I dunno, boss. Bombs aren't super chill."

Juliette shook her head. Poor Kevin. He wasn't the brightest flower on the vine. If she was ever going to convince Romeo, the owner, to sell her the shop when he retired, she had to prove she could manage it like an expert. That meant finding a trustworthy employee to help out, especially with the remodel coming up. But Kevin wasn't that person.

"Owned." He did a fist pump and glanced up, grinning. "I just beat my highest score on Junk Punk."

Juliette breathed deep, because patience was a virtue. At least that's what people said. She wouldn't know first-hand, but she was willing to give it a shot. Kevin was an okay kid, but she wasn't interested in babysitting. Most of the time, he showed up to work stoned. Just yesterday she caught him watering the orchids with a pitcher of lemonade.

She held the marijuana plant in the air, waving it to get his attention. "I found this hidden under the ferns."

Kevin's smile took an instant nosedive. "Aw, balls."

"You told me this wouldn't happen again," Juliette said, setting the plant on the cutting table. "You promised me."

"I know, but you can make anything grow. Can't you make an exception? No one has to know." The whine was teenaged to perfection with just the right notes of hope and cluelessness. "My friend has a buyer lined up for the rest of the summer. He says we'll make a killing if you help us. Besides, weed's legal now in Washington."

Juliette lifted his hoodie from a peg on the wall and handed it to him. "You can explain that to your mom when she asks why you got fired."

"Please don't tell my mom," Kevin moaned. "Wait— I'm fired?" His shoulders slumped. "*Balls*."

"Yeah, good luck with yours." She held the door open for him. "I've seen your mom when she's angry."

Kevin pulled on his hoodie, scowling.

Juliette felt a stab of pity for him. He seemed so anchor-less. "Wait." She grabbed one of her hand-wrapped soaps from a basket and held it out. "Take this."

He was clearly unimpressed with her parting gift. "I have soap at home."

"This is different. And it smells good, see?" She pressed the pine-and-sandalwood-scented bar into his hand.

He shook his head. "I use Axe body spray. I don't need—"

"Girls like this way better, trust me. It'll help you."

Finally, a flash of interest. "Get chicks?" He sniffed it cautiously.

She pressed her lips together, choosing her words. "I think it could help in a lot of ways. Just try it, okay?"

A few minutes later, Juliette watched him drive away in his mom's gold minivan. The soap was charmed to help a person gain clarity and make good choices. She hoped he'd use it, but even without the magic, it was a win for Kevin. Because . . . Axe body spray? Come on.

She closed the back door and thumped her head against it. He was the third person she'd fired in a month. Romeo wasn't going to be happy, and she really needed him happy. Her plan to buy the florist shop depended on it.

As if on cue, the door opened, and Romeo breezed in on a wave of expensive cologne. "Darling." He made a beeline for the coffeemaker. "Please tell me that wasn't Kevin I saw driving away when I pulled up."

Romeo was in his sixties, with salt-and-pepper hair and brown eyes that crinkled at the corners when he laughed. He wore impeccably tailored clothes, and with his Rhett Butler smile and easy charm, he looked like he just stepped out of an old Hollywood film. Juliette was sure he'd broken many hearts in his day, but now he was happily married to his husband, an airline pilot.

"I had to let Kevin go," Juliette said.

Romeo took a mug from the cupboard and lifted the ancient coffeepot near the sink. "You can't keep firing people, hun. I'm going to be gone on my trip for three weeks, and you need the help."

"Trust me, Kevin wasn't helping." She filled him in on her brief stint as an almost–drug lord.

"Well," Romeo sighed. "You did the right thing."

"So you see, I'm better off managing the place alone."

"Look," he said, pouring a cup of coffee. "I know you like to do everything yourself, and you're good at it. *Really* good at it. But one of these days you're going to have to let someone in. The remodel starts tomorrow. You need the help, which brings me to the reason I stopped by." He raised the mug and took a sip.

Juliette jerked her hand up. "I wouldn't—"

He choked. Coughed.

"Sorry," she said. "I tried to warn you."

"What fresh hell is this?" he wheezed, staring into the coffee mug. "It tastes like water strained through compost dirt."

"Well, Kevin made it, so you never know."

He set the cup firmly in the sink. "I'm going to go get something real. You want a hazelnut mocha?"

She grinned. "Always." Sweet, sweet nectar of the gods.

"Extra vanilla whipped cream, right?"

Juliette nodded. He was the greatest boss on earth. Possibly the greatest person. She adored him to the moon and—

"I hired my nephew to facilitate the remodel," Romeo announced.

Juliette stopped grinning. "*I'm* going to facilitate the remodel."

"I know, I know. But you'll be working in the shop. He's going to do the actual labor."

She followed him to the front entrance. "Is he qualified to build an entire deck and a greenhouse? I mean, I thought we were hiring contractors."

"Don't worry," Romeo said. "He's done this kind of

work before. And he'll have some people help out when needed."

Juliette wished Romeo had asked her before doing the hiring, or at least let her be part of the process. Romeo didn't have the best track record when it came to choosing solid employees. If he was hiring his nephew, it was obviously for personal, family reasons, and it was never a good idea to mix family with business. Not that she'd know. Aside from her cousin, Juliette was the last remaining Holloway on the island. But it didn't sound like a good idea. Who knew what his nephew's actual credentials were?

She crossed her arms in frustration. For all she knew, he was going to be some lazy deadbeat who did sloppy work. Another person she'd have to babysit. "When does he start?"

"Tomorrow," said a familiar voice behind her.

She whirled around.

Logan O'Connor stood in the doorway. He nodded to Romeo. "Uncle Ro."

Juliette's mouth fell open, and she had to force it shut. *Uncle* freaking *Ro*? She stared at Logan in disbelief. He looked like he needed someone to scrape the smirk off his face with a shovel. She happened to have one.

"You're just in time to join me for coffee," Romeo said, slapping him on the back. "But first, I want you to meet Juliette, my shop manager."

"We've already met," Logan said, holding out his hand.

She shook it because she was super managery and professional, and also because there was a shovel in the back room calling to her. But clocking him in the face with it might not seem very welcoming, so shaking hands was probably the better choice.

"Nice to see you again," she lied.

His grip was firm and strong. "Likewise."

"Logan's going to fix things up inside, too," Romeo said.

"Make it more organized. You'll have to give him some room to work, okay, hun? Show him where things are?"

She dipped her head, unable to go through with a full nod. For three years, she'd managed the shop. She had a system, and knew how things worked. Maybe it didn't look organized to others, but it worked for her. Everything was under control. And now she was just supposed to step aside and let his lumbering nephew come in and change everything?

Romeo kept talking about shelves and paint and mirrored paneling, but Juliette stopped listening. It's not that she didn't want to fix up the shop; she really did. But it bothered her that Romeo was making all the decisions without asking for her input. She planned on owning the shop someday. These changes happening now were going to be changes she'd have to live with for years to come. It was frustrating not to have any say about what was being done.

And here stood Logan, smirking at her. All she could think about was how he judged her shop—judged *her* all those years ago—and found them both lacking. All she could hear was, *I'm not really into plants.* He was the last person she wanted in her personal space, but by some jacked-up twist of fate, she was going to be stuck with him for the next few weeks.

"I'll do what I can to make it look decent in here," Logan said. "It shouldn't be too hard, even though the back room is a train wreck. Practically a fire hazard. I don't know how anyone can even work back there. But don't worry, Uncle Ro. I'll take care of it." He looked pointedly at her. "I'm always up for a challenge."

She narrowed her eyes.

"There's nothing here I can't handle," he said with an arrogant shrug.

And that was it. She made up her mind right then and there not to make things easy for him. He may have an uncle who ran the show, and he may have grown up with rich, doting parents and popular friends and family picnics with noodle salad, but she had something better. Something he didn't have. Something she could always count on.

Juliette's smile was catlike, her mind racing with possibilities.

She had magic.

Chapter Three

Juliette swung open the door to her cousin Emma's bakery. Even in her mood, Juliette couldn't help admiring the gorgeous FAIRY CAKES sign on the back wall. A gift from Emma's fiancé Hunter, it was an intricate mosaic of rainbow stones and turquoise lettering, created by the same artist who designed Hunter's restaurant & café sign on the waterfront.

"You're never going to guess the crazeballs day I've had," Juliette called to the back room. She inhaled the sweet, tangy scent of citrus fruit mixed with vanilla buttercream frosting. "And whatever you're baking, I need one."

Emma Holloway emerged from the kitchen with a tray of cupcakes topped with crystalized sugar candies that looked like tiny orange slices. Her blond hair was in its usual messy bun and she had a streak of frosting on her cheek. Juliette had never seen anyone more beautiful. Ever since Emma and Hunter had become engaged, it was as if she glowed from within.

Juliette felt a twinge of nostalgia and sadness, knowing it was no longer just her and Emma. They'd been best friends growing up, and it was always just the two of them against the world. Now that Emma had Hunter, things were different. Juliette loved Hunter, of course. He made Emma happier than Juliette had ever seen, so that made him golden in her book. But once Emma and Hunter were married, things would change. And since Juliette never planned on getting married, where did that leave her? The idea was a little too gloomy to contemplate, so she shoved the thought aside.

She gave Emma a quick hug and snagged a cupcake off the tray.

"Orange Dreamboat," Emma announced, placing them into the case. "Intended to bring back fond childhood dreams."

"If only our magic worked on us," Juliette said, plucking the orange candy slice off the top and popping it into her mouth. "I'd be all over this one. And I know exactly what dream I'd like to bring back." Logan's million-dollar smile flashed in her mind, but she ignored it. "The flying one. Remember how I used to fly all the time in my dreams? Swooping and soaring over Pine Cove Island, the ocean, the whole world. I never have that dream anymore. Maybe it's because I'm all grown up and I know flying isn't possible." She flopped onto the padded bistro chair. "Bummer. Adulting sucks."

She bit into the fluffy cupcake and closed her eyes, chewing in bliss. It reminded her of hot summer days eating popsicles on their grandmother's front porch when they were little. "Hmm." She took another huge bite. Chewed. Swallowed. It was heaven. "Something's off about these," she said with a forced frown. "I'm going to need to eat at least three more in order to pinpoint the problem."

"Then you'll have to wait until closing," Emma said, wiping down the counter. "I can't have you testing all my inventory."

"Just one more," Juliette said around a mouthful of spongy, delicious goodness. "Seriously, these are my favorite."

"I thought Raspberry Kiss was your favorite. And the week before that you said Lavender Bliss was your favorite. And the week before that—"

"You're right. I call dibs on all of these." She waved her hand at the colorful array of cupcakes in the case.

"I don't get it," Emma said. "How can you eat like Cookie Monster and never gain a pound?"

"It's my super intelligent brain." Juliette licked frosting off her finger. "Burns a lot of calories." She jumped up to grab a napkin. "I can't stay long because Gertie and Molly are freaking out about some houseboat thing and they want me to go by Dazzle so they can fill me in. Do you know what that's about?"

"No idea," Emma said. "But I'm sure we'll find out soon enough."

Gertie and Molly were their closest friends, and working at the hair salon meant they were always abuzz with the latest gossip.

"So what happened today?" Emma asked. "Did you fire another employee?"

"P'sh." Juliette sat back on the bistro chair. "Actually, I did. But this is crazier. You'll never guess who appeared in my shop today."

Emma took the chair opposite her and adjusted her apron. "Was it your owl from Hogwarts? Did you scold it for being sixteen years late?"

"I'm still waiting for my owl, but no. This is even weirder." She leaned forward. "Logan O'Connor came in to the shop."

Emma stopped arranging her apron and gaped at Juliette. "As in your ninth-grade crush, Logan O'Connor?"

"Yes." Though "crush" was putting it mildly. Back then,

Juliette was going to love him until galaxies collided and all the stars in the universe burned out.

"What's he doing here? Did he remember you? Did you still want to kiss him?"

"Moved back. Barely. And hells no." Juliette licked another scoop of frosting from her finger. "What am I, fourteen?"

Emma gave her a knowing smile. "I seem to remember he made quite an impact on you back then, what with his graduation party and the Spin the Bottle game."

Juliette cringed at the mention of that disastrous night. "Please, I'm so over it. Besides, this is the craziest part of all. He's going to be doing our remodel at the shop. He's Romeo's *nephew*."

Before Emma could respond, the front door swung open and Gertie and Molly hurried in.

"Oh, good," Gertie said breathlessly, hefting her giant tote bag over her shoulder. "You're both here, so we can kill two birds with one stone." Gertie was the lead hairdresser at Dazzle. At almost fifty, she had enough energy to power a small planet. Even though she was married with two grown sons in college, she never looked her age, due to her tiny stature and penchant for dying her hair wild colors. This week it was blond with purple tips.

"Yeah, we have to be quick," Molly added, pulling a chair to their table. "I have a blow dry in twenty minutes and it's Edna Humper, so I can't be late." She rolled her eyes. "That woman is like a sharknado. Tacky, unrealistic, and deadly if you get on her bad side." She grabbed a protein shake from her purse, cracked it open, and took a sip.

Molly had gorgeous curves, shiny dark hair, and a sweet, cherubic face. Even though they all told her she was perfect the way she was, she had an on-again, off-again relationship with fad diets.

"So what's all the talk about a houseboat?" Juliette asked.

"*Hollywood Houseboat*," Gertie said excitedly. "It's coming here."

Juliette tried to remember where she'd heard the name before. "That's a reality show, right?"

Gertie groaned. "I forget you spend all your spare time with plants. Yes, it's a reality show. The one where pampered celebrities have to live on a boat together and do outdoorsy things so we can all watch them suffer."

"I think I saw an ad for it," Emma said vaguely.

"You know," Gertie said, pointing a finger between them. "Sometimes I wonder how we became friends. It was the *best* show last season. The houseboat was stationed in Maui, and the celebrities had to swim with sharks, and one girl had a panic attack because—"

"—Even though she plays a lifeguard on her show," Molly interjected, "she doesn't actually know how to swim. She just flailed in the water, screaming while sharks circled her because of all the commotion."

Juliette gave a lopsided grin. "I'm totally up for watching some of that."

"Well, get ready, because they're filming the second season," Gertie said. "And this year they're coming here, to Pine Cove Island. They're going to be docked right in the harbor for the rest of June and most of July."

"Doing what?" Emma asked. "This place is a far cry from Maui."

"Yeah, we don't have hot surfer guys and hula dancers here," Juliette said. "Unless you count old Betty Zimmerman when she's been drinking. Did you hear she bruised a hip last week trying to dance on the pool table at O'Malley's?"

"Never mind all that," Gertie said excitedly. "This is bigger news, ladies. Because guess who's going to be on *Hollywood Houseboat* this season?"

"Thor?" Juliette asked. "Please say Thor."

Emma's eyes flew wide. "I thought you liked Loki better. I was team Thor, remember? We argued about it, and everything."

Juliette lifted a shoulder. "I mean, Thor's okay. He'll do in a pinch."

Gertie smacked her hand on the table. "Will you guys pay attention?" She looked at Molly and shook her head. "They're hopeless."

Molly nodded in agreement.

"Okay, who?" Juliette asked. "Just tell us."

"Brock Templeton, from *Surfers Down Under*." Molly bounced in her chair, her cherub face pink with excitement.

"Wow," Juliette said. Brock was a hotshot surfer who had his own TV show for a few years. He now lived in LA and did commercials for his wildly successful sports drink.

"I don't really care that he's gone through two and a half fiancées," Molly gushed. "I just want to see if he still has rock-hard abs. And I want to hear him say things in his supersexy Australian accent. Like 'G'day, lassie.'" She fanned herself, giggling.

"I think 'lassie' would be Irish," Emma said thoughtfully. "Or Scottish, maybe."

"It doesn't matter what he says," Molly said in exasperation. "He could read the instruction manual to my dishwasher and it would be sexy, as long as he did it with that accent."

"Maybe James can do an Aussie accent," Juliette teased. "Have you asked him?" Molly spent the previous year fielding disastrous online dates, before finally settling down with the local bartender, James Sullivan.

"Oh, please," Molly said. "I love James just as he is, but come on. It's Brock Templeton!"

Gertie gathered her huge tote bag and stood. "So there

you have it, ladies. *Hollywood Houseboat*'s coming to our tiny neck of the woods, and The Brock is coming with it. Who'd have ever thought they'd make it here?"

"This is going to be one wild summer," Molly announced as they waved good-bye and hurried out the door.

Juliette's mind strayed to Logan and how he was going to be hanging around for the next few weeks. All golden and gorgeous like he always was. Except now he was bigger and harder, and much more . . . well, *more*. She shook her head. Best not to think about it.

"What?" Emma asked as she cleared the table. Juliette's cousin could always tell when something was bothering her.

"It just feels like there's a lot of wild change in the air." She felt unsettled. The way she did when she was out gardening and the wind changed, and she knew in her bones that a storm was coming. "First Logan O'Connor shows up and it turns out he's Romeo's nephew. And now Pine Cove Island's going to get a hot dose of Hollywood's B-rated celebrities stirring things up for the summer. What's next?"

Emma grinned. "I'm getting married soon?"

A wave of happiness swept over Juliette, eclipsing all feelings of uncertainty. Emma's wedding was a little over a month away, and they'd been planning a lovely ceremony at the gazebo overlooking the waterfront. Originally, Emma and Hunter just wanted something small, but it wasn't every day someone got married on Pine Cove Island. By the time she and Juliette had worked out a guest list, it seemed like the whole town would be there.

"Yes, you are getting married." Juliette stood and gave her cousin a warm hug. "And that's the biggest and best news of all. Let's focus on that. Did you pick a dress yet?"

Emma shook her head. "Want to go dress shopping with me?"

"Of course. I can't let you go alone for something that important."

They chatted and planned for a while, and by the time Juliette drove home she had almost forgotten Logan's appearance earlier.

It wasn't until she pulled her car down the long road leading up to her cottage that she remembered. There was a black pickup truck stacked with lumber turning toward the other side of the woods beyond her house.

Juliette rolled the window down to breathe in the crisp evening air mingled with the scent of roses that lined the path to her house. Something shifted in the air. There was an unusual breeze coming in from the north.

Change.

She felt it coming with absolute certainty, the same way she could feel the sun rise in the east every morning.

She shivered and rolled up the window.

Chapter Four

"Oh, kiddo." Logan's uncle stood in the dusty living room, surveying the peeling wallpaper and water-stained carpet. "This place looks like it got hit with an apocalypse stick."

Logan propped his feet on the moth-eaten ottoman and took a sip of cold beer. True, the spacious living room of his grandfather's old house had seen better days. There were gaps in the wooden floorboards, peeling wallpaper, and mold forming on the window ledges, but all of it was fixable. Even in its shabby state, the room still had remnants of the warmth and charm Logan remembered growing up. The fireplace was sturdy and functional, and the red area rug—though worn—was as inviting as it had been on his ninth birthday when he'd spent an entire weekend building a Star Wars city out of Legos. The couch, an unfortunate shade of avocado green, was lumpier than it used to be, but he couldn't complain.

"It's not that bad, Uncle Ro," Logan said. "Gramps just wasn't big on decorating."

"Not that bad?" said a voice coming from the stairs. "Did you see the master bedroom? Who would paint such gorgeous crown molding that shade of mustard yellow? Who, I ask you."

"My grandmother?" Logan grinned as his uncle's husband, Caleb, glided down the stairs with effortless grace. Caleb was tall and lean, with graying blond hair and sharp eyes that missed nothing. He was outwardly appalled at the state of the house, but Logan could tell he was doing his best to be polite. Poise, after all, was Caleb's specialty. As an airline pilot of many years, he was used to being calm and cool in the face of chaos, even though he clearly thought the house was the equivalent of high turbulence.

Romeo wrapped an arm around Caleb's shoulders. "Don't worry. Logan's good at fixing things up."

Caleb sniffed. "Be that as it may, no amount of handiwork will help if he doesn't alter the color schemes in here. And the wall treatments must go, Logan, really. Stenciled grape leaves are so last century. You need an interior designer to help you. Or at the very least, someone with great taste."

Logan turned to his uncle. "Know anyone like that?"

"Hmm. Let me think." Romeo wrinkled his brow in exaggerated concentration. "I can ask around. Old Mrs. Mooney down at the curiosity shop might have some ideas."

"I heard she's good with stencils," Logan agreed.

"Oh, shut it, both of you." Caleb gave them a look and walked to the front windows. He ran a finger along one of the dusty metal blinds. "Of course I'll help you make this place look better, but it'll have to wait until we get back from Florida. You'll have three weeks to get it cleaned up. And, Logan." He inspected the mildewed curtains. "You're going to need industrial strength supplies."

"How about a flame thrower?" Logan asked. "Would that work?"

Caleb took one last look around the room. "It wouldn't hurt."

"Well, that's it, then." Romeo slapped his hands together. "You sure you've got what you need to start work on Monday?"

"I'm good." Logan rose from the couch and walked them to the front door. "And Juliette's there if I have any questions."

"About Juliette . . ." Romeo stopped in the foyer and turned to Logan. "She prefers to work alone."

"Oh, does she ever," Caleb said with a chuckle. "A real firecracker, that one."

"But she needs help," Romeo continued. "I've asked her to hire someone part-time in the shop while I'm gone."

"Fine by me," Logan said. "That's her business." He was there to build and clean things up. Whatever she wanted to do with employees wasn't his problem. She could hire or fire whomever she liked, as long as she stayed out of his way.

Romeo placed a hand on his shoulder. "Just keep an eye on things and make sure she has what she needs, okay? She's excellent with the plants. The girl has a talent like I've never seen."

"Like no one's ever seen," Caleb agreed. "Pure magic."

Logan stuffed his hands into the pockets of his jeans, glancing between them. "So you guys believe in all that?" As a kid growing up, his parents had whispered about the eccentric Holloway family and their odd lifestyle. "A bunch of fairy-tale nonsense," his father had always said. He was a practical man, whose religion was more football than anything else, and his mom had been PTA president. Neither had any interest in the "woo-woo" stuff going on with the Holloways. They just rolled their eyes if anyone brought it up, giving it as much credibility as the Loch Ness monster or Sasquatch.

Logan's mother was nothing like her brother, Romeo. She was straitlaced and uninterested in change, whereas Romeo was a kinder, gentler person when it came to other peoples' differences. It was one of the things Logan loved so much about him.

"Of course we believe in the Holloway charms," Caleb said, throwing on his jacket.

"I've worked with Juliette for three years," Romeo said. "Plants thrive around her. And those bath products she sells are like magic spells. I don't know what she puts in them, but they all do what they're supposed to. Dried tea leaves for headaches. Lotions to relieve stress. Essential oil blends to help soothe."

"I once had insomnia after a long flight," Caleb said. "She made me this lavender mist for my pillow, and I slept like a baby. Now I take it on all my trips."

"The girl has a gift," Romeo said simply.

Logan couldn't argue there. Just seeing Juliette, all grown up and surrounded by flowers, brought back the memory of a night he'd long forgotten. They were just kids, and she'd been completely innocent. He was eighteen and heading off to join the army. The world was his to conquer, and nothing could hold him back. Not even the girl with pleading turquoise eyes standing in his garden in the moonlight, asking him to stay. For one brief moment, his decision to leave had wavered. She'd been like a magnetic force of nature, drawing him toward her, making him forget everything else.

"Unfortunately," Romeo said, "she's not very good with the business side of things."

"How so?"

He rubbed the back of his neck. "She's kind of . . . scattered. She just operates on a different wavelength than the rest of us. Juliette has systems around the shop and she knows where things are, but it doesn't translate well to others. If there's anything you can do to help make the place more organized and efficient, I'd be grateful."

"Just don't step on Juliette's toes," Caleb whispered theatrically as they walked out the door. "You don't want to mess with Mother Nature."

They said good-bye, Logan assuring them that everything would be fine. He shut the door and walked back into the living room, his thoughts straying to Juliette earlier that day. Hands on her hips. Blue eyes flashing. With long dark hair, graceful limbs, and sinful curves, she looked like some wild fantasy. And when she started speaking in that soft, melodious voice, a jolt of pure animal lust had rocked him to the core. Juliette Holloway, in a faded skirt and a flimsy tank top with a smudge of dirt on her cheek, was like a sucker punch to the gut. Stunningly beautiful. But she'd been clearly annoyed at him from the start, which was a damn good thing. There was no room in his life for trouble, and she was the most alluring, delicious bundle of trouble he'd seen in a long time.

Logan shook his head, shoving away all thoughts of Juliette. His plans didn't involve wild forces of nature. His plans were much more calm and domestic.

He stretched out on the musty couch and rubbed his tired eyes. God, if only he could get a decent night's sleep. He had spent so many years on high alert. Even now that he was far away from the heat and the turmoil and the nights spent on hard-packed earth, it was difficult to rest.

He shifted on the couch and buried his face in a cushion. Bad idea. It smelled like mold and decay. Logan jerked to a sitting position and dropped his head in his hands.

Caleb was right. This house looked abysmal. The floorboards were warped, the carpet was threadbare, and the stained furniture looked like thrift store rejects. It was going to be a long work in progress. But even under the veneer of neglect, the house gave him a sense of peace, and that was something. He remembered being a young boy here, visiting his grandfather. They'd spent countless hours talking about things that seemed so important to him back then. Baseball. Dogs. Fishing. If only things could be that easy again.

Logan reached for his beer and finished it, reflexively rubbing the area just below his sternum. For more than a decade, he'd been a soldier, with a purpose and a country to protect. And he'd been a damned good one, even though he'd ended up leaving a piece of his soul back on that scorched desert.

His phone beeped. A text message from his uncle.

5:00 Sunday. Farewell dinner at my place. Brace yourself. Caleb's cooking.

Logan hesitated, then texted back.

Should I bring McDonald's, just in case?

Romeo's reply was instant.

And risk Caleb's wrath?

Logan smiled. Three tours in Afghanistan were nothing compared to Caleb scorned.

I'll just bring wine.

Chapter Five

Juliette kicked off her sandals, tucked her skirt under her, and stretched out on the grassy bank overlooking Pine Cove Island's waterfront. It was a sunny Thursday afternoon, with the kind of cool breeze and swirly white clouds that made her wish she was back at home working in her garden. She would have preferred to take full advantage of a day like this, cultivating her herb plants and maybe even fixing the broken rose trellis, but her friends had other ideas.

Gertie sat cross-legged next to Juliette, scoping out the pier through a pair of binoculars. "Oh, there's Vespa Kissman."

Molly rummaged through a picnic basket on the other side of Gertie. "Who's that?"

"Only the best actress in the nineties." Gertie lowered the binoculars. "She played the zombie prom queen in *Necromancer Two*."

"Haven't seen it," Molly said, pulling a chocolate chip cookie from the basket.

Gertie's mouth fell open. "*Necromancer Two: Undead Reckoning?*"

"I think my parents had it on videotape, but I wasn't allowed to watch scary movies back then," Molly added.

"It's official." Gertie handed the binoculars to Juliette. "I'm old as dirt."

"I saw it," Juliette said. "It's the one where the girl turns into a zombie and tells her prom date 'I want your body,' and then she attacks and eats him."

"Yes," Gertie said, brightening. "A true classic."

"No, the BBC version of *Pride and Prejudice* is a classic," Molly said around a mouthful of cookie. "Zombie movies aren't even in the same category. That's like comparing filet mignon with street meat."

Gertie pressed her lips together and pointed to a food vendor parked on the corner. "We just ate lunch from that taco truck, so don't get all hoity-toity with me. I'm not arguing that Mr. Darcy coming up out of that pond in a wet shirt isn't a top sirloin classic. I'm just saying Vespa was a great actress in that movie. She had some serious *oomph* in her day."

Juliette peered through the binoculars at the bosomy blonde teetering down the pier in six-inch platform heels. She had a glossy bag on one arm and a scruffy little dog on the other. The bow in the dog's hair was the exact same color as her orange dress. Even though Vespa had moved on from her role as zombie princess of the nineties, the woman definitely still had "*oomph.*"

The small crowd of locals around the dock seemed to buzz a little louder as a man stepped off the houseboat onto the pier. He planted his feet firmly on the wooden planks and glanced around the wharf like a pirate surveying his latest plunder.

Juliette grinned. "I think Brock Templeton just landed."

Molly gasped and yanked the binoculars from her. She shifted onto her knees and focused on the dock. "Oh, my god, look. It's him, you guys. It's really him. Look!"

"I was trying," Juliette said wryly.

Molly made a cooing sound that ended on a giggle.

Gertie poked her in the ribs. "What's he doing? Tell us."

"He's talking," Molly breathed.

"Here, let me see." Gertie reached for the binoculars with grabby hands.

"Wait." Molly dodged away. "He's coming down the pier. He's walking!"

"He walks *and* talks?" Juliette pulled a bottle of water from the basket. "The guy's got skills."

"Oh, shut up. Wait until you see him up close. Here." Molly shoved the binoculars back at her.

Juliette peered through the lenses. She sat up straighter. Adjusted the focus, and . . . *Hello, Hollywood.*

Brock Templeton looked like he just rode in on a wave from his show, *Surfers Down Under*. In cargo shorts and a T-shirt with the logo of his sports drink company, he moved with the practiced swagger of a man who was used to being in the spotlight. He had tousled dark hair, flashing white teeth, and a tan so golden, he practically glowed.

"What'd I tell you?" Molly said triumphantly. "He's a surf god."

Juliette watched as a group of women gathered around him like clucking hens. "Complete with an entourage of worshipping mortals," she said.

In a flurry of swishy hair and laughter, the women held out phones to get selfies, and waved notebooks and magazines for him to sign.

"Mmm, I wouldn't mind getting his autograph," Gertie said. "On my thigh."

Juliette threw her a look. "Walter might have something

to say about that." Walter was Gertie's beloved husband of twenty-something years.

"Oh, he knows me." Gertie waved a hand. "He'd probably congratulate me for showing restraint and getting an autograph on my thigh instead of my chest."

"Well, if that's your plan, get in line," Molly said wistfully. "It looks like Brock's going to be a little busy for the next few centuries."

More people gathered, and soon Brock was surrounded on all sides by eager fans. The *Hollywood Houseboat* production crew, dressed all in black, circled the crowd like vultures. They filmed and snapped pictures as Brock bantered back and forth with his admirers.

"Juliette, you should go down there and talk to him," Molly said. "We're all spoken for. You're the only one with skin in the game."

"Later," Juliette said. "Because . . . cookies." She reached into the picnic basket, selecting one of Emma's latest creations. The chocolate chip cookies were supposed to instill feelings of goodwill toward others. Even though the Holloway magic didn't work on her, Juliette had no problem appreciating the rich milk chocolate and brown sugary masterpiece. Her cousin was a baking goddess.

She chewed in bliss as Brock and his entourage slowly made their way down the pier. Vespa followed alongside a stocky man in a white apron. Molly was quick to point out he was the lead chef on a cooking show, and he wore the apron for publicity. Behind them sauntered a strikingly beautiful woman in micro denim shorts and a flimsy scrap of fabric masquerading as a halter top. Her sullen expression did nothing to mar the perfect symmetry of her face.

Molly smoothed her dark hair. "That has to be Mirage, the Victoria's Secret model."

"Yeah, you can tell because of her smoldering pout," Gertie said. "I think it's a job requirement. Must be proficient in all aspects of pout management."

"Hold up, who is *that*?" Molly demanded.

Juliette looked in the direction Molly was pointing. She squinted her eyes as a tall figure strode toward the boardwalk. Unlike the swaggering Brock, this man walked with purpose. He moved with an easy grace that made it clear he was completely comfortable with who he was, and where he was going. This man walked like he owned the world. A jolt of recognition slammed into her.

"I think I saw him on that *Ninja Cop* show," Molly said excitedly. "He's got that whole rugged, hard body look."

Gertie picked up the binoculars to get a closer view. "Holy crap of glorious things. Where's he from?"

Juliette sighed. She knew exactly where he was from. "The army."

"*Ninja Cop* warriors aren't from the army," Molly informed her. "They're from a different dimension. That's where they get those helmets that shoot laser beams."

"That's Logan O'Connor," Juliette said. "He went to my high school and just got back from the army."

Molly gaped at her. "You went to high school with that guy?" She turned her attention back to Logan. "How did you manage to graduate? I'd have spent all my time stalking him."

"I barely noticed him," Juliette lied. "Anyway, he just moved back here. And before you get all worked up, know this: he's Romeo's nephew and he's going to be doing the remodel at the florist shop."

Molly and Gertie gawked at her as if she'd just won the triple jackpot lottery.

"No." Juliette shook her head. "It's not like that, at all."

"Why not?" Molly said, frowning.

"Because he's my boss's nephew," she said in exasperation. "And even if he wasn't, I'm just not interested. He bothers me."

"Well, prepare to get hot and bothered," Gertie said under her breath. "Because he's headed in our direction."

Juliette tried to ignore the fluttering in the pit of her stomach at the sight of Logan coming toward her with long, easy strides. Today he wore jeans and a navy T-shirt, which was just annoying. Considering the way the clothes clung to his body in a blatant display of muscular, male perfection, he had to know he looked good. Therefore, he was flaunting it. Therefore, annoying.

She turned her attention to the very important task of brushing crumbs off the picnic blanket. Pesky little crumbs. Just everywhere. What to do, what to do?

"Hey." He stopped a few feet in front of her.

She looked up reluctantly.

"I was just heading over to the shop to find you," he said.

Juliette made an effort to keep her expression neutral. "I'm not there."

"I see that." The smile he gave her was too familiar. Full lips tilted up at one corner, a gleam of mischief in his eyes. It was the kind of smile people give when they know each other well. When they share secrets.

She gritted her teeth and squared her shoulders. They shared nothing but a common interest in Romeo's Florist Shop. If he assumed familiarity just because they grew up near each other, he was in for a big surprise. She was no longer that girl. Every interaction with him from this point on was going to be purely professional.

Molly thrust her hand out, beaming like a Ninja cop laser helmet. "You must be Logan."

"Juliette tells us you'll be working on the shop remodel," Gertie added.

Juliette only half listened as her friends introduced themselves, offering drinks and cookies and probably their firstborn children.

Logan politely declined.

"What were you doing out on the pier with the house-boat crew?" Gertie asked.

He looked back at the wave of people on the sidewalk. "I wasn't with them. I docked my boat and got stuck at the tail end of their parade."

Juliette gestured to the houseboat group. "Don't you want to check out the celebrities?"

"Not really."

Of course he wouldn't be interested. The great Logan O'Connor probably believed the world revolved around him. If people weren't in his orbit, they weren't worth his time. Well, someone needed to show him he wasn't *all that*.

"I think it's great the celebrities are here," Juliette said with forced enthusiasm. "They're exactly what this island needs. Fun. And I look forward to having some. Molly says I should sweep Brock Templeton off his feet and fly off into the sunset with him."

Molly stopped eating her cookie midbite, staring at Juliette as if she'd sprouted an extra head. "I don't remember saying that."

Logan raised a brow. "Don't you mean *ride* off into the sunset?"

Heat crept up Juliette's cheeks. Typical of him to correct her in something so insignificant.

"Not if I flap my wings," she blurted. Okay, that was bad. "You know. Like those superheroes? With the wings . . ." Yeah, that was worse.

She snagged the last bite of cookie from Molly's hand and popped it into her mouth. Must. Stop. Talking.

Molly scowled at her, watching in resentment as Juliette ate the last of her cookie. "She-demons have wings, too."

"They do," Gertie said with authority. "The red, leathery kind. Vespa had a pair in *Attack of the Succubus*."

"I remember that movie," Logan mused. "That was a classic."

Gertie tilted her head and regarded Logan thoughtfully. "You know, you're not just another pretty face. I like you." She patted the grass next to her. "Come sit with us and tell us your whole life story."

He grinned. "I'd love to, but I have to make a run to the lumberyard. I'm replacing the hardwood floors in my house."

"Nice." Gertie gave Juliette the side eye. "Hard wood is always nice."

That's it. Gertie needed to die a slow death. Preferably something involving zombies.

"I just wanted to relay a message from my uncle," Logan said to Juliette. "He's having a dinner at his house on Sunday night before he and Caleb leave on their trip. He wanted me to ask if you'd come."

Juliette felt a prickle of annoyance. Romeo could have asked her himself. They texted each other often enough. She knew he was probably running around trying to get some last minute things done before his Florida vacation. It was no big deal, really. It's just that for the past three years she'd been Romeo's right hand. They worked well together. But now that Logan was in the picture, Juliette felt a little like an outcast. She didn't like it.

"I don't know," she found herself saying. "I might be busy that night. I'll have to check my calendar."

Logan looked slightly amused, as if he knew the only thing she had planned for Sunday night was curling up with her cat and watching old *Firefly* episodes with a pint of butter pecan ice cream.

"It's at five o'clock, if you can make it," he said. "Otherwise I guess I'll see you on Monday."

"Yup."

He said good-bye and walked away.

She braced herself for impact. Three . . . two . . . one . . .

"Sweet sugary balls of—"

"That man is sooo—"

Juliette held up her hand. "I already know what you guys are going to say and the answer is, I'm not interested."

"Why not?" Gertie demanded. "He's gorgeous, and seems really nice. And he's got great taste in movies, so you know he's smart. Besides, you've been single now for how many years?"

Juliette frowned. "I date guys all the time."

"Yeah, date and then *un*date, as soon as they start asking you personal questions. Like what's your middle name."

"That's not why I broke up with Drummer Guy, and you know it," Juliette said. "Come on, what normal guy shaves his head into an eighties mullet?"

"All right," Gertie said. "What about that lifeguard over at the community center?"

Juliette made a face. "He wore a Speedo to the beach on our first date. That's just way too much information up front."

Gertie lifted an eyebrow. "Good information?"

Juliette paused. "Let's just say, it was hard to decipher."

"The bank guy didn't wear a banana hammock," Molly said, crossing her arms.

"No, the bank guy wore a Rolex," Juliette said. "His idea of a fun date was taking me to the mall so he could"— she made air quotes with her fingers—"dress me right."

"Well, I still think you should consider Logan O'Connor,"

Gertie said. "He can't be any worse than that biker guy. Remember him? Always angry and broke."

Juliette shrugged. "He had a lot of financial commitments."

"Yeah, Gertie. Don't be so judgmental," Molly said sweetly. "Beer and sawed-off shotguns don't just grow on trees, you know."

Juliette rolled her eyes. "I hate you guys. You know that, right?"

"We know," Gertie sang back. "We love you, too."

"And because we love you, we want to see you happy," Molly added. "Sometimes it seems like you don't even want to find someone."

"She's right," Gertie said. "You, my dear, are scared of commitment."

Juliette drew her knees up and hugged herself. "No, I'm not. I'm just uninterested. There's a difference." When were her friends going to understand that she didn't want the same things they did? "Look, I'm happy that you guys each have somebody, and I'm thrilled for Emma that she's getting married, but I've got everything I need. I have plans for my future, none of which involve getting all tangled up in an emotional mess with someone. Especially someone like Logan O'Connor."

Gertie looked skeptical. "You're actually telling us, your two closest friends, that you don't think he's jump-your-bones sexy?"

"I mean . . ." Juliette hesitated. "He's all right." It was the understatement of the century. No one could argue that Logan wasn't scorching hot. But he was also arrogant, overly judgmental, and part of a past she wanted to forget. There would be no jumping of bones. "I just don't find him that attractive."

It was clear from their expressions they didn't buy it.

Time to activate the deflector shields. "Besides," Juliette said brightly, "I'd much rather focus on Brock Templeton."

Gertie's face lit up. "Good idea. And Brock's a verified playboy, so he's not going to try to trap you into a fate worse than death."

"That's for sure," Molly agreed. "If you want no strings attached, Brock's your guy."

Gertie began gathering up the picnic supplies. "We need to all be at the barbeque on the beach tomorrow night. It's a kick-off celebration for *Hollywood Houseboat*, and they've invited some locals to add authenticity to the filming."

"It's going to be filmed?" Molly tugged at the hem of her blouse. "I heard the camera adds ten pounds."

"Oh, have some pity," Gertie said. "You're gorgeous, and you've got more boobs than you need. I have none. How is that fair?"

The two women chatted back and forth as Juliette helped pack up. She stood and stretched, staring at the small boat docked at the end of the pier. She remembered Logan's grandfather only vaguely, but he always seemed so devoted to Logan. They used to go fishing on that boat. Juliette once stood at the edge of the woods when she was just a girl, watching them load up the truck with the boat on a trailer hitch. His grandpa ruffled his hair and told jokes. She was too far away to hear them, but she knew they were funny because Logan threw his head back and laughed. What must it have been like to have the attention of someone who loved you so unconditionally like that? Her own father had been so quiet after her mother died. They never did anything together.

"Juliette," Gertie asked. "You in?"

She turned away from the waterfront. "For what?"

"Haven't you been listening? The celebrity barbeque is tomorrow night. You want to go, or not?"

"Think of Brock and his sexy Australian accent," Molly said dreamily. "And how much fun you'd have if you guys got together."

"Considering how many eager female fans he has," Juliette said, "it's highly unlikely."

"You never know," Molly said. "Just think: you and Brock. Together. I mean, he might ask you to marry him, but you can rest assured he'd leave you at the altar before you could seal the deal. He's done it twice before."

Juliette slapped her hand over her heart in exaggerated glee. "Well, when you put it that way . . ." No commitment. No one to get in the way of her plans. No one to *bother* her. "How could I refuse?"

Chapter Six

The beach path leading down to the celebrity barbeque was buzzing with people. A thin sliver of moonlight reflected on the surface of the water, and Juliette's body thrummed with a wild, restless energy. She adjusted the hem of her blue slip dress, loving the glint of mirrored embroidery. It was the dress she always wore when she felt adventurous.

A hum of excitement filled the air as a crowd of fans gathered behind a roped-off area in the sand.

"Everyone step back," a huge man called. He looked like a bouncer at a nightclub, with a tight shirt and steroid-induced arm muscles. Beside him stood a gaunt woman holding a small clipboard. Her pinched lips and sour expression made it very clear this was not the job she wanted.

"Only twenty people at a time," he said. "We'll rotate through every thirty minutes." He paused to listen to the sour-faced woman, then said, "Either wait your turn, or go home."

"Charming," Juliette muttered under her breath. She shifted from one foot to the other, searching for her friends in the crowd. It was difficult to find them in the jostling sea of people. Maybe they'd already been admitted into the party.

"Stop it," a female voice hissed from the bushes. "Get off me."

Juliette whirled around, searching the lilacs on the path to her right.

"Go away," the woman's voice rose. "I already told you. No means *no*."

There was a faint, scuffling sound on the other side of the bushes. Juliette felt a rush of alarm. Clearly, the woman needed help, and whoever was with her needed a swift kick to the root balls.

Juliette charged through the lilacs, grateful that she never had to worry about branches slapping her in the face or hindering her progress. Plants and trees always seemed to sway softly around her to make room. It was a perk of being connected with Mother Nature. She burst into the clearing on the other side and stopped short, blinking at the sight in front of her.

A woman with hair the color of fiery autumn leaves was arguing with what appeared to be . . . a crow? The large bird sat on a branch at face level, and she was wagging her finger at it.

Juliette lifted her brows. Maybe the woman had had one too many drinks at the bonfire.

"I told you, now's not a good time," the woman scolded. "You can't keep following me. You need to leave."

Juliette took a hesitant step forward. "You okay?"

The woman turned with an exasperated look on her pretty, heart-shaped face. "Oh, I'm fine. I'm just trying to get him to go home, but he's not listening."

"I've never seen a pet crow before." Juliette approached the bird with caution. He seemed pretty harmless, which was a far cry better than what she'd expected.

It flitted to another branch and cocked its head, fixing Juliette with a beady stare.

The woman sighed. "He's not my pet. I made the mistake of feeding him some of my Cheetos yesterday, and now he thinks we're besties."

Juliette peered at the shiny black bird in fascination. "I can't believe he's not scared of you. Birds don't usually do this, do they?"

"Sometimes." The woman made a face. "Especially if dumb people feed them." She turned back to the crow. "Listen. If you be a good bird and get out of here, I'll give you double Cheetos tomorrow."

It cawed and edged its way closer.

"Double," she repeated, putting her hands on her hips.

The bird ruffled its glossy feathers and tilted its head.

"It's a good deal," the woman reasoned. "And you're obviously a smart bird. You should take it."

After a long pause where Juliette half expected the bird to open its beak and argue, it finally spread its wings and disappeared into the night sky.

The woman watched him fly away, then turned to Juliette. "Thanks for trying to come to my rescue. Did you think I was being assaulted?"

"Well, I did hear you say 'no means no.'"

There was a familiar warmth to the woman's smile. Even though she had to be in her midtwenties, her dimples made her appear sweet and childlike. She held out a hand. "I'm Kat."

Juliette clasped her hand and introduced herself, unable to shake the feeling of familiarity. "Have we met?"

"Doubt it. I just got here yesterday with the houseboat. I'm part of the entourage." She drew the word out with mock importance, gesturing her hands wide. "Not the glamorous part though. I'm with the crew."

Juliette fell into step with her as they headed back to the beach path. "That must be an interesting gig."

Kat gave a huff of laughter. "If by 'interesting' you mean in the Chinese proverb sort of way? Then yes. I am living in very interesting times." At the top of the path, she stopped. "I have to go check on someone. See you down at the bonfire." She waved and marched toward the parking lot, her bright red hair billowing behind her.

Juliette made her way down the beach path. Odd woman, that one. Talks to birds. Has wild hair. Eats Cheetos. Clearly, she was good people. Juliette decided that she liked her on the spot.

A few minutes later, she found Emma and Molly standing in the crowd.

"There you are." Emma gave her a quick hug. "We thought maybe you were already at the party."

"Gertie's down there," Molly said, adjusting the neckline of her pink top. "She slipped past the guards about twenty minutes ago."

"Of course she did." Juliette looked over at the two crew members near the roped-off entrance to the beach. They were surveying the crowd like gods of Olympus, peering in boredom at the lowly mortals.

"All right," the man said. "We'll take five more people."

A squeal of feminine voices went up and Juliette found herself caught in a sea of fruity perfume and floaty hair. They pressed toward the front of the rope, and she had to shove against the crowd to breathe. This was ridiculous.

"You." Someone poked her on the shoulder. The bouncer guy motioned her toward the rope. "In." He didn't mince words.

The woman with the clipboard barely looked at her. "Sign here, then print your full name and phone number."

"Why?"

"In case you're chosen for the camera footage." Her

tone was short and clipped, just like her hair. "Do you want to go in or not?" she asked impatiently.

"I'll go if she doesn't want to," someone called behind her.

"Yeah, take me instead!" a giggling teenager said.

Juliette signed her name and information on the clipboard. Because . . . why not? She wanted to have fun and it was a bonfire, after all.

Once out of the crush of people, she turned back and saw Emma and Molly waving through the crowd.

"Make me proud," Molly called, laughing.

Juliette followed the thumping music to the bonfire down on the beach. The film crew was out in full force, weaving in and out of the partygoers with cameras and bright lights. People laughed and drank, some standing in small groups with beer and plates of sticky barbeque, others mingling near the fire, swaying to music.

Brock Templeton was sitting on a log with his back to the water, holding court with a group of fans. They were all listening to him talk with rapt attention. As expected, most of his admirers were women.

"Drink?" Kat appeared out of the crowd and handed her a wine cooler. She gestured to Brock and his groupies, tilting her head sideways and staring at them like they were aliens from another planet. "Everyone's always so fascinated with him. I don't get it."

"What, you're not dazzled by the surf god?" Juliette teased, taking a sip.

Kat snorted. "When you have to live with the guy day in and day out, the luster wears off fast, trust me."

"Oh, Kat," a low, sultry voice called out. "You've made a friend. How fabulous, darling."

Vespa Kissman swayed toward them with a beer bottle in each hand. Her stretchy red dress accentuated her body in a stunning display of perfectly tanned flesh. Even at her age of fifty-something, Vespa was a force to be

reckoned with. Up close, she was exactly the bombshell
Juliette expected. Sure, there were lines at the corners of
her eyes and she had that distinct wrinkling around her
mouth that indicated years of smoking, but she still knew
how to work her assets. She was like a big red fire engine.
Bright and shiny and impossible to ignore.

Vespa stumbled, then straightened. She laughed, tipped
her head back, and drained one of her beers.

"Double-fisting it tonight, Vespa?" Kat asked.

"It's a bonfire." Vespa waved her empty bottle. "We're
going wild like the natives. You should try it, sugar."

Kat held up her drink. "Working on it." She introduced
Juliette to Vespa.

"Ooh." Vespa's charm bracelets jangled as she gestured
to Juliette's dress. "I love this whole bohemian chic thing
you've got going on here. Who are you wearing?"

Juliette wanted to laugh. Was she kidding? She didn't
have the money for designer clothes. All her money went
straight into savings so she'd have enough to buy the florist
shop when Romeo retired. She'd even lined up a loan, finally managing to save enough to make him a competitive
offer. Designer clothes—even regular new clothes—weren't
high on her priority list these days. She'd bought the dress
at a thrift store and sewed the broken straps to fit her.

Before she could answer Vespa, a loud drumbeat picked
up and dancers cheered, forming a circle around the
bonfire.

Vespa tossed her now empty bottles in the sand and held
her hands out. "Ladies, come dance with me." She bounced
to the beat of the drums, her spandex dress working over-
time to keep her assets from popping free.

"Oh, I was just—" Juliette began, but Vespa grabbed
her hand and pulled her into the dancing circle.

Kat waved them off, and Juliette barely had enough

time to set her drink on a log before being swept up in the group of twirling, laughing people. Four men with hand drums kept the beat going strong, and soon Juliette was whooping and jumping with everyone else as they circled the fire.

Juliette lifted her hands and tilted her head up to the sky, grinning at the canvas of stars. The crowd's laughter was intoxicating, and soon she was moving with them, spinning in circles and laughing with wild abandon. She whirled until she was dizzy, until she couldn't catch her breath. This was exactly what she needed. Just pure, carefree fun. It was impossible to worry about anything when you danced around the fire under the stars. Finally unable to continue, she spun out of the circle and staggered to a log beyond the fire, giggling like a fool.

And then she saw Logan.

He was sitting across the circle, watching her. Firelight glinted off his tawny hair, casting shadows along the sharp, masculine angles of his face.

A pretty blond girl sat beside him, chatting away and staring up at him like he was single-handedly responsible for inventing the sun. Her hair was sleek and shiny, and her clothes were simple but elegant. In khaki shorts and a pastel blouse, she looked like the type of girl who played tennis at the country club and enjoyed yachting. Boring and basic. Perfect for someone like him.

Juliette felt a stab of some emotion she didn't care to examine.

The girl leaned in to say something and he tilted his head, but his eyes never left Juliette's face. His mouth curved up in that secret smile.

Juliette couldn't tell if it was meant for her, or if he was reacting to something the girl said. Who even cared? Definitely not her. She tore her gaze away. She did not share secret smiles with Logan O'Connor. Or anything else.

She sprang up and walked down to the water's edge, kicking off her sandals in annoyance. Why did he bother her so much? What did it matter if some girl was hanging all over him? All those old feelings she'd had for him in the past needed to stay just where they were. In the past. Hiking the skirt of her sundress high on her thighs, she waded barefoot into the water, letting the ocean breeze soothe her heated emotions. She closed her eyes and focused on the gentle sound of the waves, wishing for a distraction. Anything to get her back to that happy place she was, moments before.

"So it's true," said a voice with a smooth Australian accent. "Mermaids do exist."

Juliette turned to see Brock Templeton standing on the shore, smiling like an official heartthrob should. His teeth were bright white against his tanned face.

She smiled back. Perfect timing. He was just the distraction she needed.

He lifted his beer in salute and took a drink, then waded barefoot into the water to join her. "You must be a local mermaid."

She blinkety-blinked her eyelashes. "Yes, but very wild. You should be careful."

He studied her for a moment with interest, his gaze dipping appreciatively to her chest, then back up to her face. "Maybe I like wild women."

Molly was right. He was a player, but a charming one. "I've heard that about you."

He jerked his chin, urging her to continue. "What have you heard?"

"That you're all about living on the edge."

"It's my favorite place." He gave her another once-over,

his gaze lingering on her exposed thighs where she held her dress in her hands. "Maybe you should join me some-time."

A small wave caught her off balance and she faltered.

He reached out a hand to steady her, then leaned close and said, "What's your name, mermaid?"

Juliette could feel his warm breath against her cheek. He smelled like beer and sporty men's cologne. Axe? Surely not.

Before she could answer, the camera crew was upon them. Several women splashed into the water, squealing and laughing as they caught up to Brock. They wrapped their arms around him from behind, coaxing him to join the party again. One of the girls slid her hands up his chest and whispered something in his ear. He grinned, then gave Juliette an apologetic smile as they pulled him back to the bonfire.

"What's your name, miss?" A cameraman stood in the water, filming as she watched Brock leave. "Was that your first kiss with Brock?"

Juliette glanced at him. "We weren't kissing." And even if they were, she wasn't the kiss-and-tell type. Especially not with a TV camera aimed at her face.

"Are you upset that he left you?" a crew member called from the shore.

She frowned. "Why would I be?"

"What were you two arguing about?" The cameraman stepped closer.

Juliette squinted against the bright light.

"A lovers' quarrel?" the man on shore called hopefully.

"Of course not," she said in exasperation. This was getting stupid. She splashed back toward the shore.

The camera guy followed behind her. "Does it bother you that he left you for another woman?"

Juliette rolled her eyes. "I don't care what he does, or with whom. I just met him." Back on the beach, she located her sandals and yanked them on.

The guy on shore peered at her through thick, tortoise-shell glasses. "Is Brock seeing someone else behind your back?"

Unbelievable. It was as if they didn't have ears. "Look." She gave them both a level stare. "Just because he talked flirty to me doesn't mean we're engaged. Got it?"

"Talked flirty to me," the cameraman repeated. He looked at the other guy. "That's good. We should use that."

"So how long have you and Brock been secretly engaged?" the man with the glasses asked.

Juliette jammed her hands onto her hips. "Are you kidding me right now? What is wrong with you guys? It's like you're physically incapable of hearing the words coming out of my mouth. There's nothing going on between me and Brock."

"We're just trying to get the story," the cameraman said defensively. "It's our job."

"But there *is* no story here." She flung her hands in the air. "Nothing to tell."

"Then it's our job to make a story," the other guy said.

"Juliette." Logan was suddenly standing beside her. "Everything okay?"

She took a deep breath and let it out in a rush. "I'm fine." As much as he annoyed her, she had to admit hearing his voice snapped everything into perspective. His was a voice of reason. At least he was capable of listening when she spoke. These two idiots made her feel like she'd fallen down a rabbit hole. It was like trying to reason with Tweedle Dee and Tweedle Dum.

The man with the camera nudged his buddy. "Her name's Juliette."

"What's going on?" Logan asked. It was a casual question, but there was an edge to it that made the men shift on their feet, glancing at him nervously.

"We're just trying to get the story between her and Brock," the guy with the glasses said.

Juliette gritted her teeth. "And I keep trying to tell them, there is no story."

"We saw you two kissing out in the water," the cameraman said. "Clear as day."

"No, you didn't." Juliette seethed. "Because we *weren't*."

"Gentlemen," Logan said in a voice that brooked no argument, "if she says there's no story, there's no story. Let it go."

For one shining moment, she felt a wave of gratitude.

"Not every woman wants to sweep Brock Templeton off his feet and fly off into the sunset with him," Logan added.

Aaand the moment was gone. He was making fun of her. Typical.

Tweedle Dee's forehead creased, as though he were thinking hard. "I believe it's *ride* off into the sunset."

"Yes," Tweedle Dum agreed. "Ride, not fly."

That's it. She'd had enough. Time to climb back up the rabbit hole. She whirled and marched away without a backward glance. A familiar male chuckle may or may not have followed her up the path. It was hard to tell over the music. Either way, she ignored it.

Chapter Seven

For as long as Juliette could remember, she rose with the sun. It was both a blessing and a curse.

On a good day, she was happy to get up early so she could tiptoe out into the quiet, damp garden and breathe in the fresh scent of green things growing. She loved to feel the grass under her bare feet, run her hands over the soft petals of the rhododendrons that grew in the corner near the woods, revel in the sharp scents of pine and damp moss mingling with roses and lilies.

On a not so good day, getting up this early was a pain in the butt because she had too much time to think.

She had declined Romeo's dinner offer the previous night, preferring to say her good-byes over the phone. The idea of sitting down to dinner with Logan had been too much, and the last thing she wanted to do was participate in a family gathering with them. It would be easier to keep a professional distance if all interaction remained in the workplace, where it belonged.

Juliette sipped her cinnamon tea as she sat on the back porch swing. Her old cat Luna was curled on the bench beside her. Juliette stroked the cat's soft black fur, taking comfort in the warm, purring body.

Determined not to think of Logan, she let her gaze roam over her beloved garden. It reminded her of an old English fairy-tale painting, with all the flowers growing in no particular order. Rosebushes wound around the perimeter, some trailing over an old trellis that no longer stood upright. The broken latticework leaned at an angle, its spindly arms spread out, as though to hug the flowering vines.

Blackberry bushes flanked one side of the garden while tulips and daffodils peeked out around the spiky leaves to soak up the early morning sunshine. Many of the flowers weren't even in season, but her garden didn't care about rules. Emma often said that the garden was a reflection of Juliette's personality. Wild and carefree, laughing in the face of tradition.

It was a beautiful morning and she should've been content, but Logan's sudden presence in her life made it impossible. For the next few weeks, she was going to have to find some way to get used to him being around. With all the change happening, she couldn't shake the nagging feeling that things were going to go wildly out of control, and not in the way she expected.

She shifted restlessly on the swing, readjusting the patchwork quilt around her shoulders.

Luna grumbled and jumped off the bench.

"Sorry, your majesty. I'm edgy this morning," Juliette said. "Big changes are on the horizon. Romeo's gone, there's a remodel about to happen, and I have to hire a new employee. Lots to worry about. And let's not forget Logan. He starts work at the shop today."

Luna cocked her head.

"Yes, the same Logan from across the woods. But things are different now. He's grown up and so am I."

The cat twitched an ear, regarding Juliette through half-closed eyes.

"Don't look at me in that tone of voice," Juliette said.

"That was over a decade ago, and I have absolutely zero feelings for him now. I'll be fine. It's going to be business as usual."

Luna turned her back on Juliette and began washing a paw.

"Thanks for the vote of confidence," Juliette said wryly. Her old cat was wise beyond her years, though just how many years was a mystery. Juliette's mom had been a healer, and she'd healed Luna as a kitten. Her mom used to joke that Luna was going to live all nine of her lives at once.

Juliette finished the last of her tea, stood, and stretched. It was time to get ready for work. What were today's goals?

1) Fill bouquet orders for the annual librarians' luncheon.
2) Mix up an herbal remedy for the gardenia plants.
3) Make lavender bath bombs.
4) Ignore Logan as much as humanly possible.

The first three things on her list would be easy as springtime. But the last item . . . Images of Logan from the barbeque flashed across her mind. Tawny hair glowing gold in the firelight. Hot, dark eyes on hers. Teasing smile that made her flush with warmth, even now. Whether she wanted to admit it or not, the last item on her list was going to be tricky.

Logan parked his truck in the lot behind the florist shop, yawning. After yet another night of restless sleep, he could tell it was going to be one of those mornings. He strode toward the back door, slowing down when he saw Juliette waiting for him.

She stood in the doorway, hands on her hips, glaring at him like a barefoot Valkyrie in a rainbow-colored sundress. The early morning breeze swirled through her dark hair, and her berry-stained lips were pursed in anger.

Woah. He knew that look on a woman. Juliette was gloriously pissed.

"Morning," he said hesitantly, stopping a few feet away. He'd been around his share of minefields before. Caution was priority one.

"What," she said in her lilting, velvety voice, "is that?" She pointed to the front of the shop, where a large pile of two-by-fours were stacked outside.

Logan glanced at the supplies he'd delivered earlier that morning. "Lumber."

"Yes, I know," she ground out. "But why is it out there blocking the path to my front door?"

He stuffed his hands into the pockets of his jeans. "Well, now. I wanted to take it around back, but the manager told me to leave it out front by the fence. Remember?" He waited a beat. "Manager?"

Bright patches of color formed on her cheeks, and she crossed her arms in frustration.

An unfortunate move on her part, because now he had to try really hard not to stare at the perfect swell of her breasts above the neckline of her dress. *Don't look down.* Fail. *Don't look—* Fail. *Damn it.*

She looked like she was ready to unleash all her wrath on him . . . and he wanted it? Yeah. He was an idiot. Too many years in the army did things to a man. It reminded you that life was fleeting. And when you see something good, you want to reach out and hold on. Even if you know you'll get burned.

"I didn't know the lumber delivery would be that big," she said. "You need to move it before customers get here."

"After I have coffee."

She stiffened.

He knew he was playing with fire, but it had been a hell of a morning. He shouldn't have had so much wine at his uncle's house last night, but Caleb's attempt at cooking duck a l'orange had made it more than necessary. And it had been a long time since he'd done something as carefree and normal as having dinner with family.

Juliette shook her head, and a strand of wavy hair fell over one eye. It looked like a ribbon of dark silk against her soft skin. He wanted to run his fingers over the sleek length of it, but he wasn't that much of a fool.

"You can't have coffee," she said. "We don't have any."

Logan eyed the old coffeepot on the counter behind her. "You sure about that?"

"That thing barely works. It only makes sludge."

"I'm okay with sludge." He'd been in combat and eaten things he'd prefer not to remember. Sludge was a staple, as far as he was concerned. "As long as it's caffeinated."

"It's not," she said quickly. "We've got nothing but decaf. You'll have to go somewhere else. But not until you remove those planks of wood from the walkway."

Logan shook his head. He was tired, he needed Tylenol, and his days of taking orders were over. The sooner she understood that, the better it would be for both of them. "Coffee first."

Juliette sucked in a breath, her eyes flashing. "I can't have customers climbing over that pile of lumber to get to the front door. It's a hazard." She lifted her slender arm. A long scrape ran from the inside of her elbow to her wrist. It wasn't deep, but tiny flecks of blood still oozed from where the rough lumber had grazed her skin.

A sharp twinge of guilt stabbed him, and he closed the gap between them without thinking. "Let me see."

"I'm fine." Juliette backed away, bumping up against the cutting table in the center of the room. "It's just a scrape, but you need to move that stuff away before someone else gets hurt."

"I will," he said firmly. "But first, you need to bandage that." She was pissed at him. That was clear. But he wasn't going to let this go. It was stupid to leave the lumber on the walkway; he knew that. Romeo trusted him to take care of things, and he should have been more careful.

He walked inside and began flinging open cupboards. "Where's your first-aid kit?"

"I can do it myself," she insisted.

"Where?"

She let out a frustrated breath and pointed to the sink. "There might be something in that jar over there."

A moment later, he stood beside her as she rinsed her arm with cold water. He knew she didn't want his help, but he didn't care. She'd gotten hurt, and it was his fault. He needed to fix it.

He dug through the ceramic jar beside the sink. It was shaped like a ridiculous frog wearing a gold crown. There was nothing in it but a tiny Band-Aid, three cotton balls, and a pair of tweezers. Unacceptable.

He scowled, holding up the frog prince's head in one hand. "What kind of first-aid kit is this?"

"It's not," she said, taking in the thunderous expression on his face. Her lips curved. "It's a cookie jar."

He plunked the frog's head back on its body. "Useless."

"Not if you have cookies." She clamped her mouth together, like she was fighting not to smile.

Logan watched in fascination as her blue eyes lit with humor, her lips curving softly in spite of her efforts. The moment she gave up and smiled at him, he forgot everything.

It was like sunlight, warming him in all the right places. He glanced at her lush mouth, the soft curve of her neck, the hollow at the base of her collarbone. Alarm bells went off in his head and damn if they didn't sound like a siren song, enticing him to move closer. She smelled like fresh herbs and something sweeter. Honey, maybe. He liked honey.

Logan stepped back fast, running a hand through his hair. There was nothing he could do here. He needed to get away. Do something useful. Preferably something physical. He was only here to clean up the place and help out with the renovations. There was no room in his future plans for a wildcat like Juliette. He'd vowed to have a normal, peaceful life, and someone like her—a *Holloway*, for god's sake—was the furthest thing from it. Getting close to her was a bad idea.

Juliette's smile faded, and she turned away. "I'll be fine." She grabbed a paper towel from the roll on the counter and dried her arm. "Just go move the stuff outside, will you?"

He was out the back door before she'd finished her sentence. Holy hell. He needed to move. Logan marched to the huge stack of lumber and heaved a two-by-four onto his shoulder, balancing the weight of it as he moved it to the clearing behind the shop. It was easy, mindless work, but required just enough concentration to leave him little time to think about blue eyes and bad ideas.

Twenty minutes later, Juliette finished another floral arrangement, setting the cobalt blue vase in the front window. She paid no attention to Logan outside, who was hauling the last of the lumber to the back of the shop. She certainly wasn't watching the way his muscles bunched and flexed as he hefted the wood onto his broad shoulders.

And she barely noticed how his T-shirt clung to his narrow torso, the hard planes of muscle evident from sweat, the jeans clinging to his backside as he moved. Nope. Nothing to see there.

She flipped the CLOSED sign to OPEN and walked to the register. Time to focus on her to-do list. Especially the part where she was supposed to ignore Logan as much as humanly possible. It shouldn't be that hard. She was human and therefore, it was possible. She just needed to get a grip and focus on work. It was going to be a busy day. Mondays always were.

"Hello, again," a voice called from the doorway.

Kat walked in wearing black boots, black shorts, and a black peasant top. Her bright red hair was smoother today. It looked like lava, flowing around her shoulders in huge waves. In her arms she held a shivering scrap of fluff wearing a pink rhinestone collar.

"We were just checking out all the shops," she said, approaching the counter with the Yorkshire terrier. "This is Hank." She held the dog up for introductions. "Hank the Tank."

Juliette reached out to pat him on the head. She loved dogs. If Luna wasn't so fussy, she'd have one of her own. Hank was tiny and adorable. He couldn't have weighed more than five pounds. His tail spun like an outboard motor as he furiously licked her hand.

"You'll have to excuse him," Kat said. "He can't control his licker."

Juliette grinned. "What brings you two in?"

"We're taking a long walk, with an emphasis on *long*."

"Trouble on the houseboat?"

Kat rolled her eyes. "Mirage—she's our resident supermodel—is fighting with Vespa again. I think they enjoy arguing. It's like a cardio workout for them. Anyway,

Hank and I needed a break." She looked at the shelves of plants, the flowering baskets and small potted trees lining the front windows. "This place suits you."

"What kind of work do you do on the houseboat?" Juliette asked.

"You're looking at it." Kat gestured to Hank. "I'm Vespa's official dog handler."

Juliette glanced at the dog. "I didn't know that was a thing."

"Oh, it's a thing. Especially with the Hollywood set. Vespa likes the idea of a dog, but she doesn't want any of the work. So I basically feed, bathe, and care for him, and she accessorizes with him." Kat scratched the dog under the chin. "I think Hank's tired of being an arm charm, though. He wants to turn in his resignation and explore other options, don't you, Hank?"

He yipped.

Juliette felt a surge of warmth for them. As a person who had lengthy conversations with her own cat, Juliette had a soft spot for people who talked to their animals. "Sounds like a tough gig on that boat, dealing with all those fancy personalities."

"It's not my favorite job, I'll say that." Kat gave the dog a pat and set him on the floor to nose around. "I'm just so over the egos. I've lived in LA for five years, so I thought I was prepared, but you never quite realize just how entitled some people are until you're stuck on a boat with them."

"Well, if you and Hank ever need to get away, you're always welcome to hang out with me."

"I think I'll take you up on that offer." Kat lifted a bar of soap from a small basket near the register. She read the label out loud. "Bee Chill."

"That's one of the honey and vanilla soaps I make. It helps soothe frazzled nerves."

Kat slapped it on the counter. "Sold."

A few minutes later, Juliette waved good-bye and watched them through the window. Kat set Hank on the ground outside, chatting to him like he was a friend. Cuter still, he sat there listening, tilting his head as if he understood. When she beckoned to him, he followed along at her heels without a leash. They definitely seemed to work well together, which was more than Juliette could say for herself and her new coworker.

She went in search of the broom, catching a glimpse of Logan out the side window. He looked exactly like the sexy cover of one of Emma's romance novels. The ones with hard body SEALS or wild highlanders or hot firefighters. She had to keep reminding herself that he was just Logan. The boy from the other side of the woods.

She swept the broom closer to the side window, stealing another peek. Just to make sure he was moving all the lumber—not for any other reason. He was standing with his back to her, breathing heavily. He'd been quick and efficient, but it couldn't have been easy. Somehow, he'd managed to clear the path right on time.

Logan turned and met her gaze through the window.

She jerked her head away and busied herself with the broom.

He tapped on the glass and gestured to the café across the street.

An hour later, she heard the back door open. When she went to investigate, Logan had already gone. But there were two large boxes on the cutting table. One was a first-aid kit in a heavy-duty aluminum case. The other was a shiny new coffeemaker.

Chapter Eight

Juliette watched the sunrise from the small strip of beach along the waterfront. She'd risen earlier than usual, deciding to take a walk before heading into work. Maybe the crisp, ocean breeze would help clear her head. Yesterday shouldn't have been too bad, all things considered. Logan had mostly stayed outside, which suited her just fine. It was easier to ignore him that way. But then he'd gone and bought that first-aid kit and coffeemaker, which ruined everything. He was supposed to be self-centered and annoying. He wasn't supposed to do helpful things like that. It blurred the lines she was trying so desperately to draw between them.

She drew a hard line in the wet sand with her toe. A small wave washed over her ankles, filling the narrow ridge and smoothing it out until it disappeared. She drew the line again—deeper this time. Another wave rolled in, washing it away in a matter of seconds. She turned her back on it, rolled up her jeans, and splashed further into the water, wrapping her arms around herself.

A lone figure approached out of the corner of her eye.

Brock Templeton was jogging along the shore. It was odd to see him without his camera crew and admiring fans.

She watched him approach until he slowed to a stop in front of her, breathing heavily.

Juliette had to give Molly credit. The man did kind of look like a surf god, all tanned skin and windblown hair.

"Mermaid," he said with his trademark grin. "We meet again." Boyish dimples. Sparkling eyes. The camera loved him for a good reason.

Juliette smiled. "I thought Australians said 'G'day, mate' or something like that."

"I'll say whatever you want, if it'll make you happy."

Yeah, he was a smooth talker. The Australian accent didn't hurt, either. No wonder all the women were lining up. Juliette joined him on the shore, noting the way his dark hair waved perfectly around his face, like he'd arranged it with some kind of mousse or gel. Did he always do his hair when he went for a morning run? Not that it mattered. Some guys were just really meticulous about their appearance. She'd dated her fair share of pretty boys before, and no one could argue that Brock wasn't pretty.

"You never told me your name at the barbie the other night," he pointed out.

"No, I didn't. You got sidetracked. In fact"—Juliette picked up her flip-flops and looked out at the empty stretch of beach—"where is your entourage this morning?"

Brock chuckled. "Anywhere but here, thank god. I'm not usually a morning person, but this is the only time I can get a moment alone." He gazed out at the ocean. "It's nice, this time of day."

"Yes," she agreed. "It's one of the things I love about dawn. Nobody usually wants these hours except me. So, for just a little while"—she spread her arms wide—"I get to have the world all to myself."

"Until I show up." There went the dimples again.

"Until you intrude," she teased.

"And if I beg you to share your world with me?"

Okay, that was kind of corny. But did she care? Not so much. Maybe that's how TV stars talked. Maybe they got so used to playing a role, they didn't know how to stop.

"I guess I can make an exception just this once," she said lightly. "But if your camera crew gets here, all bets are off."

"Deal." He linked his hands behind his neck to stretch, his arm muscles flexing admirably.

Even if he did it on purpose, she wasn't complaining.

His gaze roamed over her in obvious appreciation. "I didn't expect to see anyone up this early."

"I've always been an early riser."

Brock yawned. "Me too."

"I thought you said you weren't usually a morning person," Juliette said in surprise.

"Oh, right," Brock said. "I meant, I've been getting up early since we got here. Have you lived here long?"

"All my life. It must seem pretty small compared to where you're from."

"It really is," he agreed. Then he gestured to her and added quickly, "But the scenery's lovely."

Okay, he was on perma-flirt. But there was nothing wrong with casual, meaningless flirting. In fact, that was supposed to be the plan, wasn't it? Have a fun summer fling with a nice, hot guy. No strings attached.

They strolled toward the path leading up to the waterfront. She checked the sunrise to gauge the time. She needed to get to work. There was a banquet at one of the hotels, and she had to put together a large order of bouquets for an early morning pickup.

She dusted the sand off her feet and slipped into her flip-flops. "Well, it was nice seeing you again."

"You're leaving so soon?" Brock looked surprised.

Juliette guessed people didn't usually walk away from him so fast. Maybe women usually jumped on him and he never had to make much of an effort. Maybe it was time he did.

"I have to get to work," she said. "I have to prepare bouquets before I open the shop."

"You work at a flower shop?"

"I do."

"Nice," he said with admiration. "I can just imagine you." He held his hands up and traced the air in a vague outline of her body. "Lounging around all day surrounded by flowers."

Juliette wrinkled her brow in amusement. "I don't really get a lot of time to lounge around. Because, you know. It's my job."

"Of course," he said quickly. "When will I see you again?"

Juliette hesitated. "I really can't say." Wow. Was she really doing this? Playing hard to get? Her friends would be appalled, but for some reason she just wasn't in a big hurry to climb Brock the Rock. Maybe she'd kick herself for it later. She'd been known to make poor decisions in the morning before caffeine.

"Why not?" His expression was full of so much surprise, she almost laughed. Clearly, he wasn't used to getting this answer from women.

The sound of voices floated on the wind, and Juliette saw three of the camera crew running toward them. *Oh, hells no.* She wasn't about to trip down that rabbit hole again. She turned to go.

"At least tell me your name," Brock insisted. "You know mine, so it's only fair."

"Juliette." She ran up the path toward the street before the camera crew could reach them.

"Wait. Can I get your number?" he called after her.

She didn't look back. Just kept going until she reached Front Street, still puzzling over the fact that she'd just played hard to get with a hot TV celebrity. The truth was, he didn't seem all that interesting. Still, it wasn't like her to pass up a chance to have some fun. Frowning, Juliette hurried toward the florist shop. Something was off with her this morning, but she didn't care to examine what it was.

Next time, she'd do better. Next time—if there was a next time—she'd give Brock a chance.

Chapter Nine

It was ten o'clock in the morning by the time Logan strolled in to work. Juliette tried to tell herself it didn't matter; his job was his business. But that wasn't entirely true. As the standing manager of Romeo's Florist Shop, it was her responsibility to oversee everything that went on, which included the business of Romeo's slow-moving, swaggering nephew.

"Nice of you to finally make it in," she said when he came through the back door. She'd spent the morning swamped with customers and orders, and in the middle of it she'd had to deal with Logan's lumberyard delivery all by herself.

He walked over to the coffeepot and poured himself a cup from the new machine. His face looked drawn, and there were dark shadows under his eyes.

Juliette crossed her arms and opened her mouth to speak, but Logan held up a hand.

"Before you start," he said, "you should know that my answer to everything for the next five minutes is going to be 'coffee.'"

"You should know that you're late," she tossed back. "We open at eight o'clock here."

He raised his mug in salute and took a sip.

"The lumber company stopped by this morning at eight-thirty," she continued, "and since you weren't here, they started dumping all the supplies by the front walkway. And this time, the store was filled with customers."

Logan leaned against the counter and regarded her with bloodshot eyes. He took another slow sip.

"What is wrong with you this morning?" she blurted. "You look like you drank one too many shots of tequila last night and had to crawl home on your lips."

His mouth lifted at one corner as if he found her amusing.

"It's not funny," she said with growing annoyance. "You're supposed to be here on time so you can handle all the re-model stuff."

He closed his eyes and rubbed his face with one hand. "A friend kept me up all night."

An image of the pretty blonde from the bonfire flashed across Juliette's mind. She'd been wrapped around him like a human pretzel, and it hadn't seemed to bother him.

Juliette bristled. "Look, if you want to party all night long with Suzy Sunshine, go right ahead. But you're still expected to show up on time and get some actual work done here. The rest of us have to do our jobs. I'm sure Romeo wouldn't be thrilled to know you were dragging in two hours late on your second day of work."

Logan stopped with his cup halfway to his mouth. "Suzy Sunshine?"

"That girl from the barbeque."

He frowned. "You mean Bella?"

"Whatever." She wouldn't know. Because she didn't care.

"We weren't partying," he said casually. "Not all night, anyway. I wasn't up for it."

She had the sudden urge to throw something at him. Instead, she smiled sweetly. "Stamina problems, huh? Not a shocker. It's your second day on the job and you can't even keep up."

Logan set his cup on the counter with a *thud*, an unspoken challenge in his eyes.

All Juliette's nerve endings went on high alert. She suddenly felt like a rabbit in plain sight of a wolf.

His gaze slid lazily down her body in a sensual caress, then back up to linger on her mouth before meeting her eyes. "I have no problems keeping up, *Juliette*." He drew her name out on his tongue like he could taste it. "I'd be happy to prove it to you, if you don't believe me."

Heat scorched up the back of her neck, across her cheeks, her chest, her limbs. He was looking at her as though he knew all her dark secrets, which was absurd. No man knew her that intimately. Sure, she'd been with guys before; but she never gave herself away emotionally. She just wasn't the type to go overboard into lovey-dovey territory and start blabbing all her secret feelings and desires. Juliette had learned a long time ago that the people you love tend to leave, and that's just the way it was. No one had ever looked at her the way he was looking at her now. He made her feel vulnerable and exposed. She didn't like it.

Pushing her feelings aside, she steered the conversation back into neutral waters. Must remain professional! "You should've been here on time."

"Looks like you managed just fine, without me."

"In the future," she continued, using her best manager voice, "I expect you to keep to the schedule."

Logan crossed his arms and leaned against the counter.

"See, now that's the tricky thing about expectations," he drawled. "If you set the wrong ones, you'll always be disappointed."

"Is that what you had to tell Bella last night?" she shot back.

Logan blinked. Then he did the most startling thing. He tipped his head back and laughed.

It was mesmerizing. The sound of it filling the room like a favorite song she'd play over and over on a loop if she could. The look of him, head back, broad shoulders shaking, eyes crinkling at the corners. She could've grown roots and stayed there in that moment, bathed in the warmth of his laughter, for the next million years. This was madness. Definitely not neutral waters.

"How long will it take to build the redwood deck?" she demanded.

Logan's laughter ended on a chuckle. "I'm not."

"But you're supposed to build it," she insisted. "Romeo said so." It was part of their plan to make the shop more inviting—someplace people would sit and relax. Right now, most of her bath products were on a repurposed bookshelf near the register. Once they moved the bigger plants to the deck, she'd finally have the space to set up a gift shop in the corner. That was the plan.

"I'm not building a redwood deck," Logan said through a yawn.

All her annoyance shifted to anger. No one messed with her plans. Not even him. *Especially* not him.

"I discussed it with Romeo already," she said. "We have a vision for this place, and this renovation is ours, not yours. You're supposed to just follow the orders."

All the mirth was gone now, his face unreadable. "Don't you worry about it, sweetheart," he said softly. "I've got it all worked out."

The endearment pricked against her skin like a tiny thorn. "I'm not your sweetheart."

"No?" He frowned and tilted his head to the side as though trying to remember something. "That's odd."

A twinge of unease gripped her. Surely he wouldn't remember something so stupid as a flowery love note written by a foolish girl.

"I seem to remember a note telling me otherwise."

Crap. Juliette spun away and began washing her hands at the sink. "I don't know what you're talking about."

"It's been a long time," he said casually, like he was trying to recall something as mundane as the weather forecast. "But I clearly remember a note—"

"—I was *fourteen*." She squared her shoulders and turned to face him. "Kids do stupid things."

Logan said nothing. Just stood there looking at her as if he could read all the things she wasn't saying. She hated that about him. Even back when they were kids, he always seemed to see beyond the front she put up for others.

"I'm surprised you even remember that," she said lightly.

"Well, it's not every day a guy gets a letter with . . . what were those? Pressed flowers?"

Embarrassment flooded her. She still remembered placing the forget-me-nots in the note she'd so carefully written on the full moon. He seemed so much older than her back then, but she'd been convinced he was her soul mate. The note had been an attempt at a love spell. She wanted to reveal her feelings so he wouldn't leave. Why did people always leave?

"It was such a pretty note," he said. "With swirly writing. You said you wanted to be my sweetheart. I remember that clearly."

Juliette crossed her arms, annoyed. "I was kind of an idiot back then."

Again with the secret smile. "I thought it was cute."

"Well, Denise sure didn't." Denise had been his on-again, off-again girlfriend. She was one of those students with perfect clothes and a trust fund swagger.

Juliette felt the long-forgotten humiliation swell up inside her all over again. "Did you know she made copies of that note and plastered them all over the girls' locker room to humiliate me?"

Logan's easy smile faded. "I didn't know that."

She gave a half shrug to show him it didn't bother her anymore, even though the memory was a painful one. "Denise was a mean girl, and I was just a dumb kid."

"She *was* a mean girl," Logan agreed. "And I was an idiot for going out with her."

The silence stretched between them for a few moments and Juliette found herself saying, "Well, good thing we're older and wiser now. You were a terrible judge of character back then. Hopefully that girl you were with at the bonfire is a lot nicer."

Logan dipped his head. "Bella's all right."

"Good." Juliette fidgeted with the stem cutters beside the sink.

"We're old family friends," he said, as though it needed some sort of explanation.

"Great." He might think they were just friends, but Juliette had seen the way the girl looked at him. She was obviously smitten. Juliette knew because she was pretty sure she'd once looked at him the same way.

"Our parents used to play golf together."

Juliette tried to ignore the dull ache that settled over her like a well-worn blanket. After her mom died, her dad had never really recovered. Juliette had practically raised herself. If it hadn't been for her cousin Emma, the loneliness would've eaten away at her until she was just a shell, like her dad. No one ever played golf in her family. No one played anything.

Concern etched his face. "What is it?"

Once again, he saw too much. Juliette shook off the old memories and steeled herself. It was time to focus on the important things that mattered, like the florist shop. Her future. She'd wasted enough time on Logan this morning. "Look, it's going to be a busy day, and I don't really have time to sit around and talk about your dating life. I don't care who or what you do on your off hours, okay? Just show up to work on time and stay out of my way."

He was silent for a heartbeat. Two. Three. Then he turned away and rinsed the mug in the sink. Juliette could almost feel the walls go up between them. Fine. It was better this way.

She blindly grabbed the nearest bunch of long-stemmed roses from a bucket on the floor and plunked them on the table, adding, "Please just start on the redwood deck like you're supposed to."

"Not going to happen," he said coolly. "I need to set posts for the greenhouse this week. But don't worry about the deck, sweetheart. I'll get to it when I get to it."

He was out the door before she could argue.

Juliette stood there after he left, running her fingers over the delicate blooms. The petals unfurled slowly, releasing a sweet perfume into the air. "I'm not your sweetheart," she whispered. The flowers said nothing, but their significance was loud and clear. Coral roses signified desire.

Chapter Ten

"Bella shmella," Juliette muttered as she pulled fresh carnations from a bucket, trimmed the ends with cutters, and arranged them in a glass vase. The morning rush had died down, which meant her mind could wander to places it shouldn't.

What kind of a name was Bella, anyway? *Twilight* was so ten years ago. She yanked sprigs of greenery from a pile on the table and began adding them to the floral arrangements. Bella was obviously one of those high-maintenance, golf club girls. The kind who ordered half-double-decaffeinated-skinny half-caffs at Starbucks and wore zillion-dollar sunglasses and sensible shoes.

Juliette ran a hand over her messy braid and glanced down at her jeweled flip-flops.

"So what?" she said to the eucalyptus sprigs as she tucked them into the vase. She didn't have the desire, or the inclination to be a basic Bella. And anyway, golf was just an insult to Mother Nature. All that neatly manicured grass clipped way too short. Too many chemicals for honest plants to grow. Plus, let's be real. Those horrific golf outfits! Polo shirts and khaki shorts. Who willingly wears beige, for freak's sake?

Juliette chopped the stems off a few peonies a little shorter than she should've. Really, she felt sorry for Bella. It couldn't be easy living such a beige life.

"Hello?" someone called.

Juliette set the peonies back in a bucket of water and went to go help the customer. She came to a halt in the doorway, startled. "You."

As if she'd conjured her from thin air, Bella stood in the middle of the room. Except she wasn't wearing beige at all, the traitor. She had on a pair of denim shorts and a Seahawks T-shirt, with her hair pulled back into a shining ponytail. She looked cute and normal and exactly perfect for someone like Logan.

Bella arched a pencil-thin brow. "Me?"

"Oh, I meant, can I help? You, that is." Juliette cleared her throat. "Can I help you?" She slapped dirt off her hands, suddenly feeling drab.

Bella picked her way carefully toward the back counter, sidestepping the ferns and taking extra care not to brush against a large ivy plant that spilled over one of the shelves.

"You can touch them," Juliette said. "They don't bite."

Bella gave her a once-over. "You're that Holloway, right? The one who makes all the bath bombs and stuff?"

Juliette nodded. *That* Holloway? It figured. Bella came from a family like Logan's. Fine, upstanding pillars of the community. Council members, business leaders, board directors. Those types of families didn't think much of the Holloways. In their opinion, the Holloways were just the resident weirdos.

She watched as Bella began digging through the basket of hand-wrapped soaps on the counter, grabbing each one, reading labels, then shoving them aside. She seemed to be on a mission.

Juliette gathered the discarded soaps and carefully placed

them back in the basket. "Are you looking for something in particular?"

"Sort of." Bella was now searching the old bookshelf filled with Juliette's bath products. "I'll know it when I see it." She opened testers of body lotion, sniffing each one.

After a couple of minutes, Juliette said, "I think I saw you at the bonfire."

Bella glanced up, finally showing some interest. "Yes, I was with Logan. Is he here? He told me he was working here for the next few weeks."

Juliette jerked a thumb over her shoulder. "He's out back."

"Good." Bella tightened her ponytail. "But first, I'm looking for something very important." She glanced left and right, then lowered her voice even though they were the only people in the shop, and whispered, "I need to buy one of those special potions you make."

Juliette waited for her to elaborate.

"My friends would laugh at me if they knew I was doing something so silly," she said in a rush. "But I thought I'd give it a try because what the heck, right? We're not getting any younger."

"Who's not?"

"Us." Bella wagged a finger between them. "Women our age."

"I'm twenty-seven," Juliette said defensively.

"Exactly. Our clocks are ticking, and on this island, that's a death sentence, am I right? There are like, no good guys here. Trust me, I've been on the lookout. And I've got plans, see?"

No. Juliette didn't see. Twenty-seven was still plenty young. And her clock was most definitely *not* ticking, thank you very much. If Bella was looking for a cure for aging, she was going to be disappointed. Holloway magic was special, but nothing could stop the passage of time.

"The things I make are intended to inspire good feelings and help people," Juliette said. "I don't make antiaging creams or anything like that."

Bella let out a squawk of laughter that ended on a snort. "That's not what I'm here for. Look, you know how some women love to work and do all this stuff?" She flapped her hands around, gesturing to the shop. "Well, I'm not one of those working types."

Juliette pressed her lips together. "You don't say."

"It's true. I'm a Sinclair. Sinclair women know where their place is, and that's on the arm of a good man. You know what I mean?" Her smile showed lots of teeth, and there was a glint of overeager zeal in her eyes à la Patty Simcox from *Grease*.

Juliette's brows drew together. So weird. Bella looked normal, but . . .

"I've been planning my wedding for years," Bella continued with enthusiasm. "The dress, the flowers, the colors. I even have my china pattern all picked out."

"That's . . ." *Stepford wife cray cray.* "Remarkable."

"And now," Bella said triumphantly, "I finally found the perfect groom."

"Don't you mean husband?"

"Yeah, that." Bella leaned forward, excitement saturating every word. "He's perfect for me. He's good-looking, so that means our kids will have a genetic advantage. And he's from a nice family, too. He's the kind of guy who listens to everything I say and wants to please me all the time, you know what I mean? He never argues with me, either. Just lets me talk and talk, and he hangs on my every word. I can tell he's one of those guys who'll do anything I say. *Forever.*"

Juliette half expected that last word to echo like in a scary movie. Was this lady for real? "He . . . sounds perfect for you," she managed.

"I know, right?" Bella seemed so happy that she understood.

Oh, Juliette understood, all right. She understood that Bella was the walking poster child for Crazy Ex-Girlfriends Anonymous. It was no wonder she was single. Whoever got stuck with her was in for a world of hurt. Suddenly, Juliette began to smile because she knew exactly who the lucky target was.

"It's Logan O'Connor," Bella gushed.

Bingo.

"He's The One."

"How fantastic." Juliette couldn't stop grinning, imagining all the problems someone like Bella would cause him. He had no idea what he was in for. This woman was going to sink her hooks into him and make him dance like a puppet on strings. It would be fun to watch him struggle.

Bella picked up a vial of perfume. "So do these things really work?"

"They do if you're open to change. What exactly are you looking for?"

"Never mind. I think I've found it." Bella held up a glass spray bottle labeled Desire. "What's this do?"

"It invokes yearning. But it only works if the person shows interest to begin with."

"Oh, he's plenty interested," Bella said with confidence. She gazed intently at the dark red bottle and murmured, "A love potion."

"Not exactly," Juliette said. "It's more for couples who already like each other and want to spice things up, if you get my meaning."

Bella slapped her designer bag on the counter—beige, of course—and said, "I'll take it."

* * *

Logan finished measuring off the perimeter of the greenhouse foundation and started digging a hole for one of the posts. He wiped sweat from his brow with his T-shirt, which he'd pulled off an hour ago.

"Oh, there you are, Logan," called a bubbly voice.

He turned to see Bella Sinclair walking toward him.

"Well, look at you, all working hard," she said to his bare torso.

Logan clutched his balled up shirt. "What brings you out here?"

"I came to see if you wanted to get lunch."

He checked his watch and grimaced. Past twelve o'clock, and he still needed to get the last post centered. "I can't today. I've got a lot of work to do here."

She pouted and fluffed her ponytail.

Logan's stomach growled. He was actually pretty hungry.

"I just checked out your uncle's flower shop," Bella said. "I bought one of those perfumes."

Aw, hell. What was he supposed to say next? He never quite knew how to talk to Bella, because she was always going on and on about things he didn't get. Shoes and nail salon gossip and what so-and-so said to so-and-so. And now she wanted to talk about perfume? Luckily, Bella was a chatterbox. Logan never had to say much because she usually said it all.

"Some ladies from my office told me about all the great bath products they sell here at the florist shop, so I wanted to try them out. They smell divine."

"The ladies from your office?"

"No, silly." Bella gave him a playful shove. "The bath products from that Holloway girl. You know, the one in the shop?"

"Yeah." He knew the one. Logan looked at the back

window where Juliette was busy dusting the shelf. She seemed very intent on her job. Too intent.

Bella reached into a small paper bag and pulled out a bottle. "This is one of the perfumes she makes. But I'm not going to tell you what it does. You'll have to guess."

He tried to follow along, but the woman wasn't making a whole lot of sense. She sprayed some on her wrist and giggled. He checked his watch again. He probably should go get some lunch, but he'd have to do it quickly.

"Here." Bella stuck her wrist under his nose. "Smell this."

He sniffed. It was strong. But it smelled sweet and spicy and delicious. "What is that?"

She shook her head, her ponytail swinging from side to side. "Not telling." Then she sprayed a bunch more all over herself. "You'll have to ask me later."

Logan frowned. Half the time he didn't understand her chatter. This was one of those halves. He was tired. And hungry. And her ponytail was so swishy. The color of her hair reminded him of French fries. "I think I do need to get something to eat."

She perked up. "Come get a burger with me."

Great idea. A burger was exactly what he wanted. He'd fix the foundation posts when he got back. "Let me just go to the truck and grab a clean shirt."

She followed him all the way to his truck, chatting away. By the time they reached the diner down the road, Logan knew all about her friend's neighbor's underage son's speeding ticket. Or was it her friend's son's underage neighbor? It didn't matter. What did matter was that her perfume was so strong, it filled his truck and started to give him a low-grade headache.

A chatty half hour later, Logan finished the last bite of his second cheeseburger deluxe, drained his soda, and leaned back in his chair. God, that was a good meal. He hadn't realized just how hungry he'd been. Next time he wouldn't skip breakfast.

Bella rambled on about office gossip, and he tried to make the occasional correct noise to indicate he was listening. If he just repeated the last word or two of her run-on sentences, she seemed content.

"So then Jason over in accounting, not Jason T. but Jason A.," Bella was saying.

"Jason A.," Logan repeated.

"Yes, he told Julie that if she didn't like the way he wrote the report, she could write it herself. Then he said her reports were so juvenile, she might as well write them in crayon."

"Crayon," Logan repeated.

"I know, right?" Bella giggled and sipped her pink milkshake. It smelled like strawberries. Maybe he'd order one of those. A nice, creamy shake sounded really good right now. He checked his watch. It was getting late. He needed to go.

"So," Bella said, leaning closer. "Wanna go to the beach on Saturday?" That perfume she'd sprayed earlier wafted across the table, clashing with the sweet scent of her milkshake.

Logan shook his head no, but found himself saying, "Okay." He watched in fascination as the last of the strawberry shake disappeared up the straw and into her mouth.

She giggled again, licking her lips. "I gotta get back to work. Tell that girl in your shop I said thanks."

"For what?" Logan asked, searching for the server. Maybe he could get a quick milkshake to go.

"Never you mind," Bella said. "I'll tell you later."

On the way back to the shop, her perfume and nasally voice made his head ache even worse. By the time he waved her off and entered the back door to the kitchen, he went straight for the first-aid kit.

Juliette came around the corner in her faded, patched overalls—the kind of thing a farmer would wear. Her hair was in a messy knot on top of her head, with some wispy pieces falling around her face. There was a smudge of dirt on her neck, and what looked like a fistful of weeds sticking out of one pocket. She wasn't even wearing shoes, for god's sake. She just stood there leaning against the door-jamb with one foot on top of the other, her delicate toenails painted an unusual shade of blue. There was a mischievous glint in her eye and a sprig of leaves tangled in her hair. Everything about the woman was a mess. A radiant, beautiful mess.

Logan tore his gaze away and fumbled for the Tylenol.

"How was lunch?" she asked.

"I've got a headache." And, somehow, a Saturday beach date with Bella. How had that happened? He filled a glass of water from the sink, rubbing his aching temples. The scent of that perfume still permeated his brain.

Juliette walked to the corner cupboard and drew out a vial of clear liquid. There was a sudden gentleness, a depth of concern in the way she looked at him. "This will help you."

He shook his head. "No thanks."

"But this is ten times more effective than that. It's a pain reliever. I made it."

"This is fine." He popped the Tylenol and drank.

Juliette turned stiffly and put the vial away. "What's the matter? Afraid I'll turn you into a frog with my wild voodoo magic?"

He set the glass on the counter and glanced sideways at her. "Would you?"

"Of course." She walked over to the sink and started washing her hands. "That was my special Frogman elixir. I was hoping you'd fall for it, but you didn't. Next time I'll have to slip it into your drink when you're not looking."

Logan pinched the bridge of his nose with his fingers. The woman was going to be the death of him. She was as mercurial as spring weather. Sunshine and rain. One minute trying to help him, the next trying to poison him.

"First of all, I don't buy into that magic potion stuff," he told her.

She rinsed lemon-scented soap from her hands and reached for a towel without looking at him. "Suit yourself."

"And second, I just spent an hour breathing in that perfume you made and now I feel sick, so I'd rather stick with what I know."

Juliette stopped drying her hands and glanced at him. "You didn't like the perfume?"

"Not on her," Logan said firmly. "Not at all."

She dropped the towel, then stooped to pick it up. "What do you mean?"

"I don't know. She put on way too much, I guess." Why did Juliette look so bothered? Maybe she was really sensitive about her bath products. "Don't worry. I'm sure the perfume would be fine on someone else."

She gazed at him as if he were a puzzle she was trying to solve.

"What?" he asked.

"Nothing." She was standing close enough for him to see tiny flecks of green in her blue eyes. Green like all the plants she loved. Like the sprig of leaves still stuck in her hair.

Without thinking, he reached to pull it free.

Juliette started to lean away.

"Hold on." He settled a hand on her shoulder. "There's something in your hair." He could feel the warmth of her skin underneath her flimsy cotton top. Hear the soft rise and fall of her breathing as she stilled. There was an almost palpable thrum of energy in the air between them as he worked the leaves free.

"There," he murmured, looking down at her.

She didn't look away, or turn away. She looked back, eyes half closed as though in a trance, lips soft and inviting.

With infinitesimal slowness, Logan leaned in, like he was the tide and she was the shore, and through no fault of his own, his body was drawn to her. It was as if the inevitability of them, coming together, was decided long ago by some force as old as time.

The bells on the front door jangled, snapping Juliette out of her momentary lapse of sanity. She jerked away.

What just happened? If the Desire perfume didn't work on him with Bella, so be it. That just meant he never liked her to begin with. But this—whatever this was—between him and her? This was madness. It wasn't the potion, because Holloway charms didn't work on Holloway women. They only worked to help other people; that was the nature of it. So why was there this spark between her and Logan? The only logical conclusion was that their attraction was real.

She took several shaky steps back.

Logan didn't try to follow, which was a good thing. If he did, she'd be tempted to finish what they'd almost started. What the hell was wrong with her? She couldn't afford to get tangled up with him, of all people. She knew this. But clearly, he didn't.

"We should get back to work," she said, doing her best to sound calm and unfazed. "We can't afford to waste time."

She left the room without making eye contact and walked into the front of the shop. *How to Be an Idiot, by Juliette Holloway.* Seriously, what the actual hell? She just couldn't trust herself to keep a level head around him. From now on, she was going to be strictly business. No more personal conversations. No more chats in the kitchen. Just no.

"G'day, mate," Brock Templeton said in his sexy Australian accent. He stood near the entrance in board shorts and flip-flops, holding a slushy drink with a bendy straw. "I was hoping I'd find you here."

"Oh." She was still reeling from the almost-kiss with Logan in the back room. Had it been almost a kiss? Maybe she'd misread it. Either way, it had been something too close for comfort. From now on she was going to make sure he stayed outside and worked on his stuff, while she worked on hers. There was no reason for him to be in her space at all.

Brock casually approached the florist counter, glancing around at the hanging baskets and shelves of ferns. "So this is where mermaids hang out when they're not at the beach."

"Sometimes," she said vaguely.

He didn't seem to notice that she was preoccupied. Maybe he was just used to women being tongue-tied around him.

"Didn't catch your number before you bolted, but I had one of my assistants look up the local flower shop," he said. "That's how I tracked you down."

She could hear Logan moving boxes in the back room. Why couldn't he just go? Having him close just confused her and complicated things.

She gave Brock her full attention and forced a smile. "So, you're stalking me, then?"

"I guess I am," he said with a laugh. "I can't seem to get you out of my head." His expression was so sincere, Juliette almost believed him. But actors were actors for a reason.

"So, now you've found me," she said. "Now what?"

"Now I ask if you'll go to dinner with me. I know girls

don't usually date their stalkers, but I'm hoping you'll make an exception. I promise not to kidnap you and tie you up." He took a sip of his slushy and added, "Unless that's your thing."

Before she could answer, Logan strode across the room like royalty. Back straight, head high, he didn't even acknowledge them as he carried a toolbox to the front window.

She felt like a rubber band stretched too tight, like part of her attention was on Brock, but Logan's commanding presence was pulling her in the opposite direction. If she didn't get him out of here, she was going to snap.

"What are you doing?" Juliette said to Logan, careful to keep her voice neutral.

"Working."

"I have time off Friday night, if you're free," Brock said to Juliette.

"I have to work here until six." She frowned as Logan opened the toolbox, took out a measuring tape, and started measuring the window ledge. Irritation spiked. What was he up to?

"How about I pick you up at six-thirty, then?" Brock asked.

Now Logan was taking her potted plants out of the window and setting them on the floor. Juliette balked. No one moved her plants without asking. "*No*."

"No?" Brock blinked in surprise.

"Oh, not you, sorry," Juliette apologized. "Can you hold on for a second?"

She strode across the room to where Logan was dismantling her front window display. "What are you doing?" she hissed. "You can't just come in here and rearrange my plants all willy-nilly without asking."

"I'm not rearranging them," he said, still pulling plants from the window.

She stomped her foot. "Stop. You're ruining my display."

He didn't even bother looking at her. "I'm measuring for shelves."

"I don't want shelves in this window," she said through gritted teeth. She grabbed two of the plants from the floor and placed them back in the window. "Go outside and work on the greenhouse. This is not your domain."

Logan lifted the same two plants and placed them gently on the floor again. "If you don't like it, take it up with my uncle."

She clenched her fists and backed away. "Oh, I will."

"Fine." He turned his back and continued dismantling her window display.

"Fine," Juliette ground out. She stomped back to the counter, barely managing to keep her expression neutral. Ten minutes ago, she almost wanted to kiss him, and now all she wanted to do was knock him on the head with a watering can. Not the plastic kind, either. The big, rusty metal kind.

"Trouble with the hired help?" Brock asked.

She tried not to glare at Logan's back. "Yes, but nothing I can't handle."

"So, dinner then? Friday?"

"Sure," she said loudly. "I'd love to have dinner with you, Brock."

Chapter Eleven

Logan hammered the nail into the greenhouse post, doing his best not to think of feisty, infuriating women and the preening peacocks they chose to date.

"Mr. O'Connor?"

Logan slammed another nail home and turned to see a young man near the fence by the road. He had a shock of wavy brown hair, cut too long for his angular face, but he'd plastered some kind of pomade over it to make it stay behind his ears. He eyed the florist shop nervously.

"Can I help you?" Logan asked.

The kid—he couldn't have been more than eighteen— shifted on his feet and tugged at the hem of his rumpled T-shirt. "I'm Kevin." He glanced at the shop again and stepped further into the shadow of the fence line. "You told me to meet you here?"

Logan set the hammer down. *Oh, hell no.* This was not what he'd had in mind when he put out an ad for home improvement assistance. The boy was thin as a rail with no visible upper body strength. He likely didn't know the first thing about refinishing hardwood floors or rewiring electrical outlets.

"You're the guy who answered my ad?" Logan asked. "The one with extensive home renovation experience who can start right away?"

Kevin ducked his head. "Yeah, that's me." His bony shoulders rose a few centimeters and curved inward, as if he were apologizing for being himself.

Logan searched for a way to let the kid down easy. He didn't want to turn him away, but his house needed serious work. Parts of the downstairs laundry room needed to be gutted, and he had to install a new sink. He needed a skilled handyman who could work alongside him to get the job done quickly. With his uncle's shop remodel taking up all his time during the day, he only had evenings and partial weekends to work on his house. He'd make better time with someone to help, but not with a scrawny kid like this.

Kevin seemed to gather his courage. "I know you were probably expecting someone more . . . just more. But I can do a lot. And I learn quick. And I'll work weekends, or whatever."

"I appreciate it," Logan said. "But I need someone who's a little more senior for this position. Someone with commercial contract experience working with retail buildings or custom homes, at the very least."

Kevin's face lit up. "I did my mom's whole kitchen remodel with her last summer after my dad left. We put in granite counters, and I repainted all the cupboards."

That was a lot of work. If the kid actually did it right. "Did you use a sander?"

Kevin nodded like a bobble-head doll. "Yeah, for sure."

"Did you hand paint the cabinets?"

"Better." Kevin lifted his chin with pride. "I rented a paint sprayer."

Logan tried not to imagine where he'd used the paint sprayer and the electric sanding equipment to work on the cupboards. Hopefully in a well-ventilated area like the backyard.

"It turned out really good, too," Kevin continued. "And when we finished the kitchen, my mom said she always wanted a blue bedroom, so I painted the walls in her room for her. And then I painted the rest of the downstairs."

"Did you tape everything off?"

"Of course," he said, as if that was a dumb question.

"Paint the crown molding and baseboards, too?" Logan was trying to gauge whether or not the kid was good with detail work.

Kevin's face fell. "Nah, we don't have that molding stuff. Our house is kind of small." He eyed the florist shop again, clearly uncomfortable.

"Is there something you want to tell me?" Logan asked. "About why you keep looking at the shop like it's going to bite you?"

The kid kicked a small rock with his shoe. "I used to work in there. For a little while."

"And you didn't like it?" Logan thought of Juliette's cluttered shelves and how she was fiercely protective of her plants. It might not have been easy for him.

"No, it was fine. The boss lady was cool. She just didn't like that I tried to grow my plant in her store."

That didn't sound like Juliette. "Why not?"

He kicked another rock with his shoe. "Never mind. I gotta go. Thanks, anyway."

"Wait." Logan approached Kevin until they were standing face to face. "If I were going to hire you for this job"— he couldn't believe he was saying this—"then we'd have to be straight with each other. Man to man."

Kevin looked surprised, but he stood up taller.

Logan leveled his gaze at the kid. "Why did you get fired from the florist shop? Were you stealing?"

"No!" Kevin said quickly. "I wouldn't do that. I was just

trying to grow my pot plant, is all. Because she's really good at growing stuff. But she didn't like what I did so she gave me some smelly soap and then fired me."

Logan pressed his mouth together and turned away to feign interest in the shop, but really it was because he was trying not to smile. Only Juliette would give her fired employees parting gifts. When he turned back around, his face was deadpan. "I appreciate your honesty, but I don't tolerate drugs on this job. I'll be working with power tools. Most of them are dangerous, even for a sober person."

"I don't even smoke pot anymore," Kevin said with feeling. "I haven't done it since I got fired."

"Really?" That was hard to believe.

"Swear on my life," Kevin promised, holding up his fingers in a symbolic gesture of honesty. Logan didn't have the heart to tell him that the rocker symbol didn't really count. Maybe Kevin was just that clueless. He didn't seem to have a dad in the picture.

Hell. Logan rubbed the back of his neck, sighing. He was going to do this, wasn't he? He was going to give the kid a chance. Every person deserved a chance to start fresh. He knew that better than anyone. "All right. I'll hire you for two weeks. On a trial basis."

"Yesss." Kevin did a fist pump.

"You can meet me at my house after seven. I'll send you the address. We'll be sanding floors and ripping out wallpaper later in the week."

Kevin's face lit up. "Aw, man, I'm so glad I got this gig. It was either this, or I'd have to sell dog outfits at this old lady's shop on the waterfront. Thanks, man. Uh . . . boss."

Logan shook his head.

"Boss man?"

"Just call me Logan."

"Sure thing, boss," Kevin said, before catching himself. "I mean Logan."

* * *

Juliette sat behind the front counter, balancing her feet on the bottom rung of the stool as she stared glumly at her last message to Romeo.

> Hi, Romeo!
> Hope you're having fun on your trip. Everything's going great here. We're right on schedule and I'm about to interview people for the part-time help. I'll keep you posted.
> Juliette ♥

She set her phone down and pressed her lips together. At first, she'd written him a scathing e-mail, listing all the reasons Logan was driving her crazy. It even had bullet points and sub bullet points. But the last thing she wanted was for Romeo to think she wasn't able to handle things. So she'd decided to paint a rosy picture and send a short, professional note, instead. Even though it sucked.

As for the employee interviews, it hadn't technically been a lie. She *would* be interviewing people, just as soon as she got around to putting a HELP WANTED sign in the window. She'd been dragging her feet, hoping she could conveniently overlook it. Except, Logan might notice and mention it to Romeo. Not that he'd been paying much attention to her today. Ever since their whatever-that-was yesterday, he'd been avoiding her. He didn't even come in the back room that morning. Instead he'd shown up outside and went straight to work.

She set a vase of gladiolas on a shelf near the side window. And sweet mother of steel-coated washboards, there he was. Shirtless again. It was difficult not to stare. Bella was out there, too, chatting away. She'd come buzzing around for the second time in three days. Logan didn't seem to mind, either. Probably because the stupid Desire perfume had finally kicked in.

The front door flew open and Kat rushed in with Hank the Tank tripping along at her heels. The tiny dog's head barely reached the top of Kat's combat boots. Today he wore a black leather collar with spikes.

"Hey, Juliette," Kat said breathlessly. "Can I get a dozen red roses like, in a vase or whatever? Mirage is having another one of her trademark tantrums."

Juliette went to the cold case and pulled out a ceramic vase of long-stemmed red roses. "You want me to tie a ribbon around it?"

"Barbed wire would be better," Kat said moodily. "The director says Mirage needs a peace offering. He thinks it'll make her happy. Which is dumb, because the only way a vase of flowers would make her happy is if the vase was made from solid gold and filled with French champagne."

Juliette unfurled a length of ribbon from a spool beneath the register, cutting enough to tie around the neck of the vase. "What's going on?"

"Mirage is freaking out because she gained five pounds. Which is also dumb, because what's up? That lady needs to eat." Kat groaned and scrubbed her face with both hands. "You have no idea how much I just want to hide from those people. They're all a bunch of entitled, overgrown babies. Every single one." She gave Juliette an apologetic glance. "Oh, sorry. Aren't you dating Brock, or something?"

Juliette pursed her lips to one side. "I wouldn't call it 'dating,' but we are going to dinner tomorrow night."

"Well, brace yourself," Kat said. "He's going to talk about his old surf show the whole time."

"Thanks for the warning," Juliette said in amusement.

Kat shook her head. "You know what? Don't listen to me. I'm not the best judge of character, anyway. If I had my way, I'd hang around animals all day and only deal with people when absolutely necessary. This job is just stressing me out."

"Did you try using the Bee Chill soap I made?"

"I tried it, but I'm still worked up." She lifted a hand to massage her temple. "Don't get me wrong, the soap is awesome and smells amazing, but it's hard to relax when your roommates are going into WWF smackdown mode all the time."

"Are you using it every day?" She couldn't be. Sometimes people didn't realize they needed to bathe in it a few times for the charm to take effect.

"No, I only tried washing my hands with it, to be honest."

"There's the problem," Juliette said. "You have to keep it in your shower and use it a few times in a row. Trust me—that stuff really works."

"Okay, will do," Kat said glumly. "I think I just messed up accepting this gig. There's no place to get away. Even on my two days off, I have nowhere to hide."

"Come hide here," Juliette said. "It's always peaceful and—" Her eyes flew open and she sucked in a breath.

"What?"

"You could come here and sit on this stool," Juliette said in excitement, pointing to the wooden stool behind the cash register. "On one of your days off. Or all of them—whatever you want."

"Um, okay." Kat looked doubtfully at the stool. "Sounds . . . fun?"

"I mean, you could work here," Juliette said. It would be so perfect. Kat needed to get away, and Juliette needed to hire someone to appease Romeo. And the best part of the plan was she genuinely liked Kat. She felt a connection with her that she didn't usually feel with people she'd just met.

Kat's mouth formed an O. "Well, now, I don't really

know a lot about plants. And while I do love the atmosphere . . ." She trailed off, staring in rapt attention out the window.

Juliette followed Kat's gaze to the glowing, tanned figure of Logan sawing away at a piece of lumber. His chiseled back and arm muscles flexed with every drag and push of the saw. And he was really wearing those jeans.

"That's just Logan," Juliette said with a wave of her hand. "He's doing our remodel for the next few weeks. Drives me freaking crazy, but I'm stuck with him because he's my boss's nephew. He's stubborn as a bull."

Kat nodded, still staring out the window. "I'm really good with animals."

"Look," Juliette said. "My boss has been urging me to hire someone to work at least one day a week in the shop. And lord knows I could use a day off, but so far I've had zero luck finding someone who can do the job. Do you want to work here on one of your days off?"

Kat chewed her bottom lip and took a long look around. "It is kind of like an oasis."

Juliette flushed with pride and straightened her spine. "That's because plants are my specialty. And I make sure all my plants are happy. I think this is one of the most restful places on the island. Minus the bull outside, that is. You wouldn't have to do much. Just sit here and ring up customers. The only reason I need you is to stop my boss from nagging me."

"I get the naggy boss thing, believe me," Kat said, rolling her eyes. "Vespa wants me to find a groomer who specializes in creative coloring so she can dye Hank's fur hot pink. I keep stalling, for obvious reasons."

"Poor Hank." Juliette looked over at the dog, who was trotting around the shop like he owned the place. He already fit in so well. She turned back to Kat. "When are your days off?"

"It varies," Kat said. "I always get at least a couple of days off each week. Sometimes three, if I'm lucky."

"How about working here on Saturday from noon to six? You could bring a book or a laptop—whatever you want. You can even bring Hank."

Kat paused just long enough for Juliette to think about bribery. She had a cousin who baked magic cupcakes, and friends working at the best salon on the island. Surely there was something she could offer to make the deal more appealing. Perhaps a month's supply of her newest Tranquility body spray, guaranteed to invoke peace?

"Okay," Kat finally said. "I like the idea of getting away from the houseboat. And I could use the extra money."

"Perfect." Juliette did a little jump and clapped her hands. She felt as though the sun had just come out from behind a dark cloud. Things were working out. Aside from Logan and his meddling, the shop was running smoothly. Now she could e-mail Romeo and tell him she'd found a part-time employee. He was going to be impressed with her ability to get things done, and that was priority one. Impress Romeo with her abilities, then swoop in when he announced his retirement, and swoop out with the greatest prize of all.

She just had to be patient for a little while longer, and everything was going to come up roses.

Chapter Twelve

"You have to play booty songs," Gertie insisted. "People don't want to stand around at a wedding reception drinking tea with their pinkies in the air. They want to shake it up and dance. They want to have *fun*."

Juliette scribbled the suggestion in her yellow notebook. Molly and Gertie sat next to her at a bistro table in Emma's shop. It was lunchtime on Friday, and they'd all gathered to help Emma make a song list for her wedding reception, which was turning out to be an eclectic mix of everything under the sun, now including "booty shakers."

"I'm cool with whatever you guys want the DJ to play," Emma said, joining them with a tray of cappuccinos. "As long as I don't have to walk down the aisle to 'Baby Got Back.'"

"Speaking of nice butts," Gertie said, stirring her cappuccino, "how's Logan these days?"

Juliette slouched in her chair with a cupcake and a frown. "I'm going to kill him, you guys."

"What did he do this time?" Molly checked her lipstick in a compact mirror. "Is he rearranging your seed shelf again?"

"He better not." Just the other day, she'd caught him

trying to organize her seed containers alphabetically. She was furious. Before he'd started, she knew exactly where everything was. Now she had to stop and think about alphabet letters. Sure, it made sense to everyone else, but it wasn't her system. And she wasn't happy about how he'd done it for efficiency's sake, without asking first.

"Today I sent a nicely worded, professional e-mail to Romeo," she said with growing annoyance. "Requesting that his stupid nephew focus his stupid attention *outside*, and stop messing with all my freaking stuff."

Molly tossed the compact back into her purse. "Sounds very professional. Did you capitalize the *F* in freaking?"

"Romeo hasn't responded yet," Juliette said glumly.

Gertie stirred raw sugar into her cappuccino. "Well, he is on vacation. Checking e-mails isn't going to be his first priority."

"Give it time, Jules," Emma said. "You only have to get along with Logan for another couple of weeks, or so, before Romeo's back. Just try to ignore him."

"I am trying," Juliette wailed. "But every time I turn around he's there. Changing something. I caught him measuring the front windows the other day—did I tell you guys that? He said he was going to install some glass shelves for the plants." She glared at her friends.

They stared back.

Emma cleared her throat. "That sounds . . . good?"

Juliette flung her hands in the air. "Of course it's good, but he didn't ask me first. That's the thing. He just thinks he can do whatever he wants because Romeo told him to organize things."

"And that makes you mad because you feel like you've been there longer, and you deserve to know what his plans are," Emma offered.

"Exactly." Juliette scooped frosting off her cupcake and tasted it. It was dark and sweet, with a drizzle of caramel and a hint of sea salt. As usual, Emma's latest creation was nothing short of a masterpiece. The cupcake was so good, she almost forgot to be annoyed.

"At least Logan's doing a good job building the stuff out back," Molly pointed out. "And he's easy on the eye."

"He is that, girlfriend," Gertie said. "You can't deny it."

"I don't find him attractive," Juliette lied, taking a bite of her cupcake and chewing furiously.

Gertie gave her a long-suffering glance.

Molly looked incredulous.

Emma looked like she was trying not to smile.

"What?" Juliette demanded. "I'm serious. He's just not . . . he's . . ." She searched for reasons. Anything! "Too tall, for one thing."

"Why would that be a problem?" Molly asked. "Tall's nice."

"Not when you have to crane your neck up every time you're trying to tell him what to do. And then he just stands there with those big"—she fluttered her hands in the air—"shoulders. And he stares down at you like you're funny or something. And then he says nothing. Nothing! Just stands there all silent like some big lumberjack Tarzan." She frowned and crossed her arms.

"Mmm," Molly said. "Yeah, those guys are the worst."

"And he's too *active*," Juliette said in a rush. "He's always marching into the kitchen and then marching around outside with his dumb hammer, or saw, or whatever. Just everywhere, hammering and making noise, and not even bothering to keep a shirt on. It's unbearable."

"You poor thing." Gertie shook her head slowly. "No woman should have to deal with that."

"Maybe you should try to get to know him better," Emma said. "See him outside work. He might grow on you."

"Hells no," Juliette said with feeling. "Anyway, he has this praying mantis of a girl hanging around. She'd murder me in my sleep if I got in her way." Juliette thought of Bella's plan to ensnare Logan into wedded bliss. "But once she finds out he's not the perfect man she thinks he is? She's going to bite his head off. And I'll be watching and laughing and clapping from the front row." She narrowed her eyes. "With my popcorn and Milk Duds."

Gertie lifted a brow. "Clearly you've given this some thought."

"But never mind him," Juliette said. "I have real news." She waited a few beats for impact. "I have a date with Brock Templeton."

As expected, the conversation erupted in shrieks of glee and disbelief, and she spent the rest of the lunch hour explaining how it happened. What he was wearing. How he looked when he asked. What he was wearing again—so Molly could better visualize—and all the other details.

By the time Juliette returned back to the shop, she was feeling more relaxed and actually looking forward to dinner with Brock that night.

Juliette kicked off her shoes and took her hair down, massaging her head as she walked into the front room to remove the OUT TO LUNCH sign from the window. She was so preoccupied with her thoughts, she didn't realize she wasn't alone until something landed in a garbage bin beside her.

She spun around, startled.

Logan was across the room, lounging behind the counter. Several wadded up pieces of paper were scattered near the register.

"What are you doing in here?" she demanded.

He spared her a glance, stretched his arm above his head, and sent a paper ball sailing into the wastebasket. "Taking a break."

Annoyance bubbled to the surface. "Shouldn't you be . . . I don't know . . . building something?"

"I'm waiting on the landscaper to drop off the slate rock." He focused on the garbage can.

"Well, don't you have anything to do while you wait?"

"I'm doing it." He sent another paper ball flying through the air. This time it bounced off the rim and landed on the floor.

Juliette looked at the wadded up paper, then at him. "Whatever you're doing, it doesn't look very productive."

"I'm playing Trashball," he said. "It's a great stress reliever. *You* should try it."

"I'm not stressed," she said.

A soft chuckle "Right."

She lifted her chin. "I'm not."

"Whatever you say, captain. By the way, those white cards in the back room? I think they're invitations?"

"What about them?" Emma's wedding invitations had arrived that morning, and she hadn't had a chance to look at them yet.

"They fell out of the box. All over the floor, but don't worry." He jerked a thumb at the filthy push broom in the corner. "I swept them up."

Juliette sucked in a breath, horrified that he'd swept up the silver-embossed, white linen cardstock with the shop broom. "You didn't."

"I didn't," he agreed. "Relax."

She glowered at him.

"See?" He pointed at her with a wadded up piece of paper, then aimed for the bin again. "Stressed."

"You're the reason," she said. "That's your idea of helping a person de-stress? Scaring them?"

"Okay, I'm sorry. Look, you can take the next shot." He tossed her the paper ball. "Try it."

She narrowed her eyes and threw it directly at him. It bounced off his perfect mouth.

Juliette tossed her hair and bit back a grin. She did feel better.

Logan nodded slowly. "Well, you tried. Don't beat yourself up. Not everyone can be a natural at Trashball." He stretched his hand over his head without taking his eyes off her face and tossed the ball.

It landed in the wastebasket with a soft *thunk*.

He winked.

Juliette couldn't help the tiny smile that tugged at the corners of her mouth. "Oh, please. That was dumb luck, and you know it."

"Try it," he said. "I dare you."

Never one to back away from a challenge, she strode across the room, joining him behind the counter. She grabbed a paper ball and threw. The ball bounced off the rim of the wastepaper basket. So close.

He took one, tossed, scored.

She grabbed another, sent it sailing, and missed by several feet. Before he could throw another, she grabbed one in each hand and launched them across the room at the same time. One bounced off the rim, the other landed in the bin.

"Score!" Juliette laughed and turned to him, triumphant.

Logan was grinning down at her. A shot of heat zipped through her body. Everything about the nearness of him—how his eyes glowed with pleasure, how a lock of hair waved over his brow, how he smelled faintly of evergreens and sunlight after rain—everything attracted her. Why was it so easy to fall back into old patterns? When she was young, she thought Logan shone like the moon in the sky. Now she knew not to shoot for the moon. She belonged where she was, with her feet planted firmly on the ground. She knew it, and he needed to know it. Fast.

"Just because I'm playing this game, doesn't mean I like you now," she blurted.

He raised a brow in silent challenge.

Juliette lifted her chin, heart beginning to pound in her chest. "I just—I want to make that clear."

"That you don't like me?"

She nodded.

He studied her for a long moment, then said softly, "You know what I think, Juliette?"

She shook her head, unable to answer. Whatever he was about to say, she didn't want to hear it. What she did want was to run her hands up the front of his shirt and feel the hard ridges of muscle underneath, slide her arms around his neck and dig her fingers into his thick hair, pull him closer and see if his lips were as warm and soft as they looked. *Danger!* She backed into the wall behind her.

He slowly closed the space between them, his dark eyes fixed on hers. "I think you do like me."

She tried to scoff, but it sounded too breathy. "No, I don't. You annoy me."

"I didn't always." He searched her face from beneath thick lashes. "I kissed you once before, do you remember?"

A thrill shot through her. "No." Said the lying'est liar who ever lied. She'd never forget that first kiss as long as she lived. She was fourteen. He was eighteen. It had been fleeting and unexpected and thrilling, but bittersweet. She'd foolishly thrown herself at him, and he'd treated her like a child.

"I must not have done a very good job of it, then," he said.

"Must not have." She licked her suddenly dry lips and tried to sound nonchalant. "But hey, don't beat yourself up.

Not everyone can be a natural at it. Just stick to things you're good at. Like Trashball."

With infinitesimal slowness, he leaned closer, until she could feel the heat of his body just inches from hers. "I was just a kid back then, when we kissed."

"I'm sure nothing's changed," she whispered, insides shaking like a sapling in a windstorm.

"Let's find out."

She opened her mouth to say no, but the word dissolved on the tip of her tongue.

Logan's mouth curved up at one corner. "I *dare* you."

When he dipped his head, she met him halfway. Because he dared her, so what else could she do, right?

He brushed his mouth softly against hers at first, demanding nothing. Giving nothing. It was carefully controlled, just the light slide of barely parted lips, their breaths mingling as he braced his hands against the wall behind her. Juliette squirmed, instinctively pressing closer until the full length of her body made sudden contact with his.

Logan exhaled sharply, sliding a hand around her waist, his powerful arm anchoring her against him. When he deepened the kiss, her entire body went molten. Everything about him was hot and hard and he tasted a bit like cinnamon gum and sweet, wicked promises—the kind whispered between two lovers in the dark.

When he finally drew back, they both stared at each other, their breaths mingling in the space between them.

Juliette swallowed hard and fought to get back to the place she was before. "Hated it," she whispered.

"Mmm, it was terrible." He lowered his gaze to her mouth, his large hand on the nape of her neck, thumb stroking deliciously near the sensitive spot behind her ear. "Maybe we should try again," he murmured. "Just to be sure."

She reached up and sank her hands into his hair, pulling him down so she could kiss him again. Somewhere in the back of her mind, her future self was yelling at her for acting like a lunatic and jumping into such dangerous waters, but her present self was kicking back on an inflatable raft with a mai tai shouting, "Come on in, the water's fine!"

When they finally pulled away from each other, they were both breathing hard and Logan was looking at her like he'd never seen her before. It was the kind of look a person gave when he was focusing all his attention, like a sharpshooter homing in on his target.

Juliette suddenly felt exposed. She was no man's target. She slid sideways and moved toward the entrance to the back room, their eyes still locked on each other.

A crease started to form on Logan's forehead. He seemed . . . bothered. Now he was looking at her like she was a problem.

Juliette bristled. She was no man's problem, either.

She forced a small laugh. "That was a weird experiment."

His frown deepened. "Experiment."

"Yeah." She nodded, going with it. "And I'll say it was not as horrible as I expected. But I don't plan on repeating it."

An emotion flashed across his face, too fast for her to catch. Then he stood soldier straight, his voice carefully controlled. "It was a bad idea."

Something stabbed at her insides. "Agreed."

He was still frowning when he said, "It won't happen again." Then he headed for the door.

She escaped to the back room and began scrubbing down the cutting table. When that was clean, she started in on the kitchen sink. Then the counters. The physical work made it easier not to think. *What in the holy heart attack had just happened?* She really needed to sweep the floor. *Logan kissed her.* Probably should mop it, too. *And she kissed him back. What the hell?* She dragged the mop bucket out of the closet near the bathroom and proceeded to make a mental list of all the reasons the kiss was no big deal. It was just a dumb experiment. Both of them agreed it wouldn't happen again. She squeezed water from the mop and began on the floors.

Several minutes later, she swiped a lock of hair out of her face and surveyed the squeaky-clean room. Better. She took a deep breath and let it out slowly. Everyone had momentary lapses of sanity once in a while. That thing with Logan would just have to be hers. As long as they both never spoke of it again, everything would be fine.

At six o'clock, Juliette grabbed the bag she'd brought from home and stepped into the tiny bathroom in the back of the shop. She quickly changed from overalls into a strappy sundress and combed out her hair. After touching up her makeup and slipping on a pair of sparkly sandals, she felt much better. It was impossible not to feel powerful when she was wearing amazing shoes.

In the mirror, she looked as calm and cool as an Enya song, but inside she was all head-banging Metallica. Why wouldn't she be? Her feelings were a jumbled mess. Logan O'Connor had just kissed her to the moon and back again, and as much as she hated to admit it—she'd liked it. A lot.

Juliette sighed and gathered her things, then went to make sure the shop was in order before Brock showed up. No use dwelling on one tiny, stupid mistake.

By the time Brock breezed into the shop, Juliette was ready for him. He was fifteen minutes late, but she'd been grateful for the extra time to regroup. She'd focus only on Brock tonight, and forget all about the other incident.

"Hello, gorgeous. Sorry I'm a bit late." Brock looked

rocker chic in a motorcycle jacket, dark red jeans, and alligator boots. On anyone else, it would've looked kind of ridiculous, but he somehow managed to pull it off. Mostly.

"You're all right with motorcycles, right, luv?" He gestured to a Harley parked near the front walkway.

Juliette considered her dress. The short skirt flared out from the waist in soft folds that ended above her knees. It was not the type of dress a sensible person wore to ride a motorcycle, but she wasn't in the mood to be sensible. She was determined to have fun and scrub all thoughts of Logan from her mind.

"Sure. Let's go." At least she was wearing nice underwear. A little Marilyn Monroe breeze never hurt anyone.

She locked up the shop and followed Brock to his motorcycle.

Logan was outside pushing a wheelbarrow full of slate tiles, his arm muscles straining from the load. When he saw them, he slowed to a stop and set the wheelbarrow down.

Brock jumped on and motioned to Juliette to climb up behind him.

"Stop." Logan's voice was deep and commanding. "Where's her helmet?"

Brock looked at Logan in surprise. "I don't use one myself." He dragged a hand through his hair and fluffed it up. "Not very comfortable."

"A hell of a lot more comfortable than decapitation or brain damage," Logan said darkly. He strode toward them like the god of thunder about to cast lightning. Juliette felt the sudden need to shield Brock.

"We're fine here, Logan," she said. "Go away."

He stood his ground. "You can't ride that thing without a helmet, even if he does."

"Now see here, mate," Brock began.

"I'm not your mate," Logan said in a steely voice. To her he said, "You're not getting on that thing."

Juliette clenched her hands into fists, angry heat rising up to scorch across her face. "This isn't your business. You don't get to order me around. I've lived my whole life without your interference, so I think I know how to take care of myself."

She turned to mount the motorcycle. Granted, she knew she was being reckless, but something about the way Logan was trying to control her—after he'd said their kiss had been a mistake—really pissed her off. And she and Brock were only going to dinner five blocks away. How dangerous could five blocks be?

Before Juliette could swing her leg over the bike, she felt strong hands around her waist. She was hauled into the air and pulled against the solid wall of Logan's chest.

"Let me go," she demanded, kicking her legs out. She wasn't petite, but he made her feel as though she weighed nothing more than a piece of dandelion fluff.

Logan released her. "I'm not letting you risk your life on that stupid motorcycle like this."

"It's not your concern," Juliette said, seething. "You're not here to be my watchdog; you're here to take care of the remodel."

"Romeo told me to make sure you had what you needed, and cracking your skull open on the street with this idiot"—he jerked his chin at Brock—"is not what you need."

Brock jumped off the bike, squaring his shoulders. Something flashed across his face, and if Juliette didn't know any better, she'd call it exhilaration. Brock seemed to thrive on drama. If the camera crew were here, they'd be getting some prime footage for the show. Poor Tweedle Dee and Dum. They had no idea what they were missing.

"Leave the lady alone," Brock demanded.

Lady? She wasn't sure she liked being called a lady, but it did have kind of a nice theatrical ring to it.

"You've got one of two choices," Logan said, pulling his cell phone from his pocket. "Either you ride this thing out of here and don't come back unless you have a helmet for her, or the two of you walk."

Brock held his ground, which was surprising, given that Logan towered over him by several inches. "What if I don't like those choices?"

"Then there will be consequences." Logan's voice was soft as a caress, but only a fool would miss the barely concealed threat beneath it. "I can have the police here in less than two minutes, and you can make your excuses to them."

Juliette could almost feel the testosterone crackling in the air. Logan didn't have the polished swagger and stage presence that Brock displayed, but he didn't need it.

Brock scoffed, looking every bit the arrogant celebrity. "I've no time for this." He reached out a hand to Juliette. "Come on."

She placed her hand in his and followed him down the walkway. When they reached the sidewalk, Brock turned to give Logan a mock salute. Then he draped an arm possessively around her shoulders, dropped a kiss on her cheek, and led her down the street.

Logan's chest roiled with suppressed anger. A thin crack sounded, and he glanced down at the phone he was gripping too tightly in his hand. A hairline fracture snaked across the phone screen. Easing his grip, he slipped it back into his pocket with a curse.

He paced the front walkway. What kind of an idiot would put a woman's safety in jeopardy like that? Logan knew firsthand just how easily the human body could break. He'd watched people he knew be reduced to nothing but broken bones and ashes. The idea of beautiful, vibrant Juliette getting hurt was enough to make him want to grab that stupid motorcycle and rip it apart with his bare hands.

He gave it a hard kick as he walked past. The memory of Brock kissing Juliette afforded the motorcycle another kick, making it rock precariously. Logan placed his hands on his hips and dipped his head. What the hell was he going to do about her? She was everything that drove him crazy, and nothing even close to the woman he should want. So why was he having such a hard time keeping her out of his head?

Now that he'd come home, Logan had made up his mind to seek a peaceful life. He didn't want any more chaos. He wanted to settle down and have a family—to find a woman who would make a great mother for his future children. Someone who would be calm and steady and reliable. Someone peaceful and even-tempered and *normal.*

Juliette Holloway was unpredictable. She was just as quick to anger as she was to laugh. She was disorganized and bossy. He felt a lot of strong emotions around her, but peaceful wasn't one of them. People had whispered about her family his whole life—the crazy Holloways who made magic spells. Even though Logan didn't put much belief into those things, some people did. And that made Juliette the furthest thing from normal. If there was ever a woman who was the epitome of wrong for what he wanted for his future, it was her.

And yet, he couldn't deny the intense attraction he felt. Maybe it was a throwback from his former days when he loved living on the edge and playing with fire. Juliette was like a flame he couldn't resist. He enjoyed watching her squirm, watching her get all feisty, watching her eyes go liquid with desire when he kissed her. And damn if he didn't want to kiss her again.

But he wasn't going to. If he wanted a woman to settle down with, a woman who would bring him peace, Juliette wasn't it. From now on, he was going to keep his head down and do his damn job, and hell, maybe even take Bella up on all her invitations. If a distraction was what he needed to get Juliette out of his head, then that's what he'd find.

Chapter Thirteen

"Stupid dress," Juliette muttered, tugging at the hemline as she stood in the bathroom of the Coho Grill. It must've shrunk in the wash, because she didn't remember it being so short. But that's not what bothered her. What bothered her was Logan treating her like a child. She was still silently fuming over the way he'd acted back at the shop. The entire walk to the waterfront, Brock had talked about himself, which was a godsend since she didn't have much to offer. It was difficult to make small talk when she was mad. And if there was one thing that Logan O'Connor was stellar at, it was making her insta-crazy mad.

Taking a deep breath, Juliette dug around in her purse for a brush and ran it through her hair. It was time to stop wasting good energy on thoughts of Logan. In exactly sixteen days, Romeo would be back and then things would be better.

She left the bathroom and approached a cozy table near the windows overlooking the ocean. A small group of admirers had gathered around Brock. Juliette stood back and watched. He looked like a king surrounded by his loyal subjects. The people fawned over him, and he handled it all with charm and finesse.

When he caught her eye, he said good-naturedly to the group, "Sorry to cut this short, everyone, but my date has returned."

The manager of the restaurant, a slender man with a stern expression, came and invited the people to move along.

"You look like you're holding court over here," Juliette said, taking a seat opposite him near the window.

"An occupational hazard," he said. "It doesn't matter where I go, either. Even in tiny towns like this in the middle of nowhere, it happens."

Juliette almost frowned at his reference to her hometown, then reminded herself he was a big-city television star. Of course he'd think of Pine Cove Island as being the middle of nowhere.

"Must be tough," she said, sipping her wine.

Brock assured her it was, then continued talking. He really talked a lot, actually. It wasn't a total deal breaker, but somewhere in the middle of the salad course Juliette realized she'd grown bored. He hadn't asked her a single question about herself. She had to remember she liked that about her dates. She had to remind herself that it was easier if they didn't try to get involved. Maybe Brock was really perfect for her, after all.

"So," Brock said, leaning back in his chair. "Tell me about you, Juliette."

Or maybe not. Juliette took a long sip of wine. "What do you want to know?" This was the part she hated whenever she dated a new man. This was the part where they asked her about her family, her childhood, or what her hopes and dreams and aspirations were.

"What's your favorite episode of *Surfers Down Under*?" Brock asked.

Juliette blinked. "What?"

He flashed his pearly whites. "My show. Wait, don't tell

me. You like the one where I saved the little girl from drowning, right? Most women love that one."

"Yeah," Juliette said slowly. "That's the best one." She wasn't about to admit she'd never watched the show. She only vaguely remembered seeing commercials for it, but she wasn't that interested in reality shows. The only reason she even knew his name was because of the occasional tabloid images of him with his latest breakup or engagement.

He launched into a detailed description of his top viewed shows, and by the dessert course Juliette had decided that if she was going to date him, they were better off going on activity dates like miniature golf or bowling or bungee jumping. Anywhere they could do something other than just talk. Dinner just wasn't working out.

By now, Brock had moved on to drama about *Hollywood Houseboat*. "So I told the chef on the set, the least you can do is learn the fundamental differences between vegetarian and vegan."

He laughed, and Juliette grinned to show she'd been listening, but she hadn't.

"I mean," he continued, "not everyone wants to eat garbage and throw their bodies to the wolves, you know what I mean?"

"I'm mostly a vegetarian, but I'm not religious about it or anything," she said. "I just prefer not to eat meat. I still eat dairy and things with eggs in it, though." She thought about Emma's latest creations. "Like cupcakes."

Brock's sneer was instant. "Junk food?" Then he gave her a once-over, his gaze lingering on her cleavage. "Well, I'm not going to fault you for it. I mean, look at you. You're bloody gorgeous."

Juliette made the requisite murmur of thanks before he launched into another monologue about leg day at the gym, and "getting swole," or something, but she wasn't really listening. Maybe she needed to try harder. He was polite enough. And he didn't ask her personal questions, so that was good. He was worlds better than a certain infuriating someone who had turned her life upside down and kept rearranging her stuff.

"Brock," she said suddenly. "You'd never try to rearrange my stuff, would you?"

"What's that?"

He looked so boyishly confused, Juliette found it endearing. "You'd never alphabetize my vegetable seeds or try to make me play Trashball, would you?"

"Well, I don't know much about seeds or ball trashing," he said. "And I don't like rearranging stuff. That's what my assistants are for."

"Perfect," Juliette said. "I think I like you, Brock Templeton."

"What's not to like?" He leaned across the table and took her hand in his. "You want to come out with me tomorrow evening? I'm taking the boat out for a spin."

Juliette looked down at his hand, noting the slender fingers and neatly trimmed nails. No dirt, no visible callouses, no scars. His hands would never rip out her old closet shelves or knock down the drywall in her storage room without asking.

He squeezed her hand gently. "We can meet at the dock around six?"

Juliette gave him her best smile. "Sounds like a plan."

The country club restaurant sparkled with its usual whitewashed opulence. Marble-tiled floors, white pillars, and oversized crystal chandeliers made it look like a buttercream-frosted wedding cake. Every table had snowy linen tablecloths, long-stemmed wineglasses, and ornate silverware nestled beside intricately folded napkins.

Logan knew he should be content sitting here at dinner with a perfectly acceptable woman who clearly enjoyed his company, but he couldn't shake the nagging sense of unease. After Juliette had gone off on her date with the moron, Logan had gone home in need of a diversion. He'd called Bella and asked her to dinner before he could change his mind. And now, here he was, bored and slightly uncomfortable. Bella's perfume was so strong, it was downright nauseating. Something had to be done about that. Every time he saw her, he went home feeling a little queasy.

"That was delicious," she said, as the waiter removed their dessert plates.

Logan's head was beginning to ache. Maybe he'd eaten too much. Or maybe it was the richness of the food. Or that cloying perfume. Whatever the case, something didn't agree with him.

She lifted her wineglass. "Let's have a toast."

Logan suddenly wanted to be home. The wallpaper removal project was just about ready to go, and Kevin was proving to be a great assistant. By next week they'd be able to start painting. There were still so many projects he needed to complete, but the plans were finally starting to come together.

"Logan?" Bella interrupted his thoughts. "What are you thinking about?"

He lifted his wine. "Just some future plans."

She gave him a zillion-watt smile. "To future plans, then."

They clinked glasses. When she started chatting about dinner at her parents' house, Logan did his best to follow along. If he really wanted to focus on his future, Bella should have been a decent enough prospect. She seemed to have her life together. Normal job, normal family, normal interests. He knew he should make more of an effort to get to know her, but he just wasn't feeling it.

"How about meeting for dinner at their house?" she asked.

"Whose?" He'd tuned her out again and had no idea what she was asking.

"My parents' house," she repeated. "Next week? This week they're at some car and motorcycle show, so they won't be in town."

At the mention of motorcycles, Logan set his wineglass carefully on the table. He didn't want to risk cracking glass again. The thought of that guy and Juliette made him feel hot and irrational. It was ridiculous. Why should he care?

"Hello?" Bella nudged him under the table with her foot. "Earth to Logan."

He forced his attention back to her. "Dinner with your parents. Sure." He needed to get his head in the game. Having dinner at her parents' house wasn't that big a deal. Heck, he'd already met them years ago. Maybe he'd even have a good time.

As Bella rambled on, he found himself wondering ridiculous things like what color she painted her toenails, if she drank hazelnut mochas, and whether or not she liked gardening. She didn't seem like the type to get her hands dirty, so gardening probably wasn't her thing. Nothing wrong with that. Why should it matter? Gardening wasn't really his thing either.

"Want to come over to my place after this?" Her foot snaked up his leg under the table. When it slid toward his groin, Logan's meandering thoughts came screeching to a halt.

He shifted in his chair and signaled for the waiter. "Sorry, I can't. I'm in the middle of a project."

"What project?" she asked with a pout.

"Just some work I have to do at home." He looked at

Bella and tried to paste a smile on his face, but it kept falling off. *Damn it.* She wasn't right for him, and he knew it. The more he spent time with her, the more annoying she became. Sooner or later, he was going to have to admit to himself there was only one woman he was interested in, and it sure as hell wasn't Bella.

Chapter Fourteen

Logan woke in a cold sweat, heart thumping, the sporadic sound of explosions and gunfire still ringing in his ears. He dragged himself up and sat on the side of the bed, letting his head drop into his hands.

Breathe. One in, one out. Again. He practiced this for a few minutes until the nightmare faded. It was nothing new, but it was way better than it used to be. Totally normal after what he experienced on his last tour, he was told. Wasn't that the joke for the ages? Nothing about it felt normal.

An owl hooted outside, and Logan cracked open one eye. Five-thirty in the morning. Not bad. The last time this happened was the night before work, and that made for a killer day ahead since he could never get back to sleep afterward. Juliette had accused him of partying all night when he dragged in two hours late.

With a heavy sigh, he rose from the bed and trudged outside to the back porch. He watched the sky lighten with each passing minute, the painful memories finally beginning to fade with the dawn. Something about the infinite stillness of the morning appealed to him. Who would have thought it? He'd never been a morning person before. But now he wanted to seize every moment. He didn't want to miss anything. Maybe it was because he'd seen how fleeting life could be.

The owl hooted again, and a small, dark shadow peeked around the corner of the porch.

Bright yellow eyes watched him, and he suddenly felt better. Less alone.

"You again," he said softly.

The cat stepped daintily onto the porch and sat a few feet away. It was big and sleek with ebony fur and long white whiskers.

"Where did you come from?" Logan asked.

It ignored him and proceeded to clean itself.

"Fine by me." Logan stood and stretched. "I should be taking a shower soon, too." He turned to go inside. Something in the woods caught his eye. A white, fluttering movement. He strained to see, but it floated out of sight.

Without much thought, Logan followed.

Just inside the woods behind his house, he saw it again. A flutter of white moving through the trees.

A few steps further and then he saw.

Her.

Juliette looked like a different kind of dream, floating through the woods. She was barefoot, in a white nightgown, with her dark hair streaming down her back like something out of a fairy tale. Tiny white flower petals were tangled in her hair.

Logan squinted, moving closer. The plants and trees seemed to float around her as she passed. They swayed on an unseen current to make room—the ferns and undergrowth caressing her ankles, brushing against her calves.

It was as though she were moving underwater, slowly and peacefully, a mythical creature in her element. Logan wanted to say something, but he couldn't bring himself to disturb what could only be described as perfect harmony.

Maybe it was true, what everyone used to whisper about when he was growing up. Some people called the Holloway women witches. Others called them fairy folk. They said Juliette had some special ability, some kind of pact with nature.

Logan's parents had been quick to dismiss the rumors, being completely practical people who didn't believe in any of that "wackadoo stuff," as his mother called it. But standing in the woods now, he knew she was special. And somehow, he'd always known. Even back when he was a kid visiting his grandfather, he used to sometimes see glimpses of her in the woods. She walked through them differently. Where most people would forge a path and head in a direction through the trees, Juliette seemed to wander with them. Like she was a part of them.

He watched in fascination as she crouched beside a narrow stream where ferns and small white flowers grew. She murmured to the flowers, gathering a few and breathing in their scent. He felt as if he were an intruder, watching something too rare and beautiful, not meant for his eyes. It was a ridiculous thought, but one he couldn't shake.

He backed away, intending to leave. But he had no relationship with Mother Nature, and moving silently through the woods wasn't possible.

A twig snapped under his foot, and Juliette glanced up like a startled doe.

She rose slowly, surrounded by a sea of ferns.

He leaned back into the shadows, but felt as though she could still see him, clear as day.

"What are you doing here?" she asked.

Logan tried to think of a hundred different normal things to say, but the situation felt so surreal that he said the truth. His gaze skimmed the neckline of her nightgown. "Observing the wildlife."

Juliette shifted on her feet. She reminded him of a wild animal about to take flight. "It's early. No one ever disturbs me out here."

"I'm sorry to disappoint you."

"You can easily make it up to me," she said, lifting her chin. "Go home."

A dark shadow wrapped around her ankles and Logan saw that it was the cat from his porch earlier.

"These are my woods, too," he said.

"Your woods? They belong to themselves."

"Not according to the documents my grandfather's attorney gave me. Half of them belong to me."

He could tell she didn't like it. Her blue eyes flashed, and she squared her shoulders. "Well, half is mine, but I leave them alone. They don't like to be bothered. They're like my cat. They don't like strangers."

The cat walked over to him and rubbed against his legs.

"We aren't strangers," Logan said. "Your cat hangs out at my house sometimes."

"Luna," Juliette said. "Come here."

Luna just sat near his feet, purring.

"I think she likes me." He bent to pick her up.

"Don't," Juliette called. "She'll scratch you."

Logan lifted the purring cat and gazed over its head at Juliette. "I guess I'm not a stranger, am I?"

She frowned and walked over to them, her white nightgown swirling around her calves like mist. It was simple cotton, with thin straps and a modest neckline, but sheer enough that he could almost see the shape of her underneath.

"Luna, stop that." Juliette reached out and gathered the

cat in her arms. "What has gotten into you?" She looked at him with distrust. "Did you feed her?"

"No."

"Give her salmon, or something?"

"No."

"Bathe in catnip?" she asked grumpily.

Logan stared at her for a moment. "Yes. That's exactly what I did. In fact, I order several bars of catnip soap online every few weeks, just so I don't run out."

Her lips twitched. She pressed them together.

Logan felt a lightness in his chest that he didn't expect. She was trying not to smile and that made him . . . happy.

"Seriously," she said. "Why are you out here this early in the morning?"

"I couldn't sleep."

"So you thought you'd take a walk through the wild woods at dawn?"

"Actually, I saw your"—he glanced down at her night-gown, fascinated by the thin satin ribbons that trailed between her breasts—"clothes through the trees and came to investigate. I thought you might be a ghost."

Juliette gathered Luna closer and rested her chin on the cat's head. Two pairs of eyes looked back at him. It was disconcerting to be on the receiving end of so much feminine scrutiny.

"Hasn't anyone ever told you that ghosts don't exist?" she asked.

"My parents did." Logan reached out to pet Luna. The cat started to purr again. "They told me fairy tales were just make believe. They also said monsters weren't real, but they were wrong about that."

Juliette glanced up at him. "You've seen monsters?"

"Yes." A volley of gunfire ricocheted in his mind, a

scattered remnant of the nightmare that woke him earlier. "I have."

She said nothing, just held Luna as she stroked the cat's soft fur. After a few moments, Luna wiggled out of her arms and scampered off into the ferns.

Juliette tilted her face up to the sky. "I should go back and get ready for work. It just turned six."

"How do you know?" Logan asked, entranced by the play of dappled light across her face.

"I can feel the sunrise," she said simply. "I know its exact position in the sky every morning, and I can track the hours as it progresses throughout the day." She shrugged as if it was no big deal. "Just wired that way, I guess."

"I've heard that about you," Logan said.

Juliette crossed her arms, hugging herself. "What exactly have you heard?"

"That you come from a family of gifted women and you have nature magic." Logan shifted on his feet, aware that he was talking about a subject he was brought up to ignore. But he was a different person now. He understood that his parents clung to some beliefs because it made them feel safe, but they weren't always right. "My uncle believes it. He thinks your ability to make plants grow is nothing short of a miracle."

"And what do you think?" She turned and walked away, as though she didn't expect an answer. Her hair swayed softly down her back. A few of the tiny white flowers tangled in her hair fell loose and floated to the ground. The ferns parted around her, an occasional frond curling around her legs, as she passed.

"I'm inclined to believe," he said.

She turned back in surprise. "Why?"

Because you look like a forest nymph who just sprang out of some dark fantasy. Because in the half-light you seem to glow like a rare, otherworldly creature. Because the plants flow around you in recognition, like they're paying homage to a force of nature similar to their own. He cleared his throat. "I don't know."

Her blue eyes flashed with mischief. "Well, if I were you, I'd be careful in these woods. They could be dangerous for a mere mortal like yourself."

"How so?"

"For one thing, there's poison ivy everywhere. If you don't know how to look for it, you could find yourself in a world of hurt."

"I've never been bothered by poison ivy. I'm immune."

She tilted her head and regarded him with interest. "Even still, see that plant there?" She pointed to a bright green plant with large, palm-like leaves. "That's devil's club. It's beautiful, but has hidden thorns. If it gets under your skin it can cause problems."

Exactly like someone he knew. Logan smiled.

"I'm not kidding." She gave a little stomp for emphasis, which made him smile even more. "You could get hurt out here if you're not careful."

"I played in these woods when I was a kid, Juliette. Never had a problem with sticker bushes or poisonous plants."

"Fine," she said with a toss of her hair. "Wander at your own risk, then."

Logan moved toward her. "The plants aren't what concern me. You are." The real risk was the woman standing in front of him right now, barefoot in nothing but a thin nightgown.

She frowned and bit down on her bottom lip.

Logan wanted it. The memory of the kiss they shared in the flower shop still haunted him. He wanted to taste her again.

"I'm no threat to you," she said.

Woman, if only you knew.

The forest grew very still. It almost seemed like the trees were holding their breath to see what would happen next.

"Don't worry, Logan," she said softly. "I won't put a magic spell on you. At least nothing permanent. Besides, there's no such thing as fairy tales, right? You have nothing to worry about."

He watched her go, the white nightgown like a splash of light in the shadowy woods as she walked away. When he couldn't see her anymore, he finally turned and walked slowly back to his house.

Like hell, he had nothing to worry about. She was everything he didn't need, and yet he couldn't stop himself from wanting her. She was infuriating. Alluring. Impulsive. Unconventional. He could count on both hands all the reasons she was not the girl for him. He wanted a peaceful life with a woman he could raise a family with. The type of woman who was reliable and sensible. He'd been through enough chaos. He wanted roots. Something steadfast.

Logan had dated his fair share of wild women. The fun kind who make you laugh and were always up for a good time. He spent most of his days on leave in California when he wasn't stationed overseas. He and his buddies were always up for a party, and there were always women more than willing to participate. But that was before he'd seen how bad it could get. Before the bombs. Before he watched people he cared about die.

Now all he wanted was to be home. He was done with the wild life. And Juliette was a wild, free spirit whom he'd never quite understood. Even back when he only knew her as a waif-like kid, she'd been unusual. Always with plants or flowers stuck into her pockets, hands grubby from digging in the dirt.

Logan climbed the stairs to his house, checking the loose planks in the porch floorboards. He was much better off focusing on his renovation projects. Kevin was going to come by later and help with the porch sanding. It would be good to watch the house improve over the next few weeks. God knew he could use the distraction.

He glanced back into the woods. A pair of golden eyes watched him from beneath the ferns. The cat seemed to be waiting for him. He turned and walked into the house, resolved to find a way to get Juliette out from under his skin. It was time to focus on the future. No more games.

Juliette Holloway was a wild card, and he wasn't a gambling man anymore.

Chapter Fifteen

"Hope floats," Juliette whispered under her breath as she walked toward the waterfront. It had been a good day, and she was determined that her boat date with Brock this evening was going to be even better.

Kat had proved to be a natural at greeting and helping customers. She already knew how to work the register, and customers seemed to like Kat's easy nature. They even doted on her dog, Hank. Things were looking up.

Juliette turned the corner and headed toward the pier, trying to feel more excited about her boat date with Brock. Maybe they'd hit it off, once he got away from fawning groupies. She had to admit, there was something very flattering about having *Hollywood Houseboat*'s most eligible bachelor interested in her.

She settled her purse more firmly on her shoulder, determined to have a good time.

"Miss," a voice called behind her.

Juliette turned to see the crew member with the tortoiseshell glasses from the night at the barbeque. Was he Tweedle Dee or Tweedle Dum? She couldn't remember.

"Just a few quick questions." He was holding a recording device in his hand.

"Tweedle," she said cheerfully. "So nice to see you this evening."

He held out the recorder. "What are you and Brock celebrating tonight?"

"Just a date." Juliette continued walking toward the pier. "No big thing."

"What kind of big thing?"

"The 'no' kind," Juliette said, staring straight ahead.

He tripped along behind her like Hank the Tank. "So if Brock proposes, you plan to say no?"

She whirled to face him.

He stopped fast, narrowly missing bumping into her.

"It doesn't really matter what I say to you, does it?" she asked.

His lower lip bulged out as he considered her question. "Not really."

"So even if I make up something, as long as you can work with it, you'll quit bugging me?"

He adjusted his glasses. "If you give me something good."

"Okay." She crossed her arms and thought for a few moments. "How about . . . Brock is being blackmailed by a band of ruffians, and he's hired me, an undercover assassin, to take them all out."

Tweedle scoffed. "You lost me at 'band of ruffians.' This isn't medieval England."

"Fair enough," Juliette said. "What if I told you I was a magical creature, with the ability to mix up spells from the things I grow in my garden. And this summer I plan to have my wild, wicked way with Brock—a poor, unsuspecting mortal."

"See, now you're not even trying. Magic spells?" He scoffed. "You need to give me something realistic. Something that would make a good story."

"Fine." Juliette gave him the first story that popped into

her head. "How's this? I'm from a family of all girls and one of us needs to marry a rich man so we don't all die penniless. At first, I thought Brock was arrogant, even though he's a great prospect because he makes over ten thousand a year. But after a bunch of misunderstandings, I've come to realize he's not just another hot bod in a wet pirate shirt. He has a big old mansion, too. So now I'm thinking cha-ching! I sure hope he proposes soon."

He looked mildly appeased. "That's not too bad. Any of it true?"

Juliette put her finger to her lips. "Shhh. I've said too much already."

She left him standing on the sidewalk, sending a silent prayer of thanks to Jane Austen as she made her way toward the waterfront.

Brock was already waiting for her at the pier. "Hey, babe." He leaned in to give her a kiss on the cheek, then gestured to a dinghy bobbing in the water. It had two wooden bench seats, a small outboard motor, and looked barely big enough to hold four people.

Juliette looked down at her floral dress with dismay. It wasn't that she minded the smaller boat, but she wished she'd worn jeans instead of changing into her best silk dress. For some reason, when Brock said he was going to take her on a boat date, she thought it would be a bit more glamorous.

"Sorry it's so small," Brock said with a laugh. "It came with the houseboat, and we all have to share it. Tonight's my night. I thought it'd be fun to get out on the big waves and watch the sunset."

"Sure." Juliette didn't bother pointing out that there were no big waves. Some islands had huge waves and crashing surf, like Hawaii or Tahiti, but not Pine Cove Island. Everything was usually calm and quiet. Even the ocean.

A few minutes later, they stepped carefully into the

tiny boat, and Brock maneuvered it away from the dock, pulling alongside *Hollywood Houseboat* as they passed. The "houseboat" was a sleek yacht, with two levels and both a lower and upper deck for dining and sunbathing.

The supermodel Mirage was standing on the lower deck with a glass of champagne and a pout so smoldering she was practically a fire hazard. Her gold Brazilian-cut string bikini glittered in the sunlight.

She gave Juliette a withering look, finished off her champagne in one long gulp, and turned her back on them.

"Wow," Juliette said. "She seems super nice." In a reptilian, swallow-you-whole type of way.

"Mirage? Yeah, she's a great girl," Brock agreed.

Juliette took a deep breath and let it out slowly. Maybe she just needed to lighten up a little. Lately she'd been so stressed about the renovations and dealing with Logan, she hadn't had a lot of time to relax.

"Hey, Kat's friend," Vespa called from the top deck. She leaned over the railing with a wineglass in one hand and a cigarette in the other. "If Brock gets handsy, you have my permission to slap him." She gave a raspy laugh, then took a drag on her cigarette and sashayed away.

Brock steered the boat around the marina, then took them up the island coast for several minutes before heading out into deeper water.

Juliette tipped her head back and breathed in the salty air, loving the feel of the warm sunlight on her face and the cool breeze floating in from the east. One of her favorite things about summertime in the Pacific Northwest was that the sun didn't set until around nine o'clock. It seemed to be Mother Nature's way of making up for all the rainy days throughout the rest of the year.

Seagulls called overhead, lulling Juliette into a feeling of deep contentment. This was exactly what she needed.

Just a nice, relaxing evening where she could set her cares aside and have some fun with a nice guy.

When Brock finally cut the engine, they were far enough from shore that the boats in the marina looked like small toys bobbing in the water.

He looked back at the shoreline. "It really is beautiful out here."

Juliette felt a warm sense of pride for the island she called home. "I like to think so. When you live here your whole life, you sometimes forget—"

"But it's too *quiet*, right?" Brock interrupted. "How do people do it? Day in and day out." He bent to rummage in a basket under his seat, lifting out a frosty bottle of French champagne. "Here we are."

Juliette raised her brows. "Fancy."

Dimples flashed. "I bring the party wherever I go." He popped the cork, sending it flying across the water.

"No." Juliette watched in dismay. "I can't believe you did that. It's dangerous to birds and marine life to throw—"

"Oh, I know. Sorry. Accident." Brock reached under the seat and pulled out two red plastic cups. He filled one and handed it to her, then filled another.

Annoyed at how casually he'd brushed off littering, she gripped the plastic party cup. "I've never had champagne this way before."

"Well, it doesn't matter how it goes down, as long as it goes down, right?" He tapped his cup against hers and took a champion swig. Then he topped his cup off and took several more gulps.

"Easy there, sailor," Juliette said. "Aren't we supposed to savor it?"

"Ah, no worries. I brought two more bottles." He winked. "There's plenty."

Juliette sipped her champagne, watching in reluctant fascination as Brock finished his cup and filled it again, thirstily chugging away like he'd been marooned on a desert island with his good buddy Wilson for the past five years.

Finally, he gave her his full attention. "So."

She waited.

He said nothing further.

Was she supposed to say something? "Yes?"

He gazed at her, swaying a little as the boat bobbed gently in the waves. "Juliette. Juliette," he crooned.

"Mm-hmm?"

He grinned. "The fair Juliette."

Uh-oh. Was he going to start quoting Shakespeare? She eyed the distance to the shoreline. Had to be three, maybe four hundred yards. Could she make it swimming, if she had to?

He ran a hand through his evenly spaced, caramel highlights. "I really like you."

She repeated his own words. "What's not to like?"

Brock tipped back his cup o' bubbly and drained it again, then held up the bottle. "More?"

"I'm still working on mine." *Since you only poured it forty-seven seconds ago.*

He poured more champagne into his cup and stretched back on his seat. "What I mean is, I like you a lot. I think we could really get along well together, you and I. Obviously, we're compatible." He took another swig.

"How can you tell?" Was it the matching plastic cups?

"Well, you're bloody beautiful. So, you know"—he waved his finger in the air between them—"we fit together, right?" He pronounced "right" with such a heavy accent, it sounded more like "roit."

"I don't know if you can decide compatibility just based on looks."

"Sure you can." He held his hand above his head, palm

down. "I'm on this level, see?" He raised his cup to join it. "And you're up on my level, too."

Juliette looked up at the plastic cup, wobbling above his head. "I'm not sure I follow."

He brought his hands down and leaned forward. "Just trust me on this." Another gulp of champagne. "I'm brilliant about these things, all right?"

"Roit," she said slowly. "And you're also very humble."

"I am," he agreed, nodding his head vigorously. A little too vigorously. If Juliette didn't know any better, she'd say he was drunk.

"Say, Brock, did you get a head start on the champagne before we met tonight?" She made it sound like a joke, but she needed to know. If he'd been drinking before, it would explain his weird behavior.

"Nah." Brock waved his hand. "I wouldn't start on the good stuff without you."

That was a relief.

"I did some tequila shots with the gang, though," he added. "We like to start early."

She pressed her eyes closed for a moment. "That's just great."

"I know." He refilled his mug, splashing some on the floor of the boat.

"I was kidding," Juliette said.

"About what?"

"Never mind."

Holy dunce cap. Either he was really dumb, or just stupid drunk. Maybe Kat was right about Brock all along. Juliette should've listened to her. She shouldn't have broken her own dating rule. Never date a new guy in a place you can't escape. You never know when you'll want to run screaming for the hills. Juliette looked longingly at the shoreline. It seemed farther away than ever.

"Anyway . . ." Brock rose unsteadily to his feet and plopped down on the seat beside her.

He grinned.

She showed some teeth.

"You and I make sense together," he said amiably. At least he was a happy drunk.

Juliette took a long sip of her champagne. If this was a paddleboat, she'd be backpedaling so hard right now.

Brock scooted closer. "I think we should bang."

She coughed. Gasped. "What?"

He thumped her on the back. "We should have sex. Trust me. You'd love it."

"Mmm," she said, still wheezing. "Let me think about it."

"In a few weeks I'll be gone, so don't think too long. When you decide to go for it, just give me a ring."

There would be no ringing, and no banging. Of that, she was certain.

"One of the things I've learned in life is, if you see something you want, you just gotta go for it, you know?"

"Words of wisdom, indeed," Juliette said, taking another sip of champagne.

Brock suddenly whipped off his shirt.

Juliette leaned away, startled. She eyed him warily, just in case he tried to get "handsy." His torso was so shiny, it looked waxed. There wasn't a follicle of hair on him. From a purely Mattel perspective, it was ideal. Like a glossy Ken doll. If he was up for sale on eBay, he'd be "Brand New In Box."

"Let's go for a swim," he announced.

"No way." Juliette clutched her plastic cup. "That water is freezing."

He flexed his arms and stretched. "You sure?"

She had to admit his six-pack abs were pretty impressive. The defined muscles were so symmetrical. Oddly symmetrical. She squinted her eyes and peered closer. Was he . . . ? Oh, my god, she had to ask. "Are you *airbrushed*?"

"Yeah." Brock studied his abs. "It's part of the gig. We all have to look good on camera. You know Tammy, on the set?"

Juliette shook her head. Everyone on the houseboat crew kind of blended together. Aside from the Tweedles, Kat was the only person on the crew who stood out, but maybe that was just because she liked Kat. And Kat had gorgeous red hair that no one could miss.

"Tammy's our makeup artist. Anyway, she does all our spray tans. Contouring, ab enhancements, all that stuff." He tossed the empty champagne bottle aside and grabbed a new bottle from the basket. A few moments later, he'd popped the cork and held the bottle out to her. "More?"

Why the hell not? The date was turning out to be a dud. Not only was his personality about as empty as that last champagne bottle, even his appearance was fake. Juliette took the bottle and drank directly from it. She needed to figure out how to get off this boat.

Brock let out a *whoop* of encouragement. "Drink up, luv."

Juliette handed him the bottle. "So what do you plan to do after the filming is finished? We should head to shore while you tell me all about it."

"I'm going to Burning Man, baby." He was scrutinizing his abs now, running a finger along the darker contours of his spray tan. "Ever been to it?"

Juliette shook her head. She'd heard stories about the big hippie festival out in the desert.

"You're coming with me, then," he decided. "I've already got it set up. You'd be beautiful there. And the best part about Burning Man?" He took another swig. Burped. "Clothing optional."

Yup, it was time to go.

"Um, Brock?" She forced a smile and threw in some

extra eyelash blinkety-blinks. "See that stretch of beach right there?" She pointed to the shore. "There's a really cool place where you can lay out and watch the sunset." *You, not me.*

Brock checked the champagne basket. "Beaut, let's go. We can finish the rest there." He leaned over to start the engine.

It sputtered for a few seconds, then died out.

He tried again.

Nothing.

Brock swore. "I think it's caught on seaweed or something." He stood, swaying on his feet. "I'll go take a look."

Before Juliette could protest, he launched himself into the water. The boat rocked precariously, and she grabbed on to the edge.

"What are you doing?" she called.

"It's bloody freezing," he yelled, sputtering.

"I know. I told you that. Get back in the boat."

He ignored her and swam over to the engine. "There's seaweed stuck or something. I'm going to yank it loose." He splashed around, tugging at the gnarled mass of seaweed that must have somehow caught in the propeller.

Juliette watched as he yanked at the slippery kelp. "You're making it worse," she called. The fibrous ribbons of seaweed had curled around the propeller and all his thrashing was tangling it further.

The more Brock swore, the more his Australian accent mellowed.

At first, Juliette thought he was just slurring because he was drunk. But no, his accent was definitely slipping.

"This is so jacked," he said harshly. "Now my swim trunks are stuck."

"How in the . . ." Juliette frowned and strained to see over the side of the boat.

"The string from my waistband got tangled." Brock

punched the water with his fist. "Call my assistant. Just use my phone. It's in the basket under the bench."

She searched for his phone, but the basket only held champagne. "There's nothing here."

He let out a string of curses that would make a sailor blush. "I must've left it on the houseboat. Use yours."

Juliette pulled her phone from her small purse and dialed a number he recited.

A man's voice mail picked up.

She glanced at Brock. "He's not answering."

More curses. "Yeah, he wouldn't. They're all down at the bar doing tequila shots. He probably doesn't recognize your number."

Juliette left a quick message, then put her phone down. The chances of Brock's assistant calling her back right away were slim. The quickest way out of this mess was to jump in and help him. She'd really wanted to avoid it, but it was the fastest way to get rid of him and go home. Seaweed was a plant, and plants loved her. She'd have no problem untangling it. She grumbled under her breath and kicked off her sandals.

Why did she have to wear her best dress today, of all days? It was a soft floral silk, and the only thing she had in her entire closet that was Dry Clean Only. She'd paid full price for it at a clothing boutique in Seattle on her last visit there with Emma, and she was planning to wear it to Emma's wedding rehearsal dinner. What a waste this date turned out to be.

Juliette considered her options. No use ruining her dress for Mr. Hollywood BoozeBoat. She made up her mind quickly and shimmied out of the dress, folding it and laying it neatly on the seat. Who cared if Brock saw her in her underwear? Her blue lace panties and bra were less revealing than Mirage's thong bikini. Juliette's underwear looked puritanical, by comparison. But at least they matched. Matching underwear was one of Juliette's vices. Life was just too short not to wear good underwear. Everything else was negotiable.

"I'm coming in," she said. "Don't move. You'll just tangle the seaweed further."

Brock whistled low. "Dang, girl. You are smokin' hot." His accent had definitely faded. Unbelievable. Not only were this guy's tan and muscles fake, his Australian accent was fake, too? She was so fed up with this little boating adventure.

"Tell me something, Brock," Juliette said. "You're not really Australian, are you?"

Brock's face paled and she could see him trying to decide how to answer, but he was stuck in a mess of seaweed and not really in a good position to lie. "I'm an actor, babe," he finally said. "That's what they pay me for."

Juliette scooted to the side of the boat. She dipped her hand in the water and shivered. The Pacific Northwest wasn't exactly known for balmy ocean currents, even in the summer. "So they pay you to pretend you're Australian?"

"For the ratings," he said matter-of-factly. "They said *Surfers Down Under* would be more authentic if the main character was Australian, so . . ." His voice trailed off.

She frowned. "Is anything about you for real?"

He gave her the once-over. "I f'realz think you're sexy. And I can show you what else I've got that's real, as soon as we get off this boat."

Juliette rolled her eyes. He could save it for his groupies. Brock Templeton had lost his luster for her. Kat would be so glad to hear it.

She plunged into the ocean and came up gasping from the cold, then quickly swam over to Brock to get her limbs moving.

He punched the water with his fist and swore under his

breath. Drunk and disgruntled like this, he looked nothing like the surf god he'd seemed to be a few days ago.

"Hold still." Juliette laid her hands on the knotted ropes of seaweed surrounding him. As always, she felt an instant connection with the plants. It was as simple as breathing, coaxing them little by little to slip free of the propeller. She closed her eyes and let her energy flow until she could feel the seaweed loosen, finally releasing the propeller and Brock's swim shorts. In less than one minute, he was free.

"Dude," Brock said with a loud hiccup. "How'd you do that? I was yanking on it as hard as I could." Now that he no longer cared about faking his accent, he sounded younger—like a college fraternity guy on spring break.

"You have to be gentle with that kind of seaweed," she said. "It's very sticky, and the more you pull at it, the more tangled it gets." It was much easier than telling him she had a magical connection with plants. Even if she'd wanted to tell him the truth, he'd just think she was a crazy local. Given that his entire image was contrived, he clearly had no problem with smoke and mirrors, but believing in actual magic? Not very likely.

She swam to the side of the boat to pull herself back in.

Brock reached it first and heaved himself up. The boat lurched sideways, but he managed to hook a leg over and drag himself into it. Once in the boat, he grabbed a towel from under a bench seat and started to dry off.

"Can I get some help here?" Juliette called, more than a little annoyed. The icy water lapped against the side of the boat, splashing into her face and mouth.

He looked over at her as if he'd forgotten she was there. How drunk was he?

"Sure, babe," he said lazily. "Just let me get this towel—"

"*Now*," Juliette said through chattering teeth.

Brock held his hands up, swaying with the boat. "All right, all right. Dang, you're so prickly. But you know, I like my girls sassy." He tried to lean over, but tripped on the discarded towel. "Woah." He grabbed a bench seat, chuckling as the boat rocked violently back and forth. Pushing himself up, he leaned over and held out a hand for Juliette.

She reached up and grabbed his hand.

He yanked, but nothing happened.

"On the count of three," he said with a laugh, his entire upper body hanging over the side. "Wait, let me brace my foot." He stood and put one foot on the edge, then leaned over to grab her arm.

The boat listed sideways.

"Scoot back," Juliette said in frustration. "You're going to tip it."

He made a clumsy grab for both of her hands. "Give me some credit, girl. I've done this a million times on my show. You know my show, *Surfers Down Under*?"

"Never heard of it," she muttered. "Just pull me up, all right?"

"Count of three," he slurred. "One. Two." On three, he lifted his other foot onto the edge, yanked both of her hands, and toppled straight into the water, capsizing the boat on his way down.

"No!" Juliette tried to stop it, but it was no use. The up-ended boat bobbed up and down in the waves. Her purse, her cell phone, and her prized silk dress, all disappeared into the ocean.

She slapped the water as Brock *whooped* with laughter.

"This," she said through gritted teeth, "is all your fault."

Brock stopped laughing long enough to throw her an offended look. "Take it easy, babe. It's just a dinghy. Not that big a deal."

"No?" She wanted to strangle him. Where was that sea-weed when she needed it? "Well, I just lost my purse, my

ID, my clothes, and my cell phone because of you. And now how are we going to get back to shore?"

Brock seemed to sober for a moment. Without a phone, they couldn't call for help. He looked back at the shoreline. "It's not that far. I guess we could swim for it."

"It's farther than it looks. You should know that from all your surf experience."

"Well, I'm not going to just stick around here waiting to be rescued like a loser," he said.

Juliette tried to take a calming breath. He really ought to drown, the fool. Before she could open her mouth to talk him out of it, Brock started waving his arms and yelling.

She turned in the direction he was waving and saw a motorboat coming toward them about fifty yards away. As it pulled closer, she felt her whole body flush hot with humiliation in spite of the freezing water.

Of all the capsized boats, in all the oceans, in all the world, he had to pull up next to hers.

Chapter Sixteen

Juliette watched Logan O'Connor pull beside them in his grandfather's old boat. The evening sunlight made his tawny hair glow like burnished gold. It suddenly struck her how gorgeous he was, in a very manly, down-to-earth way. He was the kind of man who made the Brocks of the world look like pampered peacocks.

Logan's dark gaze captured hers. "You look like you could use help."

"Can you please get me out of here?" She wasn't too proud to beg.

"Hey, man," Brock called. "So glad you showed up." His Australian accent was back, though a little less pronounced. "Dude, oh, my god. I totally got stuck trying to get seaweed off the propeller, and then Juliette jumped in the water and then the boat tipped over."

Juliette scowled at Brock. "That's not exactly how it happened. There were a few other steps in there you left out."

"Hey, no worries, luv," Brock said easily. "Accidents happen. Let's just get to shore." He looked up at Logan. "We're cool, right, mate?"

Logan didn't respond. He reached a hand down to Juliette. She grabbed on and he pulled her smoothly out of the water, hauling her into his boat.

Brock was babbling about the waves and the sea-weed, but Juliette didn't really hear it. She was acutely aware of Logan's hard body plastered against her wet, semi-naked one.

Their breaths mingled in the evening air. He dropped his gaze to her now transparent lace underwear. "You appear to have lost your clothes."

She pulled away and tried to cover herself. "It's a long story."

"Is it?" he murmured. She felt an odd, swooping sensation in the pit of her stomach. He was so warm. All she wanted to do was press herself against him and soak in all that heat.

"Oi!" Brock called from the water. "Can you like, lend me a hand?"

Logan's gaze stayed fixed on Juliette for several more heartbeats, then he turned away to help Brock into the boat.

Juliette took a deep breath and let it out slowly. It was impossible to deny the attraction she felt toward Logan, and she was pretty sure he felt it, too.

Logan took off his hoodie and draped it over Juliette's shoulders. It was so big, the hem skimmed past her hips to her thighs, covering her like a blanket.

She slid her arms into it and zipped it up, grateful for how huge and warm it was, then sat on one of the cushioned seats near him.

He started the engine and soon they were heading back to shore.

"You don't have anything else to wear, do you, man?" Brock asked, shivering. "Like another one of those sweatshirts, or . . . ?" He gazed forlornly at Juliette's hoodie.

Logan didn't even bother looking at him. He just shook his head.

"Do you have anything to drink, at least?" Brock whined. "A beer or something?"

"This is not a pleasure cruise. You'll have to wait until you get there." Logan jerked his chin to the houseboat docked at the end of the pier as they approached.

Brock's eyes lit up like a fireworks display. "Thank god. Civilization."

When they pulled up to the dock a short while later, Brock stepped onto the pier, swaying on his feet. He turned to Juliette. "You wanna come with me?"

"I for reals don't," she said with flawless diamond clarity.

He gave a halfhearted wave and took off toward the houseboat.

"God." She scrubbed her hands over her face. "That was a disaster."

"I won't argue with that," Logan said. "What really happened out there?"

Juliette filled him in as he docked the boat, his lips twitching suspiciously while she told him the details. By the time she was finished, he'd tethered the boat and helped her onto the dock. "I can take you home, if you want. My car's just over there."

She followed him down the pier to the street where he'd parked his truck. If only she hadn't left her car at home, but she'd caught a ride to work with Emma that morning, assuming Brock would take her home after their date. Stupid assumption. Even if Brock had wanted to drive her home, he was far too drunk to get behind the wheel.

Logan opened his truck door, and she slid into the

passenger seat, clutching his sweatshirt around her. He grabbed a blanket from the backseat and settled it over her. It smelled warm and woodsy and comforting. She snuggled under it, grateful to finally stop shivering.

Something thumped against her foot. A pile of library books were stacked on the floor. She peeked down at the heavy hardback book stacked on top. *Great Maples of the Pacific Northwest.* That was odd. She expected Logan to read political thrillers or maybe even science fiction novels, not nature books. She nudged the stack with her foot, sliding the top book over so she could see the next one. *Gardening Tips: A Healthy Tree Is a Happy Tree.* What the heck? Maybe Logan was doing some research for his yard.

Awash with curiosity, Juliette "accidentally" toppled the rest of the books onto the floor. Before she could snoop, Logan slid into the driver's seat and leaned over, gathering the books and placing them in the back.

When he started the engine, she stole a glance at his profile in the waning light. The angled planes of his face were sharper than they had been years ago. There was a hard edge to him now that made him look more dangerous, but he was still beautiful. Juliette felt a twinge of yearning, and she fought to ignore it.

The problem with Logan was that he wasn't just a gorgeous man. She'd been around handsome guys before, but with him it went deeper than that. He was part of Pine Cove Island, part of her history. She knew him back when she was young and vulnerable, before she learned that the people you love can leave and take your heart with them. He was dangerous because he made her remember that feeling. The yearning for something that was unattainable. Juliette had vowed a long time ago never to get caught up in someone so much that she'd risk herself—

risk everything she was—to be with them. Her life just wasn't destined to go down that road, and she'd accepted it.

"You okay?" Logan's deep voice cut through the cocoon of silence as they drove down the highway that led to her house.

Juliette snuggled deeper into the blanket. "Yeah. I'm just cold."

He reached over and turned on the heater.

That was the thing about him. He was always doing things to make her life easier, and it made her . . . uncomfortable. Why? Juliette frowned. Most girls would kill to have a hot guy like Logan.

"Sorry about your date," Logan said.

"Don't remind me," she moaned. "It was a disaster, but I should've seen it coming. Kat warned me about him. I guess I just didn't realize the extent of it."

"Wasn't he Australian a few days ago?"

"Yes. Shut up."

He looked suspiciously like he was trying not to laugh as he pulled into the driveway to her cottage.

"Go ahead," she said miserably. "Say what you're thinking."

"Nope."

"Why not? I bet you're dying to rub my face in it. Tell me how stupid I am. How I was an idiot to be dazzled by his nonexistent charm. How dating him was a big fat waste of time."

Logan pulled the car to a stop in her driveway. He looked straight ahead, not making eye contact. "Actually, I was thinking what an utter moron he was."

Here it came. This was the part where Logan said "I told you so" and she had to eat crow.

"Because any man lucky enough to get you would be a complete fool to ruin it."

Wait, what? He was complimenting her? Her heart thudded against her rib cage, and a warm rush of pleasure flowed over her. It felt good to be on the receiving end of his praise, especially when she was so used to arguing with him.

Logan's expression was unreadable.

What else was he thinking? Juliette wanted to ask, but she was afraid to ruin her streak of luck.

"You're too good for him, Juliette. Plain and simple."

Okay, now the world just spun out of its orbit. Logan was praising her. This had to end before it got out of hand.

"He's as fake as his accent," Logan continued. "And you're one of the most open, honest, real people I've ever met. You're too smart for him. Too beautiful for him. Too . . . everything for him."

Logan looked over at her, and she felt like she had to grab on to something or she'd float away.

"Um . . ." Juliette bit her lower lip. *Concentrate! He's praising you. Say something smart. Dazzle him with your intellect.* "Did you know that some herbal teas are believed to help cure immunodeficiency disorders?"

Logan blinked. "What?"

She opened her mouth and began spouting off the basic health benefits of herbal tea, all too aware of the way he watched her with that secret smile. He looked at her as if she was fascinating. As if she was important.

"So anyway," she continued. "I make this really good herbal tea, and you should come inside and have some. If you want."

Yup, she'd just invited him in. Juliette's head swam with all the reasons inviting him into her home was a bad idea, but none of it mattered. All that stuff meant nothing when Logan O'Connor was looking at her like this.

He threw the car into park and shut off the engine. "Okay."

Juliette jumped out and flew up the steps. Her cottage was old, but well loved. Rosebushes lined the driveway, and ivy grew up the sides of the house, as if nature was claiming it as her own. The flower boxes on the front porch railing spilled over with a profusion of brightly colored blooms, and she'd planted sweet lavender on either side of the stairs leading up to her door. There was an old stepping stone hanging on the wall by the door. It was an art project she'd made with her mother when she was five—her small handprint, surrounded by bits of colorful glass and seashells.

Since her entire purse was now at the bottom of the ocean, she searched in a planter for the spare key she kept near the door. "I can't believe he capsized the boat," she said nervously, trying to fill the space between them with words. She babbled on about plastic champagne cups and seaweed and how Burning Man was clothing optional. How Tweedle Dee didn't know Austen, and how Kat had a pet crow.

Logan came up to stand behind her as she fumbled with the lock. He was so huge, and so close, she could almost feel his warmth seeping through her wet sweatshirt. "Now I'll have to go get a new license and another key made. Luckily, I didn't have any money in there. Just my phone and my entire life and whatever." She dropped the key, bent to pick it up, and tried to open the door again. Why was she so nervous?

"Juliette," he said softly, placing a warm hand over hers on the doorknob.

She could feel his soft breath against her cheek. "Hmm?"

"Shut up."

"Okay."

He leaned in, took the key, and unlocked the door with a click that seemed to ricochet through her entire body. This was really happening. She was bringing him into her home. Her sanctuary. No man's land.

When she gathered her courage and stepped over the threshold, Logan was right behind her.

Chapter Seventeen

After quickly showering, changing into dry clothes, and toweling her hair, Juliette didn't feel any calmer. Logan O'Connor was in her house! How could she relax? Her entire body thrummed with restless energy. She was nervous. Excited. A little bit giddy.

She gathered herself together and went to the kitchen to make tea, like it was any other day. If nothing else, it gave her something to do. Chamomile tea was supposed to be soothing. It was supposed to impart feelings of calm and comfort. Juliette brewed it out of dried flowers from her garden, and she knew for a fact it made people relax. Creating tea to help soothe people was part of her special gift. Not for the first time in her life, she found herself wishing the Holloway charms worked on herself.

A few minutes later, she lifted the copper kettle from her stove, poured steaming water into two mugs, added generous dollops of honey, and went in search of Logan.

He was in the living room looking at a framed wall painting with the phrase "The Earth Laughs in Flowers."

"It's my favorite quote," Juliette said, joining him. She

handed him a cup of tea. "My cousin Emma gave it to me for my birthday a few years ago."

He lifted the mug of chamomile tea and sniffed, frowning.

"I know you're more of a beer guy, but at least try it. You never know."

He gave her a skeptical look, took a sip, and grimaced. "Now I know."

Juliette rolled her eyes. "Just drink it. Why do you always have to be so stubborn?"

He lifted a brow in challenge, but there was a teasing note in his voice. "Why do you always have to be so bossy?"

"It's one of my best qualities," she said, tossing her hair.

"Says you." He set his cup down and moved closer.

This was it. He was going to kiss her, and she was already ready, already. She tilted her face up and closed her eyes. Why not? Why not just let it happen? Who really cared if he was Romeo's nephew? She could overlook it, for now. Who cared if she'd had a crush on him since zero'th grade? Things were different. Thirteen years had passed and they were older now. They could keep it light and fun. It would be no big deal. They were obviously attracted to each other and he seemed to like her, even though he had Bella and probably a lot of other women circling him like sharks. Maybe, like her, he just wanted to have a good time. Maybe he wasn't looking for anything else.

"Can I have something else?"

Juliette opened her eyes. Blinked. Stepped back a little. "What?"

"Do you have anything else to drink besides that stuff?" He gestured to the tea.

Juliette pointed in the direction of the kitchen. "In the fridge."

"Good." He walked into the kitchen, and she stared dumbly after him.

What the hell? Yep, he was really walking away from her. Her cheeks flushed with embarrassment. This was ridiculous. Guys didn't just walk away from her. At least, not usually. Not when she was standing in front of them with her eyes closed and her lips all smoochy-smoochy. How could she have misinterpreted that moment? Maybe her brain was waterlogged after her dip in the ocean. Or maybe Brock's idiocy had worn off on her, somehow.

She found Logan sipping beer on her back patio, one hand in his pocket as he took in her garden.

He didn't say anything, but he didn't have to. Juliette knew her garden was stunning. Even though she tended it almost every day and knew every last flower, every last leaf, it never ceased to delight her. That was the wonderful thing about Mother Nature. She was always full of surprises.

She stood beside him with her head cocked to one side, trying to imagine what her garden must look like to a person who'd never seen it before. The evening summer sunlight gave the garden a warm, rich glow. A huge maple tree stood at one end, surrounded by flowering azalea bushes. Dragonflies zipped around the bright pink blooms. Tulips and daffodils danced in the breeze, tucked here and there among rosebushes and lavender plants. The scent of jasmine filled the air, and lilacs twined up an arched trellis. There was a small rockery with a waterfall tucked among the ferns, and a fairy wind chime hanging from a branch above it. The fairy's wings were spread behind her as she perched on a sliver of the moon, dangling her feet over the edge.

"This place is . . ." Logan shook his head. "Amazing."

Juliette tried to pretend it didn't matter, but it was impossible to ignore the surge of pleasure she felt at his praise. She had lived in the cottage her entire life, and tended the garden for as long as she could remember. It was where she had taken her first steps. Where she'd first learned to climb a tree. Where she came for comfort whenever life seemed too difficult to bear. The garden was an extension of herself. It shouldn't matter to her that Logan approved, but it did.

He walked toward the tree, turning in a slow circle. "Did you do all this?"

"Well, not just me." She took a seat on a swinging bench under trailing ivy. "Mother Nature had a hand in it. I still have so much I want to do. That rose trellis is breaking down." She pointed to a wild tangle of flowers woven through a weathered piece of lattice. "I'd like to replace it with an archway, and then maybe lay a rock path beyond it leading into the woods."

Logan wandered through the garden. "I've never seen anything like this. How did you do it?"

"Magic," she said impishly, drawing her knees up and linking her arms around her legs. "I'm a Holloway, remember?"

He sat beside her on the weathered bench. "How old were you when you realized you had this relationship with nature?"

She eyed him sideways. "You mean *magic*?"

"Sure." His expression held no skepticism, only curiosity. The genuine interest on his face, the openness, made her chest expand with hope. It wasn't often that someone accepted her for who she really was. Did he truly accept her?

"I don't really remember when I first realized it," she said. "I've always felt connected."

A vine from overhead landed softly on her shoulder. She lifted it absently, running the soft leaves back and forth against her cheek. "My mother said she once found me in the garden when I was a baby. I'd crawled out into the grass and fallen asleep under the tree. She said a ring of daisies had sprouted up around me, and that's when she knew what my gift was."

Logan was quiet for a long time, and Juliette wondered what he was thinking. Maybe it was too much for him to truly believe. For most people, it was. He was from a normal family, after all. Maybe he thought she was a whack job, too. Only one way to find out.

She took a deep breath and let it out slowly, gathering her courage. "You said earlier that you believed. Do you really?"

He looked surprised that she asked. "Yes."

Juliette felt her limbs go light with gratitude. It was just a single word, but it meant so much. She felt as though she'd just been given a precious gift she never knew she needed.

"Uncle Ro told me about it," he continued. "I've seen what you've done with the plants at the shop, and I've seen you in the woods. Sure, it's hard to make logical sense of it, but . . ." He swept his arm out. "I mean, look at this place. I can't think of anything other than magic that could create something this beautiful."

Warmth bloomed inside her. Logan O'Connor had just given her the best compliment in the world. She wanted to throw her arms around his neck and kiss him. Sitting next to her, unshaven in jeans and a rumpled T-shirt, he was suddenly the most desirable man she'd ever seen.

A vine from above dropped onto his shoulder.

He looked down at it in surprise.

"I think it likes you," Juliette said.

A shower of tiny jasmine flowers floated on the wind, catching in his hair.

Odd. Her plants didn't usually react this way to people.

Luna padded across the grass and sat in front of them. She peered up at Logan for a few moments, then jumped onto the bench beside him.

"Hey, cat," Logan said, reaching down to pet her.

Juliette started to tell him to be careful, but the warning died in her throat. Once again, her cat seemed to like him.

Luna was purring. Purring!

Logan stroked the back of the cat's head like they were old companions.

Okay, so hell had officially frozen over. Her cat, aka Luna the Hellcat, liked somebody. Somebody other than a Holloway. That last time in the woods wasn't a fluke.

What was going on here? First her garden seemed to approve of him, and now her cat? Something dangerously close to happiness plucked at her heartstrings. This was a little too close for comfort.

"Was it hard growing up with it?" he asked. "The magic?"

Juliette watched in fascination as Luna climbed into Logan's lap. "Sometimes."

He scratched the cat absently under her chin, and Luna just sat there. Not trying to kill him. This was madness.

Juliette sprang up and paced a few feet away. "When I was in kindergarten, my teacher got upset because one of the kids ripped her flowers out of the pot on her desk. So I walked up, placed the torn plant back in the soil, and kissed it."

"And then?"

"And then I told it to get better." She bent to pick up a

sprig of leaves off the grass, twirling it in her hands as she walked. "The next morning when I got back to school, it was."

"Was your teacher glad you fixed it?" he asked.

Juliette shook her head, saddened by the memory. She'd been so young, and wanted so much to be accepted. "She requested I be transferred to the other class."

"Why? You fixed her plant."

"Yes, I did. But I fixed it too well. It grew five times in size overnight and towered over her desk." She bit her bottom lip, still remembering the look on her teacher's face. Eyes wide with shock, trembling hand pressed to her chest. "I think I scared her. She was one of those strait-laced types, the kind who's afraid of anything that can't be explained. Even at age five, I was an enigma." She wiggled her fingers. "The Holloway family curse."

"Not a curse. A gift," he said, his hand resting on Luna's sleek black fur. "And anyone who tries to deny that it exists is either a coward, or foolish."

He was suddenly too much, sitting there all gorgeous and perfect with her cat lounging in his lap. A second vine had dropped to twine around his shoulder, and he just sat there on the bench swing, petting the cat like it was nothing. Like he belonged there.

A faded image flashed in her memory. It was so old, she couldn't have been in school yet. But even frayed around the edges, the memory glowed with a special kind of warmth that the garden had long forgotten. Juliette's dad sat on that bench with her mom. He was petting Luna, and they were smiling at her as she showed them her picked flowers. Juliette now saw Logan, superimposed against the fading memory of her parents. He fit so perfectly into her garden.

It was impossible.

She suddenly needed space.

She needed to think.

"I have to go," she said quickly. "I just remembered there's something I have to do."

He lifted Luna off his lap and stood.

"You can leave that way." She pointed to the side gate that led to the front yard. He looked like he was about to speak, but she didn't want to talk. She had to clear her head. "Thanks for everything today," she said quickly.

Without another word, she whirled and took off into the woods.

Logan watched her go until he could no longer see her dark curtain of hair and pale long skirt among the foliage.

He looked at Luna, who sat on the grass near his feet. "What was that all about?"

Luna looked up at him with eerie, golden eyes. She padded toward the woods and turned back to him.

"You think I should follow her?" Because it made so much sense to ask a cat for advice.

The cat peered into the trees, tail twitching. She meowed only once, but that's all it took.

Logan set off after Juliette. Under normal circumstances, he'd leave, but something about her always made him do the opposite of normal. It was darker under the canopy of trees, but the sun still lit the sky enough to see. The scent of pine and damp earth filled the air, and he found himself breathing in the old familiar scents, remembering a much simpler time when he was younger.

The past came tumbling back, and he remembered how magical the place had been for him. He used to charge through the woods with a makeshift branch as a sword, pretending to fight off dragons. Even though it had been years, Logan was still familiar with the stretch of woods.

If he kept walking south, it would lead to his grandfather's backyard.

In the center of the woods, he came to a small stream and found Juliette sitting on a rock with her bare feet in the water.

She looked up at him, startled.

He shoved his hands in his pockets. "What's wrong?"

"I thought you were going home." She looked down at her feet, wiggling her toes in the clear water.

Logan tilted his head toward the trees. "If I keep walking in that direction, I will be home."

"I remember your grandfather's place," Juliette said softly. "When I was little, I used to see you guys, sometimes. I remember that summer when he built you that treehouse."

"You and I played together here," Logan said. "Do you remember?" Once, when he was around eight years old, he saw her in the woods while he was playing with his action figures. He'd sized her up, decided she'd do, and held out a spaceship. She took it in her tiny hand, and for hours, they'd played in the dirt together. A couple times after that they played in the woods, in the carefree way that small children did. But one summer he brought friends from his baseball team over. The boys ran around the yard, yelling and laughing and throwing water balloons. He caught a glimpse of her standing in the trees watching him, but he turned away. She was just a baby, and he had real friends to play with.

"Mostly I just remember you running around the yard with your friends." She picked up a smooth stone and tossed it into the stream. "Or doing projects with your grandfather."

"Ah, so you were spying on me?" he teased.

Her lips curved, but she didn't make eye contact. Instead she ran a finger over a worn spot on her skirt. "My mother used to say that I spent more time in these woods than I did in my own house."

Logan watched as an expression of sadness flashed across her face. He wondered what her life had really been like as a child. He didn't know much about her back then, except that she was one of the eccentric Holloways.

Years later, she'd approached him when he was a senior in high school. He remembered the first time he saw her— all dressed up—at his graduation party. It had been a shock to realize that the wild child from the woods was transforming into a beautiful woman.

"I was so jealous of that treehouse," she said wistfully. "I remember thinking how it was wasted on you, because you were just a dumb boy."

Logan laughed. "I *was* a dumb boy."

"And if I had it," she continued, "I'd grow flowers in the windows and coax the tree branches to hide the entrance. And it would have a secret password that only my friends would know. I'd sleep in it on rainy nights, or when the moon was full, and I'd lay and just listen to the wind. I never saw the inside, but I imagined it was a mess of dumb boy things like baseball gloves and Batman comics and gym socks. And I always thought, if it were mine, I'd fill it with important things that really mattered. Like books." She grinned up at him, blue eyes flashing. "And cookies."

He liked it when she smiled at him like that. It made him wish she'd do it more often. "Just books and cookies?"

She kicked her feet out, sending water splashing in a silvery arc across the stream. "What more does a person need? Treehouses aren't that big on the inside. You have to carefully consider the necessities."

Logan felt an odd sense of melancholy, watching her in that moment. She reminded him of days long gone. Simpler times. She reminded him what it was like to feel driving optimism and hope. He suddenly wanted to hold on to that feeling as long as he could, before it slipped away.

"Come with me." He reached out his hand to help her up.

She looked at his hand, then stood on her own and dusted off her skirt. "Why?"

"I'd like you to see my treehouse." He felt like he was balancing on a ledge, and her decision would either lift him up or send him tumbling. Why did he want to show her so much? All he knew was that it mattered to him. He'd been gone so long, and after the army, his life as a young boy with his grandfather seemed so far away. But Juliette was there, even if they had never moved in the same circles. She remembered his grandfather. She remembered him. She remembered the person he was before.

"I can't," she said softly.

A tightness gripped his chest. He swallowed his disappointment. "Maybe some other time."

She dropped her head back and looked up into the canopy of trees. Logan watched as she closed her eyes and tilted her head, as if she were listening to the wind.

"I have to go home," she said. "You should, too. It's going to rain."

He glanced around. "When?"

"Right"—she spread her arms wide, her face and palms tilted to the sky—"now."

Tiny drops of rain began to fall around them, gaining momentum, faster and faster, until within moments they were cocooned in the muted sound of rain falling on leaves, and the rich scent of damp earth.

Juliette's smile seemed as ancient as the trees, her eyes liquid pools of blue, and the soft laugh that escaped her lips was mesmerizing.

Desire spiked through him, hard and fast. Without thinking, he strode over and gathered her in his arms.

She blinked up at him in surprise, her lips parting on a soft gasp.

He kissed her. Slowly. Thoroughly. Until she melted into him, her hands reaching up to grip his shoulders, her body pressing closer. The rain soaked through his clothes, running in rivulets down his face, but Logan barely noticed. All he could think about was the way she felt against him. How she tasted like raindrops and honey, and how much he wanted to sweep her up and take her home. *Home.*

Before he had the chance to try, Juliette pulled away. She looked slightly baffled, as if she was trying to figure out how the kiss had started in the first place.

Shaking her head, she turned away, moving swiftly across the forest floor. And then she was gone.

Chapter Eighteen

Game face. Game face. Game face. Juliette repeated the mantra as she parked her car behind the florist shop. She needed to pull herself together. Yesterday's boating fiasco was still a matter of humiliation, and even though she wished Logan hadn't seen her in that predicament with Brock, she was glad he'd come along to help when he did.

But it wasn't the boating incident that had her spinning like a carnival ride this morning. It was what happened afterward. Juliette squeezed her eyes shut, then checked her face in the car's visor mirror. She'd expertly applied her makeup and wove her long mass of hair into two French braids. Aside from a heightened color in her cheeks, she looked completely normal. She was totally fine.

"Liar." She stared at her reflection a moment longer, then shut the visor.

Last night had been entirely unexpected. At first she was game for whatever may have happened. In her living room, she'd actually wanted to kiss him again. Then when he finally did kiss her in the woods, she didn't want it to end. And that was bad. But what happened between them in the garden was even worse than kissing. They'd *talked*.

Juliette pressed her lips together, frowning. They talked

about the past. She even remembered her parents in the garden, back when her world was whole and happy. She remembered what it felt like before she learned that you can lose the ones you love.

She took a deep breath and straightened her spine. Better to put it all behind her. Before she left her house, she'd vowed to focus on the work that needed to get done before Romeo came back. The florist shop was finally coming together, and it was even more beautiful than she could have imagined. Romeo would see how well she'd managed everything, and her plan would fall into place. It had to. Everything else could be sorted out later. Especially her feelings for Logan.

Juliette slid out of the car. Really, how hard could it be to see him and just say "hey"? It's not like anything major had happened between them. It was just another stupid kiss. She'd survived the first one, so this one was just another slipup. She'd thank him again for rescuing her and driving her home, then laugh it all off as a crazy experience. She was a pro at keeping things light and fun with men. Dealing with Logan was going to be a breeze.

Logan's truck was already there. Her heart did a little backflip as she approached the back door.

"Hey." Kat emerged with a stack of boxes. She was wearing her usual all-black clothing, black boots, and black eyeliner. Her hair was pulled back in a tight bun, and with Hank trotting beside her, she looked like a kick-ass character from a graphic novel. Others might look at her and find her appearance unsettling, but not Juliette. There was something comforting about Kat's presence, in the same way an heirloom blanket felt soothing or a favorite sweatshirt just felt right.

Hank gazed up at Kat in adoration, his pink tongue lolling out of his mouth. Today he wore a purple lace bow in his hair, and a matching jingle bell collar.

"How's it going?" Juliette asked.

Kat dumped the boxes in the recycle bin. "Blissfully slow and quiet. There's nothing going on." She slapped dust off her hands and made a face. "And believe me, I couldn't be happier."

"More drama at *Hollywood Houseboat*?" Juliette followed her inside. Logan wasn't there, which meant he was probably working on the deck. She'd missed him. Good.

"It's insane," Kat said. "Vespa's been taking cooking lessons, and Mirage is furious because she keeps cooking."

Juliette gestured to the coffeepot. "Fresh?"

"Just made it."

"I think I love you."

Kat shrugged. "I get that a lot."

Juliette poured herself a cup and leaned against the counter. "So what's wrong with cooking food?"

"It has calories, which are basically Mirage's archnemesis. She only eats leaves and twigs. And possibly small dogs. I caught her eyeing Hank the other day, and I don't think it had anything to do with him sleeping on her cashmere sweater." She scooped the small dog up and gave him a kiss on the head. "Anyway, Mirage starts throwing a fit last night. Says Vespa's trying to sabotage her girlish figure because she's jealous. So Vespa says why would she be jealous of a stick bug, and they start fighting on the living room floor. Brock yells 'catfight,' and pretty soon the film crew's getting some classic footage for the show." Kat grimaced. "It's like a three-ring circus in there. Unbearable."

"That sucks." Juliette set her cup down and grabbed an apron off a peg on the wall.

"It does. Which is why I'm always happy to come here."

"Whenever I get all worked up or stressed out, I need to be around plants," Juliette said, looping the apron over her head and tying it around her waist. "Being surrounded by nature makes everything better."

"This place is definitely peaceful," Kat agreed as she set Hank back on the floor. "Except when Logan's prowling around outside with his power tools."

"It has been loud lately."

"Oh, I'm not talking about the noise. I'm talking about the view. That guy is seriously hot. And when he takes his shirt off?" She fanned herself. "Help me."

Juliette tried to appear neutral. "I haven't really noticed."

"Then you need to get your eyes checked," Kat said with a laugh. She reached into a box of dog treats on the counter and tossed one to Hank.

He caught it in midair, tail spinning in delight.

"Hey, I'm working on Saturday, right?" Kat asked.

"I hope so. Otherwise Emma and the girls will be out a runner. I don't know how they talked me into participating in the Mud Run." The annual Firefighters' Mud Run was a ridiculous obstacle course of mud pits, bubble foam, and forest trails. Every year people gathered into teams to compete, and all the money went to support the Seattle Children's Hospital.

"You gals are crazy," Kat said, lifting her purse off the counter. "*Hollywood Houseboat*'s all excited to win the Mud Run. Brock's been doing extra cross-fit training this week, and Mirage plans to eat carbs." She paused for a moment. "Okay, I made that up. She'd never stoop that low. Not even for a children's charity."

"How come you're not doing it?"

Kat snorted. "Like I need any more craziness? No thanks. You guys can all go get wild and filthy and whatever else. I'll be right here, eating bonbons and misting the ferns, right, Hank? He thinks all humans are nuts."

"And he'd be right." Juliette bent to pat him on the head.

Kat opened the back door. "Gotta run. I promised I'd have him back in time for the *Houseboat*'s family portrait." She made a face. "Vespa wants him in an argyle sweater with a bow tie. Do you know how hard it was to find a dog outfit like that at the last minute?"

Juliette shook her head.

"Lucky for me, that curiosity shop next door to Fairy Cakes had just what I needed. Mrs. Mooney has an entire wall dedicated to dog outfits."

Juliette gave Hank a look of pity. "Sorry, Hank."

As Kat turned to go, a large black crow swooped past the doorway. Kat *tsk*ed and called out, "Edgar, I told you to wait until I got off work."

"Edgar?" Juliette walked to the door and saw the crow flying in lazy circles around the parking lot.

He let out a loud *caw*, followed by several squawks.

"Technically, I'm off work," Kat called to him, reaching into her bag. "But next time at least give me a chance to get out the door, okay?" She pulled a small bag of Cheetos from her purse, and Edgar made a joyful dive past her head.

Juliette laughed. "Looks like your crow friend stuck around."

"We're learning to live with each other," Kat said with a shrug. "He just needs to learn boundaries. Men—am I right?"

Juliette waved good-bye and shut the door, resting her back against it for a moment. The shop suddenly felt empty without them. She spent the next few minutes stalling, cleaning up in the back room. Wiping down the cutting counter. Arranging a vase of roses. Twice. Finally she ventured out to the front of the shop, and there he was.

Logan was clearly visible through the huge side window. He was measuring a section of paving stones, his strong hands smoothing over the dark surface. Juliette tried not to imagine what those hands could do to her, but just watching him sent shivers of pleasure rippling across her skin.

He looked up.

Their eyes met. Now she couldn't look away, or it would

seem like she was nervous. And she wasn't nervous. Everything was totally normal.

Juliette lifted her hand mechanically and waved.

He held her gaze a moment longer, gave a tight nod, and went back to work.

She turned away. Why did she feel disappointed? What did she expect him to do, jump up and come running to her? Please. Obviously, he had no problem focusing on work. Fine, Mr. O'Connor. If you can do it, I can do it. Nothing to it.

An hour later, Juliette had sold the last arrangement of roses, labeled her latest batch of jasmine-scented bath bombs, and swept the entire shop. If she was aware of Logan's presence outside at all times, she didn't show it. He still hadn't come inside to talk to her, which suited her just fine.

It was late afternoon when Juliette hefted a bucket of water from the sink. She didn't hear the door open behind her, but she could feel Logan's presence the moment he stepped inside. Her hand slipped on the handle of the bucket, sloshing water down the front of her thin tank top.

Lovely. He was just in time for her wet T-shirt show. She steadied the bucket on the rim of the sink, then slowly turned and set it on the cutting table near a pile of blood-red roses.

Logan stood at the other end of the table. His dark eyes roamed over her. Juliette took a deep breath and tried to ignore the spiraling heat inside her.

"So." What should she say? How did this work again? Oh, yeah. "How's it going out there?"

He didn't say anything. Just stood there for a few moments, then started walking toward her.

Juliette felt a sudden twinge of alarm. If he came any closer, she couldn't be responsible for what she'd do. Because damn it all to Hades, even though her plan was to remain calm, cool, and indifferent about this man, her body didn't seem to be on board with it.

"Stop." She held up a hand.

Logan ignored her. He came right up beside her, then leaned forward. "Why?"

Juliette sucked in a breath, heart thumping wildly in her chest. She could feel the warmth of his body, and she wanted to touch him again.

Logan reached out and turned on the faucet. He began washing his hands.

She let her breath out slowly. "Never mind."

He seemed amused. "What did you think I was going to do?"

"I wasn't sure," she said truthfully. He was standing so close, it gave her a swooping feeling in the pit of her stomach, like she was on a wild roller coaster. She loved roller coasters. But that was neither here nor there.

"So what, am I the big bad wolf now?" he murmured, rinsing his hands.

If only you knew.

"Don't worry," he said. "I only accost unsuspecting women in the woods. You're safe here."

Somehow, she didn't quite believe it.

Customers suddenly came in through the front door. Juliette whipped out a clean apron and tied it on, side-stepping Logan.

By the time she had created four new flower arrangements, Logan's truck was gone. He left without even saying good-bye. A heavy mantle of disappointment settled over her. What did she expect?

Chapter Nineteen

On Monday evening, Juliette dropped her keys in the vine-painted ceramic bowl near her front door and kicked off her shoes. She set the disposable phone she'd purchased on the narrow entry table. It wasn't great, but it would have to do until she could afford to replace the one she'd lost in the ocean.

Juliette's stomach growled. She was starving. It had been a long day at the shop, and she'd skipped lunch. Mrs. Mooney had come in for soaps, along with her snaggle-toothed dog, Bonbon. Juliette had a soft spot for the old woman, since she'd helped the police capture Emma's terrible ex-boyfriend a year earlier. But Mrs. Mooney could talk a blue streak, and Juliette's nerves were already on high alert with Logan working outside. She was aware of him at all times. Since Logan had come to her house that night, she had no idea how to act around him. For the zillionth time that day, her stomach gave a nervous flutter. The more she thought about him, the more she wanted more.

"This is a bad idea," she said out loud.

Luna padded around the corner and rubbed against her legs.

Juliette wove her hands through her hair and massaged her scalp. "I can't stop thinking about Logan O'Connor."

Luna gave a tiny meow.

"It's a bad idea," Juliette repeated. "Very bad. It complicates things, and I don't like complications. What am I doing?" She stared down at her cat.

Luna blinked.

"I should quit now, before this situation gets any weirder. Right?"

Luna jumped onto the entry table and sniffed Juliette's phone.

"You're no help," Juliette muttered, scratching the cat behind the ears. "Did you at least cook me dinner? I'm starving. When are you going to start using those recipe books in the kitchen cupboard?" For years, a small collection of her mother's cookbooks sat on the shelf above the stove, gathering dust. But Juliette had never been that interested in cooking. She knew how to make salads and sandwiches, and she knew how to order pizza. That was good enough.

Luna nudged Juliette's phone with her nose.

"Crazy cat." Juliette ran her hand down Luna's sleek back. "I'm not ordering pizza again. I've had it three times this past week."

Luna twitched her tail and meowed loudly. She nudged the phone again.

"What is it?"

The phone began to ring.

Juliette looked at the number across the screen. It wasn't a number she recognized. She picked up her phone, walked into her living room, and flopped onto an overstuffed armchair. "Hello?"

"Hey. It's me." Logan's deep voice seemed to resonate through her entire body.

Pleasure fluttered low in her belly. She really needed to

get a grip. It shouldn't be that big a deal that he called. "How did you get my number?"

"Uncle Ro gave it to me before he left."

That made sense, since they'd be working together while he was away.

"Have you eaten?" Logan asked.

"No." The idea of going to dinner with him was so appealing, but she couldn't. She shouldn't. Staying focused was her number one priority, and Logan was a distraction she couldn't afford. Gathering her resolve, Juliette said, "I don't want to go out."

"I'm not asking you out."

"Oh." A twinge of disappointment. She smothered it.

Luna climbed into her lap, purring.

Juliette stroked the cat's sleek fur, taking comfort in her small, warm presence.

"Come over," Logan said. "I'm making dinner, and I need your opinion on something."

She almost laughed. "If you need help cooking, I'm the last person to ask for advice, I promise you. Unless it's a salad question. Salads, I can do."

There was a pause on the other end. "It's not about cooking. I need your advice about a tree."

Juliette stopped petting Luna and sat up straighter. "What tree?"

"The old maple tree in my backyard."

"The one with the treehouse?" It was the biggest maple tree Juliette had ever seen, and older than either of them.

"Yes. I think it might be sick. It was out here long before my grandfather even built his house, but it used to look so much healthier."

"Well, you were a lot younger the last time you saw it," Juliette said. "Maybe you just remember it differently."

"No." His voice rang with conviction. "I don't remember it being this brittle. Several branches have fallen off in the wind since I moved in. And the leaves are turning brown up near the top. I was going to ask an arborist to come out and take a look at it, but then I thought of you."

He thought of me. Happiness swelled inside her, and she fought to ignore it. It was a losing battle.

"You know plants," he said.

"I do."

"Will you come and have a look?"

She closed her eyes, momentarily torn. What she wanted to do was run straight over to Logan's house without even stopping to put on shoes. What she should do was politely decline any and all further interaction with him outside work. But a tree might be sick, and he was asking for her help. They needed her. How could she refuse? "Of course I'll come."

A few minutes later, she hurried through the woods drawn by an urgent desire to help. If there was any other desire that moved her swiftly toward Logan's house, she tried not to think about it. She was going because trees and plants were her "people." Mother Nature had always been there for her, so Juliette would help in any way she could.

Juliette found solace in the woods, and joy and companionship in plants, flowers, and things that grew from the earth. There was always something new to see and to experience. One of the things she loved most about her special gift was that it tended to be like most things in nature. Unpredictable. There was no precise way of knowing exactly how a spell or potion would turn out. Juliette loved surprises, and the little nuances in her spells and bath products were a constant source of delight. For the most part, they did what they were supposed to, but Mother Nature always kept her on her toes. Hers was wild magic. She knew what different herbs and plants did, but there was always something new to discover. Her own magic was a lot like her garden—an ever-changing source of wonder.

The air was crisp and cool. Juliette pulled her gray cardigan tightly around her as she stepped out of the woods into Logan's backyard.

The spicy scent of mesquite wafted through the air.

Logan looked up from the barbeque as she approached. His hair was damp and slightly mussed, as though he'd just showered, and he'd changed into clean clothes. Juliette suddenly felt like an outsider peeking into his private life. There was something so intimate about seeing him this way, relaxed and at home, without the pretense of work to define their interaction. For a moment, she wasn't sure how to act. The simple intimacy of the situation blurred the lines she'd so carefully drawn between them.

He pulled two steaks off the grill and set them on a plate. "Hungry?"

"Yes. And no." She leaned against the porch railing, eyeing the steak. "I'm hungry, but not for that. I'm a vegetarian."

He furrowed his brow, clearly not impressed with her choice. "Rabbit food, huh?"

She lifted her chin. "Smart people food."

"Says you." He was pretending to be appalled, but Juliette caught the glint of humor in his expression.

"Not all people want to eat animals," she said sternly, trying not to give in to her urge to smile.

Logan gave her a quizzical look. "If we aren't supposed to eat animals, then why are they made of meat?"

She rolled her eyes. "I bet you had that on a bumper sticker in high school."

"T-shirt," he corrected. He turned off the grill and took the plate into the kitchen, calling over his shoulder, "I also made corn on the cob."

"Good. But can I see the tree first?" Her curiosity about the sick tree overrode hunger pangs.

Logan led her to the center of the huge backyard, where the giant maple stood.

Juliette gazed up at the ancient tree. It was older than anything she knew, even older than many of the evergreens in the woods. She remembered how huge and full of vitality it had always seemed when she was little. The branches seemed to touch the sky, the leaves every brilliant shade of green. Now, the branches were gnarled and brittle. It no longer radiated health, and it was clear something was wrong.

She placed her hand on the bark, feeling its age, its weariness. An immense sadness washed over her. Even though she knew it was part of nature's ebb and flow, she always grieved when something so old had to go.

Logan was quiet while she ran her hands over the tree, checking the leaves and bending to sift the soil between her fingers.

"Is it dying?" His voice was so low, she almost didn't hear him.

Juliette looked up to see a flash of bleak hopelessness on Logan's face. She recognized the look, though she rarely saw it in other people. He truly cared for this tree. It must be the reason he'd checked out those tree books from the library.

"It's very weak," she said, choosing her words carefully. "It has blight. Sometimes it happens, even to trees this massive and old."

Logan's face remained expressionless, but there was a tightness around his eyes and mouth that Juliette didn't miss.

"This tree is important to you," she said.

Logan leaned his head back and gazed into the leafy canopy above them. The sturdy treehouse was just visible through the branches. "It was my grandfather's favorite tree. He said it was the only friend around who was older than he was. He built the treehouse for me when I was little because . . ." He paused, then shook his head. "Anyway, I just wanted to know if you could tell me what's wrong with it."

"Why did he build the treehouse?" Juliette asked. It was important to her, though she had no idea why.

"He said he wanted me and the tree to be friends." He shook his head. "It's silly, I know. My grandfather had crazy ideas. He said it was important that we were friends because someday he'd no longer be around, but a tree like this could live for more lifetimes than we could count. And he liked the idea of us still having each other, even after he was gone."

Juliette closed her eyes. They were the musings of a tired old man, a man she never even knew. But the sentiment made her throat swell with sadness. "I think I'd have liked your grandfather, if I'd known him," she said softly.

He ran his hand over the trunk of the tree. "Can you fix it?"

There it was. The question she knew he'd ask. Her heart clenched in her chest because she couldn't promise what he so obviously wanted.

"I'm sorry," she whispered. "I don't think I can."

He wouldn't make eye contact. "Why not? Don't you heal plants or make them grow, or whatever else your magic does?"

She tried to find a way to explain. "With nature, there's an ebb and flow that's almost impossible to change. This tree is huge, and ancient."

"My uncle told me you could heal sick plants." He seemed restless, as though he didn't want to accept the inevitable.

"I can, but there's always a cost. This tree would cost more than I have."

"What would you need?" he asked solemnly.

Juliette paused. She wasn't used to explaining the connection she had with nature. She couldn't even remember the last time someone had asked. It was such a personal thing, but she wanted Logan to understand. "I can make things grow, and heal sick plants if they're inclined to thrive. But when I do, it draws energy from me. It's like we share the energy. A little of mine goes into a plant to heal it. Does that make sense?"

He frowned. "So it drains your energy? It makes you sick?"

"No, but it used to. When I was younger and didn't know my limits, I was always testing what I could do. Once when I was seven years old I tried to bring our Christmas tree back to life after it had dried out at the end of the holiday. I planted it back in the ground and it ended up growing again, but I got so sick afterward. I'd used too much of my own energy to save it. I was ill for a long time and even missed school. I've since learned what's beyond my capabilities." She caressed the old tree. "I'm afraid this is just too big and too old. Its time has come. Its path is set."

"What about potions? Can you make something to help it?" Though his tone was carefully controlled, the inflections neutral, Juliette could feel his sadness. "I don't know. Like plant food, or something?"

"Maybe," she said. "I might be able to help it for a little while, but I don't know how long it would last."

The glimmer of hope in his eyes was brighter than the sun.

She wanted to shield herself from it and pretend it wasn't there. That way, if she failed to help the tree, he wouldn't be hurt. "I'll try, okay? But I can't promise anything. What I can do is try to keep it from getting worse, but even then it's difficult to say whether or not a potion would help."

Logan's expression was so full of hope, she had to turn away. It was almost painful to see, because that kind of optimism was dangerous. She knew from her own experiences. When you hoped like that, you were vulnerable. Your heart could break.

"Logan, it's important that you know. With nature . . . some things aren't meant to last."

"I understand," he said quietly. "Thank you."

A sudden gust of wind swirled through the tree's branches, and Juliette looked up at the treehouse. The large structure was still sturdy, though its sides were weathered and the tree branches had grown up and around it over the years, almost obscuring it from view. The tattered remnants of what had once been a rope ladder were barely visible through the leaves.

"Want to go check it out?" Logan asked.

She grinned and kicked off her rain boots.

"I'll go get the ladder."

A few minutes later, Logan returned with a ladder, but she wasn't there.

"Juliette?" He peered back into the woods. Maybe she'd changed her mind and gone home.

"Up here." Her head popped out of the treehouse window, her face aglow with mischief.

"How did you get up there?"

She grinned. "I'm an excellent climber."

Of course she was. He should've known that. Logan set the ladder up and climbed after her. When he reached the top, he found her in the middle of the treehouse floor sitting cross-legged with her skirt bunched around her legs.

He pulled himself inside and stood, though he had to hunch over so his head didn't hit the ceiling. The weathered floor was scattered with leaves and the wood plank walls were slightly warped with age. A tree branch had grown through the only window, making it seem as though the tree were reclaiming the space for itself. There was an old tin box beside Juliette and a beanbag chair in the corner. The place looked neglected and worn, but Logan's grandfather had built it well. It was still sturdy after all these years.

"It's smaller than I remember," he mused.

"That's because you're a giant now," Juliette said matter-of-factly.

"I am." Logan sat across from her on the floor. "You should feel sorry for me. It's hard being so big."

"It's actually very roomy in here," she said, glowing with pleasure. "A person could even sleep here, if they wanted to."

"Do you?" he asked casually, noting the heightened color in her cheeks. If she said yes, he would move mountains to make it happen. Just the idea of her sleeping in there—in a space so completely personal, a space that belonged just to him—ignited something in his blood, beginning a low, slow burn that felt anything but casual.

Juliette riffled through the tin box, a soft smile tugging at the corners of her mouth.

She was happy in this treehouse. If he'd known how pleased she would be, he'd have invited her up a long time ago. He'd do just about anything to see her looking like this.

She held up a stack of weathered comics in triumph. "I knew it."

"But you were wrong about Batman," Logan said. "Those are Spider-Man comics."

She put them back in the box. "Same thing."

Logan gasped in mock horror. "Blasphemy."

She continued her search, lifting out an old flashlight, some baseball cards, and a pack of gum. "Huh."

"Not as exciting as you'd imagined?"

"Well, it could be worse," she said impishly. "I haven't found any gym socks."

A gust of wind blew through the treehouse window, playing with the tendrils of hair around her face. The sky had grown dark in the twilight, and light rain began to fall.

Logan watched her intently. Every expression on her face was fascinating to him. A sharp yearning rose inside him, and he recognized it for what it was. Desire. He wanted this woman. Everything about her drew him in. Somehow, sitting in his old treehouse with her felt like the most natural thing in the world. It felt *right*.

A dark curl fell over her eyes. She reached up and smoothed it back. The wind swirled through the open windows, and the lock of hair fell again.

This time, Logan reached out to brush it off her face. He trailed his fingers lightly down the side of her neck, leaning closer. And closer still.

She let him.

He covered her mouth with his, sliding his fingers into her hair, cradling the back of her head as he pulled her into his arms.

She let him.

There was no slow build this time. No easing into it. The kiss was instantly hot and carnal. Combustible. Everything in the world seemed to slip away until the only thing left was her. He was drunk on Juliette Holloway. The slick, wet heat of her tongue. The curve of her hips as she straddled him. Her soft, urgent whimper as she pressed closer. And suddenly, it wasn't enough. They yanked at each other's clothes. Fabric whisked away. Hands slid against bare skin. They kissed until the last rays of sunlight disappeared and they wore nothing but shadows. When he braced her against his body and lowered her to the floor, a thrill of triumph shot through him.

Because she let him.

Juliette made her way through the woods as quickly as she could. Her limbs tingled with the enormity of what had just happened. Her legs felt rubbery, and her toes sloshed around inside her rain boots, adding to her overall feeling of unsteadiness. She felt as if the entire world had gone askew. The rain was falling in earnest now, but she didn't care. Rain never bothered her the way it did other people. Maybe it was her close connection to nature. Whatever the reason, she reveled in it. Just like she'd reveled in hot tree-house sex with Logan O'Connor.

She stopped to lean against a tree, pressing a hand against her stomach to quell the legions of butterflies battling it out there.

With other men, she'd always enjoyed herself just fine. Sex was nice. Sometimes even good. But keeping an emotional distance was priority one. She never got swept up in anything past the physical experience, and that was just how she wanted it.

But nothing had prepared her for Logan—certainly not any of her fantasies when she was younger. He was always so steady, so calculating and careful. The way he built things to precise, exact measurements. The way he carried himself. Everything about his personality seemed so calm and cool and controlled. But tonight in that treehouse, he'd been like a wild force of nature. He'd been fiercely driven in his pursuit of her pleasure and gloriously unapologetic about what he wanted. The give. The take. It was like being caught in the throes of a magnificent summer storm. She couldn't have controlled it, even if she'd wanted to. All she could do was hold on. The connection forged between them now was more than just physical; it was deeply personal.

Trembling, Juliette pushed herself off the tree and continued through the woods, trying not to think about what it all meant. She'd lost herself completely with him, gave everything she had, and took everything she wanted. And it had been the greatest, most devastatingly emotional experience of her life.

Now what?

Chapter Twenty

Belle of the Ball was the only bridal shop on Pine Cove Island. It was cool and spacious, with overstuffed seats and a low, mirrored table stacked with bridal magazines. A silver platter of biscotti sat near the magazines, along with a beautiful three-tiered serving dish of French macarons. The store was sleek, elegant, and perfectly comfortable in every way. But Juliette barely noticed.

She slumped on the pink velvet divan in the middle of the showroom floor while Molly and Gertie bickered over bridesmaid dresses.

Sighing, Juliette picked up a lavender macaron, trying for the umpteenth time not to think of Logan and their crazy treehouse escapade the night before. Every time she thought of it, her body went soft, her skin flushed with pleasure, and her mind went into overdrive with the memory of how insanely hot Logan had been.

She shook her head and sat up straighter. She had to focus on the job at hand. They'd been looking at dresses on their lunch break for almost an hour, while Emma tried on bridal gowns for her late August wedding. The sales clerk had been more than happy to bring out rolling racks of gowns and dresses, but so far, no luck.

"How about this dress?" Gertie held up a strapless mini dress that was barely long enough to cover her important bits. "It's edgy and fun."

Juliette considered it for a moment, then shook her head. "No. Way too many sequins. We'll look like backup singers."

"Agreed," Molly said with feeling. "And anyway, this bridesmaid? Wouldn't be able to fit one *boob* into that dress." She waved her hand in the air. "Next."

Gertie huffed and put the dress back on the rack.

The salesclerk Vivian came out of the back room with a smile and a subtle hint of French perfume. She was an older woman in a blush-colored shift dress, matching kitten heels, and tasteful jewelry that said, "Trust me, I know all about style." Vivian exuded the kind of soothing, understated elegance that could calm even the most ferocious of bridezillas. Luckily for her, Emma wasn't one.

Emma floated out from the dressing room looking like a frosted cake. The puff-sleeved wedding gown flared out from her waist, cascading onto the floor in a series of swags and ruffles. Alternating satin bows and rosettes were placed at intervals along each flounce.

She turned in a slow circle and whispered to Juliette, "Is it that bad?"

Juliette set her half-eaten macaron on a lacy napkin. "If you have to ask me that, then I think you already know the answer."

"It's not that you don't look gorgeous," Molly said. "It's just kind of Little Bo-Peep-ish, you know? With the ruffles and hoopskirt and stuff."

"My dears," Vivian said with quiet authority. "Ruffles are the very thing this year. Everyone's doing ruffles."

"Does it come with any accessories?" Gertie asked. "Like a bonnet, or . . . ?"

"Some sheep?" Molly giggled.

Emma rolled her eyes and marched back into the dressing room.

Vivian followed, her kitten heels clicking on the shiny tiled floor.

"When are we going to have lunch?" Juliette grumbled. "I'm not hungry anymore, I'm *hangry*. I need something more than just cookies." She'd barely eaten anything for breakfast that morning. It was hard to eat when all she kept thinking about was her wild tryst with Logan. After telling herself all morning that it was no big deal, she'd decided to call it a tryst. She liked the clandestine sound of it. No strings attached and no danger of getting hurt. Totally doable.

"Why so grumpy?" Gertie asked. "Late night with a hot guy?" She wiggled her eyebrows.

Juliette shrugged. She was trying her best to minimize the whole thing and write it off as no big deal, but it wasn't easy when her mind kept flashing back to the things they'd *done*. The way Logan had kissed her. The way she'd run her hands up under his shirt before yanking it over his head. The smooth, rigid muscles of his torso. His powerful shoulders, bunching and flexing as he gripped the small of her back. The delicious taste of him. The scrape of the floorboards against her bare skin and the slide of his hard, naked body against hers.

"Wait." Molly snapped to attention. "You just shrugged."

"She did?" Gertie's gaze shot to Juliette. "Did something happen last night?"

Juliette held up her hands. "I'll tell you guys all at once, okay? Because I really don't want to have to repeat it. It's crazy enough that it happened, and I don't want to keep going over it again and again."

"Oh, my god." Molly's eyes flew open and she pointed

an accusing finger at her. "You had sex last night. With who? You need to spill, right now."

Juliette took a deep breath, then let it out fast. "No way."

"Yes way," Molly squeaked. "You can't just say something like that and—"

"—No, I mean . . ." Juliette pointed behind Molly.

Emma shimmied out of the dressing room in a series of mincing steps. She was wearing a rhinestone-encrusted strapless gown, so tight that it hugged her like a second skin all the way to her knees. From there, it flared out into a huge flounce that dragged several feet behind her.

"I don't think that's going to work," Gertie said.

Molly tilted her head to one side. "I think she looks like a sexy mermaid."

"But she can't walk," Gertie said. "It's not sexy if you have to hobble down the aisle."

"It's true," Emma said. "I can barely move my legs." She gave Vivian an apologetic smile. "I'm sorry. I don't think this is my lucky day. We'll come back next week for that new inventory you told us about."

Vivian murmured her understanding and began rolling the racks of dresses away.

Gertie checked her watch. "We have to get back to work. But not before Juliette tells us what happened last night."

Emma looked at Juliette with concern. "What happened?"

Juliette groaned. "Okay, I haven't had a chance to tell you guys because it all happened so fast. Last night was a mistake, okay? Let me just make that very clear right now."

She pierced the three other women with a glare until they all nodded, wide-eyed. Then she proceeded to fill them in about Logan's phone call. And the sick tree. And how she'd agreed to try to help it, even though it probably wouldn't work.

"And then we climbed up into the treehouse and then one thing led to another and then we sort of had sex," she finished in a rush.

Emma's mouth fell open.

Molly squealed.

Gertie gave a knowing laugh.

"So there you have it," Juliette said, trying to wave it off like it was nothing. "The whole thing was some odd exercise in the surreal, and it's not going to happen again."

"You passed over Brock Templeton," Molly said in awe.

"Brock is not what everyone thinks, trust me." Juliette scrunched up her face at the memory of their terrible date. "He's as fake as his airbrushed abs and foreign accent. Less Melbourne, Australia, and more Melbourne, Florida." She briefly told them about the boating disaster, promising to give them more details later.

Gertie shook her head slowly. "So you went for lumberjack Tarzan instead."

"In a *treehouse*," Emma teased. "How fitting, Jules."

Molly wrinkled her forehead. "How was that? The treehouse part?"

"It was . . ." The most erotic thing she'd ever experienced. "Hard."

Gertie snorted.

"The *floor* was hard," Juliette said. "Get your mind out of the gutter."

"Why bother?" Gertie sassed. "It's where all my friends hang out."

"That's it?" Molly looked disappointed. "You had wild jungle sex with Tarzan in a treehouse and all you can say is that the floor was hard? Can't you throw us a bone? Anything?"

Juliette couldn't help the slow grin that spread across her face. "It was *hot*." They'd been like flint and tinder.

When they came together, the fire that sparked between them burned so bright, just thinking about it made her whole body flush.

Molly frowned. "Yeah, that's not gonna fly. We need details, but you're off the hook for now because we have to get back to work." She took two more macarons from the platter and stood. "This conversation is on 'pause' until a future date."

"I can assure you, there'll be no more treehouses in my future because it was a mistake," Juliette said. "We're all wrong for each other." She knew it was true, but she couldn't help the slight twinge of melancholy that nagged at her. Still, there was no use dwelling on it. She wasn't going to let one slipup with Logan change the course of her future. She had a job to do and Romeo was coming home soon.

Logan had already built the greenhouse, and the back deck would soon be finished. Juliette wasn't about to let a messy relationship get in the way of her goals. If all went well, by the end of the summer Romeo would officially retire, and Juliette could take over the running of the new shop. Then, her life would be complete. She'd have a career surrounded by her beloved plants, she'd have her friends, and she'd have Emma and Hunter. She didn't need anything, or anyone, else.

After Gertie and Molly left, Juliette and Emma sat in the bridal shop, leafing through a book of gowns.

"You know," Emma said, staring at the magazine, "I don't think it's that bad."

Juliette peered over Emma's shoulder at the picture of a puce dress with a sparkly flower appliquéd across the midsection. "Did you fall and hit your head back in the dressing room?"

"I meant Logan," Emma said, glancing up. "You and

Logan. I'm actually not surprised it happened, and I think
you should give it a chance."

"I don't want a chance with him," Juliette said. "It was
a total freak thing. I mean, how real can it be? We were in
a treehouse. There were Spider-Man comics and a beanbag
chair, for freak's sake. And that says it all, if you think
about it. The whole thing was completely juvenile."

"I remember you had a crush on him back in high
school."

"Key words: 'high school.' We shared one tiny kiss at
his graduation party, and then he was gone. And honestly,
I don't even know why I was so hung up on him. It was the
dumbest kiss. Not even real. He only saw me as a kid. Besides, he never came back." She felt that old hollowness in
her chest, and shoved it away. It was so stupid. She hadn't
felt it in years, and she'd learned long ago to guard herself
against it.

It wasn't just that she'd lost her mother in a car accident
when she was only nine. Even her father had eventually
left, when she turned eighteen. After her mother died, he'd
never been the same. He was a quiet man, and Juliette
knew he loved her, but it was as if he could never get over
losing her mother. There was no room in his life for anything except grief. Juliette had found solace in her plants,
and in her connection with Emma and their grandmother.
She'd learned to fend for herself, doing the chores and the
laundry for both herself and her father. She even tried to
make recipes from her mother's cookbook, even though
she was abysmal at cooking. But over the years, her father
became more and more disinterested. He was like a shadow
person in her life, going through the motions but not truly
present. There, but not there. Later, when he was offered a
job in California, he took it. Juliette had been heartbroken

all over again, but she couldn't bear to watch him wither away in grief.

They still kept in touch, but only through the occasional e-mail and even rarer phone call. Juliette had learned to rely on Emma, and her loyal friends. She never wanted to feel that acute ache of losing someone again.

"So you truly feel nothing for Logan?" Emma asked.

Juliette shook her head. She studied a series of orange bridesmaid dresses in the magazine in front of her. Interesting shade of coral, those.

"Maybe it could work," Emma said.

"Coral?" Juliette kept her gaze focused on the dresses. "You think?"

"Maybe," Emma repeated, nudging Juliette with her shoulder, "there's more to this thing between you and Logan than you're admitting."

Juliette shook her head. She needed to nip this in the bud before Emma got too carried away. "Look, I get what you guys have been saying, okay? I admit he's a good-looking guy. I just didn't really pay attention before." That was a fibtacular statement and they both knew it, but Juliette pressed on anyway. "I'm just not interested in letting things go any further, and I doubt he is either. Besides, I'm not even his type. He likes normal girls."

"I wouldn't bet on that," Emma said. "You're the most stunningly gorgeous, kindhearted, amazing person I've ever known. Half the island's been in love with you at some point. Why should Logan be an exception?"

Juliette wrapped an arm around Emma and gave her a lopsided hug. "Have I ever told you I love you? Because I do. Thanks for the pep talk, but I'm honestly not interested in getting serious with Logan. Or anyone else, for that matter. I have everything I need."

Emma hugged her back and said, "I just want to see you happy. You deserve so much."

"I already have so much."

"I mean, I want you to have what I have with Hunter."

Juliette felt the conversation taking a turn, and she needed to retreat. She knew where this was going with Emma; they'd had this talk before. How could Juliette ever explain that she didn't believe in love? She believed in it for others, just not herself. She was thrilled for her cousin, and couldn't be happier that she was soon getting married to one of the best men in the world. But for Juliette, that kind of relationship was too much. Too much vulnerability. Giving your heart to someone else like that was madness. She'd tried to give hers to Logan back when she was four-teen. Practically walked right up to him and begged him not to go. But he did.

"Don't you worry about me," Juliette said, standing. "I've never been more happy than I am now, and I can't wait to see you walk down the aisle." It was true. She could see how much joy her cousin and Hunter had together, and that's all Juliette could have ever wished for.

Juliette gathered her bag and dusted macaron crumbs from her jeans. "If you really want me to be happy, you'll feed me. If I don't eat soon, you're going to find me in a chalk outline on the sidewalk out there. And then, where will you be, without me to help you find a dress? You'll have to go with what Vivian suggests, and you'll be up to your eyeballs in ruffles, shuffling down the aisle with a herd of sheep."

It was past lunchtime when Juliette relieved Kat from her shift at the shop. After Kat left, Juliette nervously wiped down the cutting table even though it didn't need it.

She knew Logan was outside, but she wasn't sure what to say. What do you say after a wild fling with a childhood crush in a dusty treehouse? Before she had time to come up with something, the back door opened and Tarzan himself walked in.

He stood for a moment, saying nothing. Why wasn't he saying anything? Did he expect her to just stand there and act like everything was fine? She could do that. Because everything was fine.

"Oh, hey," she said in a high-pitched voice. She cleared her throat and zipped over to the sink to wash her hands.

He came and stood beside her. "How are you?"

She didn't look up, because the soap dispenser was stuck and she really, really had to fix it. Stupid thing. Always getting stuck. She rinsed it under the warm water, scrubbing at the bottle with a sponge.

His large hand closed over hers, and she stopped scrubbing. She still didn't look at him.

"How are you?" he asked softly.

"I'm fine," she said brightly. "Why wouldn't I be?"

"Look." He dried his hands on a towel and leaned against the sink. "We don't have to talk about—"

"—Good," she said firmly.

He paused. "And I respect that. We don't have to. But we still have to work together. So rather than pretend nothing happened last night, let's just both agree that something did."

"Of course it did," she said. "I was there, remember?"

"I remember." His voice was a husky murmur that brought the entire night back into vivid detail.

Her throat went dry, and her cheeks flushed. It was as if time stopped and suddenly they were both back in that treehouse with the rain falling outside and nothing between them but heat and the slick caress of skin on skin.

They were standing so close. She could feel his breath stirring the fine hair at her temple. If she just leaned in a fraction of an inch, they'd be touching. She had to get it together. Romeo would be back in less than ten days. She didn't need this complication.

"Um." Juliette fought for a calm she didn't feel. "We don't really need to analyze it, okay?"

"I agree."

"There's just no reason to talk about it, you know?"

"My thoughts exactly."

"It was just a slipup. Nothing special, right?"

He narrowed his eyes for a moment. "Sure."

"Cool." Because that was what she was all about. Easy breezy fun.

He reached down and looped his fingers into the waistband of her jeans, then slowly pulled her toward him.

Her limbs went soft, and her breath hitched. "What are you doing?"

"Nothing special." When his lips met hers, she didn't even try to fight it. She just gave up. Okay, she was smitten with Logan O'Connor. She was a Logan O'Connor groupie. A Logan Luster. She had to do something. Set some ground rules. Quick!

"Wait," she said breathlessly, pulling back. "If this is going to keep happening, then we need to get one thing straight."

His gaze fixed intently on hers.

"I'm just in it for fun. That's all."

Logan cocked an eyebrow.

"I mean it," Juliette said in a heated rush. "I'm not interested in anything else, and we are obviously wrong for each other in every other way. I mean, I drive you crazy."

He nodded. "You do. You really do."

"And you think I'm too bossy. You said so yourself."

"True." He slid his hands around her waist, his warm fingers caressing the small of her back.

"And you annoy me a lot." A shiver of pleasure rippled over her skin. "You're stubborn and you don't take orders well."

"Also true," he murmured.

"So we're in agreement, then?" Her voice quivered as his fingers traced delicious spirals up her spine. "This is just a fling?"

He gave her a slow, sexy smile and bent to kiss her again.

Chapter Twenty-One

"Why did I agree to this?" Juliette asked. She was standing near the starting line of the Firefighters' Mud Run, safety-pinning a race number on the back of Emma's T-shirt.

"Because Gertie said we had to show our support for the firefighters' children's charity," Emma said, gathering her hair into a ponytail. Gertie's husband, Walter, was a local firefighter, and he was in charge of running the event. "Also, Molly wants to exercise, and she says the only way she'll do it is through peer pressure."

Juliette tugged her T-shirt down over her shorts. Thanks to Molly's latest obsession with online shopping, they were all wearing bright team shirts with the phrase "Mermaids Do It Better" across the chest. "Well, at least we'll look good doing it. Which is fortunate since we're never going to win against those guys." She tilted her head in the direction of the local runners' club. Four lanky men in running shorts were stretching on the sidelines.

"What about them?" Emma whispered, gesturing to the group of jazzercise ladies in matching sparkly running skirts. "They look like they know what they're doing."

"Yeah," Juliette said. "We're definitely out of our element here."

"Who cares?" Gertie emerged from the crowd with a power bar in one hand and a water bottle in the other. She bounced with energy, shifting her weight from one foot to the other. "This will be fun. We get to be outside. Breathe fresh air."

"Wallow in the mud," Molly added, as she joined them. "Don't forget the mud. The first challenge of the race is a huge rope net we have to climb over, and on the other side is a giant mud pit." She was staring at the beginning of the obstacle course with a look of growing dread.

"That's nothing," Gertie chirped, taking a huge bite of her power bar and chewing quickly. "Wait till you see the Salmon Run."

"What's that?" Emma asked.

"It's this blow-up tunnel you have to climb through, and it's filled with bubbles up to your chin. And the whole time you have to dodge these wet sponge fish."

"Sounds like a lot of work," Molly said, scrunching up her face. "I wonder how many calories that'll burn."

"And then there's the Polar Bear Swim," Gertie continued. "A giant pool filled with ice you have to wade through to get to the Forest Run."

"Anything on the Forest Run we need to worry about?" Juliette asked.

"Just Wolves," Gertie said. "That's what they call the volunteers. Those people will be running around in there trying to catch these." She held up four red ribbons tied with Velcro elastic bands. "Everyone has to wear one of these around their waist. If one of the Wolves manages to snag yours, you're out of the race."

Molly let out a groan. "We might as well kiss Team Mermaid good-bye now."

"Hey, you never know," Emma said. "Maybe Brock's

entourage will distract most of the runners and we'll have a fighting chance."

They all turned to watch as the houseboat group gathered near the south side of the field. Brock was already surrounded by admirers, but he caught Juliette's attention over the heads of his fans and winked.

"Ooh! I saw that," Molly said. "Brock just winked at you."

Juliette turned her back on the television crew. "Hopefully he just had something in his eye."

"I think he still likes you, Jules," Emma said under her breath.

"Oh, there he goes. Looking at you again," Gertie said in a singsong voice.

"Can you guys please stop staring?" Juliette said in exasperation. "I don't want him to think we're talking about him."

"We're being discreet," Molly said.

"Yeah, it's not like we're screaming 'yowza! Awooga! Hubba hubba!'" Gertie laughed.

"Except you pretty much just screamed that," Juliette said.

Molly shook her head. "I still can't believe he's a fake Australian. I mean, the accent's always been part of the sex appeal, you know? Without the accent, he's not even . . ." She tilted her head and sized him up. "Yeah, no. I tried, but he's still hot. Even if he is fake. Maybe you should give him another chance."

"He told me we should *bang*," Juliette emphasized. "Like, he actually used that word in a sentence, and he was being serious."

"Yeah, but you know how you hate when guys get all clingy? Well, that guy is never going to be clingy. I mean, look at him." Molly pointed to Brock, who was now signing a giggling woman's thigh with a Sharpie pen.

"Juliette doesn't need to look at him," Gertie said. "She has hot lumberjack Tarzan, remember?"

"Does she?" Molly gave Juliette a questioning glance. "Are you and Logan a thing now?"

"No," Juliette said. "We're for sure not a thing. We're just . . . I don't know. We're just having fun, I guess. Maybe." She frowned and shook her head, then let out a frustrated breath. "It's nothing."

Gertie looked at Molly and mouthed, *It's a thing.*

"Jules," Emma said in alarm. "Brock's coming over here."

Sure enough, Brock's group of admirers shifted like a school of fish as he broke away and walked toward them.

"Hello, ladies." The Australian accent was back in full force. To Juliette he said, "I was hoping you'd be here."

"Yup." Juliette busied herself with some lint on her T-shirt sleeve.

"Look, I'm sorry about what happened with the boat," he said sheepishly. It looked good on him, with the puppy dog eyes and all that. "That was all my fault. I'd like to make it up to you."

"No need," she said coolly.

Brock waved his assistant over. "I brought you something."

Before Juliette could respond, his assistant ran up with a huge messenger bag slung over his shoulder. He was short and wiry, with thick glasses and slicked back hair. He looked frazzled and smelled like cigarettes. "Anything you need, Brock?"

Brock pointed to the messenger bag. "Give me one of those phones, will you?"

His assistant dug through the bag, pulled out a box, and handed it to Brock.

Brock then handed it to Juliette with a flourish. It was

the latest iPhone. "I know you lost your phone in the ocean, so I wanted to replace it."

Juliette held the sleek white box. Her current phone was a cheap, pay-as-you-go model. She'd been planning to buy a new one when she had the money, but she didn't plan on upgrading to something this fancy. "I can't accept this," she said. It was too expensive, and the last thing she wanted was to feel indebted to him.

"You're taking it," Brock announced. "It's my fault you lost your phone, and I want to make it up to you. Do you forgive me?"

Juliette looked into his faux-tanned but earnest face. He wasn't the catch everyone thought he was, but at least he was trying to say "sorry." "Sure," she said. "But I can't take this, really. It's too much."

"Don't sweat it. I've got loads of them. Don't I, Jerry?"

His greasy-haired assistant nodded dutifully.

"Wow, you must have to apologize a lot," Juliette said.

Brock looked confused, and his assistant looked alarmed. Then Brock began to laugh. Once he laughed, his assistant laughed, too.

"Look, I gotta run," Brock said. "But just keep it, okay? I get them for free, anyway. It's a publicity thing. It's the least I can do."

Juliette considered it. Apparently, it *was* the least he could do. If he wanted to give her a free iPhone, she wasn't going to put up a fight. It didn't have to mean she owed him anything. Their boat date had been a disaster. As far as she was concerned, she'd done her time. "Okay. Thanks."

"No hard feelings?" Brock asked.

"Nope." It was hard to be mad at someone as clueless as him.

He waved at Emma and the girls, then walked away with his assistant trailing after him like a puppy dog.

"Well, that was unexpected," Emma said.

Gertie took the shiny new iPhone box and turned it over in her hands. "At least he knows how to apologize."

"No kidding," Molly said. "James brought me flowers the last time we argued. Maybe he needs to step up his game."

An air horn blasted through the murmuring crowd, and people began to cheer in excitement.

"This is it," Gertie said. "Look, there's Walter." She jumped up and down, blowing kisses to her husband.

Walter stood holding a megaphone on a podium near the starting line. He was a solidly built man in his fifties with thinning hair and a kind face. He and Gertie were the perfect couple, as far as Juliette was concerned. They'd been married for years, raised two sons, and were obviously still crazy in love.

"All right, everyone," Walter said. "I want to thank you for coming out to the Mud Run this year, and for your participation in our annual charity event. I know you don't want to hear me yapping, so we're going to get this race started in just a few minutes. Whoever crosses the finish line with their red ribbon first wins for their whole team."

Juliette stuffed the phone into her backpack and set it on the sidelines with the rest of their bags. She checked to make sure her waist ribbon was tied securely and took a quick drink of water, searching the crowd. Not that she was searching for anyone in particular. Just checking out all the runners. Logan was nowhere to be found, but then she wasn't looking for him.

The first leg of the race began in a wide open field.

"Are you ready, girls?" Gertie said with excitement. "This is going to be fun."

"This is going to be painful," Molly said. "Why did I think I could do this? I'm not a runner. I hate sweating. I'm never going to make it across this field. It looks deadly."

"It's grass," Juliette said. "And it's mowed. I think you'll survive. Besides"—she shaded her eyes and squinted—"I think I see the mud pit. Just pace yourself and save your energy for that."

Molly grumbled and followed them to the starting line.

"What are the odds of us winning?" Emma asked as she surveyed the crowd.

"I'd say about a bazillion to one." Juliette dodged a group of men who looked like weight lifters. "Give or take a zillion."

"Bummer," Molly said. "The prize would've been cool."

Emma glanced up from tying her shoe. "There's a prize? I thought this was a charity event."

"It is," Gertie said. "But there's a prize for whoever crosses the finish line first. This year it's from the Donut Junkee. Whoever wins gets four dozen donuts for their team, plus a free donut every week for a year."

Juliette jammed her hands on her hips and began pacing back and forth. "Okay, this race just got real, you guys. Team Mermaid, we need to be in it to win it. Are you with me? Keep your eyes on the prize. This is the big leagues now."

"Dang," Molly said. "You're good at pep talks."

Juliette stopped pacing. "Is it working?"

"Kind of. What else you got?"

Suddenly, Walter began counting down from ten and the crowd joined in.

"Ladies," Gertie shouted, bouncing with excitement, "start your engines."

An air horn announced the beginning of the race.

Like a stampede of brightly colored cattle, the runners shot across the grassy field toward the first obstacle. The air smelled like freshly cut grass and sunscreen. Shouts of encouragement rose up from spectators on the sidelines as people dodged and wove through each other to get to the rope ladder at the end of the field.

Juliette and the girls stayed together for the first few minutes, weaving through the crowd as they rushed across the field, but by the time they reached the rope ladder, their group began to split.

"This rope is slippery," Molly yelled when she was halfway up the net.

"No it's not," Gertie said from several feet above. "Your hands are just sweaty."

"Well, it's hot," Molly complained. "This is dangerous."

"You can do it," Emma encouraged, as she pulled herself over the top and began climbing down.

Juliette had already reached the other side. The mud pit ahead of her was waist deep and about fifty yards long. People shrieked with laughter as they plunged into the sludge and began wading across.

"Are you ready for this, you guys?" Juliette said, staring out at the sea of muddy people.

"No," Molly moaned, joining them at the bottom. "This is going to suck so much."

"Mud's good for your skin," Gertie piped up. "Think of it as a spa day."

Juliette launched herself feet first into the pit, the mud squelching around her body like lukewarm Jell-O. She pushed ahead, laughing at the ridiculousness of it all. People shoved their way past each other in a jumble of muddy shoulders and elbows. Soon the mud began to migrate past Juliette's neck, splattering onto her face and hair, but she just laughed and pressed on. The truth of it was, the mud didn't bother her at all. She felt right at home surrounded by the scents of wet earth and grass. It was the hollering, shrieking people she was unaccustomed to.

Somewhere near the end of the pit, Juliette turned back to look for her friends. Emma and Gertie weren't far behind, but Molly was only halfway across. Juliette started to turn back to help her.

"Just keep going," Molly called miserably, waving a hand. Her face and hair were caked with mud. She looked like a disgruntled Cabbage Patch Kid. "Save yourselves. I'm going to be in this mud forever. I'm a mud person now."

Juliette hesitated.

"Go," Molly insisted. "Do it for Team Mermaid."

Juliette heaved herself out of the mud pit and raced toward the Salmon Run. People were slipping all over the muddy grass, some falling in laughter, some choosing to stop on the sidelines for refreshments. She kept going, managing to stay on her feet until she reached the blow-up bouncy tunnel full of bubbles.

At the entrance, she took a deep breath and plunged in. Wet sponge fish slapped at her body. One landed on her head. Bubbles tickled her nose. Somebody slid into her, and they slammed against the tunnel wall. Juliette grabbed onto the side so she wouldn't go under.

"Oi, mermaid," Brock shouted in surprise. "You're making good time, eh? Not bad for a local. Good on you." He shoved himself off the inflatable wall and pushed on, calling over his shoulder, "See you on the other side."

One of the wet sponge fish slapped Juliette square in the face. She blinked rapidly, swiping bubbles from her mouth and eyes. *Not bad for a local?* She was suddenly filled with the intense desire to show Brock Templeton that not everything on Pine Cove Island was slow. With fierce determination, she dug her heels in and charged after him.

By the time she reached the end of the tunnel, most of the crowd had thinned. From the looks of it, the less enthusiastic participants had decided to hang back at the refreshment stands set up along the course. Some people seemed content to walk toward the finish line, chatting in small groups.

Juliette didn't stop for refreshments. She shot out of the tunnel, legs pumping and lungs burning, running as fast as she could toward the Polar Bear Swim. The container of floating ice chunks was the size of a small lap pool. It loomed ahead of her like a bad omen. Some of the die-hard athletes were already wading through the frigid water, which meant there was no time to be squeamish. She gritted her teeth and kept running. It was going to be crap-tastic. She knew it for a fact. But she was caught up in the spirit of the race, and Team Mermaid deserved a fighting chance.

"Go, Juliette!" she heard Emma call from back near the Salmon Run.

Juliette sprinted. Jumped. Screeched. The icy water hit her like a shock wave, so cold she could barely catch her breath. It was worse than the mud and bubbles combined, but she had to keep going. The only way through it was through it. She forced her legs to move forward, catching sight of Brock several yards ahead of her. She couldn't let him win. On impulse, she dove forward into the icy water, kicking as hard as she could until she swam her way to the other side.

When she pulled herself out, the air felt warm against her freezing skin. She didn't stop to dry off. Flying past the volunteers holding out towels, she focused on the runners ahead of her. They'd already reached the forest. She could see them tearing through the undergrowth, their bright red ribbons fluttering behind them. But she had one advantage they didn't have. She had Mother Nature on her side. Juliette gathered every ounce of energy she had left and ran head-on into the forest.

Shouts echoed through the trees. The Wolves were on the prowl, grabbing red ribbons from the runners who were unfortunate enough to cross their paths. Unlike the rest of the people in the race, Juliette didn't have to dodge branches or worry about getting tangled in sticker bushes. The plants made way for her. She zipped over the foliage, pulling ahead of even the strongest athletes, determined to reach the finish line first. If it had been any other obstacle, she never would've stood a chance. But forests? Forests were a piece of cake.

Someone rushed at her from behind a tree. A woman made a grab for Juliette's red ribbon. Juliette spun away, slipped under a branch, and kept running.

A few moments later, another Wolf appeared in front of her. She sidestepped him, leapt over a fallen log, and flew into the bushes. Within thirty seconds, she'd left him in the dust.

Juliette was just about to congratulate herself when she saw a large group of Wolves blocking the way. They'd formed a line and were walking slowly through the trees so it would be impossible for runners to pass them undetected.

"No fair," she muttered, slowing to a stop. She slipped behind a tree to catch her breath, then hoisted herself on a low branch, climbed up into the tree, and waited.

When the line of Wolves passed, she hopped back to the forest floor and slapped dust from her hands. She was just about to tear off toward the finish line when someone stepped smoothly from the shadows.

Juliette screamed.

"My, what big lungs you have." Logan loomed in front of her, looking every bit like the big bad wolf.

She scowled. "You're in my way. Move."

"I'm doing my job." His gaze flicked to her wet T-shirt. "As a volunteer Wolf, I need to give you a hard time."

Juliette rolled her eyes. Beyond Logan's shoulder, she caught sight of Brock sneaking along the side of the forest to bypass the line of Wolves. If she didn't move fast, she was going to lose.

"You have to let me go," she said urgently. "Otherwise Brock's going to win."

Logan seemed to consider her logic for a moment. "That's a very strong argument. You can go."

She started to forge ahead.

He blocked her with his body. "For a price." He was giving her that secret look. The one that did things to her insides. Warm, sexy things. But Brock was getting away. Then again, Logan's perfect mouth looked very inviting. She didn't have time for this.

"Fine." She lifted up on her toes and stamped a kiss on his mouth. It was supposed to be a quick one, but somehow she got caught up in the feel of his hard body, and the warmth of his large hands, and the slow, sweet slide of his tongue.

When she finally pulled away, she was breathing harder than before.

"Thank you," Logan murmured. "But that's not the price."

Juliette groaned in frustration and hopped up and down. "What do you want?"

His gaze lowered to her chest, mesmerized.

She bounced one more time, just because.

"Come to dinner tonight," he said huskily. "My house."

Brock was now making his way toward the end of the trail that led to the finish line. She had to go, or *Hollywood Boozeboat* was going to win.

"Fine."

"Fine as in 'fine you'll come for dinner'?"

"Yes," she said in exasperation. "Fine means yes. Can I go now?"

Logan stepped aside. "Fine."

Juliette shot toward the finish line, ahead of the pack.

Later, her friends would shout about her amazing luck at winning the race. The surprised look on Brock's face would go down in history as one of Juliette's favorite moments of victory. And the day would end in triumph and dozens of free donuts for Team Mermaid. But the best part of that day had nothing to do with winning the race or beating an arrogant celebrity or giving her friends bragging rights.

The best part of the day, whether she wanted to admit it or not, was being accosted in the woods by a very big, very bad wolf.

Chapter Twenty-Two

"Hey, boss man. I finished the last coat of paint on those chairs," Kevin called from the garage.

Logan eyed the recipe book on his kitchen counter, making sure he'd measured everything exactly right. "That's great, Kevin. And please call me Logan." The kid was a quick study, taking directions and running with projects. The only thing he couldn't seem to remember was to stop calling him "boss man."

Logan checked the timer, opened the oven, and pulled out his latest project. The delicious scent of the spicy vegetarian stuffed peppers surprised him. Maybe it was all the melted Monterey Jack cheese. With enough cheese, anything was edible.

Someone knocked on the sliding glass door, and he glanced up to see Juliette out on the patio. Logan thought nothing could've looked hotter than the wet shirt she had on at the mud run, but he was wrong. In denim shorts and a simple white tank top, she looked sexy as sin, and she probably didn't even know it.

He slid the door open with one hand, holding the stuffed pepper dish in the other. "You're just in time."

"Wow, that looks good." She stepped inside and choked back laughter. "What happened in here?"

The kitchen looked like hell; he knew it. "Don't worry, we're not having dinner in here. Kevin and I have been ripping out the wallpaper, and we're still in the middle of it."

"Who's Kevin?"

"He's my assistant."

She leaned over to smell the stuffed peppers. "Mmm."

Logan's heartbeat kicked up a notch. Erotic images flashed through his head when she leaned in close like that. He wanted to toss the dish aside, throw her over his shoulder, and drag her upstairs to his bed. Dinner be damned. He wanted to devour *her*.

"Hey, boss," Kevin called as he came in through the garage. "I think I'm going to head out and—*oh*." He stopped in the kitchen doorway, looking at Juliette like he'd just discovered a great white shark in his swimming pool.

Juliette seemed almost as shocked as he did. She looked at Logan, incredulous. "Kevin's your assistant? *Kevin* Kevin?"

"He's been a great help," Logan said smoothly. "I understand he used to work at the florist shop."

She gave Kevin a calculating look. "He did. But we had a little disagreement."

Kevin started to squirm. Logan didn't blame him. Juliette looked like Wonder Woman about to whip out her lasso of truth.

"How's it going, Kevin?" she asked.

"I'm good," Kevin mumbled. He shrugged his bony shoulders. "I'm not doing that stuff anymore. The pot plant stuff."

"Really?" Juliette put her hands on her hips. "Since when?"

Poor Kevin was pink around the ears, but Logan had to give him credit for sticking it out. "I just quit that same week, after you fired me. My friend who was into growing, and all that? He moved to Seattle, and I don't know . . ." He rubbed the back of his neck with one hand. "I just didn't like it anymore. Kinda made me feel like I was spinning my wheels, not getting anywhere."

Juliette's expression softened, and she gave Kevin a brilliant smile that, in Logan's opinion, carried a far more powerful punch than anything Wonder Woman could dish out. "You're obviously doing great work here, so I'm glad Logan has you to help."

Kevin blinked a few times, then shuffled back and forth on his feet. "Yeah, this is a great gig. My mom's relieved. I'm saving up for a car so I don't have to keep using hers."

Logan gathered up the dinner supplies while Juliette and Kevin talked. They chatted about Kevin's plans for junior college, a girl he was dating, and something about soap. Logan only half listened, distracted by Juliette's melodious voice and her warm presence in his kitchen. There was something so domestic about it, and it made him want to cook dinner for her every night, just to keep her close.

After Kevin said good-bye, Logan led Juliette to a small table on the front porch, where he placed glasses, plates, and the stuffed pepper dish.

"I hope you don't mind eating outside. The living room and kitchen are torn apart right now."

"I noticed," Juliette said with a laugh. "You guys are making progress, though. What's your plan for the rest of the house?"

"The upstairs looks pretty good already." He set out utensils and napkins, then poured wine and offered her a glass. "I fixed up the master bedroom and the floors. It's the downstairs that looks like a nightmare. Once I'm done with that, I might start on the yard."

Juliette sipped her wine and leaned back in her chair, eyeing the stuffed peppers. "You made a vegetarian dish?"

"It's my first attempt at rabbit food," he said. "Go easy on me."

Juliette gave him a sassy look that made him think about clearing the table with one arm and throwing her on top of it so he could— *Jesus,* he needed to pull it together. Ever since they had sex in that treehouse, he felt like his body was fine tuned to hers. Whenever he saw her, whenever she got close, he wanted her. He'd wanted her before that, but now that he knew *in detail* what it was like, it was hard not to think of anything else.

He placed peppers on their plates and forced himself to think of normal, polite topics. "Have you had this before?"

She nodded. "My mom was a vegetarian, too. She used to make it." She took a bite, closed her eyes, and chewed.

Logan watched her like he was an addict and she was his drug of choice. He couldn't tear his gaze away from her mouth, and her soft moan made the blood rush from his head to lower, more demanding parts of his body.

"It's delicious," she said, her tongue darting out to lick a drop of sauce from her bottom lip.

Logan shifted in his chair. He fought to hang on to their thread of conversation. "Probably not as good as your mom used to make."

A flash of sadness crossed her face, and he could've kicked himself. Why'd he have to bring up her mother? He knew her mom had died in a car accident when Juliette was little. He vaguely remembered hearing about it when he was in middle school.

"I actually don't remember," Juliette said. "My mom was a really good cook, but it's been so long. And my dad didn't . . ." She set down her fork and picked up her wineglass. "My dad wasn't much good at anything, after my mom died."

"What happened?" Logan asked. He'd already shot the conversation to hell; he might as well go all the way.

She took a sip of wine, and for a moment Logan wondered if she was going to ignore the question or brush him off.

"I was in fourth grade," she finally said. "They sent me home early from school. My mom was driving to the grocery store and a semitruck blew through a traffic light. They said she died instantly." Juliette shrugged, as though trying to minimize the pain of it, but Logan could tell she was sinking into memories she rarely talked about. A tiny crease formed between her brows, and she rubbed a finger back and forth over a scratch on the tabletop. "Anyway, my dad sent me to my grandmother's place that day. It was supposed to be for a few days, but I didn't actually go back home for over a month. My grandmother tried to keep me with her and Emma, but I wanted to go home. I missed my mom, and I missed him. My dad and I were still a family. At least, that's what I thought."

Logan reached out and took her hand. "You were a family."

She seemed startled at the contact. "We *were*. He never got over my mom's death. For a long time he was angry at the Holloways. I think he might have even been angry at me. My mom was a healer. That was her gift. My dad was mad that she couldn't heal herself, but the Holloway gifts don't work like that. We can only help other people. After a while he stopped being angry, and then he got sad. And then, I think he just stopped feeling anything at all. He was never the same."

She drew her hand away and ran it through her hair. "When I turned eighteen, he took a job in California and moved away. He said I could go with him, but we both knew my home was here. And I had Emma and our grandmother, so I never even considered it. . . ." She trailed off and looked at him with false optimism. "Now we rarely see each other, but I think he's happier. I think this place reminded him too much of my mother." A flash of pain ghosted across her face. "I know I reminded him too much of her."

Logan wanted to hold her. The idea of Juliette as a little girl, sad and neglected, made him wish he could turn back time and change things. He wished he'd paid more attention to her. He could've been a better friend.

"I wish I could've helped you," he said.

She seemed surprised. "I think you might've been a little busy . . . oh, I don't know, growing up? Being a kid yourself?" She gave him a grateful smile. "Thanks, but that was a long time ago and I'm totally fine now." She spread her hands out. "Look how fine I turned out."

"You are fine." He knew she was joking, but he wasn't. She had turned out beautiful and kind and fascinating and caring. She had turned out perfect.

"Wow, it's late." Juliette suddenly pushed away from the table. "I should be getting home."

Disappointment gripped him. "You barely started your dinner."

"It was really good," she assured him. "Really. It's just that I actually ate a bunch of donuts after the mud run. I'm not that hungry. I just remembered I have some things to do."

Logan rose from his chair. "Let me walk you home."

"No," she said too quickly. "I'm fine. Thank you so much for dinner. You're great at cooking rabbit food."

She made her apologies, and Logan couldn't do anything except watch her go.

With a curse, he shoved away from the table, grabbed the dish he'd so carefully prepared, and stalked into the kitchen.

He was a world-class idiot. He shouldn't have brought

up her family. Of all the asinine things to do, that was near the top of his list. It was clear she didn't like talking about her past, and now the dinner he'd so carefully planned was over before it even began. He stared out the kitchen window into the woods.

"Juliette Holloway," he murmured. "What am I going to do about you?"

Chapter Twenty-Three

Soft moonlight spilled in through Juliette's bedroom window, lending a silvery, dreamlike quality to the cozy room.

Juliette ran her fingers over the faded stitching in the corner of the patchwork quilt where her mother had embroidered her name, with a tiny flower to dot the letter *i*. The blanket was almost as old as she was. Fraying around the seams, the colorful squares were faded from years of washing. But of all the things in her house, Juliette treasured it the most. She and her mom had spent countless hours snuggled in it as they read stories of pirate kings and fairy princesses and fantasy worlds shrouded in mist. Sometimes, her dad would join them, his deep baritone voice adding a dramatic note to the story villains. Juliette used to giggle and snuggle deeper into the quilt as he made growling monster noises.

She rubbed a corner of the quilt over her lips, remembering those moments of complete happiness. They had been a family back then. Whole and happy and invincible. It was like a dream. Juliette knew now that that kind of dream was just a fairy tale, like the stories her parents used to read to her. Things like that didn't last. She couldn't count on them. If she did, she'd just end up getting her heart broken. Still, even though she knew better, she cherished the memory of those times when she'd had it.

It was hard for her to believe she'd told Logan the story of her past. Sitting across from him on his porch at dinner had felt like the most natural thing in the world. She'd somehow slipped into an alternate universe where she didn't have to guard herself. Once she realized what she'd done—how easy it was to trust him—it scared her. He'd gone through all that trouble of cooking her dinner, and she'd run off like a coward.

She shifted restlessly and swung her legs over the side of her bed. No use trying to sleep when the moon was calling.

Luna meowed and jumped onto the windowsill.

"I know," Juliette said, scratching the cat between the ears. "It's too nice a night to spend sleeping. Let's go out."

With midnight approaching, Juliette decided to try one of the special potions to mix up for Logan's tree. Even though it was too far gone to save, she had to try. The look on his face when he'd asked her to heal it was painful, even in memory. She knew what it felt like to want to save something from your past.

In the garden underneath a spill of roses one summer, she'd planted aloe. It wasn't supposed to grow in this type of soil and the climate was all wrong, but like the rest of the plants in her garden, it grew anyway.

Under the stars, she broke off a small tip from the aloe plant and added it to a wooden bowl filled with healing herbs. To that, she added rainwater from a ceramic pitcher, calendula petals, and milk thistle. Then she closed her eyes and thought of the tree, of Logan's hope, and of his grandfather's kind intentions. When she opened her eyes, she whispered words of healing into the wind. Moonlight flooded the garden and the breeze kicked up around her in a swirling caress, kissing her eyelids and stirring the hair at the nape of her neck. A few moments later, the healing potion was ready. Of that, Juliette was certain. But the real question was whether or not it would make an impact on the dying tree.

Barefoot, she walked back to her house and poured the potion into an amber glass vial. It was best to use it soon, while the moon still shone bright in the sky. If it was going to work on the tree, now was the time. Without waiting to change out of her nightgown, Juliette drew on a cardigan sweater and stepped into a pair of rubber boots. Then she set off through the woods to Logan's house.

Luna followed at her heels, the cat darting like a shadow in and around the undergrowth.

"Can you please walk a straight line?" Juliette asked. "You're going to trip me up and it's hard enough to see, as it is." She hadn't thought to bring a flashlight, but then, she rarely did when the moon was so bright. Juliette knew the woods better than she knew the streets in her town. And since the trees and branches always flowed in a soft rhythm around her, she never had much trouble navigating.

A short while later, she stepped onto Logan's lawn. The old maple tree seemed shabby in the moonlight, and Juliette was overcome with sadness. Even in the dark she could sense its weakness. She walked around the tree in a circle, sprinkling drops of the potion onto the soil as she sent her intentions into the earth and roots.

When she was finished, she placed the vial into the pocket of her cardigan and lay her hands on the tree. Closing her eyes, she touched her forehead to the gnarled trunk. Why did good things have to die? Why couldn't they last forever, like they did in fairy tales?

"Juliette." Logan's deep voice settled over her like a warm blanket.

She turned around slowly.

He was fully dressed in jeans, a flannel, and work boots. An odd choice for the middle of the night, but then, who was she to judge? Most normal people didn't run around the woods in their nightgowns.

"Why aren't you sleeping?" she asked.

"I could ask the same of you." He moved closer, coming to stand just in front of her.

He was close enough to touch. She wanted to reach out and lay her hands on his chest, feel the steady thump of his heart. Instead, she wrapped her arms around herself and leaned against the tree trunk. "I never sleep well when the moon is full. It's the best time to make potions, so I thought I'd try one out for the tree."

Logan's gaze dipped to the neckline of her nightgown, traveling slowly down to her boots. "Do you ever wear normal clothes when you run around in the woods?"

"I wasn't running around in the woods. I was walking purposefully to this tree. And I put on shoes." She lifted a red polka-dot rain boot. "Besides, I don't usually have to worry about running into anyone. Come to think of it, why are you out here?"

He glanced away. "Just taking a walk."

"At this hour?"

"Why not?"

Why not, indeed. It was clear he was avoiding the subject. She wondered what would bring him outside, away from a comfortable bed and a good night's sleep.

He motioned to the tree. "Thank you."

"Don't thank me yet. I don't know if it will work. On anything else, the healing potion would work wonders. At least for a little while. The spells only last a few days, then longer if something was inclined to heal in the first place. I just don't know that it will be enough for something this huge."

"Still, thank you." There was a softness in his expression

she hadn't seen before. He was looking at her like she was special. Like she was important. It was equal parts wonderful and frightening. This man was dangerous. He made her want things she couldn't have.

A shiver of anticipation.

Logan reached for her.

When she stepped into his arms, it was as if she were melting into him. He felt familiar, like all the things she wanted to hold on to, all the things from her past that were good things. Something about the way they fit together felt easy. Always with other people, she was aware of the dance—the game of flirting and dating and eventually, breaking up. But with Logan, it wasn't a game. Whatever it was, it scared her. But maybe for a little while, she'd just run with it.

Fire licked against his face. The scent of acrid smoke and burning metal filled his nose, suffocating him. All sound had been reduced to a flat, endless ringing that wouldn't stop. He dragged himself from underneath the vehicle. Two of his men were slumped on the ground. Everything else was on fire.

Logan woke with a start. The dream always left him feeling empty. Lost.

Someone shifted in the bed against him, and then he was staring into a pair of blue eyes fringed with dark lashes.

"You were dreaming," Juliette whispered.

He sat up and leaned against the headboard.

She watched him, her beautiful face etched with concern. Everything about her was soft and warm and perfect. It was always unsettling to wake from the dream, but even more so now to be in such a hellish place, only to find her beside him.

"Do you dream about the war?"

He scrubbed a hand over his face. "Always."

She pulled herself up and leaned against the headboard next to him. "Tell me."

Logan shook his head, as though to brush the memories away. What use would it be to talk about it? He couldn't change anything. But then he looked at Juliette's face, and the words came anyway. "We were digging a well in this village out in the middle of nowhere, Afghanistan. It wasn't a big operation. Just a routine job we'd done before. But someone didn't want us there. Four days into it, a bomb went off in the well." He rubbed his face with one hand, trying to scrub the memory clean. "And two other bombs in the surrounding buildings. Six of us didn't make it. My buddy Jacob . . ." He stopped altogether, not wanting to think about it.

Juliette placed her hand in his. She didn't look at him or try to force him to talk. She just sat there next to him while they stared into the dark. Together. Her presence was like a cool breeze. Having her there beside him made the past seem less painful. How did she do that? Whatever it was, he laced his fingers through hers and held on. "Jacob and I served together for a long time. He had a wife. Two kids. I watched his baby grow up in pictures." Juliette squeezed his hand. "We had this thing where we'd flip a coin to see who had to do the worst job. On that day, I won. He was closest to the well when the bombs went off."

Logan's voice trailed off, and he didn't say anything more. He remembered trying to find his friend in the wreckage. Ears ringing from the explosions. Eyes stinging. Lungs burning from the smoke. He searched for what seemed like hours. So many villagers had died. Jacob's body wasn't found until the next day. They told Logan later he was lucky to survive, but he didn't feel lucky. He felt angry. Angry at himself. The war. Everything. Sometimes the memory of Jacob kept him up all night. How he laughed when Logan won the coin toss that day. How he'd stuffed the latest picture of his baby girl into the pocket of his shirt before he left.

Logan closed his eyes. Even now, nightmares of that explosion still haunted him. He'd joined the army because he wanted to fight for his country. He didn't regret his decision; he was proud of the men he fought with, and proud of the country he fought for. But he never realized how it could chip off a piece of your soul.

"I left here when I was eighteen and thought I knew where I was headed," he said. "I was looking for adventure. I wanted to go places—anyplace away from here. All my life, my dad told me to join the armed forces. It was my duty, he said. Fight for your country. He was a military man, and so was my grandfather, so naturally they expected me to follow in their footsteps."

She squeezed his hand again. "It wasn't what you wanted?"

"It was everything I wanted," he said. "I was young and restless and nothing could have kept me here."

He paused and turned his head to look at her. "I do remember, you know. I remember that night with you. I was on my way out, and there you were. This beautiful girl in my garden, asking me not to go."

Chapter Twenty-Four

Juliette pulled the blanket up around her, as though she could shield herself from feeling vulnerable. Logan had just reminded her of that night in high school long ago, when she'd thrown herself at him. It wasn't a memory she visited easily.

"It was a crush," she said, trying to make light of it. "I mean, I barely knew you." Not true. She felt like she'd known him her whole life. She'd watched him grow up with his doting grandfather and amazing treehouse and perfect parents. She still remembered that night because it was the first and last time she'd ever tried to give her heart to someone.

Logan's senior graduation party was supposed to be the event of the year, and nothing could have kept Juliette away—certainly not the pesky fact that she was only a freshman and barely knew anyone in the graduating class. She had managed to arrange a ride with one of her friends who was dating an older guy. Before the party, Juliette had dressed carefully, doing her best to look grown up and mature. She wore her good jeans and a new tank top, and even put on makeup.

When she first arrived at the party, she stayed in the corner, pretending to laugh and fit in while the older kids drank and blasted music. Logan was outside mingling with his buddies around a fire pit, and Juliette waited a long time before she got up the courage to walk out there.

They were all sitting in a circle on the patio, drinking and talking. Someone handed her a beer and she held it like a security blanket, even though she wasn't about to drink beer. Because, gross.

A senior girl started up a game of Spin the Bottle, and one of the boys—a huge linebacker for the football team—announced "Seven Minutes in Heaven" before spinning. When the bottle stopped on her, Juliette thought she was going to faint.

The boy gave a *whoop* and lurched drunkenly to his feet. "Let's go, baby."

She was terrified. She knew what Seven Minutes in Heaven was. A stupid game where you had to go behind the bushes with the boy, and supposedly make out in the dark. She hadn't made out with anyone before, ever. And this boy, with the pimply face and beer-soaked shirt, wasn't her first, second, or twelve-hundredth choice.

But how to get out of it without looking like a stupid kid? She slowly rose to her feet.

Nobody was even paying attention to them anymore. The rest of the kids had already started spinning the bottle again.

"I'll be right back." Juliette tried to leave, but the boy reached out and grabbed her. He wasn't rough with her, but his hand stayed clamped on her upper arm, and he towered over her. "Not so fast, baby. You and I have plans." He was so drunk, his words slurred, and he smelled like warm beer and sweat. The idea of kissing him was nauseating.

Before she could respond, Logan appeared beside her. "Leave her alone, Brian."

The boy named Brian puffed out his chest. "This isn't your business, man." He tried to drag Juliette to his side, but she wiggled out of his grip.

Brian scowled at her. "What are you, a prude or something?"

Logan took her hand and moved closer, glaring at Brian.

Juliette stared down at their clasped hands. A thrill of excitement shot through her. He was holding her hand. She was holding hands with Logan O'Connor!

"She's a freshman, you moron," Logan told him. "She's just a kid."

Juliette flinched. All the elation she felt just a few seconds before evaporated with his words. *She's just a kid.* That's what he really thought of her. Of course he thought that. Why wouldn't he? Logan was all of eighteen. He was an adult, and she wasn't even old enough to drive.

Logan led her around to the side of the house until they stood alone near a tangle of pink and yellow rosebushes. Their soft, peaceful scent made a mockery of the turmoil she was feeling inside.

Humiliation burned in her cheeks. He thought she was a baby. "You didn't have to do that," she said. "I can take care of myself."

"I know you can." Logan dropped her hand. "But Brian's an idiot, and I didn't want him mauling you."

"Because I'm just a kid, right?" she asked bitterly.

"Well . . ." Logan seemed to search for the right words. "You are a lot younger than we are. Aren't you?"

"So? Lots of girls my age do more than spinning the bottle." He needed to know she was a lot more mature than her age. He needed to realize she wasn't a kid.

"You're probably right," he said quietly.

"How do you know I'm not like those girls? Maybe I've done a lot more than you think." Her voice rose with frustration. "Maybe I've even done more than you."

Logan put his hands on her shoulders. "Juliette."

"What?" she snapped.

"You should go home."

Her heart cracked. Surely he could hear it. He didn't even want her there.

He squeezed her shoulders, then let go.

Juliette's lower lip began to tremble. She pressed them together hard, wishing he would hold her so she could bury her face in his flannel shirt and pretend things were different.

"Don't leave," she whispered. "Don't go away." It was pathetic, she knew. He didn't even really know her. But they'd grown up on opposite sides of the woods, and she'd always felt connected to him.

He would never understand that, but maybe if he got to know her, she'd matter to him. Except, how would he ever get to know her if he left Pine Cove Island and joined the army? What if he never came back?

"I have to go," he said simply. The conviction—the excitement in his tone—raked across her raw emotions. How could he be so happy about leaving?

"No, you don't," she said. "There's nothing where you're going except fighting. Why would you choose that when everything good is here?" *When I'm here?*

Logan shook his head. "You don't understand. I don't want to just sit around here for the rest of my life. I want to see the world."

"Why?"

He looked at her like she was crazy. "Because it'll be something different, and I'm tired of this place. I want to do things that matter. Not everyone's happy to just wander the woods and live on the same boring island for the rest of their life, you know."

Juliette tried to breathe past the heaviness in her chest. He didn't think much of Pine Cove Island, or her. To him, she was just a boring kid. There was nothing left to say.

She turned away so he wouldn't see the tears in her eyes.

"Hey." He placed a hand on her shoulder. "I'm sorry. What else can I say?"

Say you'll stay. And that you'll never go away. Because you love me, and I'm enough.

Her eyes were hot with unshed tears, but she wasn't going to break down. That would make him think she was even more of a baby. Instead, if he was leaving and never coming back, what did she have to lose? Juliette lifted her chin and turned to face him.

"You don't have to say anything," she said. "Let's just say good-bye."

"Sure. I'll see you around, okay?"

Juliette nodded, knowing that he wouldn't. He wouldn't see her around because he wouldn't *be* around. He was going away and probably never coming back. It was now or never.

She waited a second to gather her courage. *One, two . . .* She shot up on her tiptoes and planted her lips firmly on his. *Three.*

Logan froze, his arms lifting in surprise.

Juliette pressed her body against his, wrapping her arms around his back. He was so tall, and way warmer than she'd imagined. And he smelled like pine needles and wood smoke and warm flannel. He smelled like everything she loved. He smelled like *home.*

For a few seconds, he remained rigid, but then his body relaxed and he leaned in to the kiss. It was her first real kiss, and it was everything she'd ever imagined. Juliette felt a momentary surge of triumph.

A heartbeat later, he gripped her arms and stepped back, blinking as though he were trying to process what happened.

Juliette lifted her chin. "I'm not just a kid."

Logan's breathing was a little unsteady, his expression far more serious than she'd ever seen it. "I guess not."

She'd gotten under his skin. She'd made him feel something. *Good.*

"I'll see you around, Logan O'Connor." With a toss of her hair, she turned and walked away.

If a tiny piece of her was hoping he'd follow, she refused to acknowledge it. This was how it ended, and that was fine. This was *real* life. You could love someone, but that didn't mean you were enough to make them stay. She'd been taught the lesson before, and tonight cemented it. From now on, she'd be a real grown-up. She wouldn't lose herself in silly dreams of love and forever, because it didn't last. Not for her parents, and obviously not for her. It was better this way.

Now, here she was in his bed, over thirteen years later. And instead of feeling shocked, or worried, she felt . . . safe. It made no sense, because he represented a past heartache she'd worked so hard to forget.

"I don't regret the choices I made," he said quietly. "I gave over a decade of my life to the army and the men who counted on me. They were my friends; they became my family. But the fighting and the loss . . ." He shook his head. "It stays with you, and the years go by, and you watch some of the people you know die, and you start wondering when it ends. If it ever ends. And the longer you're out there, the more you realize that the people back home have moved on. They have lives and careers and families. And you start thinking, who's going to miss me if I'm gone?"

"Is that why you wanted to come back?" Juliette whispered.

He closed his eyes and leaned his head back. "I wanted to come home. I figured it was time to stop fighting, and time to build something that would last. And the hell of it is, it was right here the whole time."

Juliette wanted to take his hand in hers. Kiss him and tell him she was glad he came home. But something stirred deep inside her. He made her want things she'd sworn off a long time ago. He was everything she'd hoped for, back when she was naive enough to believe in dreams, and it suddenly terrified her.

She reached over the side of the bed and pulled the small vial from her cardigan. Then she placed a few drops in the water glass on the nightstand and handed it to him.

He took the glass. "Is this one of your magic potions?"

"Yes. It's the same potion I gave the tree."

He gave her a quizzical look. "But I'm not dying."

"It'll help. Trust me."

Logan held her gaze for a moment, then drank the entire glass of water, his eyes never leaving her face. He set the empty glass on the nightstand. "What's it supposed to do?"

"It's a healing potion. If you're plagued by nightmares, it should bring you some peace."

The alarm clock on the bedside table buzzed. She jumped and gave a nervous laugh. "I need to get going. The sun's about to rise."

Juliette grabbed her nightgown off the floor, slipped it over her head, and wrapped her cardigan around her like a security blanket.

Logan sat up and reached for his shirt.

"Don't bother," she said. "I know my way home."

"Let me drive you."

"No, I want to walk. See you at the shop." She gave him an awkward wave and slipped out of the room, through the kitchen, and down the back porch steps. It wasn't until she was halfway home that she began to relax. As much as she wanted to pretend he was just a summer fling, she couldn't. Logan was much more than that, and she couldn't deny it anymore. When he'd told her about the war, she wanted to throw her arms around him and hold on until the pain of it faded away. She'd never felt that way about any other man. It wasn't that she was indifferent to other men she'd been with. It's that she never let them get close enough to affect her on such a personal level. She prided herself on keeping things light, and if a guy started getting serious, that's when she started getting "gone." But this whole emotional thing with Logan was different. Something was happening between them, and she had no idea how to navigate through it.

She emerged from the woods into her garden, stopping at the trellis she'd been meaning to fix. The climbing roses were on the ground again. She grabbed an armful of the thornless stems and propped them against the broken trellis. The trailing flowers slid off the latticework and landed on the ground. Again.

"Sassy," Juliette muttered. "You guys need to stay put." She shoved them up onto the trellis once more. The roses bobbed up and down as though teasing her, their stems balancing on the broken woodwork, but this time, they stayed off the ground.

She ran her fingers over the flowers, the peach and yellow blooms glowing softly in the early morning light. She'd created a spell to keep the thorns from growing, which had been easy enough. Why couldn't the rest of life be as easy as making things grow?

Luna meowed and wandered over.

She picked up her cat and brought them nose to nose. "What am I going to do about him?"

Luna began to purr.

"Yeah, I know you like him," Juliette said, setting the cat back on the grass. "Traitor."

Luna stared at her with bright, headlamp eyes.

"Okay, fine. I like him, too. But it's not going to do me any good. Things are getting out of hand already. I mean, I spent the night over there. What do you have to say about that?"

The cat yawned.

"It is, too, a big deal," Juliette said. "You know as well as I do, it's not normal for me." She never spent the night with guys she dated. Even if they ended up getting physical, Juliette never wanted to stay the night. There was just something so "permanent" about it. And last night, she fell asleep in Logan's bed like it was nothing. Like she'd done it a million times before and it was totally normal.

They'd stayed awake for hours, doing all sorts of summer fling-ish type things. Her limbs went soft and liquid at the memory of it. Everything she said before was a lie. She loved his muscles, the strength of his arms pulling her in, and the feel of his powerful body sliding against hers. She loved his wild hair, the shades of dark gold that glowed in the afternoon sun, the feel of it in her hands last night when he moved above her. She loved . . . a lot of things about him.

And as much as she felt "home" when she was with him, she'd never felt more lost.

Chapter Twenty-Five

Logan showered and got dressed, grateful that the master bedroom had been his first overhaul project. He'd painted the walls a light gray with white trim, and replaced all the old furniture with a king set in dark mahogany. The floors were still in decent shape, but he'd added a large area rug in varying shades of blue. The overall affect was relaxing and modern, and Logan had a feeling even his uncle's husband, Caleb, would approve.

Unfortunately, the rest of the house currently looked like roadkill. He went downstairs, swearing as he passed the foyer and entered the living room. He and Kevin had begun ripping down wallpaper. They'd finally stopped yesterday evening to resume again the next day. The incredible mess, paired with the dilapidated furniture and moth-eaten curtains, gave the house a sort of crack den vibe.

Logan shook his head and walked into the kitchen. It looked even worse. In addition to ripping down wallpaper, he and the kid had gutted the laundry room sink, which now sat in a heap on the table. Normally Logan kept the kitchen spotless, but this morning every surface was covered in a fine layer of dust.

He grinned at the memory of Juliette standing in the

middle of the kitchen last night, laughing at the state of his house. She had a way of lighting up the room when she laughed. The more time he spent with her, the more time he wanted to spend. Hell, she'd only left thirty minutes ago and already he missed her. Whatever this was between them, he knew one thing for certain. He didn't want it to stop.

For the past year or two, all he could think about was getting home and settling down into a normal, peaceful routine. But his image of the perfect life was never really fleshed out. He knew he'd like to start a contracting business someday, but the family he wanted to have was just a foggy idea in his mind—a wife and kids, a dog in the yard, camping trips, baseball games. But then he got to know Juliette, and now the things he wanted were becoming much clearer.

A text message dinged on his phone. It was Juliette.

You better be on time today.

Logan grinned. We'll see.

Don't make me hurt you.

You wouldn't.

I absolutely would.

Not if I bring you a hazelnut mocha.

A long pause. Fine.

Fine.

He slipped his phone back into his pocket, feeling lighter than he had in months. The things he wanted for his future were taking shape in a way he never thought possible. Roots and family were still important, but it was Juliette who made him feel alive. Her passion. Her determination. Her fierce dedication to the people and things she cared about. Logan wanted her to care about him like that. He wanted her to care because . . . he wanted *her*.

An hour later, Logan was getting ready to leave when someone knocked at his door. It was barely eight o'clock, so it could only be Juliette.

When he opened the front door, Bella stood on the doorstep holding a pie.

Logan groaned inwardly. He'd been trying to avoid her for days, ever since he'd cancelled the dinner plans with her parents. But she was as persistent as a honey badger, not taking no for an answer. It was becoming unbearable.

"Hi," she said, peering over his shoulder in curiosity.

Logan shifted on his feet to block her view. She'd never been in his house, and he'd like to keep it that way.

"I was hoping I'd catch you before you left."

"I was just heading out. What brings you over?" And how could he make her leave as quickly as possible? It was bad enough she kept showing up at the shop when he was working, but coming to his home uninvited was a new level of irritating.

For a brief moment when he first moved back, he thought they might be compatible together. But after the first couple of dates, he knew it would never work. They were all wrong for each other. It wasn't only that she talked nonstop and rarely let him get a word in. It was that he had no desire to get a word in. If she wasn't gossiping about other people, she was usually talking about things like shoe shopping, or half-yearly sales, or lately, china patterns—whatever that was. They had next to nothing in common.

"My parents are wondering when to reschedule dinner. Since you cancelled." Her tone was light, but it was clear she wasn't happy.

"Sorry, I've been busy. My uncle's coming back in a week, and I have to make sure the remodel's finished."

"Well, you need to have dinner at some point, don't you? You can come for dinner tonight. Or tomorrow."

Logan took a frustrated breath. She just wouldn't take a hint. If he wanted to be blunt, he could tell her the truth. He wasn't attracted to her. He found her petty and pushy and annoying. And her perfume made him ill. But even though it was all true, he didn't want to hurt her feelings.

"Here, I baked you a pie." She thrust it at him and shouldered her way into the house.

Logan set the dish on the entry table and shut the door. This needed to end, but how?

In the foyer, Bella came to an abrupt halt. She stared in shock at the filthy walls and floors.

Logan was about to tell her the whole house was a work in progress, when an idea suddenly popped into his head. Like a flame, it flickered and grew brighter, roaring to life until suddenly he had a plan that was so ridiculous, it just might work. He was willing to give it a try.

"What happened in here?" Bella said, wrinkling her nose.

"Nothing," he said casually, gesturing toward the living room. "After you."

She kept her arms close to her sides and walked into the next room.

Logan followed, and even though he knew what to expect, the living room was like a punch to the face. The shredded walls, stained rug, and threadbare furniture were bad enough, but he'd recently pulled the baseboards out too. Peeling, uneven paint and exposed nails were visible along the perimeter of the floor. Dust motes floated in the air, and the room smelled faintly of mothballs and mildew. Logan planned to haul the offending furniture to the dump later that day, but Bella didn't have to know that.

She curled her lip in disgust. "Oh, my god."

"I know, right?" Logan said with enthusiasm. "This is my favorite room in the house."

She looked startled. "It is?"

"Yeah, I love the whole rustic vibe." He pointed to the avocado green couch and the stained chair with the dented armrest. "I'm a bit of a dumpster diver, myself. Someone left those on the side of the road on Ninth Street. Can you believe it?"

She made a small sound at the back of her throat that sounded like a "yes."

"Steal of a deal," he said with pride. "The only thing better than cheap is free, I always say. Hey, do you want something to drink?" He really hoped she did, because the kitchen was staged for prime time.

She followed him into the next room and gasped.

The kitchen looked like a health hazard. The old sink from the laundry room sat on the table like a centerpiece from hell. Mold, dirt, and rust flakes were scattered across the weathered Formica counter. There were no chairs to sit on because Kevin had just finished painting them in the garage. For the time being, two wooden shipping crates were shoved under the table to serve as makeshift seating.

"Sorry, let me just get this out of the way." Logan slid the discarded sink several inches across the table to clear a space. Then he dragged a crate from under the table, lifted Kevin's forgotten backpack to the kitchen counter, and said, "Have a seat."

"No, I . . ." Bella looked thunderstruck. "Is this where you *eat*?"

"Most of the time." He took a used mug off the counter, making sure she noticed. "Sometimes I eat in my bedroom while I watch *Game of Thrones*, but the ants are becoming a problem." He went to the fridge, adding, "I guess that's what happens when your mattress is on the floor, though."

Logan searched through his fridge, then pulled out a carton of milk. "I'm afraid it's expired, but only by a week. Are you okay with that?"

"I'm not thirsty," she said weakly.

"You sure? There's water." He pointed to the dusty sink faucet.

She shook her head.

"Probably a good thing," he said with a chuckle. "I've been meaning to get a filter. The pipes are kind of rusty."

Bella started looking a little queasy.

Logan shoved Kevin's backpack to the corner of the counter and lifted a plate out of the sink. He began buffing it with the hem of his shirt. "Want breakfast?"

If her face had been made of ceramic, she'd have cracked. She swallowed visibly. "No."

"Okay." He put the plate in the cupboard. "I guess I could give you a tour of the house. But fair warning: the upstairs doesn't look as good as down here. There's a tiny bit of a rat problem, so I had to set a bunch of traps. You'll just have to be careful where you step."

She adjusted her purse on her shoulder, clutching the straps like a lifeline. "I think I'm good."

Logan leaned a hip against the counter, crossed his arms, and let out a contented sigh. "I know it doesn't look like much, but I call it home. This is really my speed, you know? Just laid back, low maintenance. If there's one thing I've learned from being in the army, it's not to worry about a little dirt and some wildlife. Oh . . ." He pointed to the back patio. "There's some now."

As if on cue, Luna slinked up to the sliding glass door. Bella stifled a little scream.

A dead mouse hung from Luna's mouth. She dropped it on the mat outside, took one look at Bella, and hissed.

"Don't mind that," Logan said easily. "There's a lot of

feral cats around here, but I'm cool with them. They help with the rats."

Bella looked at Logan as if she'd never seen him before. "You like living here?"

"I'd never live anywhere else," he said, as if her question was ridiculous. "My grandparents got married in this house. Someday I'm going to honor their memory by doing the same."

Now she looked like she'd just been shot. Her face scrunched up as she gaped at him. "But this house," she sputtered. "This is not the place to raise children."

"Children?" Logan jerked his head back like he'd been slapped. "Oh, ho-ho. Not happening for me. Chances are very slim, the doc said." He gave her a meaningful look. "Jet ski accident."

She looked confused, then stared down at his crotch in horror.

Logan had to fight not to cover himself with his hands. Jesus, this facade better work. He was beginning to feel as dirty as the house.

"But who wants kids, anyway, amirite?" he said. "Dogs are way better company. A buddy of mine is a breeder, so I'm thinking about starting a business. Wouldn't mind having a few pit bulls running around to keep things interesting, you know what I mean?"

She was shaking her head no. So much no.

He shifted his weight against the counter and accidentally knocked Kevin's backpack sideways. Colorful game cards spilled all over the floor. Little cartoon monster things. What were those called? He bent to gather them up. "Dang, I really need to get a binder for these."

"Y-you . . . have Pokémon cards?"

Logan gritted his teeth as he gathered up the cards. *Just own it, man. Do you want this to work or not?* He schooled his expression and stood. "Oh, yeah. Pokey Man and I go way back. I beat the . . . grand wizard at my last tournament." Wait, was that a thing? Maybe he'd gone too far. *Run with it, you're in too deep.* "Yup. Bowser was a tough boss, but I took him down. And then I was like, yesss." He pumped a fist, channeling Kevin.

Bella looked ill.

Logan almost felt sorry for her. Hell, he was starting to feel sorry for himself.

"I need to go," she said, backing into the living room. "I just remembered there's something I have to do."

"Watch out for the ottoman," Logan called.

She bumped against it. Stumbled a little. Straightened.

"Gotta be careful," he said with concern.

"I'm fine—"

"—That's an heirloom."

She scowled at him, the moth-eaten ottoman, the room. Then she turned on her heel and stalked out of the house.

Logan waited until he heard Bella's car spin out of the gravel driveway and zoom down the street.

He tossed the cards into the kid's backpack and grinned.

Achievement unlocked.

Chapter Twenty-Six

One week later, Juliette stood in the newly remodeled florist shop with her friends.

"It's just beautiful," Emma said, glancing around. "Romeo's going to love it when he sees it tomorrow morning."

"No doubt," Gertie added, turning in a circle. "It doesn't look anything like the old place. Not that the old place was bad," she assured Juliette. "It was just kind of dark and small, and this looks so much brighter and bigger. It doesn't even look like the same place."

Juliette felt a swell of pride and she walked through the shop with them. She'd been in the process of putting the finishing touches on everything, trying to anticipate how it would look for Romeo's arrival, when they'd surprised her with a visit and a hazelnut mocha.

"I like what you did with the mirrors," Molly said. The entire back wall, previously stacked with old wooden shelves and excess planting supplies, was now fitted with floor to ceiling mirrors and glass shelves that ran the length of the space. The mirrors bounced light and made the plants appear double in size. As a result, the whole interior of the shop looked twice as large, and much brighter.

"Whose idea was this?" Molly asked, checking her lipstick in one of the mirrored panels.

"Logan's," Juliette admitted. She'd fought him on it, at first. She'd complained about how he messed up her arrangements and tracked dust over the tiled floor. But in his quiet, steadfast way, he insisted on fixing the back wall. And now, the final result was amazing. Better than she could have imagined.

"He is so handy," Gertie said, joining Molly at the back wall. "I could get used to having someone like that around, and not just because he's cute." She rummaged through her giant tote bag, pulled out a brush, and began arranging her hair in the mirror. "Walter couldn't hang a picture straight if his life depended on it. The last time he tried to replace the kitchen sink he broke a pipe and flooded the entire downstairs."

"Did Logan do the painting?" Emma said from the other end of the shop. The walls were a lovely shade of spring green, with crisp, white crown molding installed along the ceiling.

"He did," Juliette said. "He did all the improvements." There was no denying that the new shop looked fantastic, and she had him to thank. For the most part, she'd rearranged the plants to better advantage and kept the shop running smoothly, but Logan had done a lot more than she thought was possible.

"He's certainly a powerhouse of energy, isn't he?" Gertie asked, sending Juliette a sly grin. "Must be nice to have someone like him around. Someone so *driven*."

"Mmm," Molly agreed. "Drive is so important."

"He must be a really good driver. Is he?" Gertie asked innocently. "A good driver?"

Juliette rolled her eyes and took a sip of her mocha.

"She's stalling," Molly teased. "I guess he's not all that."

"It's too bad," Gertie said. "Because he looks like he'd know his way around a racetrack."

"You guys," Juliette said, setting her mocha down. "He could win the Indy Five Hundred driving a golf cart."

"Who's driving a golf cart?" Kat bustled through the door with Hank following at her heels. Today Kat's frizzing hair stood out around her head like a fuzzy halo. In a black sundress, black fishnet stockings, and black combat boots, she looked like the little mermaid gone rogue.

"You must be Kat," Molly said, beaming.

Juliette made the introductions, glad to finally have Kat meet Emma and her friends. Not only was Kat the best employee she'd ever had, Juliette genuinely liked her. They just got each other, and it was uncanny how easy it was to be around her.

Kat picked up Hank and introduced him to the girls.

"I love your style." Gertie gestured to her outfit. "We need some of that around the salon. Do you do hair?"

Kat laughed and pointed to her head. "Does this not speak for itself?" She tried smoothing it down with one hand, and it bounced right back.

"You have one of the most gorgeous heads of hair I've ever seen," Gertie said with feeling.

Emma gave Hank a pat on the head. "That's a huge compliment. Gertie knows hair. It's kind of her magical talent."

Kat's green eyes lit with interest. "I heard there was magic on this island."

"Well, you heard right. But it's not me, it's these two." Gertie pointed to Emma and Juliette. "She bakes sweet charms into cupcakes, and she has garden magic."

They all looked at Kat to gauge her reaction.

"Thank goodness," Kat said with relief. "I was getting really bored hanging around a bunch of Hollywood people who *think* they're magically gifted, but aren't. You have no idea how happy I am to finally meet the real deal."

Emma looked at Juliette. "I like her."

Juliette grinned. "I knew you would."

Later that evening, Juliette stepped onto her back patio with a steaming cup of Earl Grey. She inhaled the rich scents of bergamot and lemon, contemplating what the following day would be like.

Romeo would show up, be dazzled by all the gorgeous new changes, and tell her what a marvelous job she'd done. No, he'd congratulate her and Logan, and tell them what a marvelous job they'd done, *together*.

Was all her hoping for nothing? Was Romeo going to let her take over the shop, with his beloved nephew in the picture? Juliette paced the small back patio, Luna watching her quietly from underneath a stone birdbath.

For years, all she could think about was how much she wanted to be able to support herself comfortably with a job she loved. The retail boutique with Minerva hadn't been a good fit. The woman fired Juliette after two weeks because she was too honest with the customers. "You can't say, 'Yes, that makes you look frumpy,'" Minerva had scolded. "That's not how you sell clothes." And then there was the lifeguard job she got one summer after high school. Months of classes and swim tests, only to find out she hated it. All those hours in the burning sun. The smell of suntan lotion and chlorine and wet concrete, and not a plant in sight. Just the scorched weeds that grew between the pavement cracks. When she'd started her small at-home business of making bath products and herbal remedies, it had been a nice reprieve from job hopping. The income was enough to live on, but things hadn't been easy.

Juliette sipped her tea and wandered into her garden, taking comfort in the soft grass beneath her bare feet and the scents of honeysuckle and roses and green things growing. This was what she needed to be truly happy, and after several years of floating from one job to another, she'd finally found her place.

Walking into Romeo's Florist Shop was like going home. She'd started working there and never looked back. Once Romeo realized her ability to make things grow and thrive, Juliette's job was secure. He'd been hinting about retiring for a while, and all Juliette could think of was how badly she wanted to own the shop. She was the best candidate for the role; she knew it down to her bones. When Romeo announced the renovation project, she'd been elated, thinking this was her moment to finally prove she could run the business on her own.

But then came Logan.

Juliette sat under the maple tree in the corner of her garden, letting her head fall back against the trunk. "There's no getting around it," she whispered to Luna, who had followed her to the tree. "I'm in over my head with him."

The cat flicked an ear.

"I mean it," Juliette said. "I've really gone and stepped in it now, because I care about him."

Luna sat on the grass in front of Juliette and stared up at her.

"I'm not going to discuss it with you," Juliette said. "All you get is this simple truth. I care about Logan O'Connor. There. It's done. I can't change it. So now what?" A mixture of worry and anxiety washed over her. She drew her knees up and hugged them to her chest. "I'm screwed, is what."

Luna walked over and nudged her head against Juliette's shins.

Juliette ran her hand down the cat's sleek back. "I don't like caring about him. It's too complicated. I find myself missing him when he's not around. This entire past week, all we did was hang out together. Eat dinners together. Watch old movies, lounging at his house, or mine."

Her cat nudged her again, staring up at her with bright, golden eyes.

"He made me vegetarian lasagna," Juliette continued, scratching Luna behind the ears. "And I helped him clean up his yard. We went out on his boat, too. And did you know the other day, I got the best idea for an organization shelf at the shop? An organization shelf, Luna." She shook her head. "The first thing I wanted to do was jump up and run to tell him."

Luna began to purr.

"No, that's not good. It's bad. Don't you get it? I'm starting to get used to him being around. And it's not going to last. Sooner or later, he'll move on or something will happen, and it will be over. And then guess what? It's just going to be you and me. All over again. Like always."

Luna let out a soft *meow*.

"Deny it all you want, but it's true. And I for one am not going to just sit around and wait for the crushing blow. I'm going to just focus on the important things, until this whole silly"—she gestured to her chest—"thing I'm feeling fades away. I'll just wait for it to fade."

The cat had obviously heard enough. She turned away and walked past the lilacs to the corner of the garden.

"You don't understand—" Juliette called after her, then stopped.

There was something odd about the corner of her garden. She stood slowly and walked to the climbing rosebush. The tumble of coral blooms weren't trailing on the ground. The stems weren't tangled in a broken lattice like they usually were. In fact, the broken lattice was gone. In its place stood a gorgeous arched frame. The climbing rosebush was now twined around and through the arch, its dark green leaves dancing in the wind. The flowers had turned their golden faces up to the sky, as if basking in their newfound home. They were happy and content. She could feel it.

So why was she so . . . unsettled? Juliette stared at the smooth paving stones beyond the archway. They formed a charming footpath that led into the woods, just like she'd always wanted. Logan had taken one of her dreams and made it a reality.

Luna meowed.

"I know he did it," Juliette whispered.

The cat started off into the woods, looking over her shoulder at Juliette.

"I'm not going to thank him. Not right now." Juliette backed away and strode into the house. That was the thing about Logan. He was always making things different. Better. But it was one thing for him to fix up the shop, another thing entirely for him to steal into her yard and fix something in her garden.

She set her mug in the kitchen sink, insides roiling in confusion. Part of her was grateful, but a bigger part of her was bothered that he'd done it without asking. Her garden was a private haven. It was hers from the time she could walk. It had been her joy and her solace. When the world fell apart, Juliette had her plants and they had her. It was a bond forged by Mother Nature that no one could change. No one *should* change.

The phone rang. Emma.

Juliette picked up the phone and plopped down on a kitchen chair. "Hey, Em."

"What's the matter?" Emma asked. Her cousin always knew when something was wrong, no matter how much Juliette tried to hide it.

"Nothing. I just had a long day getting the shop ready for Romeo's return."

"Okay . . ." Emma paused. "What's really the matter?"

"He drives me crazy," Juliette blurted.

"Romeo?" Emma was smiling. Juliette could hear it in her voice.

"Shut up. You know I'm talking about Logan."

"What did he do this time?"

"He secretly built a new trellis for my climbing roses," Juliette said.

"The peach-colored ones? In the corner near that broken thing?"

"Yes. I just discovered it now."

Emma made a soothing noise. "I'm so sorry. What a complete jerk. I mean, who would do that?"

Juliette pursed her lips. "You think I'm being ridiculous."

"A little."

"And that I should thank him for building it."

"Yes."

"And that I should just be happy that we're together and not worry about the future and not care that someday he's going to rip my heart out of my chest and leave and then I'll have nothing. Again."

Emma paused. "Juliette, I love you. You know that."

She closed her eyes. "I know."

"In a few weeks I'm getting married to a man I never thought I'd find. I didn't even like him at first, remember?"

Of course Juliette remembered. When Hunter came to town with his fancy new restaurant and bakery, Emma had been devastated. She and Juliette had even gone so far as to create a magic spell to try to get him to leave the island forever.

"I thought he was the worst person in the world," Emma continued. "And then I changed. He changed. We realized we were right for each other, all along."

"So what, you're saying you think Logan is right for me?"

"I'm saying I think he's right for you, right now. Maybe don't worry too much about where it's going. We can't walk around our entire lives guarding our hearts so we don't get hurt. Trust me, I know. The thing is, it's okay to fall. It's okay to let go and fall for someone, even if it means someday you'll get hurt."

"I disagree," Juliette said in a huff. "Nobody wants to get hurt."

"That's not what I'm saying. Of course nobody wants to feel heartache. But sometimes you just have to let go, and let yourself be vulnerable. It's the only way to really live. Otherwise, you'll always just be watching from the outside. I know it's scary. And there are no guarantees. But I'm here, and I love you and always will. If you get hurt, I'm here."

Juliette stood and began pacing the kitchen. "I know, Em. I just don't know how to handle this. I'm afraid of what it means."

"It means there's a boy who likes a girl, so he built her a trellis for her flowers. It's as simple as that."

"But what does the boy want from the girl? What if they don't want the same things?"

"Hmm," Emma said. "Maybe the girl should just enjoy the moment for what it is. Maybe the girl will find out she wants to go to the prom with him, after all."

"Or, maybe . . ." Juliette said, peering out the kitchen window at the new trellis. "Maybe she should just tell him that she's willing to make out under the bleachers, but she's not interested in wearing his letterman jacket."

"Are you sure about that?"

Juliette turned away from the window. "No," she said quietly. "I'm not sure about anything. I'm so confused. Being with him has been . . . unexpected. He makes me crazy. He makes me laugh. We have fun together, and I'm not just talking about sexy times." She wandered into her living room and sank into an overstuffed chair, slumping sideways to let her feet dangle over the armrest. "The truth is, I don't remember the last time I ever felt this way about anyone. I like being with him. I think about him whenever he's not around. And he's done so much for the shop to make it better. It's like I can trust him to always do the right thing, you know?" Juliette took a deep breath and let it out in a rush. "I don't know what's wrong with me."

"Don't you?" The smile was back in Emma's voice.

That unsettling mixture of worry and anxiety washed over Juliette again. She sat up straight and cleared her throat. "Never mind me. I'm so scattered right now. It's probably just nerves because I want the shop to look perfect tomorrow."

"You're going to have to thank Logan for the trellis, sooner or later," Emma said.

Juliette lifted a hand to massage her forehead. "Then I choose later. I'm too tired to deal with that right now. Romeo's coming back from his trip in the morning. And I have to find a way to bring up buying the shop."

"Word of advice? Maybe don't bombard him with that the minute he walks through the door. Let him take a couple of breaths, first."

"I'll let him have a few," Juliette said. "But once he sees the place, he has to understand that I've got things under control. He has to see that I'm the right person to take over."

"And he will," Emma said soothingly.

Juliette hoped, more than anything, that Emma was right.

Chapter Twenty-Seven

"My god, look at this place," Romeo said as he breezed through the front door. "It got a red carpet makeover." His dark hair was sun-streaked, and his face was tanner than usual. Even after a nine-hour flight and a one-hour ferry ride, he looked as elegant as he always did in slacks and a crisp linen shirt.

Juliette jumped off the stool and ran to give him a hug. It was eight o'clock in the morning, and she'd arrived early to make sure everything looked perfect. Romeo and Caleb's flight came in at 6:00 a.m. and she knew they'd stop by the shop on the way home.

"It's insane," Caleb said, standing in the middle of the floor with his hands on his hips. "Just gorgeous. It doesn't even look like the same place." Unlike Romeo, Caleb was lobster red, his faded blond hair standing out in little wisps on his head. He wore Bermuda shorts, a wrinkled linen shirt, and a seashell necklace.

"Wait until you guys see the greenhouse out back," Juliette said. "And the patio Logan built is even better than the one we wanted."

"Not so fast; I want to take it all in." Romeo strolled

through the new and improved shop, smiling in admiration. "You painted the walls?"

"Logan did," she said. "But I picked the color."

"Nice choice," Caleb said. "Spring green with a slight tint of blue. Lovely."

"And the mirrored shelves." Romeo shook his head. "Pure genius."

"If you think that's amazing, brace yourself." Juliette walked to the closet she used to fill with boxes of seeds and planting equipment. Logan had taken off the door, and she'd hung a curtain panel embroidered with green leaves. What was once a jumbled mess of boxes she had to dig through was now a perfectly organized wall of shelving, with seed packets in neat rows, arranged alphabetically.

When she drew the panel aside, Caleb gasped. "Oh, my darling, beautiful girl. You *organized*?"

"Yup," she said with pride. They didn't need to know about the fight she'd had with Logan. One morning she'd arrived at work to find that he'd tossed all her boxes into the middle of the floor and put up shelves without asking. She didn't want to admit it, but once she started organizing, she began to realize she kind of liked it. There was something almost therapeutic about having a place for everything. Who knew?

Romeo gave a low whistle. "I'm so impressed."

The back door swung open and Juliette gathered her courage. Showtime. She had to pretend that everything between her and Logan was strictly business.

"Oh, hey, Logan." She forced her voice to go up a notch, all cheerful cheery cheerleader. "Your uncle and Caleb just got here."

They greeted each other with warm hugs and slaps on the back, then Logan led them outside to see the greenhouse and patio.

She felt his eyes on her, but she couldn't look at him. Later, she'd thank him for the trellis. For now, she had to remain calm and collected. It wasn't easy when she kind of wanted to hide. She went to the back kitchen and busied herself with her inventory list.

Caleb popped his head in. "Aren't you coming?"

"I'll be there in a minute," Juliette said.

"Something's up with you." Caleb tilted his head, staring at her like he was trying to read tea leaves. "You look different."

She tucked her hair behind her ear. "I'm wearing a different mascara."

"No, that's not it." Caleb tapped his finger against his lips, eyeing her closely. "It's something else."

Juliette felt her face grow hot. Surely he wouldn't be able to tell that she and Logan were tangled up in a "thing."

"I'm just excited to see you guys," Juliette said quickly. "I feel like you've been gone for ages."

"Huh." Caleb looked unconvinced. "I don't know what it is, but it'll come to me."

Hopefully not. "Shall we?" Juliette gestured to the door.

When the two of them joined Romeo and Logan outside, Juliette was grateful for Caleb's chatter. She hid behind it like a shield.

"You two amaze me," Romeo said. "This place looks incredible."

Juliette beamed with pride. Even though she knew Logan had done most of the work, it made her happy to be included in Romeo's praise.

"I want you both to come to dinner at our place on Tuesday," Romeo said. "We'll celebrate the successful remodel."

"I've got a new eggplant parmesan recipe I've been

wanting to try," Caleb added. "Juliette, you can eat that, right? It's vegetarian."

"Yes," she said hesitantly. "I can." The real question was, did she want to? She'd heard stories about Caleb's less than appetizing culinary skills.

Logan looked at her and winked. "Sounds delicious, Caleb." To Romeo he said, "I'll bring lots of wine."

Chapter Twenty-Eight

On Tuesday night, Juliette sat on Romeo and Caleb's back patio, making sure to keep a good distance from Logan, even though they were sharing the same sofa. The past couple of days with him had been almost like a dream. She'd gone over to his house on Saturday night to thank him for the trellis, and she ended up spending the night. Again. It was just so easy to be with him, and she'd finally decided to take Emma's advice and just relax into their relationship. It wasn't hard because with Logan, everything just felt right.

Now, it was challenging to keep up a facade of indifference with him sitting only an arm's length away. She'd grown used to lounging with him at her house or his, and it felt unnatural to be so formal.

"Who wants dessert?" Caleb called from inside the kitchen.

Juliette hesitated to answer. Dinner—and Caleb's eggplant parmesan—had finally come to an end, and she'd never been more grateful. Trying to make polite conversation while chewing through undercooked eggplant was difficult, but the several glasses of wine throughout dinner had helped.

Caleb emerged from the sliding screen door carrying a platter of cookies. "I didn't have time to make dessert, so these store-bought things will have to do."

Juliette said a silent prayer of thanks and took a cookie, leaning back into the couch cushions.

"More wine?" Romeo asked.

She shook her head. "If I have any more wine I won't be able to drive home."

"I'll take more," Logan said. His large hand gripped the stemless wineglass and Juliette had to force herself to look away. She knew exactly what his hands could do, but this wasn't the time for her mind to take a joyride down Lusty Lane. Not when Caleb was giving her that look again. He was staring at her like she was a puzzle he was trying to solve.

"You know, Juliette," Caleb said as he took the seat beside Romeo. "I still can't quite put my finger on it, but there is definitely something different about you."

She did her best to look amused. "What do you mean? You've only been gone a few weeks. Not much has changed." Not much, indeed. She was in a relationship with Logan O'Connor. Everything had changed.

"You seem more relaxed or something. Like you've been doing yoga or you went to a spa."

Juliette ran with it. "You know, I guess I am more relaxed. Probably because of all the organization Logan's done in the shop, not to mention the beautiful remodel he did." She gave Logan a warm glance, Caleb's scrutiny be damned. Logan deserved the recognition for all his hard work. The shop really was much better, and it was all because of him.

Romeo cleared his throat. "Speaking of the shop, there's something I've been meaning to tell you both."

Juliette's heart did a stutter step inside her chest.

This was it. This was the moment when Romeo was going to announce his retirement. She was absolutely positive.

Juliette set her cookie down on a napkin. She was ready for this. Her finances were in order, and she already had money lined up to buy the business. Romeo would probably be thrilled she wanted to take over the shop.

"As you know, I've been talking about retirement for a while now."

Yes! Prepare the confetti cannons. Today was going to be her day.

"So here it is," Romeo continued. "I'm retiring at the end of the summer, and Caleb and I are moving to Florida."

"Florida?" Logan exclaimed. "Near my parents? I thought you loved it here."

"We do love it here," Romeo said. "But we've been wanting to move someplace warmer for a while now, and since my sister's already there . . ." He trailed off and smiled at Caleb. The two men clasped hands, and Juliette felt a surge of happiness for them. It was clear they were more in love with each other than ever, and excited about the prospect of moving.

"I'll be sorry to see you go," she said. *But not sorry to finally own my florist shop!*

"So will I," Logan added. "It's funny—I came back home and now most of my family lives somewhere else."

"You know we'll come visit you all the time," Caleb assured him.

"Logan." Romeo set his glass on the table, looked meaningfully at Caleb, then leaned forward and rested his elbows on his knees. "I've decided to leave my shop to you, if you'll take it."

A faint buzzing sound took up residence in Juliette's

ears. She shook her head to clear it. Funny. It sounded like Romeo said—

"You're leaving me the shop?" Logan looked confused.

Juliette's mouth fell open as she looked from Romeo to Logan. Then Romeo to Caleb to Logan. And finally back to Romeo. He was giving his nephew an encouraging nod. Smiling in that charming way he always did. Smiling like her favorite boss in the entire world. Her favorite boss who just yanked the carpet out from under her, then flung that carpet into her future and lit it on fire.

No, Juliette mouthed, her fingers digging into the couch cushions.

"I've seen all the amazing things you've done to the place," Romeo continued. "And I know you don't have plans for work lined up yet. Think of it as an early inheritance. Caleb and I don't have children, so you're it for us. I want to keep the shop in the family, and I know you'll take care of it. Look how well everything's going already. And you work so well with Juliette." He gestured to her, and all she could do was blink. Her fists were clenched, and she had to bite the insides of her cheeks. If she opened her mouth, she might scream.

"This is unexpected, Uncle Ro," Logan said, running a hand through his hair. "I don't know what to say."

"You'll say yes," Caleb said, taking a cookie from the plate. "We've been planning to move for a while, and your return to the island was perfect timing. It's meant to be."

Logan leaned back on the couch and hooked a foot over his knee.

Juliette wanted to kick it. She wanted to take his wine and splash it in his face. He deserved that, and more. So did his uncle. How could Romeo do this to her? They'd worked together for years. He knew she thought of the shop—maybe even him, a little—as family. How could he ruin her plans so thoroughly?

"Well . . ." Logan paused as though waiting for something. After a long moment, he said, "I'm honored. I mean, I'd be happy to, but . . . are you sure?"

"Of course I'm sure," Romeo said with a wave of his hand. "Who else would I leave my business to? You're the only family I've got out here."

And that was it. Juliette jumped to her feet. She didn't plan it; it just happened. It was like her body heard those words, and her legs stupidly took over. Her skin felt hot and itchy, and her throat was dry. "I should probably—" She cleared her throat. "I should get home. I'm sure you guys have a lot to talk about." It was a private conversation, after all. And she wasn't family.

"Don't go." Logan started to stand. "You're part of this, too."

This time, she did look at him, all her fury simmering beneath the surface. "No," she said with finality. "I'm not." *Your uncle just made that very clear.*

Logan's eyes widened, and he sat back down. He could tell she wasn't happy. He looked confused. Concerned.

Yeah, right. Like he really cared. None of them truly cared about her, or her future. She was just Juliette to them. Good with plants. Good for a summer fling. Good for whatever they needed. But what about what *she* needed?

She walked into the house and grabbed her purse, then headed out the door to her car. She got into her car and started the engine, then pulled out of the driveway. She drove down the street, turned onto the highway, and burst into tears.

Chapter Twenty-Nine

The next morning, Juliette dug her hands into the earth, yanking fistfuls of it and scattering it behind her. She'd tossed the small hand shovel, preferring to feel the soil beneath her fingers as she worked. A potted azalea sat beside her, its cheerful pink blooms laughing in the face of her misery.

She stopped digging and wiped her forearm across her brow. For the past thirty minutes, she'd paced her garden in a fury, too upset to allow the familiar scents of earth and greenery to soothe her spirit. Nothing could soothe her spirit.

Romeo was giving the shop to Logan. His announcement had been like a dagger through her heart. How could Romeo do it, without a thought for her? How could Logan so easily agree to it? Granted, she'd never told him about her plans to own it, but that wasn't his business. It was *hers*.

"Juliette." Logan's voice behind her was careful, cautious. He stepped out of the woods into her yard.

Her anger spiked. He couldn't just step into her garden like it was his. Like he belonged there. He didn't. She hadn't invited him. They weren't family.

He stood near the arched trellis. The trellis she never asked him to build. "We should talk."

She lifted her chin and fixed her gaze coolly on his. "About what, the florist shop? No need. It's none of my business if Romeo wants you to have it. You're family, after all."

"Look, I didn't know he was going to leave it to me. I was just as surprised as you were." He approached her with measured strides, but she held out her hand. He stopped a few feet away. "Why are you so angry?"

Juliette scoffed. "For one thing, you know nothing about the business. The amount of knowledge you have about plants couldn't fit inside a teacup. For another, where does it leave me?"

"What's that supposed to mean?" he asked, frustrated. "You'd still be there."

"The shop was supposed to be *mine*." She jumped to her feet, balling her hands into fists. "I was planning to make Romeo an offer to buy it when he announced his retirement."

Logan looked shocked. "You never told me."

"Why would I?" she said angrily. "They were *my* plans. My future is none of your business."

He opened his mouth to speak, but she cut him off.

"I guess now you have more roots, don't you?" she said. "Your grandfather left you his house. Your uncle's leaving you his business. Are you planning on waiting for someone to find you a suitable wife, too?"

Now he looked pissed. Good. He could join the club.

"That's not fair," he said. "I can't help the way things have worked out with my family. And you know how I feel about you."

Right. When Logan accepted Romeo's offer, it had hurt. All along she told herself that she was in control, that she was just fine and they were just having fun. But the moment Logan agreed to take over his uncle's business, she realized a lot more than she'd wanted to believe. She'd trusted him, and not just with the shop. Opening up to him about her past, sharing their stories, spending all that time together . . . it had been special. She'd allowed herself to be vulnerable, because she trusted him with her feelings. And now he'd stepped all over them, just like he did years ago. Stupid Juliette!

"Let me guess," she said. "This is the part where you tell me how much you care about me, right? How you want us to be together and all that stuff."

A crease formed between Logan's brows. "I might as well say how I feel." His voice was low. Almost too low to hear.

"Don't bother," Juliette said. "Save it for someone who'll believe you."

His mouth drew into a hard line, and a muscle pulsed in his jaw. "What have I done to make you doubt my feelings?"

Juliette laughed. A cold, brittle sound that made the roses shiver on their stems. "You've taken the only thing I ever wanted. The one thing that mattered to me."

"How was I supposed to know you wanted to *own* it?" Logan's voice rose to match hers. "For god's sake, he's my uncle, Juliette. I was caught off guard; I didn't want to refuse him."

"How noble of you," she said, turning her back. She began digging again, ignoring him. "You can leave, now. We have nothing more to say."

"Like hell, I'll leave. I've got something to say that you need to hear."

Apprehension skittered up her spine. "I don't want to hear it."

"Too damn bad," he said. "You're going to hear this, because it's the truth."

She dug her hands into the soil, anchoring herself, wishing she could plug her ears and drown out every thought and feeling.

"I do care about you," he said quietly. "I love you."

It was three simple words. Three stupid syllables. But so powerful Juliette wanted to bury her head and sob. Why now, when everything was falling apart? When she was too old to believe in it?

"Everything that you are," Logan continued. He didn't sound angry anymore. He sounded determined.

Juliette felt as if her heart was bleeding out. She didn't want this. It was too much. "Don't."

"I want to keep what we have together, Juliette," he continued. "I want this to last."

She started pulling weeds, like it was any other normal day. Like he wasn't standing there telling her the exact thing she'd wanted so badly to hear since she was a young girl. But he was too late. Last night had been a painful reminder that she was truly on her own. She would never be safe if she wasn't in charge of her own future, and relying on a job with Logan as her boss just wouldn't work. Relationships ended. If her livelihood was tied to him, she'd always be at risk. Vulnerable. Merging her life so completely with his would just end in more heartbreak. She had to protect herself. She didn't have any more of herself to give. This had to end.

She turned slowly to face him, feigning a sense of calm she didn't feel. "We had some fun, Logan. That's all it was."

"I know you don't believe that." He looked like he could see right through her. "This thing between us is more than that."

"Is it?" If she was going to break away from him, she

needed to make it count. The first cut was always the deepest. Just get it over with. "Why do you think I sold Bella that perfume? I wanted you to get together. I knew she was into you, and I thought you guys would make a good couple. That's why she kept bothering you. That's why you kept taking her on dates. I wanted you to be with her."

Logan looked as though she'd slapped him.

It made her insides knot with guilt, but she ignored it, forcing her voice to stay even. "I never wanted this fling between us to last. It was just a silly diversion. Ask any of my friends. I was bored, anyway."

"You didn't seem bored when I met you in this garden the other night."

Juliette had a sudden flashback of them together, under the stars. The way he'd moved above her. The feeling of the damp grass beneath her naked back, and how his face blended with the night sky overhead until nothing had ever felt more perfect.

"It didn't mean anything," she managed. "If you somehow thought we'd continue working together like some happy couple? You were sorely mistaken."

"I thought you wanted to stay there forever. You said it was like your home away from home."

"Not if you're there," she threw back at him. Her voice sounded nonchalant, but inside she was dying. Why did this hurt so much? How had she let him get under her skin? "I want you to leave," she said, unable to face him. "It's over between us. Let's just call it what it was, okay? A summer fling. I don't want to see you anymore. I'm giving Romeo my two weeks' notice tomorrow."

Logan came and stood in front of her. "It doesn't have to end like this, Juliette. You're saying all these things be-cause you're afraid."

"I'm not afraid," she insisted. "I'm uninterested."

Logan shook his head, eyes snapping in anger. "For

someone who's so fiercely passionate about life, you are the biggest coward I've ever met."

Juliette jumped to her feet. "How dare you call me a coward? Don't you ever—"

"—You are. You're afraid, so you're saying hurtful things and pushing me away because you are afraid."

"If what I've told you hurts, then I'm sorry," she said. "But this is how I feel. You and I were never a thing. I don't want this." She gestured between them. "Don't you get it? I don't want . . . *you*." The words caught in her throat, raked across her tongue, snagged on her teeth, but she forced them out. The veil of apathy she was desperately trying to drape over herself chafed like a blanket of nettles. If Logan didn't leave soon, she was going to break down.

He waited. For what, she didn't know.

Luna stood beside him, glaring balefully at her.

"All right, Juliette," he said stiffly. "You got it." He walked away like a soldier. Head high, shoulders back, disappearing into the woods with purposeful strides.

Luna padded to the end of the garden, staring after him.

"He's gone," Juliette choked out. "It's better this way. We don't need him."

Luna turned to Juliette and did something she'd never done before in her life. She hissed at her.

Juliette gaped in astonishment. Her beloved cat, the cat who had been with her since birth, who had stood beside her after her mother died, and been with her after her father left. The cat who had remained her ally for everything life threw her way, was now taking sides. And it wasn't with her.

Chapter Thirty

Romeo,
    Please accept this as my official notice of
resignation, effective in two weeks. I will be accepting
another position and can no longer work here.
    Wishing you all the best in your future
endeavors,
                                    Juliette

Juliette refolded her hastily scrawled note and placed it back into her straw tote bag, then hung it on a peg near the shop sink. She'd just leave it on the cutting table for Romeo to find in the morning. The message was cold and formal, but it got the point across. As short as it was, getting the words on paper had sapped all her energy that morning. She'd risen at the crack of dawn and spent over an hour trying to gather the courage to write it. Of course, she had no other job lined up, but technically she hadn't lied. Eventually, she *would* be accepting another position, just as soon as she found one.

A hollow ache settled in the pit of her stomach. She'd never find another place to work that she loved this much. Everything had gone to hell, and here she was, sitting in the handbasket. If only Logan O'Connor had never come back to Pine Cove Island. If only her employer didn't feel obligated to leave his nephew a legacy. If only she hadn't felt so betrayed by both of them.

In a way, without realizing it, Juliette had begun to think of Romeo as family. He looked out for her and relied on her to take care of his shop. She trusted his judgment, and they'd worked very well together over the years. When he made his announcement at his house the night before, Juliette had felt as though he'd slapped her. How could Romeo betray her? His decision to leave his shop to Logan had made it very clear to Juliette that she wasn't "family." Not really. She may have spent years working and proving she belonged there, but in the end, she was still alone. Logan was Romeo's *real* family. Even though he hadn't been to Pine Cove Island in years, it didn't matter.

And then there was Logan. Hearing his casual acceptance of Romeo's offer had been like a kick to the stomach after she'd already gone down. Not only did Romeo prove through his actions that he valued Logan more, Logan had shown Juliette how little he valued her. There was a nagging ache in her chest, a heaviness that wouldn't go away, whenever she thought about the things she'd said back in her garden. But she wasn't going to waste her time looking at it too closely. What did it matter?

Juliette let out a harsh laugh. What did any of this matter? She yanked off her apron and placed the last vase of gladiolas in the walk-in refrigerator. The workday was over, and she'd fulfilled her obligations. The plants were thriving, the new floral arrangements were made, and orders had been filled. Without a future here, everything felt dull.

Her phone rang and she grabbed it, not recognizing the number. "Hello?"

"Mermaid!" Brock Templeton's fake Australian accent

boomed. "I haven't seen you in ages. What have you been up to?"

Oh, just sifting through the wreckage of my life. "Not much. What are you doing?"

"I'm standing outside your flowery store."

For a brief moment, his jovial voice lifted her spirits. Who the hell cared if his accent was fake? If his abs were airbrushed? At least he couldn't break her heart.

"Go around to the back patio," Juliette said quickly. "I'll let you in."

Brock was waiting on the patio with a boyish grin and a bottle of—giant surprise—fancy champagne. His hair was expertly tousled, which Juliette now knew was no accident. His clothes were casual, but expensive, and his shoes were so clean, they had to be brand new. There was nothing genuine about Brock, nothing sincere about the way he looked at her, and no chance in hell she could fall for anyone like him.

"Hey, girl," he said. "You want to come over to my place? We can watch Netflix and chill, or something."

Juliette blinked. That would be a rock-hard *pass*. She was suddenly so tired from everything that had happened recently. Maybe a little mindless distraction would do her some good. "Why don't we just hang out here?"

Brock's disappointed gaze roamed over the large patio. The wrought iron tables were inlaid with colorful mosaic designs, and the matching bistro chairs had multicolored cushions. There were canvas umbrellas over the tables, and the area was big enough for twenty or thirty people.

"All right," he said. "I guess this'll work."

Juliette went into the kitchen and grabbed a couple of glasses. He was just hanging up his phone when she joined him outside.

"I've only got these." She held up two drinking glasses. "Sorry we don't have any plastic beer cups."

Brock laughed. "The delivery doesn't matter." He popped open the champagne and poured them each a glass.

Juliette sat in a chair and propped her feet up on the chair opposite her. She took a gulp of champagne and leaned her head back to stare up at the sky. What was she going to do, now that owning the shop was out of the question? Where was she going to go?

"So what do you think, mermaid?" Brock said amiably.

"About what?" Juliette held out her glass for more champagne. This stuff was good. Maybe Brock's enthusiasm had merit.

"You and me," he said, pouring her some more. "I'll be out of here soon. And I think you and I should—"

"Yeah, yeah." Juliette waved her hand. "You think we should bang."

"Exactly," he said, clinking his glass against hers.

"You know you can drop the accent, right?"

Brock looked perplexed for a moment. "Well, it's easier to stay in character if I maintain it—you feel me?"

Yeah, she felt him. If only her life were as simple as his. If only all she had to worry about was looking good, drinking champagne, and keeping up appearances.

Two glasses of champagne later, a group of people came around from the side walkway, chattering and laughing.

"Oi! We're back here," Brock called. He leaned forward to refill her glass. "I invited some of my mates from the camera crew, if that's all right. We've grown tired of hanging out on the houseboat, and O'Malley's Pub is all right, but the *plebs*." He shuddered.

"What do you mean?"

He made a face. "You know, those z-grade scrubbers and blokes yelling at the game on TV all the time. They're so basic."

"They're locals." Irritation pricked at her skin. Brock obviously thought the people of Pine Cove Island were beneath him. She held out her glass for more champagne. Nothing like some liquid sunshine to drown out everyone's shady flaws.

He poured her another glass and waved to his buddies.

Juliette was not surprised to see they were all wearing black. Three of the guys had on baseball caps and carried a cooler between them. Two others had messenger bags.

"Do you guys always dress in black?" Juliette asked. But it was more like a giggle. She was beginning to feel fuzzy from all the bubbly.

"It's in our contract," one of the younger guys said. He looked like he was in his early twenties, with wispy brown hair and a barely there goatee. The other two guys set the cooler down and opened the lid to reveal more bottles of champagne.

The guy with the goatee seemed unimpressed with the patio. "So this is where you work?"

She shook her head. "Not for long. I gave my notice today." She kept her tone light, trying desperately to mask the sharp pain clawing at her insides. "So I'm almost out of here."

"Well, this is a celebration then," Brock said cheerfully. "It's your going away party."

Sure it was. Juliette downed the rest of her champagne, and Brock refilled it. Why the hell shouldn't she party? A few drinks never hurt anyone. And she'd just closed the shop for the day, so it wasn't like they'd be bothering any customers. Romeo wasn't coming in until tomorrow, and she might as well enjoy what little time she had left there.

For the next two hours, Juliette drank and chatted with Brock and his equally shallow buddies. They talked about celebrities sleeping with other celebrities, who had the best cars, how much money people were worth, and all things wonderfully superficial. None of them asked her about herself, her past, or what she liked or didn't like.

Nobody expected her to say much of anything. All she had to do was hang out and be Brock's arm charm. And drink. There was something comforting about it. In the back of her mind, she knew she'd have to go back to real life, but for now, this was an easy escape.

She peered down into her empty glass and hiccupped. "I'm tanked."

Brock, who was discussing workout routines with one of the crew members, turned and laid a hand on her knee. "What's that, luv?"

"I said"—Juliette showed him her glass—"I'm deep in my cups."

He cocked his head. "Ay?"

"Three sheets to the wind," Juliette explained with a giggle. "Hammered. Wasted."

"Oh, right. You and me both," Brock said, holding up his beer.

Wait, there was beer? She looked around, her vision a little foggier than usual. A large group of people were smoking and drinking, lounging on the patio furniture. Someone had brought in a keg, and two guys were filling cups for a milling group of revelers.

She frowned. There had to be about twenty or thirty people on the patio now. Someone had turned on a portable speaker and a group of girls in shorts and bikini tops were dancing on the freshly planted grass, the tiny green shoots trampled beneath their feet.

Juliette pointed at the grass. "Stop that."

No one seemed to hear her. One guy had turned on the garden hose, causing shrieks of laughter as he sprayed people at random. Two guys were arm wrestling at one of the patio tables. Somebody dropped a beer bottle and it shattered on the slate, causing more laughter.

The entire back patio looked like a scene from one of Brock's stupid beach shows.

This wasn't good. She shook her head, trying to clear it. Her limbs felt heavy, like she was moving underwater.

"Here you go, luv," Brock said, handing her another glass.

"No." Juliette pushed it away and rose unsteadily to her feet. "You guys should go."

"But it's barely sundown," Brock said. "Come on. Dance with me." He took their drinks, set them on the table, and snaked his arms around her waist.

The patio seemed to tilt as he jostled them back and forth, completely off beat to the song playing on the speakers.

Juliette's stomach lurched. "I need to sit down."

"Okay, but first, give us a kiss," Brock teased. Before she could protest, he covered her mouth with his. His lips were clammy, and he tasted like warm beer and cigarettes.

She grabbed his shoulders and yanked away, causing them both to stumble.

Brock caught her in his arms and started to laugh.

But Juliette wasn't laughing. She was staring over Brock's shoulder at the man standing near the side gate. The man who was looking at her with an expression she didn't care to analyze. He wasn't laughing, either.

Chapter Thirty-One

The look on Logan's face was worse than anything she could've imagined. It was cold and distant, and such a far cry from the way he used to look at her.

She yanked herself out of Brock's arms and staggered back, falling into a cushioned seat with a jarring thud. Everyone else seemed too busy partying to notice Logan's glowering presence.

For the longest ten seconds of her life, Logan stared at her, unmoving, unblinking. His eyes were creased at the corners, his jaw clenched in what she could only guess was anger and condemnation.

Juliette dropped her head. She couldn't look at him right now. She needed to go home and curl up in a ball and die.

Logan walked swiftly over to the music and shut it off.

"Party's over," he said. "Everyone leave." It was the voice of a commanding officer, a voice that suffered no fools. Took no prisoners. There was absolutely no mistaking that he was the man in charge. "Now."

People grumbled, but gathered their things and began shuffling out of the yard through the side gate. All except Brock.

"Come on, you gotta lighten up, mate," Brock said,

oblivious to the tension in the air between Logan and Juliette. "Sometimes it's good to just hang, you know?"

A muscle clenched in Logan's jaw as he pointed to the side gate. "Get. Out."

Brock's lip curled, and he looked at Juliette. "Can you believe this tosser? No wonder you quit your job." He picked up his beer, finished it off, then tossed it onto the patio in smug defiance.

Logan's eyes narrowed. He walked up to Brock. "Pick it up."

"Sod off," Brock said with a sneer. He started to shove Logan away.

Logan gripped Brock by the shirt and lifted him as easily as if he were a cardboard cutout.

"Oi! Get your hands off me." Brock jerked away, staggering. For a moment, he looked like he wanted to start a real fight with Logan, then seemed to think better of it. Maybe he wasn't so stupid after all. "I'm out of here," Brock said, turning to Juliette. "But the party's not over for us, right, luv?" He cocked his head toward the side gate. "Let's go back to the houseboat."

"No." She was tired of everyone, and everything. "I've had enough."

His expression turned petulant. "What about the plan? You know, we were going to . . ." He wiggled his eyebrows. Because he was the king of subtlety. If he'd made a hole with one hand and repeatedly stuck his pointer finger in and out of it, she wouldn't have been surprised.

Juliette shook her aching head. "Not happening."

Brock looked angry now. He glanced back and forth between Logan and Juliette. "All you locals suck, you know that?"

Before Logan could react, Juliette rushed to stand between them. "Just leave, Brock. You're better off sticking with people way up on your level."

When he didn't move right away, Juliette gave a little wave. "Cheerio, mate."

She watched him storm away, then she went into the kitchen to get a broom.

When she came back out, Logan was standing on the patio looking at the mess.

Juliette cringed. There was broken glass on the slate rock and spilled beer on the seat cushions.

Humiliation reared its ugly head, and she squeezed her eyes shut. She'd messed up, bad. Inviting Brock to hang out had been the stupidest of ideas. And now Logan was here to witness her disgrace.

Logan took the broom from her hands and began sweeping.

Now she felt worse. Why was he helping her? Oh, yeah, because the place was going to be his.

"I'll do it," Juliette said irritably. She tried to take the broom, but he held it away.

"Just go home, Juliette." He didn't look her in the eye. It was clear he was disappointed in her.

Why did it hurt so much? Why did she even care? She shouldn't. He was the one who'd betrayed her and ruined everything. "I can clean this up myself," she said sharply.

"Like hell you can," Logan shot back. "You're drunk, Juliette. If you don't call a ride, I'll drive you home. But either way, you're leaving."

"I don't need you to drive me home," she said. "You've done enough to *help* me, thanks."

"I'm not the one who trashed the patio with my drinking buddies," he said in an icy voice. "You say you just want to have fun and you don't want to take things seriously, but you expect Romeo to just turn over his business to you when it's clear you haven't grown up."

"Oh, I haven't grown up?" Who the hell did he think he was, lecturing her? "I've taken care of myself my whole life. You're the one who's been given everything. Don't you dare accuse me of not being grown up."

Logan stopped sweeping and pierced her with a cold, penetrating stare. "You say you care about the shop. That you love plants and this place is everything you've ever wanted." He swept his arm out wide. "Is this what you want?"

The backyard was completely trashed. Empty plastic cups and fast food wrappers were scattered on the ground. Crushed cigarette butts littered the tall flower urns, and water spewed from the forgotten garden hose, flooding the trampled grass.

She suddenly felt ill. Logan had a point, and she didn't like it. She couldn't think of a single thing to say that would fix things. It was clear he thought she was incapable. By morning, the note she'd left for Romeo wouldn't even matter. Logan would have told him about tonight's mess, and Romeo would probably fire her.

She went into the kitchen and called Emma to come get her. Twenty excruciating minutes later, Juliette was on the highway heading home.

Logan placed the last glass in the kitchen sink and put away the broom. After Juliette left, he'd spent the hour cleaning up the mess. Now all evidence of the party was gone, with only the trampled seedlings to tell the story of what had transpired. In the morning, he could easily reseed the grass, and it would grow in no time. He'd learned that from Juliette. She'd inadvertently taught him a lot about growing things. Plants were her "people," after all.

A sharp ache lanced through him when he'd watched Juliette leave in Emma's car. The bond between them was broken. He'd ruined it by accepting Romeo's offer without thinking it over. He'd had no idea how much it would hurt her. And now she didn't want anything to do with him.

Logan squeezed his eyes shut and rubbed a hand over his face. Juliette was as complicated as the wild roses growing in the woods near her house. Gorgeous and alluring and prickly and unforgiving. What had ever made him think things could work between them?

When Romeo had announced his news, Logan had felt a fierce sense of relief. He'd believed it was a starting point for Juliette and him to have a life together. He already knew he wanted her, and this was a way to guarantee that their lives would be intertwined. She'd never be happy without the florist shop, and if he was a permanent part of it—the owner—then they could stay together. Now he realized what a mistake he'd made. He shouldn't have tried to force it.

But none of that mattered because she didn't want him anyway. Hell, she'd even tried to get Bella and him together. If he'd somehow hoped Juliette would come to her senses and take back the painful things she'd said in her garden, the scene on the patio—her in Brock's arms—finally brought home what he should've known earlier. She really didn't want him. He needed to accept it. They were all wrong for each other, and he'd been too stupid to see it. Until now.

He let out a frustrated breath and did a final check of the back patio and gardens. Everywhere he looked, he saw Juliette's influence. Her love and care of the plants was evident in all the details, from the carefully chosen terra-cotta pots for the gardenias along the walkway, to the hanging flower baskets under the eaves.

Back in the kitchen, a folded piece of paper lay in the middle of the table. He felt a deep sense of foreboding as he opened the single sheet and read the short note.

So she really was leaving.

Logan gripped the note in his hand, overcome with anger and frustration and guilt and sadness. This place was hers, more than it could ever be his. Even though she'd made it clear she didn't want him, she could still have the shop. There was no way he'd ever be able to continue running the business without her. He didn't even want to. She'd poured everything she was into this place.

Logan crumpled the piece of paper in his fist and tossed it in the trash. In two strides, he was out the door and headed to his truck, with only one destination in mind.

Chapter Thirty-Two

The dawn came earlier than usual. Or maybe she just wanted to hide from the things that felt too raw to face in the light. Juliette cracked open one eye and scowled. The sun shoved its way over the horizon, surprising her at its audacity, bathing the world outside her window in rosy streaks until everything glowed fresh and warm and new.

She turned away and drew the covers up under her chin.

Luna meowed loudly from the bedroom doorway.

"I'm not going."

Another meow.

"Because it's my day off. I'm going to sleep in like a normal person, for a change."

A soft growl.

"I am sleeping. Or I would be, if you weren't bothering me."

Juliette felt the cat jump onto the bed, stepping gingerly over the coverlet until she reached the pillow. A cold nose nudged her temple.

Mrreow!

"Ugh." She sat up and rubbed her face. Freaking cat. "Has anyone ever told you that you're a pain in the butt?"

Luna licked her paw, ignoring her.

"Don't pretend like you don't understand me." Juliette pointed to the cat. "You." She held her arms out wide. "Big pain." She pointed to her backside. "Butt."

The cat turned her back on Juliette and jumped onto the windowsill.

Juliette shook her head, then winced. Her temples throbbed with one of the worst hangovers she'd ever had. It had been a terrible last few days. She'd broken up with Logan, lost her chance at owning the shop and securing her future, and was now soon-to-be jobless. What next?

Her cell phone rang, and she checked it. Romeo.

Nope. She wasn't up for that conversation. By now, he'd have heard about the after-hours party she'd thrown on the back patio. No doubt, Logan had given Romeo all the details of the disaster, and the mess her little Hollywood "friends" had caused. Romeo was probably calling to tell her not to bother with the two weeks.

"Yesterday was the biggest pile of crap, ever," she said to Luna's back.

The cat was clearly sulking, because she didn't bother turning around.

Juliette raised a hand to her pounding head. "And today's going to be even worse."

After zombie-shuffling to the medicine cabinet for some aspirin, she stepped into the shower and tried to scrub herself awake. By the time she emerged ten minutes later, her headache was still going strong but at least she was clean.

She didn't bother getting dressed, choosing instead to slip on a clean nightgown and towel dry her hair. But the friction of the towel against her pounding head was too much, so she left her hair to dry on its own and padded toward the kitchen. How much did she drink last night?

The phone rang again. Romeo again.

She ignored it. Again.

Coffee, and then she'd figure out what to do. Coffee was nectar of the gods. It always helped. She dug around in the bottom of the canister with a growing sense of dread. The plastic scoop scraped against the empty metal container.

"You have got to be kidding me." This was boss-level bad. If caffeine didn't enter her bloodstream within the next five minutes, she was going to implode like a dying star.

Juliette tossed the scoop into the empty canister and turned away in disgust. Her car was still parked outside the shop, which meant she couldn't leave until Emma showed up later.

What now? Get in bed and ignore the world?

The phone rang a third time. Romeo, of course.

Why not talk to him and get it over with? The conversation would be the rotten cherry on top of her rotten life. She grabbed her cell and jumped in. "Hello."

"Hey, hun. I've been trying to call you all morning," Romeo said.

He was still calling her hun, even though she'd screwed up royally and he was going to fire her ass. It made it almost worse.

"I was sleeping," she said in a shaky voice.

"Sleeping? You're usually up with the sun. Are you sick?"

She took a deep breath. Obviously, he knew she was hungover. Logan would've told him everything by now. "What do you want to say, Romeo?"

"I wanted to tell you that Logan came to see me last night."

Yeah, I'll bet he did. "Great."

"And he and I had a long talk."

"Look, you don't have to drag it out," Juliette said. "Just tell me I'm fired."

"Fired?" Romeo started to laugh. "You're crazy, hun."

"You wouldn't be the first person who's told me that."

"Of course you're not fired. I'm calling to tell you that Logan and I had a long talk about you. We've both decided that the shop should be yours. You're the one who cares most about it anyway, and I know you'll take good care of it. So I'm calling to find out if you still want it."

Juliette's heart did a little tap dance along her rib cage. "What?"

"My florist shop. Logan convinced me that no one can love the business more than you. He said you were the only person who could ever do a better job than me, and I have to agree. To be honest, it didn't take much convincing on his part. All your hard work and dedication, and the leaps and bounds you've made with organization—all of it's proof that you're the best fit. So I'm just calling to let you know it's yours, if you still want it."

Juliette gripped her phone and gave a tiny exhale. "Yes."

"I only offered it to Logan because I wanted my nephew to start a life here. He came home with no set plans after leaving the army. I wanted to give him a chance to have roots here again. I thought he wanted to stay, but I was wrong."

"What do you mean?"

"He said he's grateful for the opportunity I offered, but it's not really what he wants. He's moving to Florida, too."

Panic sliced through her. "He's leaving?"

"Yes. He's putting the house up for sale, just after he finishes dealing with the yard. I guess there's a sick tree that needs to come down. After that, he'll be moving on."

Juliette felt as if a jagged rock was lodged in her throat. She kept trying to swallow around it, but the pain didn't ease. Romeo kept talking, but she barely heard what he was saying. Somewhere in the back of her mind, she knew she should be thrilled with this news. Her dream of owning the shop was finally happening, but the emptiness eating away at her insides felt nothing like victory, and everything like defeat.

She hung up the phone, cutting Romeo off midsentence, and ran for the door.

Chapter Thirty-Three

Her body ached from the hangover, but Juliette didn't care. She felt as if someone had run her entire life through a blender with no lid on. Everywhere she turned, everything was a mess.

She ran through the woods to Logan's house, her mind in a state of chaos. Branches snagged in her hair. Roots caught underfoot. Always before, the natural ebb and flow of nature surrounded her and the trees swayed to let her pass, but today the turmoil inside her was too much to contain. It permeated every thought, every movement. For the first time in her life, she felt out of sync with nature. She was moving too quickly for the breeze to make room for her. The anxious energy flowing through her set the woods on edge. She could feel it, but she had to get to Logan.

She pushed aside a heavy pine branch and sidestepped a fallen log, continuing toward the only thing that truly mattered.

When Romeo told her that Logan had given up the shop and was planning to leave, everything seemed to slow down. When Romeo announced he was leaving the shop to her, she felt a flicker of comprehension followed by a tiny leap of pleasure, but it sputtered and died out. None of it seemed to matter. Logan was leaving.

Juliette ran faster, just a hundred feet away from Logan's property now. Pain sliced through her throbbing head. She'd forgotten to drink water, which made it even worse, but she didn't care. She wasn't even properly dressed, in bare feet and her nightgown, but none of that mattered, either. She needed to talk to him. She needed to tell him so many things.

By the time she emerged onto his property, she was gasping for breath. She ran onto his back porch and banged her fist on the door.

When he didn't answer, she banged again.

Nothing.

Juliette ran to the front of the house and tried the doorbell, knocking again and again. His truck was in the driveway, so he had to be home. Maybe he was ignoring her. It was a terrible thing to contemplate. Worse, still, was the FOR SALE sign at the end of the driveway.

She slumped against the door. It was all true. He was really leaving. She bumped the back of her head against the door. How had everything gone so horribly wrong?

The door swung open and she stumbled back, catching herself on the door frame. When she turned around, Logan was there.

His hair was damp and he was shirtless, in nothing but a pair of unbuttoned jeans. He held a towel in one hand, and he smelled like fresh soap. His expression was carefully neutral. Controlled.

Juliette swallowed past the ache in her throat. "I thought you weren't home."

"I was in the shower."

She opened her mouth, but nothing came out.

A bird cried somewhere in the distance.

The wind kicked up and Juliette shivered, rubbing one

bare foot over the other. Get it together. Say what you need to say. Grow up! "I . . ." She faltered. Tried again. "I just came to say thank you. For convincing Romeo to let me have the shop."

A slight incline of his head. Nothing else.

She still couldn't read his expression. It had never occurred to her how good he could be at closing himself off. He'd always been so open with her.

She cleared her throat. "Why did you do it?" *Say it was because you want me. Say you're not leaving. Tell me you'll stay.*

Logan's eyes were as cold and dark as the sky on a moonless night. "I decided it just wasn't what I wanted. I thought I could start a life here, but I've changed my mind."

Juliette bit the inside of her cheek, feeling as if the ground was crumbling underneath her.

"Why?" she whispered.

Logan gave a half shrug. "There's nothing here that interests me. Least of all, the shop. It was always meant for you."

She crossed her arms, digging her fingernails into her hands. *There's nothing here that interests me.* "Logan," she began. *Don't go. Don't leave me. Please.* "You don't have to leave."

"I want to."

She steadied herself on the door frame.

"I'm heading down to Florida where my parents are," he continued. "Just as soon as I clean up the yard and . . ." His expression faltered. For the first time since he'd opened the door, Juliette saw pain in his eyes. "As soon as the arborists take down the tree."

She looked at the dying tree in the yard, its branches brittle and mottled. Dead leaves were piled beneath it. "What about your treehouse?"

Logan's expression was blank again. "Some things aren't meant to last, remember?"

They were her own words, and she hated them. She suddenly hated the natural order of things. Why did things have to die? Why did the people she loved always have to leave?

A bolt of shock slammed into her.

Juliette blinked rapidly, stumbling backward. People she *loved*.

Logan reached out, but she caught herself on the porch railing. "I'm fine." Except she loved him. *She loved him.* She felt sick. Anchorless. Like she was careening out into the atmosphere where the air was much thinner and she had nothing to hold on to. She took an unsteady breath.

"Are you sick?" He started to move toward her.

"No." She held out a hand, as if she could keep her feelings for him at arm's length. As if somehow, she could save herself from the crushing revelation that, even though she'd been so careful, she lost her heart to him anyway. "I'm just tired." *And also, I'm an utter fool because I love you.*

Maybe she should tell him. Maybe it wasn't too late. Or maybe it was too late, and he'd leave and her heart would crack wide open all over again, just like when she was a kid. Only this time, it would be way worse. This time she truly knew him. They'd shared more than just an awkward teenage kiss. Somehow, without her even realizing it, they'd become wrapped around each other like the vines in her garden—so intertwined that if you tried to untangle one from the other, they'd break.

"Logan," she began.

"Juliette, don't. Let's not draw this out any further than it needs to. We both know this was never going to go anywhere. I only think you knew it before I did. Look, I want you to be happy, and I'm glad you're getting the shop. You deserve it more than I ever did."

From inside his house, the phone rang.

"I have to go," he said. "I've got things to take care of."

"I'm sorry," she whispered. She didn't want him to go. She was suddenly a little girl again. Nine years old at her mother's funeral, watching the coffin lowering into the ground. Watching people scatter soil over the lid. Watching her yellow rose land on the polished casket, its petals breaking off and falling apart. She was suddenly eighteen years old again, waving good-bye to her father. Watching him place the last of his suitcases in the trunk of his car. Feeling Luna's soft fur rub soothingly against her ankles as her father shut the trunk. Hearing his promise to call, once he reached California. Knowing he probably wouldn't.

She squeezed her eyes shut and opened them again, trying to see a way out. But all she saw was him. "I don't want you to leave," she said shakily.

"Stop," Logan said. A muscle clenched in his jaw. "Don't make this more than it is. You were right. I was trying to force things that were just never there. I don't want to stay anymore. There's nothing here for me except my dead grandfather's house and a dying tree."

Tears pricked the corners of her eyes.

"I'm going," he said resolutely. "You should go, too." He backed into the house. "Good-bye, Juliette."

The door shut on a soft *click* that hit her like a bullet through the heart.

Chapter Thirty-Four

Juliette backed away, stumbling blindly down the porch steps, making her way through the overgrown grass toward the woods.

Just inside the tree line, she lowered herself to the ground and gasped. What had she done? All this time she thought she'd been shielding her heart from pain. Never letting anyone get too close. Never getting involved. All this time she thought she'd mastered the trick of staying out of the game and staying safe. But now, Logan was leaving for good, and there was a crushing ache inside her chest and limbs that proved she'd been a fool. Somewhere along the way, she'd let him into her heart. That's why she'd been so happy with him. The thing she'd always been afraid of—being vulnerable—was the only thing that had made it possible.

She pushed to her feet and looked back at the house, the yard, the dying tree.

Some things aren't meant to last, remember?

But some things were. She understood that now. Some things never went away. Her love for her mother, who'd died too young. Her love for her father, whose grief took him away. Her love for her cousin Emma, and their grandmother who'd left them the Holloway legacy. People came and went, but Juliette's love for them never wavered. She loved all of them, and that would never change.

The ancient tree swayed in the wind, its brown leaves rustling on the dying branches.

She stared at it through her tears, her heart aching for the majestic thing it used to be.

Logan loved this tree.

A gust of wind plucked withered leaves from the branches, sending them scattering into the yard.

She loved Logan.

When a small branch snapped and dropped to the ground, Juliette felt as if a dam was cracking inside her. She was suddenly flooded with the desire to make things right. It was too late to fix what she'd broken between them, but she could fix one thing. She could at least prove to him that some things were meant to last. Maybe he'd leave forever, but she could save his tree. Save the memories they'd shared in it. And even though she may never see him again, she'd still have it to remind her.

Juliette wiped a shaking hand over her eyes. Her limbs were weak, and her body was dehydrated, but she didn't care. Tongue like sandpaper, head screaming in protest, she marched toward the tree with one precious goal. She had to fix it. What mattered was saving the tree. Mother Nature had always been on her side. Juliette knew if she threw her whole heart into it, she could do it. Everything else might be falling down around her, but this one thing, she could fix.

At the base of the tree, she placed her hands on the trunk and closed her eyes, concentrating on the earth beneath her feet, and searching for the spark of recognition—the connection with Mother Nature that always stirred inside her.

When she found it, she pressed her fingers into the bark, throwing her energy into it, straining to connect to the withered fibers and the damaged cells. Without thinking, she climbed higher into the branches, her hands brushing delicately over the brittle limbs. With every breath, she poured everything she had into the ancient tree, willing it to heal.

Again and again, Juliette breathed life into the tree. She could feel the energy from her body flowing into it, healing it from the inside. She was distantly aware of Logan leaving his house, getting into his truck and driving away, but she didn't have the energy to think about it. With every movement and every breath, she focused on healing. She climbed higher, ignoring the throbbing pain in her body. If she could just save this one thing he loved, then she would have done something right.

Somewhere near the entrance to the treehouse, hope surged inside her. Juliette sensed the exact moment something shifted within the heart of the tree. New growth pushed its way up through the trunk from deep within the earth. Suddenly, everything sprang to life and the sickness began to fade. Her limbs shook, and it took everything she had to cling to the branch, but inside she rejoiced.

The old maple tree began healing before her eyes, its branches stretching and reaching toward the sky. Tiny leaves unfurled, lush and vibrant, growing and multiplying and spreading into a kaleidoscopic canopy of green above her. Within minutes, the tree was larger and healthier than it had ever been. The sickness was gone.

She'd saved it.

Juliette could barely stay awake. The treehouse entrance was only a few inches to her left. If she could reach it, she could drag herself inside before she collapsed. Slowly, feeling as though she were moving underwater, she reached out, stretching her fingertips toward the ledge. She lifted both hands, braced her feet against a lower branch, and jumped.

Her hands slapped against the floorboards of the tree-house entrance. She scrabbled to grab on to something, but her hands felt clumsy. Her fingertips scraped against the rough wooden planks. For one fraction of a second, she thought she was going to make it. Then she slipped.

Falling wasn't so bad, Juliette thought dimly. The leaves blurred past her in myriad shades of green. The wind was cool against her heated cheeks, and the breeze caught at her nightgown, floating it around her in a peaceful arc.

It was the unforgiving earth that surprised her.

Logan sat in his real estate agent's office, watching her gather the final documents together for the sale of his house. Her office was as gray as her simple, pinstriped suit. Everything was angular and modern, with nothing but a small plastic plant on the corner of her desk to indicate a semblance of life. She was all business, which he'd do well to appreciate. He wanted to sell his house as quickly as possible.

"Even though it needs some work, your house should sell fast," she told Logan, placing his file on the desk in front of her. "It's near a greenbelt overlooking the ocean, so it's a prime location."

Logan slid his chair back and stood, focusing on the tasks ahead of him. He refused to allow himself to think of anything else. Especially not Juliette. "Everything's in order then?"

The agent assured him things were fine and that she'd contact him soon.

Logan left the office with a dark sense of resignation

and got into his truck to head home. His parents had called to say that they were looking forward to seeing him, and the Florida weather was beautiful. He even had a job waiting for him. An old military buddy owned a construction company and needed someone to manage it. All things considered, his future looked promising.

He turned his truck onto the highway, gripping the steering wheel with bleak determination. It was pointless to think about Juliette and the future he'd wanted with her. She'd made it more than clear she didn't feel the same way. Learning she'd purposefully sold Bella that Desire perfume had been a blow to his pride. It hurt to know Juliette was behind all that nonsense, even though the magic never worked on him. Hell, the only desire he ever felt with Bella was the desire to eat. No wonder he was always starving whenever she came around.

Then when Juliette told him he had just been a casual fling, it had been a blow to much more than just his pride. All this time, he'd been falling in love with her. He wanted her more than anything he'd ever wanted in his life, but she didn't want him. She never did. And he just had to get on with it.

Logan pulled into his driveway, feeling a heavy sense of defeat when he saw the FOR SALE sign in his front yard. Juliette had been right. For all his intentions of keeping his grandfather's house and rebuilding his life, some things just weren't meant to last. Even the old tree in the backyard had tried to tell him.

He glanced over at it and slammed on the breaks, his car skidding to a halt in the gravel driveway.

The tree was enormous and bursting with life. It now stood like a mighty sentinel in his yard. Where once the branches were withered and brittle, they now stretched twice as large as before, reaching toward the sky in a thick canopy of vibrant green leaves.

Impossible.

Something white fluttered in the tall grass beneath it. It was like a scrap of cloth, or— Cold fear gripped him.

He shot out of the car and ran, heart thumping in panic, dread coursing through his veins at what he would find.

Juliette lay sprawled under the tree in the grass. One arm was twisted under her, the white nightgown bunched around her legs. Mud caked her feet, and there was a scrape on her forehead against skin so pale, she looked . . .

"Juliette!" Logan fell to the ground beside her. He pressed his ear to her chest. She was still breathing, thank god. He pulled his cell phone from his pocket and dialed 911. In a steady, monotone voice he told the operator the necessary details.

When he hung up, he checked her vital signs again and smoothed her hair gently back from her face with a shaking hand. She'd done the impossible. She'd healed his tree, but the cost had been far too precious. Nothing was worth her life. Nothing. A cold terror gripped him. What if she didn't wake up? "Why, Juliette?" he said shakily. "Why did you do this?"

Her eyelids fluttered.

Logan's heart flatlined, then kicked into overdrive. "Juliette. Can you hear me?"

She opened her eyes a fraction and winced.

"Don't move," Logan commanded, fear raising his voice to a near shout. "Help is coming. Stay completely still, do you understand?" He sounded harsh, he knew, but it took every ounce of willpower he had to stay calm. "Keep still."

Her lips moved like she was trying to say something.

Logan leaned down until his face was only inches from hers.

A faint whisper. "Bossy."

He squeezed his eyes shut. She was killing him. He wanted to throw his head back and roar. He should never have asked her to help save the tree. He should've been there to stop her. "Why did you do it, Juliette?" he choked out. "Why would you risk your life for nothing?"

"Not nothing." Her whisper was barely audible over the wind. "Everything."

The next morning, Juliette sat in her hospital bed feeling exhausted and heartsick. It was past six o'clock, and she'd slept like the dead. On any other day she'd be in her garden by now, curled up in her favorite quilt with Luna. And after everything that had happened yesterday, it was the only place she could think of that would bring her comfort. She rubbed her aching head. "How much longer is this going to take?"

Emma patted her hand from a chair by the bed. "You have a concussion, and you were dehydrated when you got here yesterday. They're not going to just let you dance out of here first thing in the morning."

"I'm totally fine," Juliette insisted, even though it wasn't true. Her mind strayed to Logan and she squeezed her eyes shut. Her heart ached, her body ached, and yesterday had been a disaster. But she'd saved the tree. That was something. She'd saved Logan's tree.

"Logan was here all night," Emma said, as if reading her mind. "He was a wreck, Juliette. Pacing back and forth in the waiting room like a caged lion until the nurse said we could come in. And once he saw you passed out with that IV in your arm, he looked even worse."

Juliette glanced at the cotton ball taped to the inside of her elbow where they'd given her an IV drip. Thankfully, she didn't need it anymore. "He came to see me?"

Emma nodded. "He stayed here all night until I finally made him go home. I told him I planned to stay at your house for the next couple of days, and the doctor had to assure him three times that you were completely fine, before he'd leave."

Juliette twisted the corner of her bedsheet between her fingers. "Did he . . ." She swallowed. "Did he say anything?"

Emma's eyes filled with compassion and understanding. It made Juliette want to cry. "He said he was sorry. He wanted me to tell you that."

Juliette closed her eyes. He was sorry. So was she. How had everything gone so wrong between them?

"And when he left, he said he had to go take care of something, but he'd be back."

Juliette looked at Emma. "Back when?" Was he coming back to say a final good-bye? She didn't want him to. Not today. Not when she already felt so broken. It would be too much to bear.

Emma shook her head. "I don't know. He wasn't very talkative. Mostly he just hovered in here like a silent thundercloud, glaring at the poor doctor and nurse whenever they came to check on you. And when I finally convinced him it was okay to go, he stormed out like he was on a mission. I think the nurse would've kicked him out long before I did if she hadn't thought he was part of the family."

At the mention of Logan being a part of the family, Juliette turned to stare at the wall. She didn't want Emma to see how bleak and hopeless she felt. If only she hadn't hurt him with her careless words that day in her garden. If only she hadn't been so afraid to tell him the truth.

Chapter Thirty-Five

Several days later . . .

"Ms. Holloway?"

Juliette glanced up from the inventory list she'd been putting together.

Her new employee, Felicity, walked into the back room with a watering can. She was a bright seventeen-year-old with thick glasses, a quirky grin, and a genuine interest in plants. "Should I water the ferns by the front window?"

"Yes, that would be perfect. Thank you." Juliette watched the young woman go, grateful for her new hire. Ever since the accident several days ago, so much had changed. She gripped the splint on her wrist and flexed her fingers. They said she'd been lucky. It was just a sprain and it would be better in no time. The doctor had been mystified that she'd only suffered a mild concussion when she fell from the tree, but Juliette imagined the tree had something to do with it. She vaguely remembered the branches reaching out to break her fall.

"Hey, you." Kat bustled through the back door with

Hank at her heels. Edgar the crow was perched on her shoulder. If a bird could have an expression, his could only be described as pure triumph.

Juliette grinned. "Do you know there's a bird on your shoulder?"

Kat rolled her eyes. "Yeah, I've given up. He follows me everywhere, anyway. Stupid Cheetos. I should've known better." She gave Edgar an affectionate pat, then turned back to Juliette. "I came to see if you're meeting us for lunch. Emma and the girls said to tell you the bridesmaid dresses are ready for fitting."

Juliette put the inventory list neatly into her small desk drawer. "Tell them I'll be there in twenty minutes."

"You bet. Oh." Kat pointed to Juliette's hair on her way out the door. "I'm loving your new look, by the way. It makes you look like a superhero." She waved good-bye, then closed the door behind her.

Juliette brushed a lock of hair behind her ear. A one-inch streak near her temple was now snowy white. Emma said it was probably because she gave so much of her energy to heal the tree. Neither of them knew if it would stay, but Juliette didn't mind it. Every time she looked in the mirror, it reminded her of Logan.

Her heart ached at the thought of him. He hadn't returned that morning at the hospital, and she still hadn't seen him. She tried to tell herself that it was fine; she'd saved his tree and that's what mattered. But it still hurt that he hadn't come back. Even if only to say good-bye.

"Ms. Holloway?" Felicity poked her head around the corner. "There's a customer out front who wants to buy some flowers."

Juliette nodded absently. "The summer bouquets are in the cold case."

"No, not a bouquet. This." Felicity held up a ceramic pot

of petunias. It was the same petunia plant Logan had been mangling the first day he walked into her shop. The bitter-sweet reminder of it made Juliette's heart ache even more.

"How much is it?" Felicity asked.

Juliette shook her head. She'd been meaning to take the plant home. "That's not for sale. Show them the geraniums instead."

Felicity left to deal with the customer, returning a few moments later. "He says it has to be this exact plant, and no other will do." She gave the flowers a dubious look. "And he says not to worry because he's really good at handling petunias?"

Juliette's mouth opened on a tiny inhale. She rose un-steadily from her desk chair, unlacing the dirt-smudged apron from around her waist and hanging it on a peg near the kitchen sink. Or at least, she tried. It fell to the floor, but she didn't care. With slightly shaky hands, she smoothed her hair and walked into the front room.

Logan stood near the large window looking tired, but otherwise the same as always. Beautiful.

He gave her that half smile full of secrets. "Hi."

Sadness washed over her because she missed his smile. She wished she could have it back. She wanted it all for herself. But he was leaving soon, and she had to accept that. The old Juliette would've tried to act cool and easy-breezy, but that's not how she felt. She didn't want to fake anything anymore. Especially not with him.

"Where've you been?" She gathered her courage. "I've missed you."

"I had to go to Florida for a couple of days to take care of some things. I just got back."

"Of course." He was selling his house and moving across the country. It only made sense that he'd be busy taking care of last minute details. Saying good-bye to her must be one of them. Her chest tightened in grief and she swallowed hard.

Logan took a step closer and said in a low voice, "Juliette, I'm so sorry. I should never have asked you to save the tree. I never meant for you to get hurt. You could've died, and I should've been there to—"

"—No," she interrupted. "Please don't apologize. I wanted to do it. I'm glad it worked."

He shook his head and glanced down for a moment. "I need to ask you something."

The old Juliette also would've frozen up, raised the drawbridge and got out the brick and mortar to build walls. But she wasn't going to be that person anymore. She wasn't going to shy away from her feelings. "What is it?"

His gaze was all serious intent. "Why did you do it? Why did you risk your life to save my tree?"

That was easy. "Because you love it." But now came the hard part. It was now, or never. If she was going to live courageously, this was her moment. He was leaving and that wouldn't change. But at least he'd leave with the truth. She lifted her chin and looked him straight in the eyes. "And because I love you." His expression was unreadable, but she kept on before she lost her nerve. "And I want you to know that I loved you before. Those things I said in my garden . . . I didn't mean them. I was angry and hurt. I'm sorry. I just want you to know that the thing we had between us . . ." She fought to steady her voice and forged on. "That was real for me, too. All of it was real. I was just too scared to admit it."

There. She said it. And now he would go, and she would love him forever, and life would go on as normal. For everyone else. Just not for her.

A small crease formed between his brows. Slowly, he reached out to brush his fingers along the white streak at her temple. "Your hair."

"Yeah, it's because—" Wait, what? She just bared her soul and he was commenting on her hair? "I said I love you. Did I say it out loud, or just think it?"

His mouth curved into a smile. "You said it out loud." Then he held her sprained wrist, cradling the splint between his large hands.

Juliette felt confused, but also elated that he was touching her and looking at her like she was precious. "Well, I do," she said shakily. "So there you have it."

He lifted her wrist and kissed her fingertips. "I know."

"You know what?" she asked, sidetracked by the delicious nearness of him.

"I know you love me," Logan said simply.

"You do?"

"Mmm-hm. That's why I went to Florida to meet with my buddy who runs a construction company. We're going to open a branch out here, and I'm going to manage it. That's also why I took my house off the market."

Juliette stared blankly at him. "You're not leaving?"

"I'm not leaving."

Juliette swore she felt the earth come screeching to a halt. Time stood still and everything froze. Nothing moved or breathed. She felt like they were the only two people on the entire planet.

"Um." Felicity cleared her throat from the back of the shop. "So did you still want the petunias, or . . . ?"

Logan didn't take his eyes off Juliette's face. "I absolutely do."

Felicity mumbled something and wandered into the back room.

"You're staying," Juliette said, just to make sure she'd heard him right.

"Yes."

He's staying. She repeated it in her head until the reality of it surrounded her like a favorite song, enveloping all her senses, sinking into her skin. "Why?"

"Because I love you, too." He took both her hands in his. "And you're just going to have to get comfortable with that. We're going to make this work, Juliette."

Something warm unfurled inside her because nothing had ever sounded better. She needed to know it was going to last. She wanted the whole thing. She wanted the fairy tale. "You promise?"

He lowered his head and whispered, "I promise." Then he sealed it with a kiss.

And in that moment, Juliette knew it was true. She felt it in her bones, in the same way she knew exactly when the sun would rise, or when it was going to rain, or when new spring grass was just about to emerge. She would always remember that kiss as the exact moment her future bloomed into something beautiful.

Epilogue

Later that summer . . .

"Would you look at them?" Gertie nudged Juliette's shoulder and popped a candied almond in her mouth. They were seated at the wedding table of honor, surrounded by all their closest friends and relations. "Have you ever seen a more beautiful bride and groom?"

Juliette shook her head, beaming as Emma and Hunter took to the floor for their first dance as husband and wife. Their restaurant Haven was the perfect spot for the wedding reception, with its sparkling glass art, white tablecloths, and panoramic views of the ocean. Emma looked radiant with her classic A-line lace dress and white gardenias in her hair. Juliette decided the wedding ceremony had been almost as beautiful as the bride, thanks to the gorgeous weather—courtesy of Mother Nature—and the stunning flower bouquets—courtesy of herself. And then there was the flock of white doves flying into the air at the end of the ceremony, which was a lovely touch—courtesy of Kat.

Juliette looked across the room at Kat, who was seated at one of the guest tables near the DJ. She had pretended she had nothing to do with the birds, but Juliette knew better. The black crow soaring joyfully in the midst of all those doves kind of gave it away. There was something very special about Kat. No question. One of these days, Juliette planned to have a long talk with her.

She watched as Kat cut a small piece of steak from her plate and tossed it on the floor, to the obvious delight of the tiny dog hidden under the tablecloth.

Juliette grinned and picked up her champagne glass. As far as she was concerned, Kat was the only good part of having *Hollywood Houseboat* on Pine Cove Island that summer. Now that the celebrities were finally gone, she was thrilled that Kat had decided to stay. Almost as thrilled as Kat had been when Vespa decided to leave Hank behind.

"Juliette, I need to have a word with you." Romeo walked up to her table, looking dapper as always in a tuxedo with a white rose in his breast pocket. He was holding Caleb's hand, and both of them were scrutinizing her like she was a specimen under glass.

"Is this about the new sign?" Juliette asked nervously. She'd shared with Emma the name she wanted to give her new florist shop, and Emma and Hunter secretly commissioned an artist to make the new sign for the storefront. They'd surprised her with it earlier in the week. It was an exquisite mosaic in varying shades of green, with vines and leaves surrounding the name, ROMEO & JULIETTE'S.

"I was hoping you wouldn't mind," Juliette said.

Romeo slapped a hand over his heart. "My dear, I am honored. I love the idea."

"He really does," Caleb assured her. "He even said he should've thought of it sooner. 'Romeo & Juliette's' has such a romantic ring to it."

Juliette smiled in relief. Romeo had been a great mentor, and his good opinion would always matter. "I'm so glad you approve."

"That's not what we wanted to talk to you about." Caleb

fixed her with a look that made her feel like she'd just got caught passing notes in class. "You need to settle a little dispute we're having."

"What dispute?"

"It's my belief that you fell in love with Logan while Romeo and I were on vacation. That's why you were so glowy when we first got back, and I couldn't put my finger on it. Romeo thinks you never liked Logan at all, based on an e-mail you sent—something about Logan messing with all your stuff? Anyway, Romeo thinks you didn't fall for Logan until after we got back from our trip. So which is it, before or after?"

"Neither," Juliette said with a laugh. "I fell for Logan twenty-three years ago in the woods by my house. He was pretending to be Han Solo, and he gave me his *Millennium Falcon*. We played Star Wars for hours. After that, I was pretty much a goner."

"Ah, yes," Caleb said. "Han Solo and the *Millennium Falcon*. That's powerful stuff. Pilots, you know." He winked at Romeo, and they wandered off toward the bar.

Juliette watched them leave with an overwhelming sense of gratitude. Even though they weren't related, she considered them part of her family. Romeo and his husband would always have a special place in her heart, because knowing them led her to Logan.

"There you are." Logan dropped a kiss on top of her head, taking the seat beside her at the table of honor. In a dark suit, with his golden hair smoothed back and a slight stubble on his jawline, he looked like a bad boy Prince Charming.

He fixed her with a hot, dark gaze that made her insides flutter. Sometimes, she still couldn't believe he was hers.

"You look beautiful," he said. "Have I told you that yet today?"

Juliette dipped her head and smoothed her blue satin dress. "Twice, I think."

"Actually, I take that back. You look really tired." His dark eyes twinkled with mischief as he bent to nuzzle her neck. "We should leave early so I can get you into bed."

"We can't leave," Juliette said, shivering with pleasure as Logan began planting delicious kisses along the sensitive spot where her neck met her shoulder. "They haven't even cut the cake yet."

"It's a tower of cupcakes," he murmured. "There's no cutting necessary."

"You two lovebirds should be dancing," Molly said as she and her boyfriend, James, rose from the table.

"Yeah, come on. They're playing a booty song." Gertie led her laughing husband out onto the dance floor.

"Come with me. I have a surprise for you." Logan linked his hand with hers and led her through the front doors of Haven and out into the parking lot.

"Where are we going?"

He pulled her toward his truck. "I'm stealing you away for a few minutes. Don't worry, we'll be back soon."

"I can't leave," she said with a laugh. "I'm the maid of honor."

"Actually, this was Emma's idea. I was going to wait, but she insisted I show you now. Bride's orders. I couldn't say no."

"Show me what?"

"Have patience." Logan opened the passenger door for her.

She shot him a look as she slid inside. "Patience has never been one of my virtues."

"Believe me, I know."

A short time later, Logan pulled his truck into the driveway of his house. Juliette had to take off her high-heeled sandals to follow him across the yard.

"Why are we at your tree?" she said, half complaining, half delighted. "Not that I mind being barefoot. This is heaven." She squished her toes into the grass, grateful to feel the earth under her feet. Dressing up was fun, but nothing would ever compare to this feeling of being close to nature.

Logan pointed up.

She tipped her head back and gasped.

The treehouse gleamed shiny and new, much bigger than it was before. A sturdy rope ladder hung from the entrance, and flower boxes lined the windows. Luna was draped lazily along one of the window ledges like a queen, her tail twitching in contentment. Beside her sat the ceramic pot of petunias.

Juliette's mouth fell open. "When did you do all this?"

"You were distracted these past few weeks with the wedding plans, so I wanted to surprise you."

She gazed at the new treehouse, stunned. She knew Logan and Kevin had been working extra hard on the re-model lately, but she'd never dreamed this was the project.

He gestured to the rope ladder. "Come up."

She paused, considering her bridesmaid dress. The fitted sheath hugged her curves and didn't leave much room to maneuver. "I'd love to, but my dress . . ."

"Take it off," Logan said innocently. "That way you won't get it dirty."

She narrowed her eyes at him.

He gave her a wicked grin. "I *dare* you."

A few moments later, the blue satin dress hung from a low branch, swaying in the breeze.

Juliette stood in the middle of the treehouse, turning in awe. The inside was more than twice its former size, with shiny floors, a comfy chair in one corner, and a wall of shelves at the back. Several books were stacked on the shelves, along with the frog prince cookie jar that had once been her makeshift first-aid kit.

He'd filled the treehouse with cookies and books. Just the necessities.

Juliette swallowed past the lump that formed in her throat.

"Emma helped pick out the books," Logan said almost shyly. "And she made cookies for the jar."

Juliette felt as though her heart had never been so full. It was everything she'd dreamed of having when she was little. Once again, Logan had managed to make one of her wishes come true.

He shifted on his feet. "Do you like it?"

She turned to him, blinking back happy tears. "It's better than I ever imagined your treehouse could be."

"Not mine. It's yours now," he said, glancing down at his hands. "If you want it."

"You can't give me your treehouse. It's too much."

"It's not enough," he insisted. "Nothing I have could ever be enough. But I'm going to spend the rest of my life trying to be worthy of you anyway, Juliette. If you'll have me." He gazed at her intently. "Will you?"

Juliette's breath hitched in her chest. Was he doing what she thought he was doing? Did she want him to? Every cell in her body rose up in a resounding chorus of yeses. She was so overcome with emotion that she couldn't find words.

Logan began to frown. "I'm botching this up, aren't I? I was going to wait and do it right, but every moment I'm with you feels right. Hell, I don't even have the ring yet. It's still at the jewelers." He ran a hand through his hair in frustration. "I'm sorry, I—"

"—Shh. You're doing it exactly right," Juliette whispered shakily. She stepped into his arms and buried her face in his chest, breathing in the familiar scent of him.

Logan O'Connor. The boy she loved when she was a little girl. The man she loved now.

He held her close and said in a husky voice, "Marry me, Juliette."

She smiled against his chest. "Fine."

A soft chuckle. "Fine."

Luna meowed and brushed against their legs. The cat was purring so loud, the joyful rumbling seemed to echo off the treehouse walls.

They laughed. Then they were whispering secret things to each other that only the old cat and the ancient tree could hear. Then they were kissing and then, for a while, they weren't saying anything at all.

Don't miss Kat's story in

DON'T GIVE ME BUTTERFLIES

by Tara Sheets.

Available from Zebra Books
in Summer, 2019.

Read on for a special preview . . .

Chapter One

Kat Davenport was many things, but wealthy wasn't one of them. After plunking down her last twenty bucks at the store that morning for dog food, Cheetos, and shampoo, she vowed to take whatever job came her way, no matter what it was.

"Beggars can't be choosers," she told her dog Hank as they left their motel room that afternoon. "And anything's better than being hungry and homeless."

But now, as she yanked on the ridiculous yellow chicken costume and prepared to stand in the sweltering August heat at the Pine Cove Island farmer's market, the life of a hobo wasn't looking all that bad.

"Your beak's broken," her supervisor said in a voice like fine grit sandpaper.

Kat glanced at the woman lounging on the single fold-out chair inside their booth. Smitty Bankston was on the hard side of sixty, with a sour expression that said she knew it. Deep lines etched her face, and her hair was teased and sprayed into a frothy style that had seen better days and wanted to go back.

"Your chicken beak," Smitty said. "It's all crunched up."

She took a long drag on her cigarette and flicked the ashes into the grass.

Kat blinked through the fumes. "I'll figure something out." If she'd learned one thing in her twenty-six years, it was how to improvise. She zipped the feathered costume up to her neck. The chicken head was a stuffed hood that snapped under her chin, but the plastic beak was crushed beyond repair.

"Just wear it without the beak, so your face shows," Smitty said, exhaling another plume of smoke. "That way people can hear you better when you ask for donations."

"Great." Kat tucked her frizzing red hair into the chicken hood, wondering how it had all come to this. When she saw the ad for a one-day job working with the Daisy Meadows Pet Rescue, she'd jumped at the chance. Animals were her specialty. She was born with the magical ability to communicate with them, and she'd always taken jobs involving animals. But this wasn't the cakewalk she'd expected. It was more like a pie in the face.

"Here's your basket," Smitty said, handing her a pink basket with the words PLEASE PAWS FOR DONATIONS on one side, and THANK YOU FURRY MUCH on the other. "Now get out there and work the crowd."

Thirty-seven minutes later—because she was counting—Kat had exactly zero dollars in donations. The afternoon sun was brutal, and the costume chafed in all the worst places. She wandered past vegetable stands, candle makers, and flower booths, trying not to make eye contact with people.

"Big Bird!" a small child said, pointing at her.

"No, honey." His mother gave Kat a tight smile, then pulled him away. "That's something else."

A baby in a stroller stared at Kat with wide eyes, then started to howl.

Kat hurried past as fast as her chicken feet would allow. This gig was going on her Worst Jobs Ever list, no question. She felt like one of those costumed scam artists wandering Times Square in New York City. Nobody in their right mind was going to "PAWS" and donate.

An old man with a cane hobbled over and tossed a quarter in her basket. "Shake those tail feathers, Bessie!" He wiggled his bushy eyebrows and grinned.

Kat glanced at the single coin. How had she fallen this low? Oh, yeah. Because she was the Queen of Impulsive Decisions. Three weeks ago, she was working as a pet sitter on *Hollywood Houseboat*, a reality show from southern California. Then on a crazy whim, she'd decided to stay in the Pacific Northwest for good. Pine Cove Island was far away from her ex-boyfriend and therefore, blissful, but now her bank account was empty again. And there was nothing blissful about that.

She shoved a sweaty lock of hair from her face and pushed on through the crowd.

On her second lap around the market, Kat had no further donations to show for her efforts. Fed up and needing a break from the sun, she made a bee-line toward a shady spot underneath a large tree. A white farmer's tent filled with bundles of lavender stood beside it, but no one was there.

She plopped down on a bale of hay underneath the tree, then yanked off her chicken hood and shook out her hair.

A sudden gust of wind kicked up and the fresh scent of lavender soothed her heated emotions.

She closed her eyes and breathed deeply, trying to embrace the moment. She needed to find her zen, or whatever it was called. But she also needed to find a permanent job, and a place that actually felt like home. A hollow ache settled in her chest. If a place like that even existed.

Leaning forward, Kat dropped her face into her hands. *Zen*. She massaged her temples with her fingers, trying to quiet her mind, but it didn't work. It was like asking a tornado to stop spinning. *Zen harder*. She tried for several more seconds, then let out a heavy sigh. It was no use. Maybe she could just hang out here in the shade for an hour or five.

"Excuse me," a deep voice said behind her. "I believe you're sitting on my lunch."

Kat spun around, or at least she tried. The costume's bulk made it difficult to maneuver. Her spiky tail feathers swished in an arc, sending her donation basket, a paper plate, and a sandwich flying into the grass.

"Oh!" She scrambled for the crushed sandwich and plate, setting them back on the bale of hay. Then she glanced up to apologize, but the words died in her throat.

The man loomed over her like a thundercloud, with broad shoulders, deeply tanned skin, and dark hair. He wore black jeans and a charcoal gray T-shirt, and he was so tall, Kat took an involuntary step back.

"I'm sorry," she managed. "I didn't notice your sandwich. It's this stupid costume. I can't even see my feet."

His gaze swept slowly over her.

She tried to appear calm and unfazed, but it wasn't easy. He was one of those gorgeous-by-accident types of people. The kind who didn't even have to try. Not like the carefully groomed pretty boys she'd worked with in LA. Certainly not like her ex-boyfriend who had more clothes and hair products than she did. Nothing about this man was soft or pretty. He had sharp, masculine features, unusual amber eyes, and a thin scar across his left cheekbone. He was in need of a haircut and his face was unshaven, which—paired with the scar—made him look like some wicked character from a fairy tale.

The Beast, Kat decided. He reminded her of the dark prince who got turned into a beast because of his wicked ways.

His mouth curved into an almost-smile, and a fluttering sensation began in the pit of Kat's stomach.

Uh-oh. Butterflies. This was not a good sign. In fact, getting butterflies in her stomach was the exact opposite of a good sign. The Queen of Impulsive Decisions started to smile back, but Kat shut her down fast. She was here to start fresh. That was the plan. She was not going to get all fluttery over the first hot guy who looked her way. Been there, done that, bought the T-shirt too many times to count.

"Why are you dressed like a turkey?" he asked.

Heat scorched up the back of her neck. Here she was, fantasizing about him as a dark prince being all edgy and epic, and all he saw was a stuffed turkey. So much for fairy tales.

"I'm not—" She broke off with a sigh. Really, what did it matter? She grabbed her toppled basket off the ground and set it on the bale of hay. Unfortunately, her only donation of twenty-five cents was now lost somewhere in the weeds. She searched the grass, aware that he was still watching her.

"Did you lose something?" he asked.

Just my dignity. She abandoned her search for the quarter. "It's not a big deal." With quick, frustrated movements, she began twisting her hair into a bun. If she didn't get back out there soon, Smitty was going to smoke her on a spit.

"You look pretty hot in that," he said.

She glanced sharply at him.

His face was all polite concern, but there was a glint of mischief in his eyes. "The costume." He gestured to the pear-shaped mess of feathers. "It's really hot."

Was he teasing her? She ignored him and shook out the chicken hood, preparing to put it on. The sooner she escaped into the boiling sea of humanity, the better. It was one thing to feel ridiculous, but another thing entirely to have a man like him witness it.

"But why a turkey?" he asked conversationally, leaning one shoulder against the tree trunk. "I don't get it."

"It's for a rescue shelter," she said, securing her hair with an elastic band from her wrist. "They thought it would draw attention to help get donations."

"For turkeys." He did not seem impressed.

"No." She threw him a look like *he* was the ridiculous one, then jammed on the feathered hood. "It's a rescue facility for animals. Mostly cats and dogs. And I'm a chicken, if you must know."

"Ah." He nodded solemnly, but she had the distinct feeling he was laughing at her. "I see that now."

She took a deep breath and let it out fast. "I know it's dumb, all right? Just give me five seconds and I'll be off to terrorize small children and leave you in peace."

He shrugged. "Take your time. I like chickens." He looped his thumbs into the pockets of his jeans and glanced at the crumpled plate. "My sandwich was chicken."

She tried to snap the hood under her chin. The clasp wouldn't catch. She tried again, muttering under her breath.

He pushed off the tree and stepped closer. "Do you need some help?"

"No," she said quickly. If he had to help, her humiliation would be complete. Why couldn't he just go away?

He kept watching as she fumbled with the clasp under her chin. Spiky feathers poked her neck. Brushed against her nose. Scraped along her collarbone. She bit the insides of her cheeks, frustration mounting with every second.

"Maybe you should consider an easier costume next time," he said.

She almost laughed. There wasn't going to be a "next time." Even if that meant she had to pack up a bindle stick and go moseying down the train tracks with her dog Hank.

A prickly feather jabbed her ear. She plucked the offending feather out, tossed it to the ground, and continued trying to snap the hood.

"You could try a flamingo costume," he said amiably.

Another feather dug into her temple. She shoved it back. Sweat trickled between her shoulder blades. Her arms itched. Everything itched.

"Or an albatross," he suggested. "You know, something that really says 'cat and dog shelter.'"

Kat slapped feathers away from her face. It was too much. She was fed up. With the job. The day. Her life.

"Look." She pierced him with a glare, fighting to steady her voice. "I get that this might be entertaining to you, but it's no picnic for me. I took this gig because I needed the money. I'm supposed to be collecting donations and so far, all I've gathered is twenty-five cents from an old man who told me to shake my tail feathers. So just give me a break, okay? This is not my idea of a fun afternoon."

She turned her back on him, still grappling with the hood clasp. After several moments in which she considered ripping the hood off, dousing it with gasoline, and lighting it on fire with one of Smitty's cigarettes, it finally snapped closed. Hallelujah! Now she could get on with her glorious day.

"What is?" he asked.

She spun to face him, plucking a downy feather from her mouth. "What is what?"

He was studying her with those whiskey-colored eyes, his head cocked to one side like he was trying to figure out a puzzle. A dark lock of hair fell over his brow, and Kat was struck again by how attractive he was. Or, would be. If she were into those wild, wicked beast types. Which, she wasn't.

The butterflies in her stomach started to say otherwise, but she drew out a mental fly swatter and shut them up, fast.

"What is your idea of a fun afternoon?" he asked.

Kat blinked. It had been a long time since anyone asked her opinion on something like that. There were so many ways to answer it. She'd rather be almost anywhere right now. Like the beach, or an outdoor music concert, or a sidewalk café. She'd rather be curled up with her dog watching old black-and-white movies, or browsing thrift stores for treasures nobody wanted. But none of these things would seem particularly interesting to someone who looked like he roamed the halls of enchanted castles and slayed dragons in his spare time.

Instead, she just shrugged. "I don't know. Watching movies. Shopping."

His expression faded to a look of mild boredom. "Of course."

Kat bristled. His dismissive tone bothered her. *He* bothered her. She lifted her chin. "Oh, is that not exciting enough for you?"

He shrugged. "Hey, whatever floats your boat. Not everyone has the same idea of fun, that's all. You are who you are."

She pressed her lips together. He had no idea who she was. "Well, what's your idea of a fun afternoon? Swimming with sharks? Jumping off cliffs in a wingsuit?"

His lips twitched. He ran a hand through his hair and looked away.

Kat couldn't help noticing his muscular arms, and how broad his shoulders were in comparison to his lean hips. He was built like a professional athlete. Maybe he really did do extreme sports.

"Nothing that complicated," he said, turning back to her. A soft smile played at the corners of his mouth. "Sometimes I just like to hang out and enjoy lunch with friends, or . . ." His gaze flicked to her costume, then back up to her face. "A hot chick."

Kat rolled her eyes. She grabbed her basket and marched away, tail feathers bouncing with each step.

A deep, masculine chuckle followed her until she lost herself in the crowd.

She was on the other side of the farmer's market before she looked in her basket. On the bottom was a folded twenty-dollar bill.

By six o'clock that evening, the farmer's market vendors were packing up for the day. Kat stood in the Daisy Meadows Pet Rescue booth and unzipped her chicken costume with a tortured sigh. The cool air felt like heaven on her sweaty skin. It was good to finally be free.

Smitty sucked on a cigarette and dug through the donation basket with her free hand. She held up the twenty-dollar bill. "Who's the big tipper?"

"I didn't catch his name," Kat said. In fact, she didn't see Mr. Tall, Dark, and Bothersome again after their first encounter.

Smitty shoved the donations into a glass jar and screwed the lid shut. "Well, old man Winthrop didn't donate twenty bucks, that's for sure. Bessie never got more than a quarter out of him."

Kat glanced up from tying her shoes. "Bessie?"

Smitty's expression curdled. "The gal who normally works the fair. She up and quit yesterday, which is why we needed a stand-in. And good riddance to her, if you ask me." She opened a metal box on the table and pulled out several bills. "Here's your pay. You did all right today."

"Thanks." Kat took the money and stuffed it in her pocket. Not a bad haul for an under-the-table gig.

Hank crawled out from his sleeping spot behind the tablecloth, tail spinning in joy to see her.

She scooped him up and kissed him on the head.

Smitty eyed her closely. "You good with animals?"

"I'm excellent with animals," Kat said. "It's kind of my thing." And by "thing," she meant super power. At least, that's what she liked to call it. By some freak of nature, she just always knew what animals were feeling, and she could communicate with them. But that's not something she could come right out and say. That was the kind of thing that got you beat up on the playground, or kicked out of a house.

"I need to hire another receptionist," Smitty said. "You good with paperwork and office stuff?"

"Sure." Kat pasted an extra big smile on her face, hoping it would make up for the lie. Organization was not a close friend of hers, but work was money. And money was security. And security was everything. "I'm good with animals, and office stuff."

Smitty reached into her bedazzled denim purse, pulled out a business card, and handed it to her. "Come by Monday morning. Eight o'clock sharp. It's a full-time position, if you want it."

Kat glanced at the card with the words DAISY MEADOWS PET RESCUE across the top. This time, her smile was genuine. "Sounds perfect."

Chapter Two

"Room for Rent," Kat read aloud from her laptop screen later that evening. She was leaning against the headboard of her motel room, scrolling through the Pine Cove Island classified ads. "Looking for someone to share light chores."

She glanced down at her dog Hank on the coverlet beside her. "That sounds promising, right? I'm fine with light chores."

Hank thumped his tail in agreement.

She grabbed a chip from a bag on the nightstand and continued reading aloud. "Cooking a plus. Daily massage a must. Big tool provided . . ." Kat began to frown and continued reading under her breath. "For more details call X.L. Dickerson." She made a face and set the laptop aside.

Hank whined and shook his head.

"Yeah, that one's a definite no," Kat said with a sigh. She'd been searching for a cheap room to rent for the past hour. Most of the rooms available were either too expensive, or too far away from her new job. She'd purchased an ancient Ford sedan with the last of her savings, but it wasn't the most reliable commuter vehicle.

Hank crawled into her lap and she scratched him under the chin.

An ad suddenly popped up at the top of the rental list. Kat glanced over at her laptop, reading aloud with hesitation. "Room for Rent. Willowbrook Lavender farm, 37 Griffin Road. Discount on rent in exchange for light help with barn animals. Prior knowledge a must. All utilities included."

Kat sat up straighter. The animal shelter was on Griffin Road. She leaned sideways and typed in the farm's address on her laptop. It was less than a quarter of a mile away from the shelter. Quickly, she fired off an email asking if the room was still available. Almost immediately, she got a response from an O. Prescott, and within minutes she had a plan to meet the following day to see the room.

"Hank, this might just work," Kat said, shutting her laptop. She snuggled under the covers with her dog and whispered, "We live another day."

On Saturday morning, Kat parked her car in front of Willowbrook Lavender farm with mixed feelings.

The fresh, herbal scent of lavender permeated the air, and the field beyond the house was beautiful. Rows of lavender in varying shades of purple and blue stretched for an acre along the west side of the property. A red barn with white trim stood near the south field, with a trailer hitch and wheelbarrow out front.

But the farmhouse had seen better days. It was a dingy white structure with a wraparound porch. The flower boxes on the railing were cracked and empty. The stairs leading up to the porch were sagging with age, and the turquoise front door was faded and peeling.

Next to the house was a detached garage with an apartment above it. Her future living space, if things worked out. She eyed the single window above the garage, hoping the room was decent. For the rental price, she wasn't expecting much.

Kat crossed the lawn, trying to shove off the mantle of disappointment settling over her. She had hoped Willowbrook Lavender farm would be a little more cheerful. Maybe a purple farmhouse with fluffy chickens pecking around in the yard. Come to think of it, there were no barn animals anywhere. Strange, considering that was part of the rental arrangement. Even the fenced paddock beside the house was empty and overgrown with weeds. The place looked abandoned.

She climbed the steps to the front door where a silver dragonfly knocker hung at eye-level. A mermaid wind chime beside the door danced in the breeze, its cheerful, tinkling sound eerily out of place in the somber atmosphere.

Kat paused to gather her thoughts, smoothed her hair, then knocked three times.

A few moments later, the door swung open and a man appeared.

Her mouth fell open in surprise.

Mr. Tall, Dark, and Bothersome stood on the threshold. He was younger than she'd first assumed—maybe in his late twenties or early thirties. His hair was damp and smoothed back, and he was cleanshaven, so the angles of his face were more clearly defined. He wore jeans and an unbuttoned flannel shirt, revealing a glimpse of muscled torso and tanned skin. Kat thought he'd been attractive before, but now he looked downright sinful.

His gaze traveled over her hair, her clothes, her shoes.

She shifted self-consciously on her feet. She was wearing an old tank top, shorts, and chunky boots. All her clothes were black, which was a requirement for her last job as part of the working crew on the houseboat. She hadn't had the time or money to buy new clothes yet. Now, under his scrutiny, she felt inappropriately dressed, which was absurd, considering he barely had a shirt on.

"I didn't expect to see *you* here," she blurted.

He lifted a dark brow. "Sorry to disappoint you."

"I'm not," she said quickly. But it wasn't entirely true. She'd expected a wizened old farmer in overalls with a grandpa smile. Or maybe a little old lady in an apron with lots of cats. Someone sweet and comforting. This man was the exact opposite. He gave her that unsettling, butterflies-in-her-stomach feeling.

Kat cleared her throat and tried to sound calm, even though she wasn't. "I just didn't expect . . . I mean, you don't seem like a lavender farm type of person."

His expression flickered with bitter amusement. "I won't argue with that." He began buttoning his shirt. "You're early."

Kat glanced away. Watching him dress felt almost as intimate as if she were watching him undress. "I was supposed to come at ten o'clock, right?" She pulled her phone from her pocket and checked the time. Nine forty. She must have rushed through the morning in her eagerness to see the room. "I didn't realize how early it was. Do you want me to come back in twenty minutes?"

"No need." He finished buttoning his shirt and held out a hand. "I'm Jordan Prescott."

"Kat Davenport." She reached out to shake his hand. It was a simple, everyday gesture, but the sudden skin-on-skin contact made her hyper aware of how big and warm he was, and how close they were standing. She quickly let go. "I thought I was meeting with an O. Prescott."

"My grandmother, Opal," Jordan said. "I posted the ad for her."

"You live here with your grandmother?" Another oddity.

He looked away. "Not for long."

Kat suddenly wondered what his story was. Everybody had a story. Some people got the happy Hallmark Channel ones with the parents and the family traditions and the fresh baked cookies after school. Other people got *Les Misérables*. But that's what made them resourceful and self-sufficient and strong. That's what made them capable of handling whatever life threw their way.

She squared her shoulders and lifted her chin. "Is your grandmother here?"

"No. She's at the community center playing Bingo. Or knitting." He shook his head in dismissal. "Whatever it is, she'll be back by ten o'clock."

Kat nodded in relief. A little old lady who knitted and played Bingo made sense. That was the kind of landlord she'd expected. A sinfully attractive, slightly annoying grandson wasn't part of the plan, but Kat wasn't going to let that stop her. She needed the room. It was cheap, which was her favorite price, and she had no problem taking care of animals. She had to make this work. Besides, he said he wasn't going to be there for long.

"I'm heading out, Jordan," a sultry female voice said from down the hall.

A pretty woman in a red dress suit and mile-high stilettos sauntered up beside him. She had sleek, dark hair and lips painted the exact shade of her dress. "Who's this?"

"Kat Davenport. She's here about the room for rent," Jordan said. "Kat, this is Layla Gentry."

"Oh, that's right," Layla mused. "The room above the garage. I forgot about that." She swept Kat from head to toe in an appraisal so thorough, Kat felt like she was on an auction block. Apparently, Layla decided she wasn't worth the investment, because she gave Kat a tight smile and promptly dismissed her.

Layla placed a hand on Jordan's upper arm and squeezed. "I have to run. Come by my office later." She brushed past Kat and sailed away on a river of Chanel No. 5.

"Does she live here, too?" Kat asked.

"No. She was just doing some work for me."

Kat wasn't going to ask what kind of work. It wasn't any of her business. He could do whatever he wanted with as many friends as he wanted. All she cared about was having a convenient place to live.

"Come in." Jordan stood back and waved her into the house. "I'll show you around."

Kat paused in the doorway. It was dark in the hall, except for a splash of sunlight from a window on the upstairs landing. She stole a glance at Jordan Prescott. Her potential new roommate.

He was standing half in shadow. An errant sunbeam slanted across his face, which made his eyes appear even brighter and more golden than usual.

"Are you coming in, or . . . ?"

She hesitated for a few heartbeats.

His expression lit with amusement, and his mouth curved into a smile. It wasn't the sweet, comforting kind of smile one would expect from grandpa farmers and little old cat ladies. It was an enchanted, wicked-prince smile. The kind that could lure a woman into all sorts of delicious trouble, if she were willing.

"Chickening out?" he asked softly.

Kat narrowed her eyes. She could think of several good reasons why she might be better off with a different living arrangement. But the Queen of Impulsive Decisions just tossed her hair, stepped over the threshold, and followed the beast into his lair.